About [...]

Reading and writing h[...]
Barbara Hannay's life[...]
at the age of eight for t[...]
was about a girl who w[...]
had to move from the city to the Australian Outback.

Barbara and her husband live on a misty hillside in Far North Queensland's Atherton Tableland. When she's not lost in the world of her stories she's enjoying farmers' markets, gardening clubs and writing groups, or preparing for visits from family and friends.

Barbara records her country life in her blog, *Barbwired*, and her website is: www.barbarahannay.com

Annie O'Neil spent most of her childhood with a leg draped over the family rocking chair and a book in her hand. Novels, baking, and writing too much teenage angst poetry ate up most of her youth. Now, quite a few years on from those fevered daydreams of being a poet, Annie splits her time between corralling her husband (and real-life Scottish hero) into helping her with their cows or scratching the backs of their rare breed pigs, and spending some very happy hours at her computer, writing. Find out more about Annie at her website: www.annieoneilbooks.com

Leah Martyn loves to create warm, believable characters for the Mills & Boon Medical Romance series. She is grounded firmly in rural Australia, and the special qualities of the bush are reflected in her stories. Browsing in bookshops and buying an armful of new releases is high on her list of enjoyable things to do.

Australian

AFFAIRS

Australian Affairs: Wed

BARBARA HANNAY

ANNIE O'NEILL

LEAH MARTYN

MILLS & BOON

First Published in Great Britain 2019
By Mills & Boon, an imprint of HarperCollins *Publishers*
1 London Bridge Street, London, SE1 9GF

AUSTRALIAN AFFAIRS: WED © 2019 Harlequin Books S.A.

Second Chance with Her Soldier © 2013 Barbara Hannay
The Firefighter to Heal Her Heart © 2015 Sheila Creighton
Wedding at Sunday Creek © 2015 Leah Martyn

ISBN: 978-0-263-27529-2

0519

MIX
Paper from
responsible sources
FSC™ C007454

This book is produced from independently certified FSC™ paper
to ensure responsible forest management.

For more information visit: www.harpercollins.co.uk/green

Printed and bound in Spain
by CPI, Barcelona

SECOND CHANCE WITH HER SOLDIER

BARBARA HANNAY

PROLOGUE

CORPORAL JOE MADDEN waited two whole days before he opened the email from his wife.

Avoidance was not Joe's usual MO. It went against everything he'd learned in his military training. *Strike swiftly* was the Australian Commandos' motto, and yet…here he was in Afghanistan, treating a rare message from Ellie as if it were more dangerous than an improvised explosive device.

Looming divorce could do that to a guy.

The fact that Joe had actually offered to divorce Ellie was irrelevant. After too many stormy years of marriage, he'd known that his suggestion was both necessary and fair, but the break-up certainly hadn't been easy or painless.

Now, in his tiny hut in Tarin Kot, Joe scanned the two other email messages that had arrived from Australia overnight. The first was his aunt's unhelpful reminder that she never stopped worrying about him. The other was a note from one of his brothers. This, at least, was glib and slightly crude and elicited a wry chuckle from Joe.

But he was left staring at Ellie's as yet unopened email with its gut-churning subject heading: *Crunch Time*.

Joe knew exactly what this meant. The final divorce

papers had arrived from their solicitor and Ellie was impatient to serve him with them.

Clearly, she was no longer prepared to wait till the end of his four years in the army, even though his reasons for suggesting the delay had been entirely practical.

Joe knew no soldier was safe in Afghanistan, and if he was killed while he and Ellie were still married, she would receive an Army widow's full entitlements. Financially, at least, she would be OK.

Surely this was important? The worst could so easily happen here. In his frequent deployments, Joe faced daily, if not hourly, danger and he'd already lost two close mates, both of them brilliant, superbly trained soldiers. Death was a real and ever-present danger.

Joe had felt compelled to offer Ellie a safety net, so he'd been reassured to know that, whatever happened to him, she would be financially secure. But, clearly, getting out of their marriage now was more important to her than the long-term benefits.

Hell, she probably had another bloke lined up in the wings. Please, let it be anyone but that damn potato farmer her mother had hand-picked for her.

But, whatever Ellie's reasons, the evidence of her impatience sat before Joe on the screen.

Crunch Time.

There was no point in avoiding this any longer. The coffee Joe had recently downed turned sour as he grimly clicked on the message.

It was a stinking-hot day at Karinya Station in Far North Queensland. The paddocks were parched and the cattle hungry as Ellie Madden delivered molasses to the empty troughs. The anxious beasts pushed and shoved at her, trying to knock the molasses barrel out of her hands, so of course she was as sticky and grimy as a candy bar dropped in dirt by the time she arrived back at the homestead.

Her top priority was to hit the laundry and scrub up to her elbows. That done, she strode through the kitchen, grabbed a jug of chilled water from the fridge, filled a glass and gulped it down. Taking another glassful with her to the study, she remained standing in her molasses-smeared jeans as she fired up her laptop.

Tension vibrated and buzzed inside her as the latest messages downloaded. Surely Joe would send his answer today?

She was so sick with apprehension she closed her eyes and held her breath until she heard the ping of the final message's arrival. When she forced herself to peek at the screen again, she felt an immediate plunge of disappointment.

Nothing from Joe.

Not a word.

For fraught minutes, she stood staring at the screen, as if somehow she could *will* another email to appear. She hit 'send and receive', just to be sure.

Still nothing.

Why hadn't he replied? What was the hold-up? Even if he'd been out on a patrol, he was usually back at camp within a day or two.

A ripple of fear trembled through her like chilling wind over water.

Surely he couldn't have been injured? Not Joe.

The Army would have contacted her.

Don't think about that.

Ever since her husband had joined the Army, Ellie had schooled herself to stomp on negative thoughts. She knew other Army couples had secret 'codes' for when they talked about anything dangerous, but she and Joe had lost that kind of closeness long ago. Now she quickly searched for a more likely explanation.

Joe was probably giving her email careful thought. After all, it would have come as a shock, and no doubt he was weighing up the pros and cons of her surprising proposal.

Wanting to reassure herself, Ellie reread the email she'd sent him, just to make sure that it still sounded reasonable.

She'd tried to put her case concisely and directly, keeping it free of emotion, which was only fitting now they'd agreed to divorce. Even so, as she read, she found herself foolishly trying to imagine how Joe would feel as her message unfolded.

Hi Joe,
I hope all is well with you.

I'm writing on a practical matter. I've had another invoice from the fertility clinic, you see, and so I've been thinking again about the frozen embryos. (Surprise, surprise.)

Joe, I know we signed that form when we started the programme, agreeing that, in the case of divorce, we would donate any of our remaining embryos to another infertile couple. But I'm sorry—I'm having misgivings about that.

I've given it a lot of thought, Joe. Believe me, a LOT of thought.

I'd like to believe I would be generous enough to

hand over our embryos to a more deserving couple, but I can't help thinking of those little frozen guys as MY babies.

I've thought around and around this, Joe, and I've decided that I really do want to have that one last try at IVF. I know you will probably be horrified. You'll tell me that I'm setting myself up for another round of disappointment. I know this will come as a shock to you, and possibly a disappointment as well.

However, if by some amazing miracle I did become pregnant, I wouldn't expect to change our plans re the divorce. I promise I wouldn't try to use the baby to hold on to you, or anything manipulative like that.

As you know from past experience, success is EXTREMELY UNLIKELY, but I can't go ahead with IVF without your consent and I wouldn't want to, so obviously I'm very keen to hear your thoughts.

In the meantime, stay safe, Joe.

All the very best,

Ellie

Joe felt as if a grenade had exploded inches from his face.

I know this will come as a shock to you...

Hell, yeah. Never in a million years could he have imagined this possibility...

He'd assumed that the stressful times when he and Ellie had tried for a family were well and truly behind him.

Since he'd left Karinya Station, he hadn't allowed himself to give a single thought to those few remaining embryos. How many were there? Two? Three?

A heavy weight pressed against his ribs now as he

remembered the painful stretch of years when the IVF clinic had dominated his and Ellie's lives. All their hopes and dreams had been pinned on the embryos. They'd even had a nickname for them.

Their *sproglets*.

So far, none of them had survived implantation...

The ordeal had been beyond heartbreaking.

Now... Joe had no doubt that Ellie was setting herself up for another round of bitter disappointment. And yet, for a crazy moment he almost felt hope flare inside him, the same hope that had skyrocketed and plunged and kept them on edge through those bleak years of trying.

Even now, Joe couldn't help feeling hopeful for Ellie's sake, although he knew that her chances of a successful pregnancy were slimmer than a hair's breadth. And it stung him to know that she planned to go ahead this time on her own.

Truth was, he didn't want to think about this. Not any aspect of it. He'd joined the Army to forget his stuffed-up life. Here, he had a visible, assailable enemy to keep him focused day and night.

Now Ellie was forcing him to once again contemplate fatherhood and all its responsibilities. Except, this time, it would be fatherhood in name only. She'd made it very clear that she still wanted the divorce, and Joe totally understood why. So even if there was an against-all-the-odds miracle and he found himself technically a father, his kid would never grow up under his roof.

They would be more or less strangers.

Almost as an accompaniment to this grim thought, an explosion sounded outside, too close for comfort. Through the hut's window Joe saw bright flashes and smoke, heard frantic voices calling. Another rocket-propelled grenade had dumped—a timely reminder that danger and death were his regular companions.

There was no escaping that and, if he was honest, there was absolutely no point in going over and over this question of Ellie's. It was a waste of time weighing up the pros and cons of his wife's request.

Already Joe knew his answer. It was a clear no-brainer.

CHAPTER ONE

Three years later...

'ELLIE, IT'S MUM. Do you have the television on?'

'Television?' Ellie's response was incredulous. 'Mum, I've just come in from the paddocks. Our dams are drying out. I've been wrestling with a bogged cow all afternoon and I'm covered in mud. Why? What's on TV?' The only show that interested Ellie these days was the weather.

'I just saw Joe,' her mother said.

Ellie gasped. 'On TV?'

'Yes, darling. On the news.'

'He...he hasn't been hurt?'

'No, no, he's fine.' There was a dismissive note in her mother's voice, a familiar reminder that she'd never approved of her daughter's choice of husband and that, eventually, she'd been proved right. 'You know he's home for good this time?'

'He's already back in Australia?'

'Yes, Ellie. His regiment or squadron or whatever it's called has just landed in Sydney. I caught it on the early news, and there was a glimpse of Joe. Only a few seconds, mind you, but it was definitely him. And the reporter's saying these troops won't be going back to Afghanistan. I thought you should know.'

'OK. Thanks.' Ellie pressed a hand to her chest, caught out by the unexpected thud of her heart.

'You might be able to catch the story on one of the other channels.'

'Yes, I guess.'

Ellie was trembling as she hung up. Of course she'd heard the news reports about a staged withdrawal of Australian troops, but it was still a shock to know that Joe was already home. For good this time.

As a Commando, Joe had been on dozens of short-term missions to Afghanistan, returning each time to his Army base down in New South Wales. But now he wouldn't be going back.

And yet he hadn't made any kind of contact.

It showed how very far apart they'd drifted.

Almost fearfully, Ellie glanced at the silent blank TV screen in the corner of the homestead lounge room. She didn't really have time to turn it on. She was disgustingly muddy after her tussle in the dam with the bogged cow and she needed to get out of these stinking clothes. She wasn't even sure why she'd rushed inside to answer the phone in this filthy state, but some instinct had sent her running.

She should get changed and showered before she did anything else. She wouldn't even look for Nina and Jacko until she was clean.

But, even as she told herself what she *should* do, Ellie picked up the remote. More than one channel would cover the return.

It took a few seconds of scrolling before she found a

scene at Mascot Airport and a journalist's voiceover reporting an emotional welcome for the returning troops.

The screen showed the airport crowded with soldiers in uniform, hugging their wives and lifting their children high, their tanned, lean faces lit by unmistakable excitement and emotion.

Tears and happy smiles abounded. A grinning young man was awkwardly holding a tiny baby. A little girl hugged her daddy's khaki-clad knee, trying to catch his attention while he kissed her mother.

Ellie's throat ached. The scene was crammed with images of family joy. Tears pricked her eyes and she wondered where Joe was.

And then she saw him.

The man who would soon be her ex.

At the back of the crowd. Grim-faced. He was skirting the scenes of elated families, as if he was trying to keep out of camera range while he made his way purposefully to the exit.

He looked so alone.

With his green Commando's beret set rakishly on his short dark hair, Joe looked so tall and soldierly. Handsome, of course. But, compared with his laughing, happy comrades, he also looked very severe. And so *very* alone.

Ellie's mouth twisted out of shape. Tears spilled. She didn't know why—she simply couldn't help it.

Then the camera shifted to a politician who'd arrived to welcome the troops.

Quickly, she snapped the remote and the images vanished.

She let out her breath in a despairing huff. She felt

shaken at seeing Joe again after so long. To her dismay, it had been more like a horse kick to her heart.

She drew a deeper calming breath, knowing she had to set unhelpful sentimentality aside. She'd been braced for Joe's return and she'd known what was required.

Their divorce would be finalised now and it was time to be sensible and stoic. She knew very well there was *no* prospect of a happy reunion. She and Joe had made each other too miserable for too long. If she was honest, she wasn't surprised that Joe hadn't bothered to tell her his deployment was over. She didn't mind really.

But she *did* mind that he hadn't even asked to see Jacko.

Joe stood at the motel window on Sydney's Coogee Beach, looking out at an idyllic moonlit scene of sea cliffs and rolling surf.

So, it was over. He was home—finally, permanently. On the long flight back from Afghanistan he'd been dreaming of this arrival.

For most Australians, December meant the beginning of the long summer holidays and Joe had looked forward to downing a cold beer at sunset in a bar overlooking the beach, and sitting on the sand, eating hot, crunchy fish and chips straight from the paper they were wrapped in, throwing the scraps to the seagulls.

This evening he'd done all of these things, but the expected sense of joy and relaxation hadn't followed. Everything had felt strangely unreal.

It was unsettling, especially as his Commando training had taught him to adapt quickly to different environments and to respond effectively to any challenges.

Now he was home, in the safest and most welcoming

of environments, and yet he felt detached and disconnected, as if he was standing on the outside, watching some stranger trying to enjoy himself.

Of course, he knew that the transition to civilian life would be tricky after years of strict training and dangerous combat. At least he'd been prepared for the Happy Family scenes at the airport today, but once he'd escaped those jubilant reunions he'd expected to be fine.

Instead he felt numb and deflated, as if nothing about this new life was real.

He stared at the crescent of pale sand below, silvery in the moonlight, at the rolling breakers and white foam spraying against the dark, rocky cliffs, and he half-wished he had new orders to obey and a dangerous mission to fulfil.

When his phone buzzed, he didn't have the heart to answer it but, out of habit, he checked the caller ID.

It was Ellie.

His gut tightened.

He hadn't expected her to call so soon, but perhaps she'd seen the TV news and she knew he was back in Sydney. No doubt she wanted to talk, to make arrangements.

His breathing went shallow as hope and dread warred inside him. Was he ready for this conversation?

It was tempting to let her call go through to voicemail, to see what she had to say and respond later. But in the last half-second he gave in. He swallowed to clear his throat. 'Hi, Ellie.'

'Oh? Hello, Joe.'

They'd spoken a handful of times in the past three years.

'How are you?' Joe grimaced, knowing how awkward he sounded. 'How's the kid?'

'We're both really well, thanks. Jacko's growing so fast. How are you?'

What could he say? 'Fine. Home in one piece.'

'It must be wonderful to be back in Australia for good,' she said warmly.

'Yeah, I guess.' Too late he realised he should have sounded more enthusiastic.

'I…ah…' Now, it was Ellie who seemed to be floundering for words.

They weren't good at this. How could they be? An unhappy silence ticked by.

'I hear you've had a very dry year up north,' Joe said, clumsily picking up the ball.

'We have, but the weather bureau's predicting a decent wet season.'

'Well, that's good news.'

Joe pictured Karinya, the Far North Queensland cattle station that he and Ellie had leased and set up together when they'd first been married and afloat on love and hope and a thousand happy dreams. In his mind's eye, he could see the red dirt of the inland and the pale, sparse grass dotted with cattle, the rocky ridges and winding creeks. The wide blue overarching sky.

When they'd split, Ellie had stubbornly insisted on staying up there and running the place on her own. Even when the much-longed-for baby had arrived she'd stayed on, hiring a manager at first while she was pregnant, and then a nanny to help with the baby while Ellie continued to look after the cattle business as well as her son.

His son. Their son.

'Joe, I assume you want to see Jacko,' Ellie said quickly.

He gritted his teeth against the sudden whack of emotion. There'd been opportunities to visit North Queensland between his many missions, but he'd only seen their miracle baby once. He'd flown to Townsville and Ellie had driven in to the coast from Karinya. They'd spent an awkward afternoon in a park on Townsville's Strand and Joe had a photo in his wallet to prove it.

Now the kid was two years old.

'Of course I'd like to see Jacko,' he said cautiously. How could a father not want to see his own son? 'Are you planning to come in to Townsville again?'

'I'm sorry, Joe, I can't. It's more or less impossible for me to get away just now. You know what it's like in December. It's calving time, and I'm busy with keeping supplements and water up to the herd. And Nina—that's the nanny—wants to take her holidays. She'd like to go home to Cairns for Christmas, and that's understandable, so I'm trying to manage here on my own. I…um…thought you might be able to come out here.'

Joe's jaw tightened. 'To the homestead?'

'Yes.'

His brow furrowed. 'But even if I fly to Townsville, I wouldn't be able to make it out to Karinya and back again in a day.'

'Yes, I know…you'd have to stay overnight. There…there's a spare bed. You could have Nina's room.'

Whoa.

Joe flinched as if he'd been hit by a sniper. He held the phone away at arm's length as he dragged a shaky breath. He'd been steeling himself for the heart slug of another meeting with his son, but he'd always imagined another half hour in Townsville—a handover of gifts, maybe a walk in the park and another photo of himself with the kid, a memory to treasure.

Get it over, and then goodbye.

He wasn't sure he was prepared to stay at Karinya, spending all that time with young Jacko, as Ellie called him, spending a night there as well.

That had to be a bad idea.

Crazy.

'Joe, are you still there?'

'Yeah.' The effort to sound cool and calm made him grimace. 'Ellie, I'm not sure about going out there.'

'What do you mean? You *do* want to see your little boy, don't you?'

The hurt in her voice was crystal freaking clear.

'I…I do… Sure, of course I want to see him.'

'I thought you'd want to at least give him a Christmas present, Joe. He's old enough now to understand about presents.'

Joe sighed.

'But if you'd rather not…' Her voice was frosty now, reminding him of the chill factor that had caused him so much angst in the past.

'Look, I just got back. I'm jet-lagged, and there's all kinds of stuff to sort out here.' It wasn't totally the truth and Ellie probably guessed he was stalling.

'You and I have things to sort out, too.'

Joe drew a sharp breath. 'Do you have the papers from the solicitor?'

'All ready and waiting.'

'OK.' He felt the cold steel of a knife at his throat. 'Can I call you in the morning?'

By then he'd hopefully have his head together.

'Sure, Joe. Whatever.' Again, he heard the iciness that had plunged their once burning passion to below freezing point.

'Thanks for the call, Ellie.' With an effort he managed to sound non-combative, aware they were already falling into the old patterns that had eroded their marriage—constantly upsetting each other and then trying to placate, and then upsetting each other yet again. 'And thanks for the invitation.'

'No worries,' she said, sounding very worried indeed.

Damn him!

Ellie stood beside the phone, arms tightly crossed, trying to hold herself together, determined she wouldn't allow her disappointment to spill over into tears. She'd shed enough tears over Joe Madden to last two lifetimes.

It had taken considerable courage to ring him. She was proud she'd made the first move. But what had she expected? Warmth and delight from Joe?

What a fool she could be.

If Joe came to Karinya, it would be to sign the papers and nothing more. He would be businesslike and distant with her and with Jacko. How on earth had she once fallen for such a cold man?

Blinking and swiping at her eyes, Ellie walked softly through the house to the door to Jacko's room. Her little boy slept with a night light—an orange turtle with a purple and green spotted bow tie—and in the light's glow she could see the golden sheen of his hair, the soft downy curve of his baby-plump cheek.

He looked small and vulnerable when he was asleep, but in the daytime he was a ball of energy, usually good-natured and sunny, and gleefully eager to embrace life—the life he'd been granted so miraculously.

Ellie knew Joe would melt when he saw him. Surely?

Perhaps Joe sensed this possibility. Perhaps he was afraid?

Actually, that was probably close to the truth. The Joe Madden she remembered would rather face a dangerous enemy intent on death and destruction than deal with his deepest emotions.

Ellie sighed. This next phase of her life wasn't going to be easy, but she was determined to be strong while she and Joe sorted out the ground rules for their future. The impending divorce had been hanging over them for years like an axe waiting to fall. Now, she just wanted it to be over. Finalised.

But she planned to handle the arrangements with dignity and good sense, and she aimed to be mature and evolved in all her dealings with Joe.

It probably helped that they were more or less strangers now.

This was a bad idea. Crazy.

The more Joe paced in his motel room, the more he was sure that going back to the homestead was a risk he didn't want to take. Of course he was curious to see his son, but he'd always anticipated that his final meeting with Ellie would be in a lawyer's office. Somewhere neutral, without memories attached.

Going back to Karinya was bound to be painful, for a thousand different reasons.

He had to remember all the sane and sensible reasons why he'd suggested the divorce, beginning with the guilty knowledge that he'd more or less trapped Ellie into marriage in the first place.

The unexpected pregnancy, their hasty marriage followed by a miscarriage and a host of fertility issues.

Now, since Jacko's arrival, the goalposts had shifted, but Joe had no illusions about a reconciliation with Ellie. After four years in the Army, he was a hardened realist and he'd seen too much injury and death to believe in second chances.

Of course, today hadn't been the only time Joe had landed back in Australia to find himself the sole father in his unit with no family to greet him. He was used to seeing his mates going home with their wives and kids, knowing they were sharing meals and laughter, knowing they were making love to their wives, while he paced in an empty motel room.

Until today, his return visits had always been temporary, a short spot of leave before he was back in action. This time, it was unsettling to know he wouldn't be going back to war. His four years of service were over.

Yeah, of course he was lucky to still be alive and uninjured. And yet, tonight, after one phone conversation with Ellie, Joe didn't want to put a name to how he felt, but it certainly wasn't any version of lucky.

Of course, if he hadn't been so hung up on leaving a widow's pension for her, they would have been divorced years ago when they'd first recognised that their marriage was unsalvageable. They could have made a clean break then, and by now he would have well and truly adjusted to his single status.

Almost certainly, there wouldn't have been a cute complication named Jackson Joseph Madden.

Jacko.

Joe let out his breath on a sigh, remembering his excitement on the day the news of his son's birth came through. It had been such a miracle! He'd even broken his habitual silence about his personal life and had made an announcement in the mess. There'd been cheering and table-thumping and back slaps, and he'd passed his phone around with the photos that Ellie had sent of a tiny red-faced baby boy wrapped in a blue and white blanket.

He'd almost felt like a regular proud and happy new father.

Later, on leave, when his mates quizzed him about Ellie and Jacko, he was able to use the vast distance between the Holsworthy Base and their Far North Queensland cattle station as a valid excuse for his family's absence.

Now that excuse no longer held.

He and Ellie had to meet and sign the blasted papers. He supposed it made sense to travel up to Karinya straight away.

It wouldn't be a picnic, though, seeing Ellie again and looking around the property they'd planned to run together, not to mention going through another meeting with the son he would not help Ellie to raise.

And, afterwards, Joe would be expected to go home to his family's cattle property in Central Queensland, where his mother would smother him with sympathy and ply him with questions about the boy.

As an added hurdle, Christmas was looming just around the corner, bringing with it a host of emotional trapdoors.

Surely coming home should be easier than this?

CHAPTER TWO

WHEN ELLIE'S PHONE rang early next morning, Jacko was refusing to eat his porridge and he was banging his spoon on his high chair's tray, demanding. 'Eggie,' at the top of his voice.

For weeks now, Nina, the nanny, had supervised Jacko's breakfast while Ellie was out at the crack of dawn, delivering supplements to the cattle and checking on the newborn calves and their mothers.

Now Nina was in Cairns with her family for Christmas and as the phone trilled, Ellie shot a despairing glance to the rooster-shaped kitchen wall clock. No one she knew would call at this early hour.

Jacko shrieked again for his boiled egg.

Ellie was already in a bad mood when she answered. 'Hello? This is Karinya.'

'Good morning.' It was Joe, sounding gruff and businesslike. Very military.

'Good morning, Joe.' Behind Ellie, Jacko wailed, 'Eggie,' more loudly than ever.

'Would Friday suit?'

She frowned. Did Joe have to be so clipped and cryptic? 'To come here?'

'Yes.'

Friday was only the day after tomorrow. It wasn't much warning. Ellie's heart began an unhelpful drumming, followed by a flash of heat, as if her body had a mind of its own, as if it was remembering, without her permission, the fireworks Joe used to rouse in her. His kisses, his touch, the sparks a single look from him could light.

In the early days of their marriage, they hadn't been able to keep their hands off each other. Back in the heady days before everything went wrong, before their relationship exploded into a thousand painful pieces.

'I could catch a flight that arrives in Townsville around eight a.m.,' Joe said. 'If I hire a car, I could probably get to Karinya around mid-afternoon.'

'Eggie!' Jacko bawled in a fully-fledged bellow.

'Is that the kid crying?'

His name's Jacko, Ellie wanted to remind Joe. Why did he have to call him 'the kid'?

Holding the receiver to one ear, she filled a cup with juice and handed it to Jacko, hoping it would calm him. 'He's waiting for his breakfast.'

Jacko accepted the juice somewhat disconsolately, and at last the room was blessedly silent.

'So how about Friday?' Joe asked again.

At the thought of seeing him in less than forty-eight hours, Ellie took a deep, very necessary breath. 'Friday will be fine.'

It would *have* to be fine. They *had* to do this. They had to get it over and behind them. Only then could they both finally move on.

Joe was an hour away from Karinya when he noticed the gathering clouds. The journey had taken him west from Townsville to Charters Towers and then north through Queensland's more remote cattle country. It was an unhappily nostalgic drive, over familiar long, straight roads and sweeping open country, broken by occasional rocky ridges or the sandy dip of a dry creek bed.

The red earth and pale, drought-bleached grass were dotted with cattle and clumps of acacia and ironbark trees. It was a landscape Joe knew as well as his own reflection, but he'd rarely allowed himself to think about it since he'd left Queensland five and a half years ago.

Now, he worked hard to block out the memories of his life here with Ellie. And yet every signpost and landmark seemed to trigger an unstoppable flow.

He was reliving the day he and Ellie had first travelled up here, driving up from Ridgelands in his old battered ute. No one else in either of their families had ventured this far north, and the journey had felt like an adventure, as if they were pioneers pushing into new frontiers.

He remembered their first sight of Karinya—coming over a rise and seeing the simple iron-roofed homestead set in the middle of grassy plains. On the day they'd signed up for the long-term lease they'd been buzzing with excitement.

On the day their furniture arrived, Ellie had raced around like an enthusiastic kid. She'd wanted to help shift the furniture, but of course Joe wouldn't let her. She was pregnant, after all. So she'd unpacked boxes and filled cupboards. She'd made up their bed and she'd scrubbed the bathroom and the kitchen, even though they'd been perfectly clean.

She'd baked a roast dinner, which was a bit burnt,

but they'd laughed about it and picked off the black bits. And Ellie had been *incredibly* happy, as if their simple house in the middle of hundreds of empty acres represented a long and cherished dream that had finally come true.

When they made love on that first night it was as if being in their new bed, in their new home, had brought them a new level of connection and closeness they hadn't dreamed was possible.

Afterwards they'd lain close and together they'd watched the stars outside through the as yet uncurtained bedroom window.

Joe had seen a shooting star. 'Look!' he'd said, sitting up quickly. 'Did you see it?'

'Yes!' Ellie's eyes were shining.

'We should make a wish,' he said and, almost without thinking, he wished that they could always be as happy as they were on this night.

Ellie, however, was frowning. 'Have you made your wish?' she asked.

'Yes.' He smiled at her. 'What about you?'

'No, I haven't. I...I don't know if I want to.' She sounded perplexingly frightened. 'I...I don't really like making wishes. It's too much like tempting fate.'

Surprised, Joe laughed at her fears. He ran a gentle hand down her arm and lightly touched her stomach, where their tiny baby lay.

'Do *you* think I should make a wish?' Ellie's expression was serious now.

'Sure.' Joe was on top of the world that night. 'What harm can it do?'

She smiled and nestled into his embrace. 'OK. I wish for a boy. A cute little version of you.'

Three weeks later, Ellie had a miscarriage.

Remembering, Joe let out an involuntary sigh. *Enough.*

Don't go there.

He forced his attention back to the country stretching away to the horizon on either side of the road. Having grown up on a cattle property, he was able to assess the condition of the cattle he passed and the scant remaining fodder. There was no question that the country needed rain.

Everywhere, he saw signs of drought and stress. Although Ellie would have employed contract fencers and ringers for mustering, she must have worked like a demon to keep up with the demands of the prolonged drought.

He found himself questioning, as he had many times, why she'd been so stubbornly determined to stay out here. Alone.

He stopped for bad coffee and a greasy hamburger in a tiny isolated Outback servo, and it was only when he came outside again that he saw the dark clouds gathering on the northern horizon. Too often in December, clouds like these merely taunted graziers without bringing rain, but, as he drove on, drawing closer to Karinya, the clouds closed in.

Within thirty minutes the clouds covered the entire spread of the sky, hovering low to the earth like a cotton wool dressing pressed down over a wound.

As Joe turned off the main road and rattled over the cattle grid onto the track that led to the homestead, the first heavy drops began to fall, splattering the hire vehicle's dusty windscreen. By the time he reached the house the rain was pelting down.

To his faint surprise, Ellie was on the front veranda, waiting for him. She was wearing an Akubra hat and a Drizabone coat over jeans but, despite the masculine gear, she looked as slim and girlish as ever.

She had another coat over her arm and she hurried down the front steps, holding it out to him. Peering through the heavy curtain of rain, Joe saw unmistakable worry in her dark brown eyes.

'Here,' she yelled, raising her voice above the thundering noise on the homestead's iron roof, and as soon as he opened the driver's door, she shoved the coat through the chink.

A moment later, he was out of the vehicle, with the coat over his head, and the two of them were dashing through the rain and up the steps.

'This is incredible, isn't it?' Ellie gasped as they reached the veranda. 'Such lousy timing.' She turned to Joe. Beneath the dripping brim of her hat, her dark eyes were wide with concern.

He wondered if he was the cause.

'Have you heard the weather report?' she asked.

He shook his head. 'Not a word. I haven't had the radio on. Why? What's happening?'

'A cyclone. Cyclone Peta. It started up in the Gulf yesterday afternoon, and crossed the coast mid-morning. It's dumping masses of rain further north.'

'I guess that's good news.'

'Well, yes, it is. We certainly need the rain.' She frowned. 'But I have a paddock full of cattle down by the river.'

'The Hopkins paddock,' Joe said, remembering the section of their land that had flooded nearly every wet season.

Ellie nodded.

'We need to get them out of there,' he said.

'I know.' Her soft pink mouth twisted into an apologetic wincing smile. 'Joe, I hate to do this to you when you've just arrived, but you know how quickly these rivers can rise. I'd like to shift the cattle this afternoon. Now, actually.'

'OK. Let's get going, then.'

'You don't mind?'

''Course I don't.' In truth, he was relieved to have something practical to do. A mission to rescue cattle was a darn sight more appealing than sitting around drinking tea and trying to make polite conversation with his beautiful soon-to-be ex.

'It's flat country, so we won't need horses. I'll have to take Jacko, though, so I thought I'd take the ute with the trail bike in the back.'

Joe nodded.

'One problem. I'd probably have to stay in the ute with Jacko.' Ellie swallowed, as if she was nervous. 'Would you mind…um…looking after the round-up?'

'Sure. Sounds like a plan.' He chanced a quick smile. 'As long as I haven't lost my touch.'

As he said this, Ellie stared at him for longer than necessary, her expression slightly puzzled and questioning. She opened her mouth as if she was going to say something in response, but then she shook her head as if she'd changed her mind.

'I'll get Jacko. He's having an afternoon nap.' She shrugged out of her coat and beneath it she was wearing a neat blue and white striped shirt tucked into jeans. Her waistline was still as trim as a schoolgirl's.

When she took off her hat, Joe's gaze fixed on her

thick dark hair, pulled back into a glossy braid. Her hair had always been soft to touch despite its thickness.

'Come on in,' she said awkwardly over her shoulder. 'You don't mind if we leave your gear in your car until later?'

He shrugged. 'It's only Christmas presents.'

'Would you…ah…like a cup of tea or anything?'

'No, I'm fine.' The muddy coffee he'd had on the road would take a while to digest. 'Let's collect the kid and get this job done.'

They took off their boots and hung their wet coats on the row of pegs that Joe had mounted beside the front door when they'd first moved in here. To his surprise, his own battered elderly Akubra still hung on the end peg.

Of course, he'd known it would feel strange to follow Ellie into the house as her guest rather than her partner, but the knife thrust in his gut was an unpleasant addition.

The house was full of the furniture they'd chosen together in Townsville—the tan leather sofa and the oval dining table, the rocking chair Ellie had insisted on buying when she was first pregnant.

Joe wouldn't take a stick of this furniture when they divorced. He was striking new trails.

'I'll fetch Jacko,' Ellie said nervously. 'I reckon he'll be awake by now.'

Unsure if he was expected to follow her, Joe remained standing, almost to attention, in the centre of the lounge room. He heard the creak of a floorboard down the hall and the soft warmth in Ellie's voice as she greeted their son. Then he heard the boy's happy crow of delight.

'Mummy, Mummy!'

Joe felt his heart twist.

Moments later, Ellie appeared in the doorway with Jacko in her arms. The boy was a sturdy little fellow, with glowing blue eyes and cheeks still pink and flushed with sleep. He was cuteness personified. Very blond— Joe had been blond until he was six and then his hair had turned dark.

The last time Joe had seen his son, he'd been a sleepy baby, barely able to hold his head up. Now he was a little man.

And he and Ellie were a winsome pair. Joe couldn't help noticing how happy Ellie looked now, with an extra aura of softness and womanly warmth about her that made her lovelier than ever.

She was complete now, he decided. She had what she'd so badly wanted, and he was truly happy for her. Perhaps it was fitting that this miracle had only occurred after Joe had stepped out of the picture.

Jacko was grinning at him. 'Man!' he announced in noisy delight.

'This is Joe,' Ellie told him, her voice a tad shaky. 'You can say *Joe*, can't you, big boy?'

'Joe!' the boy echoed with a triumphant grin.

'So he's going to call me Joe? Not Dad?'

Ellie frowned as if he'd let fly with a swear word.

'You've been away,' she said tightly. 'And you're going away again. Jacko's only two, and if you're not going to be around us he can't be expected to understand the concept of a father. Calling you Daddy would only confuse him.'

Joe's teeth clenched. He almost demanded to know

if she had another guy already waiting in the wings. A stepfather?

'Jacko's bound to understand about fathers eventually,' he said tersely.

'And we'll face that explanation when the time is right.' A battle light glowed in Ellie's dark eyes.

Damn it, they were at it already. Joe gave a carefully exaggerated shrug. *Whatever.* He'd had enough of war at home *and* abroad. On this visit he was determined to remain peaceful.

He turned his attention to his son. 'So how are you, Jacko?'

The boy squirmed and held out his arms. 'Down,' he demanded. 'I want Man.'

With an anxious smile, Ellie released him.

The little boy rushed at Joe's legs and looked up at him with big blue eyes and a grin of triumph.

What now? Joe thought awkwardly. He reached down and took his son's tiny plump hand and gave it a shake. 'Pleased to meet you, Jacko.'

He deliberately avoided noting Ellie's reaction.

They drove down to the river flats with their son strapped into the toddler seat between them, and Ellie tried not to mind that Jacko seemed to be obsessed with Joe.

The whole way, the little boy kept giggling and making eyes at the tall dark figure beside him, and he squealed with delight when Joe pulled faces.

A man's presence at Karinya was a novelty, of course, and Ellie knew that Jacko had been starved of masculine company. He was always intrigued by any male visitor.

Problem was that today Ellie was almost as intrigued as her son, especially when she watched Joe take off on the trail bike through the rain and the mud. He looked so spectacularly athletic and fit and so totally at home on the back of a motorbike, rounding up the herd, ducking and weaving through patches of scrub.

He certainly hadn't lost his touch.

'Show-off,' she muttered with a reluctant grim smile as he jumped the bike over a pile of fallen timber and then skilfully edged the stragglers forward into the mob, heading them up the slope towards the open gate where she was parked.

'Joe!' Jacko cried, bouncing in his car seat and pointing through the windscreen. He clapped his hands. 'Look, Mummy! Joe!'

'Yeah, he looks good, all right,' Ellie had to admit. In terms of skill and getting the job done quickly, Joe might never have been away.

And that felt dangerous.

Out of the blue, she found herself remembering their wedding day and the short ceremony in the register office in Townsville. She and Joe had decided they didn't want to go through awkward explanations about her pregnancy to their families, and neither of them had wanted the fuss of a big family wedding.

They'd both agreed they could deal with their families later. On that day, all they'd wanted was to commit to each other. Their elopement had seemed *soooo* romantic.

But it had also been reckless, Ellie thought now as she saw how brightly her son's eyes shone as he watched Joe.

'Don't be too impressed, sweetheart. Take Mummy's word; it's simply not worth it. That man will only break your heart.'

Jacko merely chortled.

It was dark by the time Joe came into the kitchen, having showered and changed into dry clothes. Outside, the rain still pelted down, drumming on the roof and streaming over the edge of the guttering, but Ellie had closed the French windows leading onto the veranda and the kitchen was bright and cosy.

She tried not to notice how red-hot attractive Joe looked in a simple white T-shirt and blue jeans, with his dark hair damp from the shower, his bright eyes an unforgettable piercing blue. The man was still unlawfully sexy.

But Joe seemed to have acquired a lone wolf aura now. In addition to his imperfect nose that had been broken in a punch-up when he was seventeen, there was a hard don't-mess-with-me look in his eyes that made her wonder what he'd been through over the past four years.

Almost certainly, he'd been required to kill people, and she couldn't quite get her head around that. How had that changed him?

The Army had kept the Commandos' deployments short and frequent in a bid to minimise post-traumatic stress, but no soldier returned from war unscarred. These days, everyone knew that. For Ellie, there was the extra, heavily weighing knowledge that their unhappy marriage had pushed Joe in the Army's direction.

And now, here they were, standing in the same room, but she was painfully aware of the wide, unbridgeable chasm that gaped open between them.

She turned and lifted the lid on the slow cooker, giving its contents a stir, wishing she was more on top of this situation.

'That smells amazing,' said Joe.

She felt a small flush of satisfaction. She'd actually set their dinner simmering earlier in the day, hoping it would fill the kitchen with enticing aromas, but she responded to Joe's compliment with a casual shrug and tried not to look too pleased. 'It's just a Spanish chicken dish.'

'Spanish?' Joe raised a quizzical eyebrow.

No doubt he was remembering her previously limited range of menus. 'I've broadened my recipe repertoire.'

Joe almost smiled, but then he seemed to change his mind. Sinking his hands into his jeans pockets, he looked around the kitchen, taking in the table set with red and white gingham mats and the sparkling white cupboards and timber bench tops. 'You've also been decorating.'

Ellie nodded. 'Before I became pregnant with Jacko I painted just about every wall and cupboard in the house.'

'The nesting instinct?'

'Something like that.'

Joe frowned at this, his eyes taking on an ambiguous gleam as he stared hard at the cupboards. His Adam's apple jerked in his throat. 'It looks great,' he said gruffly.

But Ellie felt suddenly upset. It felt wrong to be showing off her homemaker skills when she had absolutely no plans to share this home with him.

'Where's Jacko?' he asked, abruptly changing the subject

'Watching TV. Nina's recorded his favourite programmes, and he's happy to watch them over and over. It helps him to wind down at the end of the day.'

This was met by a slow nod but, instead of wandering off to check out his son, Joe continued to stand in the middle of the kitchen with his hands in his pockets, his gaze thoughtful.

'He doesn't watch a lot of TV,' Ellie felt compelled to explain. 'I…I usually read him story books as well.'

'I'm sure he loves that.' Joe's blue eyes blazed. 'Chill, Ellie. I'm not here to judge you. I'm sure you're a great mum. Fantastic.'

Her smile wobbled uncertainly. Why would this compliment make her want to cry?

They should try to relax. She should offer Joe a pre-dinner beer or a glass of wine.

But, before she could suggest this, he said, 'So, I guess this is as good a time as any for me to sign those divorce papers?'

Ellie's stomach dropped as if she'd fallen from the top of a mountain. 'Well…um…yes,' she said, but she had to grip the bench behind her before her knees gave way. 'You could sign now…or after dinner.'

'It's probably best to get it over with and out of the way.'

'I guess.' Her reply was barely a whisper. It was ridiculous. She'd been waiting for this moment for so long. They'd arranged an out of court settlement and their future plans were clear—she would keep on with the lease at Karinya, and Joe had full access to Jacko, although she wasn't sure how often he planned to see his son.

This settlement was what she wanted, of course, and

yet she felt suddenly bereft, as if a great hole had opened up in her life, almost as if someone had died.

What on earth was the matter with her? Joe's signature would provide her with her ticket of leave.

Freedom beckoned.

The feeling of loss was nothing more than a temporary lapse, an aberration brought on by the unscheduled spot of cattle work that she and Joe had shared this afternoon. Rounding up the herd by the river had felt too dangerously like the good old days when they'd still been in love.

'Ellie?' Joe was standing stiffly to attention now, his eyes alert but cool, watching her intently. 'You're OK about this, aren't you?'

'Yes, of course. I'm totally fine.' She spoke quickly, not quite meeting his gaze, and then she drew a deep, fortifying breath, hoping it would stop the trembling in her knees. 'The papers are in the study.'

'Ellie.'

The unexpected gentleness in his voice brought her spinning around. 'Yes?'

'I wish…'

'What?' She almost snapped this question.

What do you wish? Tell me quickly, Joe.

Did he wish they didn't have to do this? Was he asking for another chance to save their marriage?

'I wish you didn't look so pale and upset.'

Her attempt to laugh came out as a hiccup. Horrified, she seized on the handiest weapon—anger. It was the weapon she'd used so often with this man, firing holes into the bedrock of their marriage. 'If I'm upset, Joe, it's because this is a weird situation.'

'But we agreed.' He seemed angry, too, but his anger

was annoyingly cold and controlled. 'It's what you want, isn't it?'

'Sure, we agreed, and yes, it's what I want. But it's still weird. How many people agree to a divorce and then put it on hold for four years?'

'You know why we did that—so you'd be looked after financially if I was killed.'

'Yes, I know, and that was generous of you. Just the same, it hasn't been a picnic here.' Suddenly, Ellie could feel the long months of tension giving way inside her, rushing to the surface, hot and explosive. 'While you were away being the hero in Afghanistan, you were distracted by everything over there. But I was *here*, supposed to be divorced, but surrounded by all of this.'

Flinging her arm dramatically, she gestured to the homestead and the paddocks beyond. 'Every day, I was left with the remnants of our lives together. A constant reminder of everything that went wrong.'

'So why did you stay?' Joe asked coolly.

Ellie gasped, momentarily caught out. 'I'm surprised you have to ask,' she said quickly to cover her confusion.

He shrugged a cool, questioning eyebrow.

And Ellie looked away. She'd asked herself the same question often enough. She knew exactly why she'd stayed. Even now, she could hear her dad's voice from all those years ago. *If you start something, Ellie, you've got to see it through.*

Her dad had told her this just before her thirteenth birthday. She'd been promised a horse for her birthday and he'd been building proper stables instead of the old two-sided tin shelter they'd had until then.

Ellie had helped him by holding hammers or the long

pieces of timber and she'd handed up nails and screws. While they worked her dad had reminded her that owning a horse was a long-term project.

'You can't take up a responsibility like a horse and then lose interest,' he'd said. 'I've known people like that. They never stick at anything, always have to be trying something different, and they end up unhappy and wondering what went wrong.'

Tragically, her father had never finished those stables. He'd also he'd been mending a windmill and he'd fallen and died three days before Ellie's birthday. In the bleak months that followed, Ellie's mum had sold their farm and moved into town, and the horse that should have been Ellie's had gone to another girl in her class at school.

In a matter of months, Ellie lost everything—her darling father, her beloved farm, her dreams of owning a horse. And the bittersweet irony of her father's words had been seared into her brain.

If you start something, you've got to see it through.

Years later, with a failed marriage and failed attempts at parenthood weighing her down, she'd been determined that she wouldn't let go of Karinya as well.

'So why did you stay here?' Joe repeated.

With her arms folded protectively over her chest, Ellie told him. 'I love this place, Joe. I'm proud of it, and I've worked hard to improve it. It was hard enough giving up half a dream without giving up Karinya as well.'

Joe's only reaction was to stand very still, watching her with a stern, unreadable gaze. If Ellie hadn't been studying him with equal care, she might have missed the fleeting shadow that dimmed his bright blue eyes, or the telltale muscle twitching in his jaw.

But she did see these signs, and they made something unravel inside her.

Damn you, Joe. Tell me what you're thinking.

Painful seconds ticked by, but neither of them moved nor spoke. Ellie almost reached out and said, *Do we need to talk about this?*

But it wasn't an easy question to ask when it was Joe who'd originally suggested their divorce. He'd never shown any sign of backing down, so now her stubborn pride kept her silent.

Eventually, he said quietly, 'So, about this signing?'

Depressed but resolute, Ellie pointed to the doorway to the study. 'The papers are in here.'

As she reached the study, she didn't look back to check that Joe was following her. Skirting the big old silky oak desk that they'd bought at an antique shop in Charters Towers, she marched straight to the shelves Joe had erected all those years ago and she lifted down a well-thumbed Manila folder.

She sensed Joe behind her but she didn't look at him as she turned and placed the folder on the desk. In silence she opened it to reveal the sheaf of papers that she'd lodged with the courts.

'I guess you'll want to read these through,' she said, eyes downcast.

'There's no need. Geoffrey Bligh has sent me a copy. I know what it says.'

'Oh? All right.' Ellie opened a drawer and selected a black pen. 'So, I've served you with the papers, and all you need to do now is sign to acknowledge that you accept them.' She still couldn't look him in the eye.

She was trembling inside and she took a deep breath.

'There,' she said dully, setting the appropriate sheet

of paper on the desk and then stepping away to make room for Joe.

His face was stonily grim as he approached the desk, but he showed no sign of hesitation as he picked up the pen.

As he leaned over the desk, Ellie watched the neat dark line of his hair across the back of his neck and she saw a vein pulsing just below his ear. She noticed how strong his hand looked as he gripped the pen.

Unhelpfully, she remembered his hand, those fingers touching her when they made love. It seemed so long ago and yet it was so unforgettable.

There'd been a time in their marriage when they'd been so good at sex.

Joe scrawled his spiky signature, then set the pen down and stood staring fiercely at the page now decorated with his handwriting.

It was over.

In the morning he would take this final piece of paper with him to their solicitor but, to all intents and purposes, they were officially and irrevocably divorced.

And now they had to eat dinner together. Ellie feared the Spanish chicken would taste like dust in her mouth.

CHAPTER THREE

IT SHOULD HAVE been cosy eating Ellie's delicious meal in the homestead kitchen to the accompaniment of the steadily falling rain. But Joe had dined in Kabul when a car bomb exploded just outside and he'd felt more relaxed then than he did now with his ex.

It shouldn't be this way.

All their tensions were supposed to be behind them now. They were no longer man and wife. Their marriage was over, both in reality and on paper. It was like signing a peace treaty. No more disputes. Everything was settled.

They were free. Just friends. No added expectations.

And yet Ellie had barely touched the food she'd taken so much trouble to prepare. Joe supposed she wished he was gone—completely out of her hair.

As long as he hung around this place, they would both be besieged by this edgy awareness of each other that kept them on tenterhooks.

Ellie was meticulously shredding the tender chicken on her plate with her fork. 'So what are your plans now?' she asked in the carefully polite tone people used when they were making an effort to maintain a semblance of normality. 'Are you staying in the Army?'

Joe shook his head. 'I have a job lined up—with a government team in the Southern Ocean—patrolling for poachers and illegal fishermen.'

'The Southern Ocean?' Ellie couldn't have looked more surprised or upset if he'd announced he was going to mine asteroids in outer space. 'So…so Jacko won't see you at all?'

Annoyed by this, Joe shrugged. 'If you plan to stay out here, it wouldn't matter what sort of work I did—I still wouldn't be able to see the boy very often.'

'There's an Army base in Townsville.'

This was a surprise. He'd expected Ellie to be pleased that he'd be well away from her. 'As I said, I'm leaving the Army.'

Ellie's eyes widened. 'I thought you loved it. I thought it was supposed to be what you'd always wanted.'

'It was,' Joe said simply. For possibly the first time in his life, he'd felt a true sense of belonging with his fellow Commandos. He'd grown up as the youngest in his family, but he'd always been the little nuisance tagalong, hanging around his four older brothers, never quite big enough to keep up, never quite fitting in.

In the Army he'd truly discovered a 'band of brothers', united by the challenge and threat of active service. But everything about the Army would be different now, and he couldn't bear the thought of a desk job.

Ellie dipped her fork into a pile of savoury rice, but she didn't lift it to her mouth. 'I can't see you in a boat, rolling around in the Southern Ocean. You've always been a man of the land. You have all the bush skills and knowledge.'

It was true that Joe loved the bush, and he'd especially loved starting his own cattle business here at

Karinya. But what was the point of rehashing ancient history?

'I guess I feel like a change,' he said with a shrug.

'When do you have to start this new job?'

'In a few weeks. Mid-January.'

'That soon?'

He shrugged again. He was pleased he had an approaching deadline. Given the mess of his private life, he needed a plan, somewhere definite to go with new horizons.

'Will you mind—' Ellie began, but then she swallowed and looked away. 'Will it bother you that you won't see much of Jacko?'

Joe inhaled a sharp, instinctively protective breath. He was trying really hard not to think too much about his son, about all the milestones he'd already missed and those he would miss in the future—the day-to-day adventure of watching a small human being come to terms with the world. 'Maybe I'll be more use to him later on, when he's older.'

It was clearly the wrong thing to say.

Ellie's jaw jutted. She looked tenser than ever. Awkward seconds ticked by. Joe wished he didn't have to try so damn hard, even now, after they'd broken up.

'What about you?' he asked. 'I haven't asked how you are now. Are you keeping well?'

'I am well, actually. I think having Jacko has made a big difference, both mentally and physically. I must admit I'm a lot calmer these days. And I think all the hard outdoor work here has paid off as well.' She touched her stomach. 'Internally, things…um…seem to have settled down.'

'That's fantastic.' He knew how she'd suffered and he was genuinely pleased for her. 'So, do you have plans?'

'How do you mean?'

'Are you planning to move on from here?' Joe steeled himself. If there was a new man in her life, this was her chance to say so.

But her jaw dropped so hard Joe almost heard it crack.

'You're joking, aren't you?'

'Not at all.'

'You really think I could willingly leave Karinya?'

'Well, it's got to be tough for you out here on your own. You need help.'

'I hire help if I need it—fencing contractors, ringers, jillaroos…'

The relief he felt was ridiculous. He covered it with a casual shrug. 'I've heard it's hard to find workers these days. Everyone's heading for the mines.'

'I've managed.'

Joe couldn't resist prying. 'I suppose you might have a boyfriend lined up already?'

'Oh, for pity's sake.' Ellie was angry now.

And, although he knew it was foolish, he couldn't help having one last dig. 'I thought your mother might have had a victory. What was the name of that guy she picked out for you? The potato farmer near Hay? Orlando?'

'Roland,' Ellie said tightly. 'And he grows all sorts of vegetables—lettuce, pumpkins, tomatoes, corn—much more than potatoes. He's making a fortune, apparently.'

'Quite a catch,' Joe said, more coldly than he'd meant to.

'Yes, and a gentleman, too.' Ellie narrowed her eyes

at Joe. 'Do you really want me to give up this lease? Are you worried about the money?'

'No,' he snapped tersely. He couldn't deny he was impressed by Ellie's tenacity, even if it suggested that she was prepared to work much harder at the cattle business than she had at their marriage. 'I just think it's too big a property for a woman to run on her own, especially for a woman with a small child to care for as well.'

'Nina will be back after Christmas. She's great with Jacko.'

Joe recognised a brick wall when he ran into it and he let the subject drop. He suspected Ellie was as relieved as he was when the meal was finally over.

With the aid of night vision goggles, Joe made his way through a remote Afghan village, moving with the stealth of a panther on the prowl. In every dark alley and around every corner the threat of danger lurked and Joe was on high alert, listening for the slightest movement or sound.

As forward scout, his responsibilities weighed heavily. Five Australian soldiers depended on his skills, trusting that he wouldn't lead them blindly into an ambush.

As he edged around another corner, a sudden crash shattered the silence. Joe's night vision vanished. He was plunged into darkness.

Adrenaline exploded in his vitals. How had he lost his goggles? Or—*hell*—had worse happened? Had he been blinded?

He couldn't even find his damn rifle.

To add to the confusion, a persistent drumming sounded above and around him.

What the hell had happened?

Even more bizarrely, when Joe stepped forward he felt carpet beneath his feet. His *bare* feet. What was going on? Where was he?

Panic flared. Had he gone raving mad? Where were his boots? His weapon?

Totally disoriented, he blinked, and at last his vision cleared slightly. He could just make out the dimmest of details, and he seemed to be naked apart from boxer shorts and, yes, his feet were bare and they were definitely sinking into soft carpet.

He had absolutely no idea where the hell he was, or how he'd got there.

Then he heard a small child's cry and his stomach lurched. As a Commando, in close contact with the enemy, his greatest fear was that he might inadvertently bring harm to Afghan children.

It was still difficult to see as he made his way through the pitch-black night, moving towards the child's cry, bumping into a bookcase.

A bookcase?

A doorway.

Ahead, down a passage, he saw a faint glow—it illuminated painted tongue-and-groove timber walls. Walls that were strangely familiar.

Karinya.

Hell, yeah. Of course.

A soft oath broke from him. He'd woken from a particularly vivid dream and he was back in North Queensland and, while he couldn't explain the crashing sound, the crying child was…

Jacko.

His son.

Joe's heart skidded as he scorched into Jacko's room. In the glow of a night light, he saw the toddler huddled and frightened on the floor in the wreckage of his cot. Without hesitation, Joe dived and swept the boy into his arms.

Jacko was shaking but, in Joe's arms, he nestled against his bare chest, a warm ball sobbing, seeking protection and clearly trusting Joe to provide it.

'Shh.' Joe pressed his lips to the boy's soft hair and caught the amazing smell of shampoo, probably baby shampoo. 'You're OK. I've got you.'

I'm your father.

The boy felt so little and warm in Joe's arms. And so scared. A fierce wave of emotion came sweeping through Joe—a surge of painful yearning—an urge to protect this warm, precious miniature man, to keep him safe at all costs.

'I've got you, little mate,' he murmured. 'You're OK.' And then he added in a soft, tentative whisper, 'I'm your dad. I love you, Jacko.' The words felt both alien and wonderful. And true.

'What happened?' Ellie's voice demanded from the doorway. 'I heard a crash.'

Joe turned and saw her in the dimmed light, wearing a white nightdress with tiny straps, her dark hair tumbling in soft waves about her smooth, bare shoulders. She looked beautiful beyond words and Joe's heart almost stopped.

'What happened?' she asked again, coming forward. 'Is Jacko all right?'

'I think he's fine, but he got a bad fright. Looks like his cot's collapsed.'

Jacko had seen Ellie now and he lurched away from Joe, throwing out his arms and wailing, 'Mummy!'

Joe tried not to mind that his Great Three Seconds of Fatherhood were over in a blink, or that Jacko, now safely in Ellie's arms, looked back at him as if he were a stranger.

Ellie was staring at Joe too—staring with wide, almost popping eyes at his bare chest and at the scars on his shoulder. Joe hoped her gaze wouldn't drop to his shorts or they'd both be embarrassed.

Abruptly, he turned, forcing his attention to the collapsed cot. It was a simple timber construction with panels of railings threaded on a metal rod and screwed into place with wing nuts. Nothing had actually broken. It seemed the thing had simply come apart.

'Looks like the wing nuts in the corners worked loose,' he said.

'Oh, Lord.' Ellie stepped forward with the boy on her hip. 'Jacko was playing with those wing nuts the other day. He was trying to undo them, but I didn't think he had a hope.'

'Well, I'd say he was successful. He must have strong little fingers.'

Ellie looked at her son in disbelief and then she shook her head and gave a wry smile, her dark eyes suddenly sparkling. Joe so wished she wouldn't smile like that, not when she was standing so close to him in an almost see-through nightdress.

'You're a little monkey, Jacko,' she told the boy affectionately. Then, more businesslike, she turned to Joe. 'I guess it shouldn't be too hard to fix?'

'Piece of cake.' He picked up one of the panels. 'A

pair of pliers would be handy. The nuts need to be tight enough to stop him from doing it again.'

Ellie nodded. 'I think I have a spare pair of pliers in the laundry, but don't worry about it now. I'll take Jacko back to my room. He can sleep with me for the rest of the night.'

Lucky Jacko.

From the doorway, she turned and frowned back at Joe. 'Do you need anything? A hot drink or something to help you get back to sleep?'

She must have seen the expression on his face. She quickly dropped her gaze. 'I keep forgetting. You're a tough soldier. You can sleep on a pile of rocks.'

With Jacko in her arms, she hurried away, the white nightdress whispering around her smooth, shapely calves.

Joe knew he wouldn't be sleeping.

Jacko settled quickly. He was like a little teddy bear as he snuggled close to Ellie and in no time he was asleep again. She adored her little miracle boy, and she relished this excuse to lie still and hold him, loving the way he nestled close.

Lying in the darkness, she inhaled the scent of his clean hair and listened to the soft rhythm of his breathing.

His perfection constantly amazed her.

But, tonight, it wasn't long before she was thinking about Joe and, in a matter of moments, she felt a pain in her chest like indigestion, and then her throat was tense and aching, choked.

She kept seeing Joe's signature on that piece of paper.

And now he was about to head off for the Southern

Ocean. Surely, if he wanted adventure, he could have caught wild bulls or rogue crocodiles, or found half a dozen other dangerous activities that were closer to home?

Instead, once again, he was getting as far away from her as possible, risking his life in stormy seas and chasing international poachers, for pity's sake.

Unhelpfully, Ellie recalled how eye-wateringly amazing Joe had looked just now, standing bare-chested in Jacko's room. With the little boy in his arms, he'd looked so incredibly strong and muscular and protective.

Man, he was *buffed*.

He'd always been fit and athletic, of course, which was one of the reasons the Army had snapped him up, but now, after all the extra training and discipline, her ex-husband looked sensational.

Her ex.

The word hit her like a slug to the heart. Which was crazy. *I don't want him back. Looks aren't everything. They're just a distraction.*

Tonight, it was all too easy to forget the pain she and Joe had been through, the constant bickering and soul-destroying negativity, the tears and the yelling. The sad truth was—the final year before their separation had been pretty close to hell on earth.

Unhappily, Ellie knew that a large chunk of the tension had been her fault. During that bleak time when she'd been so overwhelmed by her inability to get pregnant again, she'd really turned on Joe until everything he'd done had annoyed her.

Looking back, she felt so guilty. She'd been a shrew—constantly picking on Joe for the smallest things, even the way he left clothes lying around, or the way he left the lid off the toothpaste, the way he'd assumed she was happy to look after the house and the garden while he swanned off, riding his horse all over their property, enjoying all the adventurous, more important outdoor jobs, while she was left to cook and clean.

Ellie hadn't been proud of her nagging and fault-finding. As a child, she'd hated the way her mother picked on her dad all the time, and she'd been shocked to find herself repeating that despicable pattern. But she'd become so tense and depressed she hadn't been able to stop herself.

Naturally, Joe hadn't accepted her insults meekly. He'd slung back as good as he got. But she'd been dev-astated when he finally suggested divorce.

'It's clear that I'm making you unhappy,' he'd said in a cold, clipped voice she'd never heard before.

And how could Ellie deny it? She *had* been unhappy, and she'd taken her unhappiness out on Joe, but that hadn't meant she wanted to be rid of him.

'Do you really want a divorce?' she'd asked him and, although she'd been crying on the inside, for the sake of her pride, she'd kept a brave face.

'I think it's the only solution,' Joe had said. 'We can't go on like this. Maybe you'll have better luck with an-other guy.'

She didn't want another man, but why would Joe believe that when she'd been so obviously miserable?

'What would you do?' she'd asked instead. 'Where would you go? What would we do about Karinya?'

He'd been scarily cool and detached. 'You can make up your mind about Karinya, but I'll apply to join the Army.'

She hadn't known how to fight this. 'The Army was what you wanted all along, wasn't it? It was what you were planning before we met.'

Joe didn't deny this.

It was then she'd known the awful truth. Falling for her had been an aberration. A distraction.

If she hadn't been pregnant, they wouldn't have married...

The bitter memories wrung a groan from Ellie and, beside her in the darkness, Jacko stirred, throwing out an arm and smacking her on the nose. He didn't wake up and she rolled away, staring moodily into the black night, thinking about Joe lying in his swag on the study floor. He'd insisted on sleeping there rather than in Nina's room.

'It's only for one night,' he'd said. 'Not worth disturbing her things.'

Ellie wondered if Joe was asleep, or whether he was also lying there thinking about their past.

Unlikely.

No doubt he was relieved to be finally and permanently free of her. He certainly wouldn't be as mixed-up and tied in knots as she was.

Joe didn't want to think about Ellie. She was part of his past, just as the Army was now. Every time visions of her white nightdress arrived, he forcibly erased them.

He'd signed the final papers.

Ellie. Was. No. Longer. His. Wife.

And yet...

Annoyingly, he felt a weight that felt like grief pressing on his chest. Grief for their loss, and for their fail-

ure, for their past mistakes and for how things used to
be at the beginning.

And, despite his best efforts, he couldn't stop the
blasted memories.

He'd been a goner from the moment he first saw
Ellie, which was pretty bizarre, given that his first sight-
ing had been at long distance.

Ellie had been walking with her back to him at the
far end of their tiny town's one and only shopping street.
And, from the start, there'd been something inescapably
alluring about her. The glossy swing of her dark hair
and the jaunty sway of her neat butt in long-legged blue
jeans had completely captured his attention.

Of course, it was totally the *worst* time for Joe to become romantically entangled. He'd been on the brink
of joining the Army. After struggling unsuccessfully
to find his place in the large Madden family, overrun
with strapping sons, he'd been lured by the military's
promise of adventure and danger.

So, on that day that was etched forever in his memory, he should have been able to ignore Ellie's attrac-
tions. He should have finished his errands in town and
headed back to their cattle property. And perhaps he
would have done that if Jerry Bray hadn't chosen that
exact moment to step out of the stock and station agency
to speak to Ellie.

Jealousy was a strange and fierce emotion, Joe
swiftly discovered. He hadn't even met this girl, hadn't
yet seen her front-on, hadn't discovered the bewitching
sparkle in her eyes. And yet he was furious with Jerry
for chatting her up.

To Joe's huge relief, Jerry's boss interrupted his employee's clumsy attempts at flirtation and called him back inside.

Alone once more, Ellie continued on to the Bluebird Café, and this was a golden opportunity Joe couldn't let pass.

After a carefully calculated interval, he followed her into the café, found her sitting alone at one of the tables, drinking a milkshake and engrossed in a women's magazine.

She looked up when he walked in and Joe saw her face for the first time. Saw her eyes, the same lustrous dark brown as her hair, saw her finely arched eyebrows, her soft pale skin, the sweet curve of her mouth, her neat chin. She was even lovelier than he'd imagined.

And then she smiled.

And *zap*. Joe was struck by the proverbial lightning flash. His skin was on fire, his heart was a skyrocket.

'So what d'ya want?' asked Bob Browne, the café's proprietor.

Joe stared at him blankly, unable, for a moment, to think. It was as if his mind had been wiped clean by the dark-eyed girl's smile.

Bob gave a knowing smirk and rolled his eyes. 'She's not on the menu.'

Ignoring this warning, Joe shrugged and ordered a hamburger and a soft drink. Unable to help himself, he crossed the café to the girl's table. 'Hi,' he said.

'Hello.' This time, when she smiled, he saw the most fetching dimple.

'You must be new around here. I don't think we've met. I'm Joe Madden.'

'Ellie Saxby,' she supplied without hesitation.

Ellie Saxby. Ellie. Had there ever been a more delightful name?

'Are you staying around here?' he asked super-casually.

'I'm working for the Ashtons. As a jillaroo.'

Better and better.

There was a spare chair at Ellie Saxby's table. 'OK if I sit here?' Joe was again carefully, casually polite.

Ellie rewarded him with another dazzling smile. 'Sure.'

Her eyes were shining, her cheeks flushed. The atmosphere was so electric, Joe felt as if he was walking on clouds.

And yet there was nothing remarkable about that first conversation. Joe was too dazed to think of anything very clever to say. But he and Ellie chatted easily about where they lived and why they'd come to town.

By the time his hamburger arrived, he was halfway in love with Ellie and she was giving out all the right signals. They left the café together and Joe walked with her to her vehicle.

They exchanged phone numbers and Ellie remained standing beside her car, as if she wasn't ready to drive away.

She looked so alluring, with her sparkling eyes and shiny hair, her soft skin and pretty mouth.

Joe had never been particularly forward with girls, but he found himself saying, 'Look, I know we've just met, and this out of line, but I really need to—'

He didn't even finish the sentence. He simply leaned in and kissed her. Ellie tasted as fresh as spring and, to his amazed relief, she returned his kiss with just the right level of enthusiasm, and a simple hello, exploratory kiss became the most thrilling, most electrifying kiss ever.

It was the start of a whirlwind romance. Before the week was out, he and Ellie had found an excuse to meet again and, within the first month, they drove together to Rockhampton for dinner and a movie, followed by a night in a motel, which proved to be a night of blazing, out of this world passion.

When Ellie discovered she was pregnant, Joe had to make a quick decision. Ellie or the Army?

No contest.

In a blinding flash of clarity, he knew without question that his plan to join the Army had been a crazy idea. In Ellie he'd found his true reason for being. He asked her to marry him and, to his delight, she readily agreed.

The ink on their marriage certificate was barely dry before they headed north in search of their very own cattle property and the start of their bright new happy-ever-after.

When Ellie miscarried three weeks after they'd moved into Karinya, they'd been deeply disappointed but, in the long run, not too downhearted. After all, they were young and healthy and strong and in love.

But it was the start of a downhill run. A diagnosis of endometriosis had followed. Joe had never even heard of this condition, let alone understood how it could blight such a fit and healthy girl. Ellie was vivacious, bursting with energy and life and yet, over the next few years, she was slowly dragged down.

He remembered finding her slumped over the kitchen table, her face streaked with tears.

He'd touched her gently on the shoulder, stroked her

hair. 'Don't let it get you down, Ellie. It'll be OK. We'll be OK.'

We still have each other, he'd wanted to say.

But she'd whirled on him, her face red with fury. 'How can you say that? How can you possibly *know* we'll be OK? I'm sorry, Joe, but that's just a whitewash, and it makes me *so* mad!'

She'd lost all hope, had no faith in him or their future. He'd felt helpless.

Now, with hindsight, he could see the full picture. He and Ellie had rushed at marriage like lemmings to a cliff, expecting to build a lasting relationship—for richer or poorer, in sickness and in health—having based these expectations on little more than blazing lust.

It was his fault.

Joe had always known that. Looking back, it was blindingly obvious that he hadn't courted Ellie properly. They hadn't taken anywhere near enough time to get to know each other as friends before they became life partners. They hadn't even fully explored their hopes and dreams before they'd embarked on marriage.

They'd simply been lovers, possessed by passion, a heady kind of madness. And Ellie had found herself trapped by that first pregnancy.

Small wonder their marriage had hit the rocks as soon as the seas got rough and, instead of offering Ellie comfort, Joe had taken refuge, working long hard hours in Karinya's paddocks—fencing, building dams, mustering and branding cattle. Later he'd joined the Army. Had that been a kind of refuge as well?

Whatever. It was too late for an extensive post-mortem. Tomorrow he'd be leaving again and Ellie would finally be free. He wished he felt better about that.

CHAPTER FOUR

NEXT MORNING IT was raining harder than ever.

Out of habit, Ellie woke early and slipped out of bed, leaving Jacko curled asleep. She dressed quickly and went to the kitchen and, to her surprise Joe was already up, dressed and drinking a mug of tea.

He turned and greeted her with only the faintest trace of a smile. 'Morning.'

'Good morning.' Ellie flicked the kettle to bring it back to the boil and looked out of the window at the wall of thick grey rain. 'It's been raining all night. You won't want to waste time getting over the river.'

Joe nodded. 'I'll need to get going, but I'm worried about you and Jacko. You could be cut off.'

'Yeah, well, that happens most wet seasons.' She reached for a mug and a tea bag. 'I'm used to it and we're well stocked up.'

Joe was frowning, and Ellie wondered if frowning was his new default expression.

'It's hardly an ideal situation,' he said. 'A woman and a little child, isolated and alone out here. It's crazy. What if Jacko gets sick or injured?'

'Crikey, Joe. Since when has that worried you? We've been living here since he was born, you know.'

'But you haven't been cut off by flood waters.'

'I have, actually.'

He glared at her, and an emotion halfway between anger and despair shimmered in his eyes.

Ellie tried for nonchalance as she poured boiling water into her mug.

Joe cleared his throat. 'I think I should stay.'

Startled, Ellie almost scalded herself. 'You mean stay here with us?'

'Just till the river goes down again.'

'Joe, we're divorced.'

His blue eyes glittered. 'I'm aware of that.'

'And…and it's almost Christmas.' Last night they'd struggled through an unbearably strained meal together. They couldn't possibly manage something as festive as Christmas.

Ellie was supposed to be spending Christmas Day with her neighbours and good friends, the Andersons, although, if the creek stayed high, as well as the river, that might not be an option.

Of course, her mother had originally wanted her to go home to New South Wales, but Ellie had declined on several grounds. Number one—she wasn't comfortable around her stepfather, for reasons her mother had turned a deaf ear to. As well as that, up until yesterday, she'd been dealing, ironically, with drought. Her priority had been the state of her cattle—and then clearing things up with Joe.

The Joe factor was well and truly sorted, and sharing Christmas with him would be a disaster. Being divorced and forced to stay together would be a thousand times bigger strain than being married and apart.

'There's absolutely no need for you to stay, Joe. I really don't think it's a good idea.'

'It was just a suggestion,' he said tightly. 'I was only thinking of your safety.'

'Thanks. That's thoughtful.' Feeling awkward, Ellie fiddled with the handle of her tea mug. 'You know drought and floods are part and parcel of living in this country.'

With a brief shrug, Joe drained his mug and placed it in the sink. 'I should head off then, before the river gets any higher.'

'But you haven't had breakfast.'

'As you pointed out, it wouldn't be wise to wait. It's been raining all night and the river's rising every minute. I've packed the solicitor's papers. I'll drop them in at Bligh's office.'

'Right.' Ellie set her tea mug aside, no longer able to drink it.

Joe's duffel bag was already packed and zipped, and the swag he'd used for sleeping on the study floor was neatly rolled and strapped. Seemed the Army had turned him into a neat freak.

'I've also fixed Jacko's cot,' he said.

'You must have got up early.'

Without answering, he reached for his duffel bag and swung it over one shoulder. 'I wasn't sure where to put the Christmas presents, so I stowed them under the desk in the study. Hope that's OK?'

'That…that's fine, thanks, Joe.' Ellie wished she didn't feel quite so downbeat. 'I hope you haven't spoiled Jacko with too many presents.'

She winced as she said this. She didn't really mind how many presents Joe had bought. This was one of his few chances to play the role of a father. She'd been trying for a light-hearted comment and had totally missed the mark.

Now, Joe's cold, hollow laugh chilled her to the bone.

His face seemed to be carved from stone as he turned to leave. 'Well, all the best, Ellie.'

'Hang on. I'll wake Jacko so you can say goodbye to him, too.'

'Don't disturb him.'

'You've got to say goodbye.' Ellie was close to tears. 'Actually, we'll come out to the river crossing with you. We can follow you in the ute. Just in case there's a problem.'

'There won't be a problem.'

To her dismay, her tears were threatening to fall. 'Joe, humour me. I want to see you safely off this property.'

For the first time, a faint smile glimmered. 'Of course you do.'

Ellie parked on a ridge above the concrete causeway that crossed the river and peered through the rain at the frothing, muddy flood rushing below.

She could see the bright blue of Joe's hire car parked just above the waterline and his dark-coated figure standing on the bank, hands on hips as he studied the river.

'I think it's already too high,' she said glumly to Jacko. The river level was much, much higher than she'd expected. Clearly, the waters from the north had already reached them overnight.

She felt a flurry of panic. Did this mean that Joe would have to stay with them for Christmas after all? How on earth would they cope with the strain?

Even as she wondered this, Joe took off his coat, tossed it back into his vehicle, then began to walk back to the swirling current.

He wasn't going in there, surely?

'Joe!' Ellie yelled, leaping out of the ute. 'Don't be mad. You can't go in there.'

He showed no sign that he'd heard her. No doubt he was as keen to leave her as she was to see him go, but marching into a racing torrent was madness.

Ellie rushed down the track. 'Joe, stop!' The river was mud-brown and seething. 'You can't go in there,' she panted as she reached him.

He scowled and shook his head. 'It's OK. I just need to check the condition of the crossing and the depth. It's too risky to drive straight in there, but I can at least test it on foot. I'll be careful. I think it's still shallow enough to get the car across.'

'But look how fast the water's running. I know you're keen to get away, but you don't have to play the tough hero now, Joe.' Knowing how stubborn he could be, she tried for a joke. 'I don't want to have to tell Jacko that his father was a moron who was washed away trying to cross a flooded river.'

Joe's blue eyes flashed through the sheeting rain. 'I've been trained to stay alive, not to take senseless risks.' He jerked his head towards the ute. 'If you're worried about Jacko, you should get back up there and stay with him.'

Ellie threw up her hands in despair. She'd more or less encouraged, or rather *urged*, Joe to leave. But as she stood there debating how to stop her ex from risking his neck, she heard her little son calling to her.

'Go to him,' ordered Joe.

Utterly wretched, she began to walk back up the slope, turning every step to look over her shoulder as Joe approached the river. By the time she reached the ute, Joe was already in the water and in no time he was up to his knees.

Anxiously, she watched as he carefully felt the ground in front of him with one foot. He edged forward but, despite the obvious care he was taking, a sudden swift surge in the current buffeted him, making him sidestep to regain his balance.

'Joe!' she yelled, sticking her head out into the rain. 'That's enough! Get out!'

'Joe, that's 'nuff!' parroted Jacko.

A tree branch hurtled past Joe, almost sweeping him with it.

Turn back. Ellie was urging him, under her breath now, so she didn't alarm Jacko.

To her relief, Joe must have realised his venture was useless. At last he turned and began to make his way back to the bank.

But Ellie's relief was short-lived, of course. Sure, she was grateful that Joe hadn't drowned himself, but she had no idea how they could live together amicably till the river levels dropped. It would take days, possibly weeks, and the strain would be intolerable.

She was so busy worrying about the challenge of sharing Christmas with her ex that she didn't actually see what happened next.

It seemed that Joe was standing perfectly upright one moment, and then he suddenly toppled sideways and his dark head disappeared beneath the ugly brown water.

Joe had no warning.

He had a firm footing on the causeway, but with the

next step there was no concrete beneath him and he was struggling to regain his balance. Before he could adjust his weight, he slid off the edge.

He felt a sudden jarring scrape against his leg as he was pulled down into the bowels of the dark, angry river.

He couldn't see, couldn't breathe.

Scorching pain shot up his calf, and now he discovered that he also couldn't move. His foot was jammed between the broken section of the concrete causeway and a rock.

Hell. This was it. He'd survived four years of war and now he was going to die here. In front of Ellie and Jacko.

He was a brainless idiot. What had Ellie called him? A moron. She was dead right. No question.

And now… As his lungs strained for air, frantic memories flashed. The first time he'd seen Ellie in the outback café. The first time they'd kissed.

Last night and the chubby, sweet weight of Jacko in his arms.

His signature, acknowledging their divorce.

Don't freaking panic, man.

This was a major stuff-up, but he'd been trained to think.

He had to forget about the pain in his leg and his dire need for air and he had to work out a plan. Fast.

Clearly, his first priority was to get his head above water, but he was anchored by his trapped leg and the massive force of the rushing river. There was only one possible course of action. He had to brace against the current and use every ounce of his upper body strength, especially his stomach muscles, to pull himself upright.

Almost certainly, he couldn't have done it without

his years in the Army and its daily routine of rugged physical training.

As he fought his way upright, his arm bumped a steel rod sticking out of the concrete. As soon as he grabbed it, he had the leverage to finally lift his head above the surface.

He dragged a great, gasping gulp of air. And immediately he heard Ellie's cry.

'Joe! Oh, God, Joe!'

She was in the river, making her way towards him through the seething, perilous water. Her dark hair was plastered to her head, framing her very white, frightened face, and she looked too slender and too fragile and too totally vulnerable.

At any moment, she would be whipped away downstream and Joe knew he wouldn't have a chance in hell of saving her. In the same moment, he thought of trusting little Jacko strapped in his car seat, needing Ellie.

'Get back,' he roared to her. 'Stay on the bank. I'm OK.'

'You're not. Let me help you.'

'No,' he bellowed angrily. '*Get back!*'

He, at least, had something to hang on to, which was more than Ellie had. 'There's no point in both of us getting into trouble. If you're washed away, I won't be able to help you. For God's sake, Ellie, stay there. Think of Jacko. What happens to him, if neither of us gets out?'

This seemed to get through to her at last. She stood there with the river seething about her ankles, clearly tormented by difficult choices, but at least she'd stopped stubbornly coming towards him.

Joe knew he had to get moving. His foot was still

jammed and his only hope was to ignore the pain and to haul his foot out of the trapped boot.

Clenching his teeth, he kept a death grip on the steel rod as he concentrated every sinew in his body into getting his foot free. The force of the river threatened to push him off balance. Slicing pain sheared up his leg as if it was once again sliced by something rough and hard, but somehow, miraculously, his foot was finally out.

Now he just had to stay upright as he fought his way back. He was limping and he stumbled twice, his bare foot slipping on rocks, but he didn't fall and, as he reached the shallows, Ellie was there beside him.

'Don't argue, Joe. Just give me your arm.'

He was happy to let her help him to the bank.

At last…

'Thanks,' he said. And then, with difficulty, 'I'm sorry.'

'Yeah, well, thank God it's over.' Ellie seemed to be suddenly self-conscious. She quickly let go of him and stepped away. Her hair was sleek and straight from the rain and her clothes were plastered to her slender body. And, now that they were safe, Joe probably looked at her for longer than he should have as they stood on the muddy bank, catching their breath.

'You're bleeding!' Ellie cried suddenly, her eyes widening with horror as she pointed to his injured leg.

Joe looked down. Blood was running from beneath his ripped jeans and spreading in bright red rivulets over his bare foot.

'I think it's just a cut,' he said.

'But we need to attend to it. I hope it won't need stitches.'

'I'm sure it's not urgent. Go to Jacko.'

As if backing up Joe's suggestion, a tiny voice in the

distance screamed, 'Mama!' The poor little kid was wailing.

'He needs you,' Joe said, shuddering at the imagined scenario of poor Jacko abandoned in the car while both his parents were swept away.

At least Ellie was already on her way to him. 'You'd better come too,' she called over her shoulder.

There was only one option. While Ellie comforted Jacko, Joe found a towel to wrap around his bleeding leg and, after that, they drove their respective vehicles back to the homestead.

'Nuisance, I know,' Joe said as he set his luggage on the veranda again. 'This totally stuffs up your plans.'

Ellie shrugged. She'd morphed from the bravely stubborn warrior woman who'd rescued him from the river back to a tight-faced, wary hostess.

'We should take a closer look at your leg,' was all she said.

'I don't want to bleed all over the house.' Joe's leg was stinging like crazy and he'd already left bloody footprints on the veranda.

'Let me take a look at it.' Ellie dropped to her knees beside him, frowning as she carefully parted the torn denim to examine his leg more closely.

This was the first time Ellie had touched him in years, and now she was kneeling at his feet and looking so worried. He felt momentarily deprived of air, as if he was back in the river.

Ellie felt incredibly flustered about patching up Joe's leg.

She'd been hoping for distance from her ex, and here

she was instead, tending to his wounds. And the task felt impossibly, disturbingly intimate. She knew she had to get a grip. It was only a matter of swabbing Joe's leg, for heaven's sake. What was wrong with her?

Of course, she was still shaken from the shock of seeing him almost drown in front of her. She kept reliving that horrifying moment when his dark head had disappeared beneath the swirling flood water.

She'd believed it was the end—Joe was gone for ever—and she'd been swamped by an agonising sense of loss. A slug of the darkest possible despair.

Even now, after they were both safely home and showered and changed, she felt shaky as she gathered bottles of antiseptic, tubes of cream and cotton wool swabs and bandages and anything else she thought she might need.

Now she could see the contrariness of their situation. She and Joe had made every attempt to split, finally and for ever, and yet fate had a strange sense of humour and had deemed it necessary to push them together again.

Here was Joe in her kitchen, dressed in shorts, with his long brown leg propped on a chair.

It wasn't fair, Ellie decided, that despite an angry red gash, a single limb could look so spectacularly masculine, so strongly muscled and large.

'Blood,' little Jacko announced solemnly, stepping closer to inspect the bright wound on Joe's calf.

'Jacko's always seriously impressed by blood,' she explained.

Jacko looked up at Joe with round worried eyes, blue gaze meeting blue. 'Band-Aid,' he pronounced solemnly.

'Thanks, mate.' Joe smiled at the boy. 'Your mum's looking after me, so I know I'm in good hands.'

To Ellie's dismay, she felt a bright blush heat her face. 'I'm afraid Joe will need more than a Band-Aid,' she said tightly as she drew a chair close. 'Jacko, why don't you go and find Teddy? I'll give him a Band-Aid, too.' With luck, she would get most of this task done while the boy was away, looking for his favourite stuffed toy.

But, to her annoyance, she couldn't quite meet Joe's eyes as she bent forward to examine his torn flesh. 'It looks like a very bad graze—and it's right down your shin.' She couldn't help wincing in sympathy. 'It must have hurt.'

'It's not too bad. I don't think it's too deep, do you?'

'Perhaps not, but it's had all that filthy river mud in it. I'd hate you to get infected.' Gently, conscientiously, Ellie washed the wound with warm water and antiseptic, then dabbed at the ragged edges with a cotton wool swab and extra antiseptic. 'I hope this doesn't sting too much.'

'Just slosh it on. I'll be fine.'

Of course. He was a tough guy.

Ellie wished she was tougher. She most definitely wished that being around her ex-husband didn't make her feel so breathless and trembling. And overheated.

She forced herself to be businesslike. 'Are you up-to-date with your tetanus shots?'

'No worries there. The Army made sure of it.'

'Of course. OK. I think I should put sterile dressings on these deeper patches.'

'I'm damn lucky you have such a well stocked first aid kit.'

'The Flying Doctors provided it. There are antibiotics, too, if you need them.'

'You're an angel, Ellie.'

Joe said this with such apparent sincerity she was terrified to look him in the eye, too worried he'd read her emotions, that he'd guess how upset she'd been by his accident, that he'd sense how his proximity set her pulses hammering.

Carefully, she tore the protective packaging from a dressing patch and placed it on his leg, gently pressing the adhesive edges to seal it to his skin. Then, without looking up, she dressed another section, working as swiftly and efficiently, and as gently, as she could.

'The Florence Nightingale touch suits you.'

Ellie's head snapped up and suddenly she was looking straight into Joe's eyes. His bright blue gorgeous eyes that had robbed her of common sense and stolen her heart at their very first meeting.

Joe responded with a slow shimmering smile, as if he liked looking at her, too. Her face flamed brightly. Dismayed, she clambered to her feet.

'Teddy!' hollered Jacko, suddenly running into the room with his fluffy golden bear.

Excessively grateful for the distraction, Ellie found a fluorescent green child-pleasing Band-Aid and ceremoniously applied it to the bear's furry leg. Jacko was suitably delighted and he showed the bear to Joe, who inspected the toy's injury with commendable attention for a man not used to children.

'OK,' Ellie told Joe brusquely as Jacko trotted off again, happily satisfied. 'You can throw your things into Nina's room. You should be comfortable enough sleeping in there.'

This time she was ready when a blush threatened at the mere mention of his sleeping arrangements. A deep breath and the sheer force of willpower kept it at bay, but she didn't miss the flash of tension in Joe's eyes.

Almost immediately, however, Joe recovered, and he gave her an easy shrug. 'I'm fine with sleeping in the swag.'

'Don't be silly. You can't sleep on the study floor with an injured leg.'

His shoulders lifted in a shrug. 'OK. I'm not fussy. I'll sleep wherever's most convenient for you.'

Their gazes locked and Ellie's pulses drummed. She knew Joe must have been thinking, as she was, of the big double bed where she slept. Alone. The bed they'd once shared so passionately.

Hastily she blocked out the dangerously stirring memories of their intimacy, but, as she put the first aid kit away, she wondered again how she was going to survive several days of Joe's presence in her house. She felt quite sure she'd already stumbled at the first hurdle.

CHAPTER FIVE

JOE'S BROTHER, HEATH, answered when Joe rang home with the news that he couldn't make it for Christmas,

'Jeez, mate, that's bad luck.'

'I know. I'm sorry, but with all this rain it's impossible to get through.'

'Mum will be upset.'

'Yeah.' Joe grimaced. It was way too long since he'd been home. 'So, how are Mum and Dad?'

'Both fighting fit.' Heath laughed. 'Excuse the pun. Should remember I'm talking to a soldier.'

'Former soldier.'

'Yeah. Anyway, they were really excited about seeing you.'

Joe suppressed a sigh. 'I suppose Dad's busy?'

'He and Dean are out in the paddock helping a heifer that's having twins. But Mum's around.'

'I'd like to speak to her.'

'Sure. She's just in the kitchen, up to her elbows in her usual Christmas frenzy. Making shortbread today, I think. I'll get her in a sec—but first, tell me, mate—if you're stuck at Karinya, does that mean you'll have to spend Christmas with Ellie?'

'Looks that way.' Joe tried hard to keep his voice neutral.

'But you're still going ahead with the divorce, aren't you?'

'Sure. Everything's signed, but I can't deliver the final paperwork till the rivers go down. As far as we're both concerned, though, it's a done deal. All over, red rover.'

'Hell. And now you're stuck there together. That's tough.'

'Well, at least I get to spend more time with Jacko.'

'That's true, I guess,' Heath said slowly, making no attempt to hide his doubts. 'Just the same, you have my sympathy, Joe.'

'Thanks, but I don't really need it. Ellie and I are OK. We're being perfectly civil.'

'Civil? Sounds like a load of laughs.'

'You were going to get Mum?' Joe reminded his brother.

'Yeah, sure. Well, Happy Christmas.'

'Thanks. Same to you, and give my love to Laura and the girls.'

'Will do. And good luck with you know who!'

Joe didn't have long to ponder his brother's final remark. In no time he heard his mother's voice.

'Darling, how lovely to hear from you. But Heath's just told me the terrible news. I can't believe you're stranded! What a dreadful shame, Joe. Are you sure there's no way you can get across that darned river?'

'I nearly drowned myself trying.' Joe wouldn't normally have shared this detail with his mother, but today it was important she understood there was no point in holding out hope.

'Oh, good heavens,' she said. 'Well, I guess there's no hope of seeing you for Christmas.'

'Impossible, I'm afraid.'

'That's *such* a pity.'

In the awkward silence, Joe tried to think of something reassuring to tell her. He'd felt OK before talking to his family but, now that he'd heard their voices, he felt a tug of unanticipated emotion. And nostalgia. He was remembering the happy Christmases of his past.

'So, how are you?' his mother asked after she'd digested his news.

'I'm fine, thanks. Copped a bit of a scrape on the leg, trying to cross the river, but nothing to worry about.'

'And how's Jacko?' His mother's voice softened, taking on a wistful quality.

His parents had never met Jacko, their grandson, and now the sadness in her voice was a stinging jolt, like a fish hook in Joe's heart. He'd told himself that his parents probably didn't mind—after all, they had six other grandkids—but there was no denying the regret in his mother's voice.

'Jacko's a great little bloke,' he told her. 'I'll email photos.'

'That would be lovely. I'm sure he's a dear little boy, just like you were.'

It was hard to know how to respond to this, especially as his throat had tightened painfully. 'He's a cute kid, all right. Gets up to mischief.'

'Oh, the little sweetheart. I can just imagine. Joe, we'll still get to meet Jacko, won't we? Even though you're divorced?'

'Yes. I'll make sure of it.' *Somehow. Some time.* Joe added silently. He wasn't sure when. But it hit him now that it was important for Jacko to meet his side of the family.

He imagined the boy meeting the raft of Madden uncles and cousins—meeting Joe's parents. It hadn't occurred to him till now, but he wanted the boy to know the whole picture. It was important in shaping his sense of identity.

Hell. He'd been so busy carving out a new life for himself that he hadn't given his responsibilities as a father nearly enough thought.

Now, he thought about Christmas at Ridgelands. He could picture it clearly, with the long table on the homestead veranda groaning beneath the weight of food. There'd be balloons and bright Christmas decorations hanging from posts and railings. All his family around the table. His parents, his brothers and their wives and their kids…

They would have a cold seafood salad as a starter, followed by roast turkey and roast beef, all the vegetables and trimmings. Then his mother's Christmas pudding, filled with the silver sixpences she'd saved from decades ago. Any lucky grandchild who scored a sixpence in their pudding could exchange it for a dollar.

There would be bonbons and silly hats and streamers. Corny jokes, family news and tall stories.

When Joe had first arrived back from Afghanistan, he'd been too distanced from his old life to feel homesick. Now, he was seized by an unexpected longing.

'Oh, well,' his mother was saying, 'for the time being, you'll have to give Jacko an extra hug from me.'

'Will do.' Joe swallowed. 'And I'll make sure I come to see you before I leave for the new job.'

'Oh, yes, Joe. Please do come. It's been so long. Too long.'

'I know. I'll be there. I promise. Give my love to Dad, and everyone.'

'Yes, darling. We'll speak again. Can we call you on this number?'

'Sure.'

'And you give my love to—' His mother paused and ever so slightly sighed. 'Perhaps I should say—give my *regards* to Ellie.'

'You can send Ellie your love.' Joe's throat was extra-sore now, as if he'd swallowed gravel. 'She's always liked *you*, Mum. *I'm* her problem.'

'Oh, darling,' An unhappy silence lapsed. 'I just hope you and Ellie manage to have a stress-free Christmas together.'

'We'll be fine. Don't worry. We're on our best behaviour.'

Joe felt a little shaken as he hung up. While he'd been a soldier on active duty, his focus had been on a foreign enemy. With the added problem of an impending divorce hanging over him, he'd found it all too easy to detach himself from home.

Now, for the first time, he began to suspect that avoiding his family had been a mistake. And yet, here he was, about to run away again.

He'd barely put down the receiver when the phone rang almost immediately. He supposed it was his mother ringing back with one last 'thought'.

He answered quickly. 'Hello?'

'Is that Joe?' It was a completely different woman's voice.

'Yes, Joe speaking.'

'Oh.' The caller managed to sound disappointed and put out, as if she was wrinkling her nose at a very unpleasant smell. 'I was hoping to speak to Ellie.'

'Is that you, Angela?' Joe recognised the icy tones of his ex mother-in-law.

'Yes, of course.'

'Ellie's out in the shed, hunting for Christmas decorations. I'll get her to call you as soon as she gets in.'

'So where's Jacko?' Angela Fowler's voice indicated all too clearly that she didn't trust Joe to be alone with her grandson.

'He's taking a nap.'

'I see,' Angela said doubtfully and then she let out a heavy sigh. 'I rang, actually, because I heard about all the rain up there in Queensland on the news. There was talk of rivers flooding.'

'Yes, that's right, I'm afraid. Our local creeks and rivers are up and Karinya's already cut off.'

'Oh, Joe! And you're still there? Oh, how dreadful for poor Ellie.' Ellie's mother had always managed to imply that any unfortunate event in their marriage was entirely Joe's fault. 'Don't tell me this means... It doesn't mean you'll be up there with Ellie and Jacko for Christmas, does it?'

'I'm afraid we don't have a choice, Angela.'

There was a horrified gasp on the end of the line and then a longish bristling pause.

'I'll tell Ellie you called,' Joe said with excessive politeness.

'I suppose, if she's busy, that will have to do.' Reluctantly, Angela added, 'Thanks, I guess.' And then... 'Joe?'

'Yes?'

'I hope you'll be sensitive.'

Joe scowled and refused to respond.

'You've made life hard enough for my daughter.'

His grip on the phone receiver tightened and he was tempted to hurl the bloody phone through the kitchen window. Somehow he reined in his temper.

'You can rest easy, Ange. Ellie has served me with the divorce papers and I've signed on the dotted line. I'll be out of your daughter's hair just as soon as these rivers go down. In the meantime, I'll be on my best behaviour. And I hope you and Harold have a very happy Christmas.'

He was about to hang up when he heard Ellie's footsteps in the hall.

'Hang on. You're in luck. Here's Ellie now.'

Setting down the phone with immense relief, he went down the hallway. Ellie was on the veranda. She'd taken off her rain jacket and was hanging it on the wall hook, and beside her were two large rain-streaked cardboard cartons.

'Your mother's on the phone,' Joe told her.

A frown drew her finely arched eyebrows together. 'OK, thanks.' She was still frowning as she set off down the hall. 'I think Jacko's awake,' she called back to Joe. 'Can you check?'

'Can do.'

Even before Joe reached the boy's room, he heard soft, happy little chuckles. The lively baby talk was such a bright, cheerful contrast to his recent phone conversation.

In fact, Joe couldn't remember ever hearing a baby's laughter before. It was truly an incredible sound.

He slowed his pace as he approached the room and

opened the door slowly, carefully, and he found Jacko, with tousled golden hair and sleep-flushed cheeks, standing in his cot. The little boy was walking his teddy bear, complete with its fluoro Band-Aid, along the railing. He was talking to the bear in indecipherable gibberish. Giggling.

So cute.

So damn cute.

Joe felt a slam, like a fist to his innards. The last time he'd seen his son, he'd been a helpless baby, and now he was a proper little person—walking and talking and learning to play, beginning to imagine.

He'd missed so many milestones.

What will he be like next time I see him?

It was difficult enough that Joe had to spend this extra time with Ellie, while trying to ignore the old tug of an attraction that had never really died. But now, here was his son jerking his heart-strings as well.

As soon as Jacko saw Joe, he dropped the teddy bear and held up round little arms. 'Up!' he demanded.

Joe crossed to the cot and his son looked up at him with a huge, happy grin. It might even have been an admiring grin. A loving grin?

Whatever it was, it hefted a raw punch.

'Up, Joe!'

'OK, mate. Up you come.'

Jacko squealed with delight as Joe swung him high, over the side of the cot. Then, for a heady moment, Joe held the boy in his arms, marvelling at his softness, at his pink and gold perfection.

Hell. He could remember when this healthy, bouncing kid had been nothing more than a cluster of frozen invisible cells in a laboratory—one of the *sproglets* that had caused him and Ellie so much hope and heartbreak.

Now the collection of cells was Jacko, their miraculous solo survivor.

And, after everything they'd been through, Joe found himself in awe.

'Wee-wee!' announced Jacko, wriggling with a need to be out of Joe's arms.

He quickly set the kid down. 'Do you want the toilet?'

Jacko nodded and clutched at the front of his shorts, pulling a face that made the matter look urgent.

'Let's go.' With a hand on his shoulder, Joe guided him quickly down the hallway to the bathroom, realising as he did so that, despite having several young nieces and nephews, *this* was a brand new experience.

'I think you have to stand on this fellow,' he said, grabbing a plastic turtle with a flat, step-like back and positioning it in front of the toilet bowl.

Jacko was red-faced as he climbed onto the step and tugged helplessly at the elastic waistband on his shorts. It was a moment before Joe realised he was needed to help the boy free of his clothing, which included pulling down a miniature pair of underpants printed with cartoon animals.

'OK. There you go. You're all set now.'

And then, out of nowhere, a fleeting memory from his own childhood flashed. Tearing a corner of paper from the roll on the wall, Joe dropped it into the bowl.

'See if you can pee on the paper,' he said.

Jacko looked up at him with open-mouthed surprise, but then he turned back and, with commendable concentration, did exactly as Joe suggested.

The kid was smart.

And right on target.

'Bingo!' Joe grinned. 'You did it. Good for you, Jacko!'

Jacko beamed up at him. 'Bingo, Joe!'

'You've earned a high five!' Joe held out his hand.

'What are you two up to?'

They both turned to find Ellie in the hallway behind them, hands on hips. Beautiful but frowning.

'I did Bingo, Mummy,' Jacko announced with obvious pride as he stood on the turtle with his shorts around his ankles.

'Bingo? What are you talking about?' She directed her frown at Joe.

He pointed into the bowl. 'Jacko hit the piece of paper. I thought it would help him to aim.'

'Aim?' Ellie stared at him, stared at both of them, her dark eyes frowning with disbelief. As comprehension dawned, her mouth twisted into the faintest glimmer of a smile—a smile that didn't quite make it.

'He's not in the Army *yet*,' she said tightly. 'And don't forget to wash your hands, Jacko. It's time for your afternoon tea.'

'So, do you have a job for me?' Joe asked once Jacko was perched on a stool at the kitchen bench and tucking into a cup of juice and a plate of diced cheese and fruit.

Ellie looked pained—an expression Joe was used to seeing after a phone call from her mother. No doubt Angela Fowler had once again piled on the sympathy for her poor daughter's terrible fate—this time, being forced to spend Christmas with her dropkick ex.

In the past, that pained look had irritated Joe. Today, he was determined to let it wash over him.

'Perhaps I could assemble the Christmas tree?' he suggested.

'That would be helpful.' Ellie didn't follow through with a smile. 'The tree's in one of the boxes on the veranda.'

'You'd like it in the lounge room?'

'Yes, please.'

Ellie took a deep breath as she watched Joe head off to the veranda.

Conversations with her mother had always been heavily laced with anti-Joe sentiments and today had been a doozy.

This is a dangerous time for you, Ellie. I don't like the idea of the two of you alone up there. You'll have to be very careful, especially if Joe tries anything.

Tries what, Mum?

Tries to...to win you back.

Of course, Ellie had assured her mother there was no chance of that. Absolutely. No. Chance. But she wished this certainty hadn't left her feeling quite so desolate.

These next few days were going to be hard enough with the two of them stuck in the house while the rain continued pelting down outside. It would be so much easier if she could carry on with the outside work, but the cattle were safe and until the rain stopped there wasn't a lot more she could do.

Unfortunately, she couldn't even give Joe a decent book to read. Since Jacko's birth, she'd only had time for cattle-breeding journals, women's magazines and children's picture books.

Ellie decided to let Joe get on with the tree while she cooled her heels in the kitchen with Jacko, for once letting him dawdle over his food, but as soon as he'd finally downed his afternoon tea, he was keen to be off.

'Where's Joe?' was the first thing he asked.

So they went back to the lounge room and, to Ellie's surprise, Joe had almost finished assembling the six-foot tree. He made it look dead easy, of course.

Jacko stared up at the tree, looking puzzled, as if he couldn't understand why adults would set up a tree inside the house. As an outback boy, he hadn't seen any of the city shops with brightly lit trees and Santa Clauses, although he had vague ideas about Christmas from books and TV.

'This is our *Christmas* tree,' Ellie explained to him. 'Mummy's going to make it pretty with lights and decorations, and soon there'll be lots of presents underneath it.'

At the mention of presents Jacko clapped his hands and took off, running in circles.

'Well, that got a reaction,' said Joe, amused.

'He can still remember the pile of presents he scored for his second birthday.'

Too late, Ellie remembered that Joe hadn't sent the boy anything. Lordy, today there seemed to be pitfalls in even the simplest conversation.

Joe was grim-faced as he fitted the final top branches in place.

Ellie went to the CD player and made a selection— a jaunty version of *Jingle Bells*. She hoped it would lift the dark mood that had lingered since her mum's annoying dire warnings on the phone.

Determined to shake off the grouchiness, she went

to the second carton and took out boxes of exquisite tree ornaments. Decorating the tree had always been her favourite Christmas tradition. Today it was sure to lift her spirits.

'Ooh! Pretty!' Jacko squealed, coming close to inspect.

'Yes, these ornaments are very pretty, but they're made of glass, Jacko, so you mustn't touch. They can break. I'm going to put them on the tree, and they'll be safe there. They'll make the tree beautiful.'

Jacko watched, entranced, as Ellie hooked bright, delicate balls onto the branches. She knew it was too much to expect him not to touch but, before she could warn him to be *very* gentle, he batted with his hand at a bright red and silver ball.

Ellie dived to stop him and Joe dived too, but they were both too late. The ball fell to the floor and smashed.

Ellie cried out—an instinctive response, but probably a mistake. Immediately, Jacko began to wail.

It was Joe who swept the boy into his arms and began to soothe him.

Ellie was left watching them, feeling strangely left out. She waited for Jacko to turn to her, to reach out his arms for her as he always did when he was upset. But he remained clinging to Joe.

Joe. Her son's new, big strong hero.

She refused to feel jealous. If she was honest, she could totally understand the appeal of those muscular, manly arms.

Once upon a time Joe was my hero, too. My tower of strength.

Now, she would never feel his arms around her again.

Yikes, where had that thought sprung from? *What's the matter with me?*

She hurried out of the room to get a dustpan and broom and, by the time she returned, Jacko had stopped crying.

Joe set him down and the boy stood, sniffling, as he watched Ellie sweep up the glittering broken pieces.

'I told you to be careful,' she felt compelled to remind him as she worked. 'You mustn't touch these pretty ornaments, or they'll break.'

'He's too little to understand,' said Joe.

Ellie glared up at him. 'No, he's not.' *What would Joe know about little kids?*

Joe shrugged and looked around the room. 'Perhaps we can find something more suitable for him to play with. Something like paper chains? They might distract him.'

Ellie had actually been thinking along the same lines and it annoyed her that Joe had made the suggestion first. 'So you're suddenly an expert on raising children?'

'Ellie, don't be like that.'

'Like what?'

Joe simply stared at her, his blue eyes coolly assessing.

Oh, help. It was happening already. All the old tensions were sparking between them—electricity of the worst kind. Dangerous. Lethal.

All she'd wanted was a simple, relaxing afternoon decorating the tree.

'There are paper chains in those shopping bags,' she said, pointing to one of the cartons. Then, summoning her dignity, she rose and took the dustpan back to the kitchen.

By the time she returned, Jacko and Joe had trailed bright paper chains along the shelves of the bookcase and they were now looping them around a tall lamp stand.

The CD was still playing. The singer had moved on to *Deck the Halls*, and Ellie set about decorating the tree again, hoping for peace on Earth and goodwill towards one particular man.

She couldn't deny that Joe was great at playing with their son. Every time Jacko became too curious about the tree, Joe would deflect him. They played hide and seek behind the sofa, and Joe taught Jacko how to crawl on his belly, Commando style. Watching this, Ellie winced, sure that Joe's injured leg must have hurt.

She almost said something about his leg, but held her tongue. He was a big, tough soldier, after all.

Joe hid Jacko's teddy bear behind a cushion and the boy squealed with delight every time he rediscovered the toy. After that, Jacko played the game again and again, over and over.

Ellie tried really hard not to feel left out of their games. She knew that the nanny, Nina, played games like this all the time with Jacko, while she was out attending to chores around the property. But she'd never imagined macho Joe being quite so good with the boy.

It shouldn't have bothered her. It *didn't* bother her. If Joe was proving to be an entertaining father, she was pleased. She was even grateful.

She was. Truly.

Meanwhile, the Christmas tree became a thing of beauty, with delicate ornaments and shiny stars, and trailing lines of lights and silver pine cones.

After Jacko's umpteenth game of hiding the toy bear

behind the cushion, Joe strolled over to inspect Ellie's progress.

'It's looking great,' he said. 'Really beautiful.'

His smile was genuine. Gorgeous? It sent unwanted warmth rippling through her. 'At least it helps to make the house look more festive.'

Joe nodded and touched a pretty pink and purple glass spiral with his fingertips. 'I remember these. We bought them for our very first Christmas.'

To Ellie's dismay, her eyes pricked with the threat of tears. Joe shouldn't be remembering those long ago times when they were still happy and hopeful and so blissfully in love.

'I'd rather not rehash old memories, Joe. I don't think it's helpful.'

She saw a flash of emotion in his eyes. Pain? Her comment hadn't hurt him, surely? Not Joe. He had no regrets. Not about them. He'd gone off to war without a backward glance.

And yet he definitely looked upset.

Ellie wondered if she should elaborate. Try to explain her caution.

But what could she explain? That she hadn't meant to hurt him? That, deep down, she still cared about him? That the memories were painful *because* she cared?

How could those sorts of revelations help them now? They couldn't go back.

Confused, Ellie felt more uptight than ever. She spun away from Joe and began to gather up the empty boxes and tissue paper that had housed the decorations, working with jerky, angry movements.

To her annoyance, Joe simply stayed where he was by the tree, watching her with a thoughtful, searching gaze.

'You could always help to clean up this mess,' she said tightly.

'Yes, ma'am.' He moved without haste, picking up the shopping bags that had housed the paper chains. Crossing the room, he dropped them into one of the cartons and, when he looked at her again, his eyes were as hard and cool as ice. 'You can't let up, can you, Ellie?'

'What do you mean?'

'You're determined to make this hard for both of us.'

'I'm not *trying* to make it hard,' she snapped defensively. 'It *is* hard.'

'Yeah? Well, you're not the only one finding it hard. And it doesn't help when you make it so damn obvious that you can't stand the sight of me.'

Ellie smarted. 'How can you say that?'

'How?' Joe looked at her strangely, as if he thought she'd lost her marbles. 'Because it's the truth. It's why I left four years ago.'

No! The protest burst on her lips, but she was aware that Jacko had stopped playing. He was standing very still, clutching his teddy bear, watching them, his little eyes round with worry.

They were fighting in front of him, which was terrible—the very last thing she wanted.

'If we're going to survive this Christmas,' Joe said tightly, 'you're going to have to try harder.'

Ellie felt her teeth clench. 'I know how to behave. I don't need a lecture.'

'Well, you certainly need something. You need to calm down. And you need to think about Jacko.'

'Are you serious?'

'This atmosphere can't be good for him.'

How dare you? Of course she was thinking about Jacko.

Ellie was stung to the core. Who did Joe think he was, telling her off about her parenting? Was he suggesting she was insensitive to Jacko's needs? Joe, who hardly knew the boy?

She was Jacko's *mother*. She knew *everything* about her son—his favourite food, his favourite toy and favourite picture books. She knew Jacko's fears, the times he liked to sleep, the way he liked to be cuddled.

She'd been through his pregnancy on her own, and she'd given birth to him alone. She'd raised Jacko from day one, nursing him through colic and croup and teething. Later, chickenpox. Jacko's first smile had been for Ellie alone. She'd watched him learn to roll over, to sit up and to crawl, to stand, to walk.

Around the clock, she'd cared for him, admittedly with Nina's help, but primarily on her own.

She and Jacko were incredibly close. Their bond was special. Incredibly special.

How dare Joe arrive here out of the blue and start questioning her mothering skills?

Without warning, her eyes filled with tears. Tears of hurt and anger. Scared she might start yelling and say things she'd regret, she turned and fled from the room.

Damn. What a stuff-up.

As Ellie hurried away, Jacko stared up at Joe with big, sad blue eyes. 'Mummy crying.'

Joe swallowed the boulder that jammed his throat. Why the hell had he started a verbal attack on Ellie? This was *so* not the way he'd wanted to behave.

How do I tell my two-year-old son that I'm the reason his mother's crying?

Anxiety and regret warred in Joe's gut as he crossed the room to the boy and squatted so they were at eye level. 'Listen, little mate. I'm going to go and talk to your mum. To...ah...cheer her up.'

Joe had to try at least. It took two to fight. Two to make peace. He had to pull in his horns, had to make an effort to see this situation from Ellie's point of view.

'I need you to be a good boy and stay here with Ted.' Joe dredged up a grin as he tickled Jacko's tummy.

Obligingly, Jacko giggled.

The kid was so cute. Already Joe knew it was going to be hard to say goodbye.

'How about we hide your bear behind the curtain over there?' he suggested, pointing to the floor-length curtains hanging either end of the deep sash windows that opened onto the veranda. He showed Jacko how to hide the bear behind them, just as they had with the cushions, and the little boy was thrilled.

'Ted!' he squealed, astonished by the big discovery when they lifted the curtain. 'Do it again, Joe!' At least he was all smiles again.

'You have a go at hiding him,' said Joe.

Jacko tried, frowning carefully as he placed the bear behind the curtain. Once again, he lifted the fabric and saw the bear, and he was as excited as a scientist discovering the Higgs boson particle.

'OK, you can play with him here,' Joe said. 'And I'll be back in a tick.'

'OK.'

Reassured that Jacko would be happy for a few minutes at least, Joe went in search of Ellie.

CHAPTER SIX

ELLIE STOOD AT one end of the long front veranda, elbows resting on the railings, staring out at the waterlogged paddocks. The rain had actually stopped for now, but the sky was still heavy with thick, grey clouds, so no doubt the downpour would start again soon.

She wasn't crying. She'd dried her tears almost as soon as she left the lounge room and she was determined that no more would fall. She was angry, not sad. Angry with herself, with her stupid behaviour.

She'd been determined to handle Joe's return calmly and maturely, and when he'd been forced to stay here she'd promised herself she would face that with dignity as well. Instead she'd been as tense and sharp-tongued as a cornered taipan.

She was so disappointed with herself, so annoyed. Why couldn't her behaviour ever live up to her good intentions?

You make it so damn obvious that you can't stand the sight of me.

Did Joe really think that? How could he?

It seemed impossible to Ellie. The sad truth was— the sight of Joe stirred her in ways she didn't want to be stirred. She found herself thinking too often about the way they used to make love.

Really, despite their troubles, there'd been so many happy times, some of them incredibly spontaneous and exciting.

Even now, *irrationally*, she found herself remembering one of the happiest nights of her life—a night that had originally started out very badly.

It had happened one Easter. She and Joe were driving down the highway on their way to visit her mum, but they'd been so busy before they left that they hadn't booked ahead, and all the motels down the highway were full.

'Perhaps we should just keep driving,' Joe had said grimly when they reached yet another town with no spare rooms.

'Driving all night?' she'd asked. 'Isn't that dangerous, Joe? We're both pretty tired.'

He'd reluctantly agreed. 'We'll have to find a picnic ground then and sleep in the car.'

It wasn't a cheering prospect, but Ellie knew they didn't have much choice. While Joe went off to find hamburgers for their dinner, she tried to set the car up as best she could, hoping they'd be comfortable.

She'd shifted their luggage and adjusted their seats to lie back and she'd just finished making pillows out of bundles of their clothing when Joe returned. He was empty-handed and Ellie, who'd been ravenous, felt her spirits sink even lower.

'Don't tell me this town's also sold out of hamburgers?'

'I don't know,' he said simply.

Her stomach rumbled hungrily. 'Are all the shops closed?'

'Don't know that either. It doesn't matter.' Joe's sudden cheeky smile was unforgettably gorgeous. He held up a fancy gold ring, dangling keys. 'I've booked us into the honeymoon suite in the best hotel in town.'

Ellie gasped. 'You're joking.'

Still smiling broadly, Joe shook his head. 'Ridgy-didge.'

'Can…can we afford a honeymoon suite?'

He shrugged, then slipped his arm around her shoulders, pressed a warm kiss to her ear. 'We deserve a bit of comfort. We never had a proper honeymoon.'

It was the best of nights. Amazing, and so worth the extravagance.

All thoughts of tiredness vanished when they walked into their suite and saw the champagne in an ice bucket, a huge vase of long-stemmed white roses and chocolate hearts wrapped in gold foil on their pillows.

Like excited kids, they bounced on the enormous king-sized bed and then jumped into the spa bath until their room service dinner arrived. And they felt like film stars as they ate gourmet cuisine dressed in luxurious white fluffy bathrobes.

And, just for one night, they'd put their worries aside and they'd made love like honeymooners.

I shouldn't be thinking about that now…

Ellie was devastated to realise that she was still as physically attracted to her ex as she'd been on that night. The realisation made her panic.

What a mess.

With a despairing sigh, she sagged against a veranda post. How had she and Joe sunk to this? She'd thought about their problems so many times, but she'd never pin-pointed a particular event that had killed their marriage. It had been much the same as today. Ongoing bicker-ing and building resentments had worn them down and eroded their love.

Death by a thousand cuts.

But why? How? How could she be so tense and angry with a man she still fancied? It wasn't as if she actively disliked Joe.

She supposed they should have seen a marriage guid-ance counsellor years ago.

Joe had been too proud, of course, and Ellie had been too scared—scared that she'd be psychoanalysed and found lacking in some vital way. But if she'd been braver, would it have helped?

She probably would have had to tell the counsellor about her father's death and how unhappy she'd been after that. Worse, she would have had to talk about her stepfather and how she'd run away from him.

Ellie didn't actually believe there was a connection between Harold Fowler and her marriage breakdown, but heaven knew what a counsellor might have made of it. Even now, she still shuddered when she thought about Harold.

And here was the thing: it was the sight of *Harold* that Ellie couldn't stand. Not Joe.

Never Joe.

Her mum had married Harold Fowler eighteen months after her father died, after they'd sold the farm and moved into town. Harold owned the town's main hardware store—he was loud and showy and popu-lar, a big fish in a small country pond. And a couple of years later he was elected mayor. Ellie's mum was thrilled. She loved being the mayor's wife and feeling like a celebrity.

Harold, however, had given Ellie the creeps. Right from the start, just the way he looked at her had made her squirm and feel uncomfortable, and that was before he touched her.

She'd been fifteen when he first patted her on the bum. Over the following months, it had happened a few more times, which was bad enough, but then he came into the bathroom one night when she was in the shower.

He was full of apologies, of course, and he backed out quickly, claiming that he'd knocked and no one had answered. But Ellie had seen the horrible glint in his eyes and she was quite sure he hadn't knocked. Her mother hadn't been home that night, which had made the event extra-scary.

And Harold certainly hadn't knocked the second time he barged in. Again, it had happened on a night when Ellie's mum was away at her bridge club. Ellie was seventeen, and she'd just stepped out of the bath and was reaching for her towel when, without warning, Harold had simply opened her bathroom door.

'Oh, my darling girl,' he said with the most ghastly slimy smile.

Whipping the towel about her, Ellie managed to get rid of him with a few scathing, shrilly screamed words, but she'd been sickened, horrified.

Desperate.

And the worst of it was she couldn't get her mother to understand.

'Harold's lived alone for years,' her mum had said, excusing him. 'He's not used to sharing a house with others. And he hasn't done or said anything improper,

Ellie. You're just at that age where you're sensitive about your body. It's easy to misread these things.'

Her mother had believed what she wanted to, what she needed to.

Ellie, however, had left home for good as soon as she finished school, despite her mother's protests and tears, giving up all thought of university. University students had long, long holidays and she would have been expected to spend too much of that time at home.

She had realised it was futile to press her mother about Harold's creepiness—mainly because she knew how desperate her mother was to believe he was perfect. Harold was such a hotshot in their regional town. He was the mayor, for heaven's sake, and Ellie was afraid that, if she pushed her case, she might cause the whole thing to blow up somehow and become a horrible public scandal.

So she'd headed north to Queensland, where she'd scored a job as a jillaroo on a cattle property. Over the next few years, she'd worked on several properties—a mustering season here, a calving season there. Gradually she'd acquired more and more skills.

On one property she'd joined a droving team and she'd helped to move a big mob of cattle hundreds of kilometres. She was given her own horses to ride every day. And, finally, she was living the country life she'd dreamed of, the life she'd anticipated when she was almost thirteen. Before her father died.

Whenever she phoned home or returned home for the shortest possible visits, she was barely civil to Harold. He got the message. Fortunately, he'd never stepped out of line again, but Ellie would never trust him again either.

Trust…

Thinking about all of this now, Ellie was struck by a thought so suffocating she could scarcely breathe.

Oh, my God. Is that my problem? Trust issues?

That was it, wasn't it?

She clung to the railing, struggling for air. Her problems with Joe had nothing to do with whether or not she was attracted to him. The day they met remained the stand-alone most significant moment of her life.

She'd taken one look at Joe Madden, with his sexy blue eyes, his ruggedly cute looks, his wide-shouldered lean perfection and nicest possible smile, and she'd fallen like a stone.

But I couldn't trust Joe.

When it came to coping with the ups and downs of a long-term marriage, she hadn't been strong enough to deal with her disappointments. She'd lost faith in herself, lost faith in the power of love.

Ellie thought again about her father climbing a windmill and dying before he could keep his promise to her. She thought about her creepy stepfather, who'd broken her trust in a completely different way. By the time she'd married Joe…

I never really expected to be happy. Not for ever. I couldn't trust our marriage to work. It was almost as if I expected something to go wrong.

It was such a shock to realise this now.

Too late.

Way too late.

She'd never even told Joe about her stepfather. She'd left it as a creepy, shuddery, embarrassing part of her past that she'd worked hard to bury.

But that hadn't affected how she'd truly felt about him.

She'd loved Joe.

Despite the mixed-up and messy emotional tornado that had accompanied her fertility issues and ultimately destroyed their marriage, she'd *truly* loved him—even when he'd proposed their divorce and he'd told her he was leaving for the Army.

And now?

Now, she was terribly afraid that she'd never really stopped loving him. But how crazy was that when their divorce was a fait accompli?

No wonder she was tense.

Ellie thumped the railing with a frustrated fist. At the same moment, from down the veranda she heard the squeaky hinge of the French windows that led from the lounge room. Then footsteps. She stiffened, turned to see Joe. He was alone.

She drew a deep breath and braced herself. *Don't screw this up again. Behave.*

'Are you OK?' Joe asked quietly.

'Yes, thanks.'

He came closer and stood beside her at the railing, looking out at the soggy paddocks. 'I'm sorry, Ellie. I'm sorry for getting stuck into you. My timing's been lousy, coming back here at Christmas.'

She shook her head. 'I'm making too big a deal about the whole Christmas thing.'

'But that's fair enough. It's the first Christmas Jacko's been old enough to understand.'

She sighed, felt emotionally drained. Exhausted. 'Where's Jacko now?'

'In the lounge room. Still hiding the bear, I hope. Persistent little guy, isn't he?' Joe slid her a tentative sideways smile.

She sent a shy smile back.

Oh, if only they could continue to smile—or, at the very least, to be civilised. Joe was right. For Jacko's sake, they had to try. For the next couple of days—actually, for the next couple of *decades* till Jacko was an adult, they had to keep up a semblance of friendship.

Friendship, when once they'd been lovers, husband and wife.

'I got my knickers in a twist when you suggested I wasn't sensitive about Jacko,' Ellie admitted. 'It felt unfair. He's always been my first concern.'

'You've done an amazing job with the boy. He's a great little guy. A credit to you.'

The praise surprised her. Warmed her.

'I don't know how you've done it out here on your own,' Joe added.

'The nanny's been great. But I'll admit it hasn't always been easy.' She stole another quick glance at him, saw his deep brow, his wide cheekbones, his slightly crooked nose and strong shadowed jaw. She felt her breathing catch. 'I guess this can't be easy for you now. Coming back from the war and everything.'

When he didn't answer, she tried again, 'Was it bad over there?'

A telltale muscle jerked. 'Sometimes.'

Ellie knew he'd lost soldier mates, knew he must have seen things that haunted him. But Special Forces guys hardly ever talked about where they'd been or what they'd done—certainly not with ex-wives.

'I was one of the lucky ones,' he said. 'I got out of it unscathed.'

Unscathed emotionally? Ellie knew that the Army had changed its tactics, sending soldiers like Joe on shorter but more frequent tours of duty in an effort to minimise post-traumatic stress, but she was quite sure that no soldier returned from any war without some kind of damage.

I haven't helped. This hasn't been a very good home-coming for him.

Quickly, bravely, she said, 'For the record, Joe, it isn't true.'

He turned, looking at her intently. 'What do you mean?' His blue eyes seemed to penetrate all the way to her soul.

Her heart began to gallop. She couldn't back down now that she'd begun. 'What you said before—that I can't bear the sight of you—it's not true.' *So not true.*

'That's the way it comes across.'

'I know. I'm sorry. Really sorry.'

She could feel the sudden stillness in him, almost as if she'd shot him. He was staring at her, his eyes burn-ing. With doubt?

Ellie's eyes were stinging. She didn't want to cry, but she could no longer see the paddocks. Her heart was racing.

She almost told Joe that she actually *fancied* the sight of him. Very much. Too much. *That* was her problem. That was why she was tense.

But it was too late for personal confessions. Way too late. Years and years too late.

Instead she said, 'I know I've been stupidly tense about *everything*, but it's certainly not because I can't stand the sight of you.' *Quite the opposite.*

She blinked hard, wishing her tears could air-dry.

Joe's knuckles were white as he gripped the veranda railing and she wondered what he was thinking. Feeling. Was he going over her words?

It's certainly not because I can't stand the sight of you.

Could he read between the lines? Could he guess she was still attracted? Was he angry?

It felt like an age before he spoke.

Eventually, he let go of the railing. Stepped away and drew a deep breath, unconsciously drawing her attention to his height and the breadth of his shoulders. Then he rested his hands lightly on his hips, as if he was deliberately relaxing.

'OK, here's a suggestion,' he said quietly. 'It's Christmas Eve tomorrow. Why don't we declare a truce?'

'A truce? For Christmas?'

'Why not? Even in World War One there were Germans and our blokes who stopped fighting in the trenches for Christmas. So, what do you reckon?'

Ellie almost smiled. She really liked the idea of a Christmas truce. She'd always liked to have a goal. And a short-term goal was even better. Doable.

'I reckon we should give it a shot,' she said. If soldiers could halt a world war for a little peace and goodwill at Christmas, she and Joe should at least make an effort.

He was watching her with a cautious smile. 'Can we shake on it?'

'Sure.'

His handclasp was warm and strong and, for Ellie, just touching him sparked all sorts of flashpoints. But now she had to find a way to stay calm. Unexcited. Neutral.

Her goal was peace and goodwill. For Christmas.

Their smiles were uncertain but hopeful.

But then, in almost the same breath, they both re-membered.

'Jacko,' they exclaimed together and together they hurried down the veranda to the lounge room.

There was no sign of their son, just his teddy bear lying abandoned on the floor near the empty cartons.

Ellie hurried across the room and down the hall-way to the kitchen. 'Jacko?' she called, but he wasn't there either.

Joe was close behind her. 'He can't have gone far.'

'No.' She went back along the hallway to the bed-rooms, calling, 'Jacko, where are you?' Any minute she would hear his giggle.

But he wasn't in his room. Or in her bedroom. Or in the study, or Nina's room. The bathroom was empty. A wild, hot fluttering unfurled in Ellie's chest. It was only a small house. There wasn't anywhere else to look.

She rushed back to the lounge room as Joe came through the front door.

'I've checked the veranda,' he said.

'He's not here.' Ellie's voice squeaked.

'He must be here. Don't panic, Ellie.'

She almost fell back into her old pattern, hurling defensive accusations. *How could you have left him?*

But she was silenced by the quiet command in Joe's voice, and by the knowledge that she'd been the one who stormed out.

'What was Jacko doing before you came outside to talk to me?' she asked with a calmness that surprised her.

'He was playing hide and seek with the bear. Here.'
Joe swished aside the long curtain beside the door.

Ellie gasped.

Jacko was sitting against the wall, perfectly still and
quiet, peeping out from beneath his blond fringe, hugging his grubby knees.

'Boo!' he said with a proud grin. 'I hided, Mummy.'

They fell on him together, crouching to hug him,
laughing shakily. United by their mutual relief.

It wasn't a bad way to start a truce.

Dinner that night was leftover Spanish chicken. For
Joe and Ellie the atmosphere was, thankfully, more relaxed than the night before, and afterwards, while Ellie
read Jacko bedtime stories, Joe did kitchen duty, rins-
ing the plates, stacking the dishwasher and wiping the
bench tops.

By the time he came back from checking the station's working dogs and making sure the chicken coop
was locked safely from dingoes, Ellie was at the kitchen
table, looking businesslike with notepaper and pen, and
surrounded by recipe books.

'I need to plan our Christmas dinner menu,' she said,
flipping pages filled with lavish and brightly coloured
Christmas fare.

'I don't suppose I can help?'

She looked up at him, her smile doubtful but curious.
'How are your cooking skills these days?'

'About the same as they were last time I cooked for
you.'

'Steak and eggs.' Her nose wrinkled. 'I was hoping
for something a little more celebratory for Christmas.'

'Well, if you insist on being fussy...' He pretended

to be offended, but he was smiling as he switched on the kettle. 'I'm making tea. Want some?'

'Thanks.'

At least the truce seemed to be working. So far.

While Joe hunted for mugs and tea bags, Ellie returned to her recipe books, frowning and looking pensive as she turned endless pages. As far as Joe could tell, she didn't seem to be having much luck. Every so often she made notes and chewed on her pen and then, a few pages later, she scratched the notes out again.

'Our Christmas dinner doesn't have to be lavish,' he suggested as he set a mug of tea with milk and one sugar in front of her. 'I'm fine with low-key.'

'I'm afraid it'll have to be low-key. We don't have much choice.'

With an annoyed frown, Ellie pushed the books away, picked up the tea mug and sipped. 'Nice tea, thanks.' She let out a heavy sigh. 'The problem is, I didn't order a lot of things in for Christmas. Jacko and I were supposed to be spending the day with Chip and Sara Anderson on Lucky Downs. All they wanted me to bring was homemade shortbread and wine and cheese. But now, with the creeks up, we won't be able to get there.'

She waved her hand at the array of books. 'Some people spend weeks planning their Christmas menus and here am I, just starting. Yikes, it's Christmas Eve tomorrow.'

Joe helped himself to a chair and picked up the nearest book: *Elegant and Easy Christmas*.

'Those recipes are gorgeous,' Ellie said. 'But they all need fancy ingredients that I don't have.'

He flicked through pages filled with tempting pictures—a crab cocktail starter, turkey breast stuffed with pears and chestnut and rosemary, a herb-crusted stand-ing rib roast, pumpkin and caramel tiramisu.

'I see what you mean,' he said. 'These are certainly fancy. Would it help if we make a list of the things you have in store?'

'Well, yes, I guess that's sensible.' Ellie rolled her eyes. 'I've a pretty good range of meat, but my problem is the trimmings. I don't have the sauces and spices and fancy herbs and that sort of thing. So I'm afraid we're stuck with ordinary, boring stuff. For Christmas!'

'Hmm.'

She looked up, eyeing Joe suspiciously. 'You're frowning and muttering. What does that mean?'

'It means I'm thinking.' Truth was—an exciting idea had flashed into his head. Crazy. Probably impossible.

But it was worth a try.

'Excuse me,' he said, jumping to his feet. 'I need to make a phone call.'

'There's a phone here.' Ellie nodded to the wall phone.

'It's OK. I've bought a sat phone, and I have the numbers stored.'

She looked understandably puzzled.

Adorably puzzled, Joe thought as he left the room.

By the light of the single bulb on the veranda, he found the number he wanted. Steve Hansen was an ex-Army mate and, to Joe's relief, Steve answered the call quickly.

'Steve, Joe Madden here. How are you?'

'I'm fine, Joe, heard you were back. How are you, mate? More importantly, where are you? Any chance of having a Christmas drink with us?'

'That's why I'm ringing,' Joe said. 'I've a huge favour to ask.'

'Well, ask away, mate. We both know how much I owe you. If it wasn't for you, I would have flown home from Afghanistan in a wooden box. So, what is it?'

CHAPTER SEVEN

MIDAFTERNOON ON CHRISTMAS Eve and the Karinya kitchen was a hive of activity.

At one end of the table, Ellie and Jacko were cutting shortbread dough into star shapes—with loads of patience on Ellie's part. At the other end, Joe, having consulted an elderly everyday cookbook, was stuffing a chicken with a mix of onion, soft breadcrumbs and dried herbs. To Ellie's amusement, he was tackling the task with the serious concentration of a heart surgeon.

By now the rain had stopped and the air was super-hot and sticky—too hot and sticky for the ceiling fan to make much difference. Flies buzzed at the window screens and from outside came the smell of once parched earth now turned to mud.

With the back of her hand, Ellie wiped a strand of damp hair from her eyes. She was used to hot Christmases and she'd come to terms with the ordinariness of this year's Christmas fare so, despite the conditions, she was actually feeling surprisingly upbeat.

She was certainly enjoying her truce with Joe.

And yet she was nervous about this situation. Playing happy families with her ex *had* to be risky. It was highly possible that she was enjoying Joe's company far too much. Already, today they'd caught themselves laughing a couple of times.

Surely that had to be dangerous?

Could laughter lead to second thoughts? Could she find herself weakening and becoming susceptible to Joe's charms, just as her mother had warned?

Then again, she knew these happy vibes couldn't last. By Boxing Day, she and Joe would be back to normal.

Normal and divorced and leading separate *peaceful* lives.

'OK,' she said briskly, whipping her attention from her broken marriage to her neat sheets of shortbread stars and her small son's not-so-neat efforts. 'I think it's time to pop these gourmet masterpieces into the—'

She stopped in mid-sentence as an approaching sound caught her attention.

Thump-thump-thump-thump-thump-thump-thump...

Jacko squealed. 'Heli-chopper!'

Joe looked up from his task of stitching the chicken and grinned. 'That's probably Steve.'

'Steve?' Ellie frowned as the roar of the chopper blades grew louder. Closer.

'Steve Hansen. A mate of mine from the Army. He got out last year.'

'Oh.'

In a heartbeat Ellie guessed exactly what this meant. Joe was no longer stranded here. She went cold all over. Joe had found an escape route. A friend with a helicopter was coming to his rescue. He was about to leave her again.

Ridiculously, she began to shiver in spite of the heat. *This* was the reason for last night's mysterious and secretive phone call. Joe had never explained, and all morning she'd been wondering.

Now, with an effort, she dredged up a smile. 'Well, that's *your* Christmas sorted.'

Joe looked at her strangely, but anything he might have said was drowned by the helicopter's noisy arrival directly above the homestead roof.

There'd been helicopters at Karinya before. They'd come to help with the mustering, so little Jacko wasn't frightened by the roaring noise. In fact he was squealing with delight as he dashed to the window.

The chopper was landing on the track beside the home paddock and, with a whoop of excitement, Joe picked the boy up and flipped him high onto his broad shoulders.

Ellie gulped. The sight of her son up on his father's big shoulders was...

Breathtaking...

'Are you coming to say hello to Steve?' Joe called to her before he hurried outside, leaving her with her arms akimbo and a table covered with raw chicken and unbaked cookies.

Ellie had no idea how long this interruption would take, so she found space for the uncooked food in the fridge.

By then, the helicopter had landed and Joe and Jacko were waiting at the bottom of the front steps until the blades stopped whirring. Jacko was jigging with excitement. Ellie's stomach felt hollow as she joined them.

It's OK. I'll be fine. Joe has to leave some time, and it's probably easier to say goodbye now, without going through the whole business of Christmas first.

Joe was grinning at her, his rugged face relaxed and

almost boyish with excitement. He looked a bit like Jacko. Or Jacko looked like him.

It wasn't a cheering thought now, when he was about to leave them. Ellie's heart did a sad little back-flip.

The rotor blades slowed. A door in the helicopter opened and a beefy red-haired pilot with a wide friendly grin appeared.

'Ho! Ho! Ho!' he called jauntily as he climbed down.

'Merry Christmas!' responded Joe and the two men greeted each other with handshakes and hearty back slaps. Joe's smile was wide as he turned back to Ellie and Jacko. 'Come and meet Steve. He was in Afghanistan with me, but he's set up in Townsville now and he's started his own chopper charter business.'

Pinning on her brightest smile, Ellie took Jacko's hand and encouraged him forward. 'Hi, Steve. Nice to meet you.'

'You, too,' Steve said warmly. 'Merry Christmas.' He shook hands with Ellie, then bent to ruffle Jacko's hair. 'Hello, young fella. You're a chip off the old block if ever I saw one.'

'This is Jacko,' Joe said proudly, adding a bright-eyed smile that included Ellie.

'Hi, Jacko.' Steve waggled his eyebrows comically, making the little boy giggle.

To Ellie, he said, 'I remember how excited Joe was when this little bloke was born. The news came through when we were all in the mess. You should have seen this man.' He slapped a big hand on Joe's shoulder. 'He was so damn proud, handing around his phone with a photo of his son.'

'How...how nice.' Ellie was somewhat stunned. She

glanced at Joe, saw the quick guarded look in his eyes, which he quickly covered with an elaborate smile.

'And now Jacko's a whole two years old,' Joe said.

'You're a lucky little bloke, Jacko,' announced Steve and then he nodded to the helicopter. 'And you're certainly in for an exciting Christmas.'

An exciting Christmas? Ellie frowned. What was this about?

She was struck by a ghastly thought. Surely Joe wasn't planning to take Jacko with him? 'What's going on?' she demanded.

Now it was Steve who frowned.

'Everything's fine, Ellie,' Joe intercepted quickly in his most soothing tone. 'Steve's brought out extra things for Christmas.' Turning to Steve, he said, 'I haven't told Ellie about this. I was keeping it as a surprise.'

'Ah!' Steve's furrowed brow cleared and was replaced by another grin. He winked at Ellie. 'Romantic devil, isn't he?'

Clearly Joe's Army mates didn't know about their divorce. Ellie found it difficult to hold her smile.

'Stand back then, Mrs Madden, while we get this crate unloaded.'

Dazed, she watched as Steve Hansen climbed back into the helicopter and began to hand down boxes and packages, which Joe retrieved and stacked on the ground.

There was an amazing array. Boxes, supermarket bags, wrapped parcels. A snowy-white Styrofoam box with *Townsville Cold Stores* stamped on the side.

As the last carton came out, Joe turned to Ellie with a complicated lopsided grin. 'I thought you deserved a proper Christmas. You know, some of the fancy things you were missing.'

She gave a bewildered shake of her head. 'You mean this is all fancy Christmas food? For me?'

'North Queensland's freshest and best,' responded Steve from the cockpit doorway. 'I set my wife Lauren on the hunt and she's one hell of a shopper.'

Ellie was stunned. 'Thank you. And please thank Lauren.' Again she was shaking her head. 'I can't believe you and your wife have gone to so much trouble, especially on Christmas Eve. It's such a busy time.'

Steve shrugged. 'Joe knew exactly what he wanted, and bringing it out here has been my pleasure.' He gave another of his face-splitting smiles. 'Besides, I'd do anything for your husband. You know Joe saved my life?'

'No,' Ellie said faintly. 'I didn't know that.' She hardly knew anything about Joe's time in the Army.

'Out in Oruzgan Province. Your crazy husband here broke cover to draw enemy fire. I was literally pinned between a rock and a hard place and—'

'Steve,' Joe interrupted, raising his hand for silence, 'Ellie doesn't need to hear your war stories.'

But Steve was only silenced momentarily. 'He's way too modest,' he said, cocking his thumb towards Joe. 'They're saying we're all heroes, but take it from me— your husband is a *true* hero, Ellie. I guess he's never told you. He risked his life to save mine. He was mentioned in despatches, you know, and the Army doesn't hand those out every day.'

'Wow,' Ellie said softly.

Wow was about all she could manage. The admiration and gratitude in Steve's eyes was so very genuine and sincere. She had difficulty breathing.

He risked his life to save mine.

But Joe obviously hadn't told Steve that he was now divorced, which made this moment rather confusing and embarrassing for Ellie, not to mention overwhelming. Her throat was too choked for speech. Her lips were trembling. She pressed a hand to her mouth, willing herself not to lose it in front of these guys.

'Thanks for sharing that, Steve,' she managed to say eventually. 'Joe never tells me anything about Afghanistan.' To keep up the charade, she tried to make this sound light and teasing—a loving wife gently chiding her over-protective husband.

'Well, it's been a pleasure to finally meet you and Jacko,' Steve said. 'But I'm afraid I have to head back. We're throwing a Christmas party at our place tonight. Pity you guys can't join us, but Lozza will have my guts for garters if I'm late.'

Already, he was climbing back into the cockpit.

Without Joe.

'You'd better hurry and get your things,' Ellie told Joe.

'My things?'

'You're not leaving without your luggage, surely?'

His blue eyes shimmered with puzzled amusement as he stepped towards her. Touched her lightly on the elbow. 'I'm not leaving now, Ellie,' he said quietly. 'I'm not going anywhere till the floods go down.'

'But—'

He cupped her jaw with a broad hand. 'Relax. It's cool.' His smile was warm, possibly teasing. His touch was lighting all kinds of fires. 'I couldn't let you eat all this stuff on your own.'

And then his thumb, ever so softly, brushed over her lips. 'Let's wave Steve off, and get these things inside. And then we can really start planning our Christmas.'

Our Christmas.

Joe was free to leave. Steve Hansen would have taken him back to the coast in a heartbeat—no questions asked. Instead Joe had *chosen* to stay.

And the way he'd looked at her just now was like the Joe of old.

But that was crazy. He couldn't… They couldn't…

She mustn't read too much into this. It was Christmas and Joe wanted to spend more time with Jacko. It was the only logical, believable explanation—certainly, the only one Ellie's conscience could accept.

But as Steve took off with the downdraught from his chopper flattening the grass and sending the cattle in the next paddock scampering, she had to ask, 'So, if you knew Steve could fly out here, why didn't you get him to rescue you?'

Joe shrugged. 'It would have been difficult, leaving the hire car stranded here.'

It was a pretty weak excuse and Ellie didn't try to hide her scepticism.

'Besides,' Joe added smoothly, 'you and I decided on a truce, and how can you have a truce between two people if one of the combatants simply walks away?'

As excuses went, this was on the shaky side too, but Ellie wasn't going to argue. Not if Joe was determined to uphold their truce. And not when he'd gone to so much trouble and expense to celebrate Christmas with her and Jacko.

'Come on,' he said, hefting the white box of cold stores. 'Let's see what Steve's managed to find.'

* * *

The packages were piled into the kitchen and it was just like opening Christmas presents a day early.

In the box from the cold stores, nestling in a bed of ice, they found the most fantastic array of seafood—export quality banana prawns, bright red lobsters, a slab of Tasmanian smoked salmon, even a mud crab.

'I may have slightly over-catered,' Joe said with a wry grin. 'But seafood always looks a lot bigger in the shell.'

In another cold bag there was a lovely heritage Berkshire ham from the Tablelands. This brought yet another grin from Joe. 'If the wet closes in again, we'll be OK for ham sandwiches.'

The rest of the produce was just as amazing—rosy old-fashioned tomatoes that actually smelled the way tomatoes were supposed to smell; bright green fresh asparagus, crispy butter-crunch lettuce, further packets of salad greens, a big striped watermelon. There were even Californian cherries, all the way from the USA.

In yet another box there were jars of mustard, mayonnaise and marmalade. Pickles and quince paste from the Barossa Valley. Boxes of party fun—bonbons and sparklers, whistles and glow sticks.

And there was a plum pudding and brandy cream, and a bottle of classic French champagne, and another whole case of wine of a much classier vintage than the wines Ellie had bought.

She thanked Joe profusely. In fact, on more than one occasion, she almost hugged him, but somehow she managed to restrain herself. Joe might have been incredibly, over-the-top generous, but Ellie was quite sure a newly ex-wife should *not* hug the ex-husband she'd so recently served with divorce papers.

It was important to remember that their Christmas truce was nothing more than a temporary cessation of hostilities—*temporary* being the operative word.

Ellie forced her mind to safer practical matters—like what they were going to do with the stuffed chicken and shortbread dough sitting in the fridge.

'We'll have them tonight,' suggested Joe. 'They'll be perfect for Christmas Eve.'

So the chicken and assorted roast vegetables, followed by shortbread cookies for dessert, became indeed the perfect Christmas Eve fare.

A cool breeze arrived in the late afternoon, whisking away the muddy aroma, so Ellie set a small table on the veranda where they ate in the gathering dusk, sharing their meal with Jacko.

Joe stuck coloured glow sticks into the pot plants along the verandah, lending a touch of magic to the warm summer's night.

Jacko was enchanted.

Ellie was enchanted too, as she sipped a glass of chilled New Zealand white wine, one of Joe's selections.

She had spent the past four years working so hard on Karinya—getting up at dawn, spending long days out in the paddocks overseeing the needs of her cattle, and then, after Jacko was born, fitting in as much time as possible to be with him as well.

Most nights, she'd fallen into bed exhausted. She'd almost forgotten what it was like to take time out to party.

Putting Jacko to bed on Christmas Eve was fun, even though he didn't really understand her explanation about the pillowslip at the end of his cot. He would soon work it out in the morning, and Ellie's sense of bubbling anticipation was enough enthusiasm for both of them.

When she tiptoed out of Jacko's room, she found Joe on the veranda, leaning on the railing again and looking out at the few brave stars that peeked between the lingering clouds.

He turned to her. 'So when do you fill Jacko's stocking?'

She smiled. 'I've never played Santa before, so I'm not exactly an expert, but I guess I should wait till I'm sure he's well and truly asleep. Maybe I'll do the deed just before I go to bed.'

'I'd like to make a contribution,' Joe said, sounding just a shade uncertain. 'I asked Steve to collect something for Jacko.'

'OK. That's nice. But you can put it under the tree and give it to him in the morning.'

'I'd like to show it to you now. You might want to throw it in with the Father Christmas booty.'

'Oh, there's no need—'

But already Joe was beckoning Ellie to follow him inside, into the study, where he promptly shut the door behind them.

'This makes a bit of a noise and I don't want to wake him.' He was trying to sound casual, but he couldn't quite hide the excitement in his eyes.

Intrigued, Ellie watched as he pulled a box from beneath the desk and proceeded to open it.

'Oh, wow!' she breathed as Joe drew out the world's cutest toy puppy. 'A Border Collie. How gorgeous. It looks so real.' She touched the soft, furry, black and white coat. 'It almost feels real and it's so cuddly. Jacko will love it!'

'Watch this.' Joe pressed a button in the puppy's stomach and set it on the ground. Immediately, it sat up and barked, then dropped back to all fours and began to scamper across the floor.

'Oh, my goodness.' Ellie laughed. 'It's amazing.'

The puppy bumped into the desk, backed away and then proceeded to run around in circles.

'I knew Jacko was too little for a real dog,' Joe said. 'But I thought this might be the next best thing.'

'It is. It's gorgeous. He'll be over the moon.' *The presents I bought won't be half as exciting.*

Joe was clearly pleased with her reaction. 'One of the guys in our unit bought a toy like this for his kid's birthday, and his wife put a movie of the boy and the puppy on the Internet. It was so damn cute it more or less went viral at the base.'

'I can imagine.' Ellie was touched by how pleased Joe looked, as if it was really important to find the right gift for his son.

'The other present I brought back with me was totally unsuitable,' he said. 'A kite. What was I thinking?'

'A kite from Afghanistan?'

Joe rolled his eyes to the ceiling. 'Yeah.'

'But their kites are supposed to be beautiful, aren't they?'

'Well, yes, that's true, and it's a national pastime for the kids over there, but a kite's not really suitable for a two-year-old. I just didn't think. I'll keep it for later.'

The puppy had wound down now and Joe scooped it up, unselfconsciously cradling it in his arms.

It wasn't only *little* boys who looked cute with toy dogs, Ellie decided.

'So you might like to put this in with the Santa stash,' he said.

'But then Jacko won't know *you* bought it for him.'

'That's not important.'

Ellie frowned. 'I think it is important, Joe. If you're going to go away again for ages at a time, a lovely gift like this will help Jacko to remember you.'

Perhaps this was the wrong thing to say. Joe's face turned granite-hard—hard cheekbones, hard eyes, hard jaw.

Silence stretched uncomfortably between them.

Ellie wished she knew what he was thinking. Was he regretting his decision to work so far away? Perhaps he felt differently about leaving Jacko now that he'd met the boy and so clearly liked him?

It was more than likely that Joe loved Jacko. For Ellie, just thinking about Joe heading off there to that freezing, lonely, big ocean made her arms ache strangely. They felt so empty and she felt sad for Joe, sad for Jacko too—for the tough, complicated father and his sweet, uncomplicated son.

Maybe she even felt sad for herself?

No. I've made my choices.

It seemed like an age before Joe spoke. 'I'd rather my son remembered *me*, not the toys I've given him.'

Ellie swallowed. It was hard to know whether he was taking the high moral ground or simply being stubborn. But he was sticking to his decision.

She held out her hand. 'In that case, I'd love to add this puppy to the Santa bag. Jacko will adore it. He'll be stoked.'

'You want to keep it in this box?'

'No. It looks more true-to-life out of the box.' Ellie hugged the puppy to her stomach. 'Joe, you haven't bought a Christmas present for me, have you?'

The hard look in his eyes lightened. 'There might be a little something. Why? Does that bother you?'

'Yes. I don't have anything for you. I never dreamed—'

He smiled crookedly. 'Chill, Ellie. It's no big deal. I know you haven't been anywhere near shops.'

Just the same, she was going to worry about this and it would probably keep her awake.

This is damn hard, Joe thought as Ellie left with the dog. Coming home was *so* hard. So much harder than he'd expected.

Of course, he'd always known he would have to make big adjustments. Soldiers heard plenty of talk about the challenges they would face as they transitioned from the huge responsibilities and constant danger of military life to the relative monotony and possible boredom of civilian life.

But Joe had been convinced that his adjustments would be different, easier than the other men's. To begin with, he wasn't coming home to a wife and family.

Or at least he hadn't planned to come home to a wife and family.

And yet here he was—on Christmas Eve—divorced on paper, but up to his ears in family life and getting in deeper by the minute.

He had to face up to the inescapable truth. No matter how much distance he put between himself and his family, there would always be ties to Ellie and Jacko.

It was so obvious now. He couldn't believe he hadn't seen it before.

And here was another thing. By coming back to Karinya, he was forced to see his absence in Afghanistan from Ellie's point of view, and he didn't like the picture he discovered.

While he'd played the war hero, earning his fellow soldiers' high regard, his wife—she'd still been his wife, after all—had slogged for long, hard days on this property, and she'd done it alone for the most part. As well, with no support whatsoever from him, she'd weathered the long awaited pregnancy and birth of their son.

On her own.

After the years of heartbreak and invasive procedures that had eroded their marriage, Joe knew damn well that the nine months of pregnancy must have been a huge emotional roller coaster for Ellie.

And what had he done? He'd tried to block out all thoughts of her pregnancy. And he'd let her soldier on. Yes, Ellie had most definitely *soldiered* on. Alone. Courageously.

Just thinking about it made Joe tremble now. During that whole time, Ellie must have believed he didn't care.

Hell. No wonder she had trouble trusting his motives today. No wonder she'd expected him to escape in Steve's chopper as soon as he had the chance.

And yet, strangely, escape had been the last thing on his mind. Shouldn't he be worried about that?

CHAPTER EIGHT

WHEN ELLIE WOKE early next morning, she felt an immediate riff of excitement, a thrill straight from childhood.

Christmas morning!

She went to her bedroom window and looked out. It was raining again, but not too heavily. She didn't mind about the rain—at least it would cool things down.

'Happy Christmas,' she whispered to the pale pink glimmer in the clouds on the eastern horizon, and then she gave a little skip. Rain, hail or shine, she was more excited about this Christmas than she had been in years.

Having a child to share the fun made such a difference. And this year they had all Joe's bounty to enjoy, as well as his pleasant company during their day-long truce.

The truce was a big part of the difference.

Don't think about tomorrow. Just make the most of today.

On the strength of that, Ellie dressed festively in red jeans and a white sleeveless blouse with a little frill around the neckline. When she brushed her hair, she was about to tie it back into its usual ponytail when she changed her mind and left it to swing free about her shoulders.

Why not? They might be in the isolated outback, but it *was* Christmas, so she threaded gold hoops in her ears as well, and sprayed on a little scent.

On her way to the kitchen she passed Jacko's room, but he was still asleep, still unaware of the exciting bundle at the end of his cot. He normally wouldn't wake for at least another hour.

As Ellie passed the open door of Joe's room, she glanced in and saw that his bed was made, so he was already up, too. She felt pleased. It would be nice to share an early morning cuppa while they planned their day together.

Maybe they could start with a breakfast of scrambled eggs and smoked salmon with croissants? And they could brew proper coffee and have an extra croissant with that new, expensive marmalade.

Joe might have other ideas, of course. He wasn't in the kitchen, however.

Ellie turned on the kettle and went to the doorway while she waited for it to come to the boil. Almost immediately, she saw movement out in a paddock.

Joe?

She crossed the veranda to get a better view through the misty rain. It was definitely Joe out there and he was bending over a cow that seemed to be on the ground.

Ellie frowned. Most of her pregnant cows had calved, but one or two had been late to drop. She hoped this one wasn't in trouble.

Grabbing a coat and Akubra from the pegs by the back door, she shoved her feet into gumboots and hurried down the steps and over the wet, slippery grass, dodging puddles in the track that ran beside the barbed wire fence.

'Is everything OK?' she called as she reached Joe.

He'd been crouching beside the cow, but when Ellie called he straightened. He was dressed as she was in a dark oilskin coat and broad-brimmed hat. In the dull grey morning light, his eyes were very bright blue.

Ellie had always had a thing for Joe's eyes. This morning they seemed to glow. They set her pulses dancing.

'Everything's fine,' he said. 'You have a new calf.'

And now she dragged her attention to the cow and saw that she had indeed delivered her calf. It was huddled on the ground beside her, dark red and still damp, receiving a motherly lick.

'Her bellowing woke me up,' Joe said. 'So I came out to investigate, but she's managed fine without any help.'

'That's great. And now we have a little Christmas calf,' Ellie said, smiling.

'Yes.' Joe smiled too and his gaze rested on her. 'Happy Christmas, Ellie.'

'Happy Christmas.' Impulsively, she stepped forward and kissed him lightly on the cheek.

He kissed her in reply—just a simple little kiss on her cheek, but, to her embarrassment, bright heat bloomed where his lips touched her skin.

Awkwardly, she stepped away and paid studious attention to the little calf as it staggered to its feet. It was incredibly cute, all big eyes and long spindly legs.

'It's a boy,' Joe said, and almost immediately the little fellow gave a skip and tried to headbutt its tired mum.

Ellie laughed, but the laugh died when she saw Joe's suddenly serious expression.

'I've been thinking about you,' he said. 'I never asked what it was like—when Jacko was born.'

She felt winded, caught out. 'Oh, God, don't ask.'

He was frowning. 'Why? Was it bad?'

You shouldn't be bothering with this now. Not after all this time.

'I know I should have asked you long ago, Ellie.' Joe's throat worked. 'I'm sorry, but I'd like to know. Was…was it OK?'

Even now, memories of her prolonged labour made her wince. She'd been alone and frightened in a big Townsville hospital, and she'd been unlucky. Rather than having the assistance of a nice, sensitive and understanding midwife, the nurse designated to look after her had been brusque and businesslike. Unsympathetic.

So many times during her twenty plus hours of labour, Ellie could have benefited from a little hand-holding. A comforting companion. But she wouldn't tell Joe that. Not now.

Especially not today.

She dismissed his concern with a wave of her hand. 'Most women have a hard time with their first.'

A haunted look crept into his eyes. 'So it was tough?'

OK, so he probably wouldn't give up without details. She told him as casually as she could. 'Almost twenty-four hours and a forceps delivery.'

She wouldn't tell him about the stitches. That would totally gross him out. 'It was all perfectly normal in the end, thank heavens, but it had its scary moments.'

Joe looked away. She saw the rise of his chest as he drew a deep breath.

'But it was worth it,' Ellie said softly. 'It was so worth every minute of those long hours to see Jacko.' And suddenly she had to tell Joe more, had to help him to see the joy. 'He was the most beautiful baby ever born, Joe. He had this little scrunched up face and dark hair. And he was waving his little arms. Kicking his legs. He had long feet, just like yours, and he was so amazingly perfect. It was the biggest moment of my life.'

You should have been there.

Oh, help. She was going to cry if she kept talking about this. Joe looked as if he was already battling tears.

It was Christmas Day. They should *not* be having this conversation.

Forcing herself to be practical, Ellie nodded to the new calf and its mother. 'I'll bring them some supplements later but, right now, I'm hanging out for breakfast. Are you coming?'

It took a moment for the furrows in Joe's brow to smooth. He flashed a scant, uncertain smile. 'Sure.'

'Let's hurry then. I'm starving.'

On the homestead's back veranda, Ellie pulled off her gumboots and removed her hat and coat. Joe shouldn't have been paying close attention. But, beneath the outdoor gear, she was dressed for Christmas in skinny red jeans and a frilly white top. Winking gold earrings swung from her ears and her dark glossy hair hung loose.

'So I was thinking scrambled eggs and smoked salmon?'

Breakfast? With his emotions running high, Joe's thoughts were on tasting Ellie's soft pink lips and hauling her red and white deliciousness close. He wanted to peel her frilly neckline down and press kisses along the delicate line of her collarbone. Wanted to trace the teasing seams of her jaunty red jeans.

Yeah, right, Brainless. Clever strategy. You'd land right back where you started with this woman. Ruining her life.

'Joe?'

He blinked. 'Sorry?'

With evident patience, Ellie repeated her question. 'Are you OK with scrambled eggs and smoked salmon?'

'Sure. It sounds—'

'Mummy!' cried a high-pitched voice from inside the house. 'Look, Mummy, look! A puppy!'

Ellie grinned. 'Guess we'll deal with breakfast in a little while.'

For Joe, most of Christmas Day ran pretty much to plan. Jacko loved his gifts—especially the little dog, and the colourful interlocking building set that Ellie had bought for him. The three of them enjoyed Ellie's leisurely breakfast menu, and Joe and Ellie took their second cups of coffee through to the lounge room where they opened more presents from under the tree—mostly presents for Jacko from their respective families.

Ellie loved the fancy box of lotions and bath oils and creams that Steve Hansen's wife had selected for her. And, to Joe's surprise, she handed him a gift.

'From Jacko and me,' she said shyly.

It was very small. Tiny, to be accurate. Wrapped in shiny red paper with a gold ribbon tied in an intricate bow.

'I know I said I didn't have anything for you, Joe. I meant I hadn't *bought* anything. This…this is homemade.'

Puzzled, he opened it and found a USB stick, a simple storage device for computers.

'I've put all Jacko's photos on there,' Ellie said. 'Everything from when he was born. I…um…thought you might like to—'

She couldn't go on. Her mouth pulled out of shape and, as her face crumpled, she gave a helpless shake of her head.

Dismayed, Joe dropped his gaze and stared fiercely at the tiny device in his hand.

'It'll help you to catch up on Jacko's first two years,' Ellie said more calmly.

But Joe was far from calm as he thought about all the images this gift contained. Two whole years of his son's life that he'd virtually ignored.

He saw that his hand was trembling. 'Thanks,' he said gruffly. 'That's—'

Hell, he couldn't make his voice work properly. 'I…I really appreciate this.'

It wasn't enough, but it was the best he could do.

They phoned their families.

'It's bedlam here,' Joe's mother laughed. 'Wall to wall grandchildren.'

'Jacko loves the picture books you sent, Mum. And the train set from his cousins. They were a huge hit.' The phone line was bad after all the rain and he had to almost yell.

'We miss you, Joe. And we're dying to meet Jacko, of course. Everyone sends their love. I hope you're having a nice day, darling.'

'We are, thanks. It's been great so far. Everything's fine.'

He and Jacko went into the lounge room and built a tall tower with the new blocks while Ellie phoned her mother. Joe had no intention of listening in, but she also had to speak loudly, so he couldn't help but hear.

'Harold gave you a diamond bracelet? How…how thoughtful. Yes, lovely. Yes, Mum, yes, Joe's still here. No, no. No problems…No, Mum. Honestly, you didn't have to say that. All right. Apology accepted. No, it doesn't mean I'm giving in. Yes, we're having beautiful seafood. One of Joe's Army mates brought it out in a helicopter. Yes, I thought so. *Very* nice. And Happy Christmas to you, too!'

Ellie came back into the lounge room and pulled a heaven-help-me face. 'I think I need a drink.'

'Right on time.' Joe grinned. 'The sun's well over the yardarm.'

They opened a bottle of chilled champagne and chose a CD by a singer they'd both loved years and years ago. And the music was light and breezy and the day rolled pleasantly on.

Jacko romped with his toy dog and played the new game of hide and seek, putting the dog behind cushions and then the curtains. Joe and Ellie made a salad with avocado, three kinds of lettuce and herbs. They set the dining table for lunch with the seafood platter taking pride of place. They added bowls for the crab shells and finger bowls floating with lemon slices.

They pulled bonbons that spilled rolled-up paper hats and corny, groan-worthy jokes. Jacko blew whistles and pulled crackers that popped streamers. The adults ate seafood and drank more champagne, while Jacko had orange juice and chicken. They laughed.

They laughed plenty.

Over plum pudding with brandy cream, while Jacko enjoyed ice cream with chocolate sprinkles, Joe told some of the funnier stories from Afghanistan. Ellie recalled the bush yarns the ringers had told around the campfire during last winter's cattle muster.

Joe couldn't drag his eyes from Ellie. She was glowing—and not from the wine. Her smiles were genuinely happy. Her dark eyes shone and danced with laughter. Even in an unflattering green paper hat, she looked enchanting.

And sexy. Dangerously so.

Seafood in the outback was a rare treat and she ate with special enthusiasm, sometimes closing her eyes and giving little groans of pleasure.

One time she caught Joe watching her. She went still and a pretty pink blush rose from the white frill on her blouse, over her neck and into her cheeks.

Watching that blush, Joe was tormented.

This truce was perilous. It was setting up an illusion. Messing with his head. Encouraging him to imagine the impossible.

After their long leisurely lunch, Ellie bundled a sleepy Jacko into his cot. The new black and white puppy, now named Woof, took pride of place next to his much-loved teddy bear. He was one very happy little boy.

On leaving his room, she found, to her surprise, that the dining table had already been cleared. Joe was in the kitchen and he'd cleared away the rubbish. He'd also rinsed their plates and glasses, and had almost finished stacking the dishwasher.

'Goodness, Joe. The Army's turned you into a domestic goddess.' *And a sex god*, she thought ruefully. *Or is it just too long since I've had a man in my kitchen?*

Grabbing the champagne bottle from the fridge, Joe

held it up with a grin. 'Want to finish this? There are a couple of glasses left.'

Ellie smiled. She was loving everything about this Christmas. 'It would be a crime to let those bubbles go flat.'

They took their glasses back to the lounge room. Outside, it was still drizzling and grey, but it was cosy inside with the coloured lights on the Christmas tree and a jazz singer softly crooning, and with Joe sprawled in an armchair, long legs stretched in close-fitting jeans and a white open-necked shirt that showed off his tan.

Ellie thought, *I'm almost happy. I'm so close to feeling happy that I can almost taste it.*

She *might* have been completely, unquestionably happy if this truce were real and not a charade.

It was scary—*super*-scary—to be having second thoughts, to wish that she and Joe could somehow time-travel back into their past and right a few wrongs. OK, right a *mountain* of wrongs.

It wasn't going to happen, of course. This pleasant and charming interlude was nothing more than time out. Time out for Christmas. From reality.

It was important to remember that. Ellie planned to make sure she remembered it. She hadn't needed her mother's phone call to remind her.

Joe hoped he looked relaxed, but it was getting harder and harder to stay cool and collected while Ellie kicked off her shoes and made herself comfortable on the sofa.

She arched and stretched like a sleepy cat and then sank against the cushions, offering him an incredibly attractive view of her long legs in slinky red jeans. She wriggled her bare toes and sipped champagne with a smile of pure bliss.

The urge to join her on the sofa was a major problem.

And here was an inconvenient truth.

Ellie was the only woman Joe had ever truly wanted and, despite the bitterness and sorrow that had blown apart their marriage, the wanting was still there. Had never really left. It was an involuntary, visceral, inoperable part of him. And right now it was—

Driving him crazy.

Ellie took another sip of her champagne and held the glass up to the light, admiring the pale bubbles. Then she looked at Joe and her gaze was thoughtful, almost…

Wistful?

He held his breath. It was so hard to sit still when all he wanted was to be there on the sofa with her, helping her out of that frilly blouse.

Almost as if she could read his thoughts, Ellie's smile turned wary. Colour warmed her cheeks again and her eyes took on a new heightened glow. She shifted her position, and Joe wondered if she was feeling the same fidgety restlessness that gripped him.

His head was crammed with memories of making love to her. He could remember it all—the sweet taste of her kisses, the silky softness of her skin, the eager wildness of her surrender—

'So,' Ellie said with an awkward little smile, 'how would you like to spend the afternoon?'

She was joking, right?

'Are you interested in watching a DVD?'

'Might be dangerous,' Joe muttered.

'A DVD? Dangerous?'

He pointed to the positioning of the TV screen. 'We'd have to share that couch.'

Ellie looked startled, as well she might. She tried to cover it with a laugh. 'And that's a problem?'

'When you're wearing those tempting red jeans— yes, a big problem.'

Her expression switched from startled to stunned. And who could blame her? It had probably never occurred to her that her ex still had the hots. For her.

Joe grimaced.

Ellie simply sat very still, clutching her champagne flute in two hands, staring at him with a hard to read frown.

To his surprise, she didn't look angry. Or sad. Merely bemused and thoughtful.

His heart pounded. What was she thinking? If she showed the slightest hint that she was on the same wavelength, he would be out of this chair...

Then Ellie dropped her gaze to her glass and ran a fingertip around its rim. 'That's part of our problem, isn't it?'

Joe waited, unsure where this was heading.

'There's always been an attraction.' Ellie swallowed, gave a self-conscious shrug. Kept staring at her glass. 'But perhaps we would have been better off if we'd spent more time talking. I know you hate getting too deep and meaningful, Joe, but I don't think we ever spent enough time just talking, did we?'

'Not without arguing, no.'

'Have you thought about it very often?' She looked away and swallowed nervously. 'Have you given much headspace to what went wrong for us?'

'Some.' Joe's throat was so tight he could barely speak. 'Yes.'

Ellie drained her champagne and set the glass on the coffee table. 'I must admit I don't like failing or giving up, so I've given quite a bit of thought to our problems since you left. Too much, I guess.'

'What conclusions have you come to?'

Ellie regarded him with a narrowed, doubtful gaze. 'I can't imagine you'd really want to talk about this now.'

'No, it's OK. Go on. I'm listening. I'd actually like to hear your point of view.'

She seemed to think about this for a moment and then suddenly dived in. 'Well, I've always thought we were like that old song. Married in a fever. One minute we were the world's hottest lovers. Next, we were trying to set up a cattle business and start, or I should say restart, our family.'

'And then it all got so hard.'

'Too hard,' Ellie agreed with a frown. 'And that's when we didn't talk enough. Or when we tried to talk we just ended up yelling.'

Joe nodded, recalling the distressing scenes he'd tried so hard to forget.

'But there's one thing I'm very grateful for, Joe. Even in the heat of it, you never raised a finger to hurt me.'

'I wouldn't. I couldn't.'

Ellie had tears in her eyes now. 'But I think, in the middle of it all, we somehow lost sight of each other.'

'Or maybe we never really took the time to know each other properly.'

'Yes, that too.' She looked down at her hands and rubbed at a graze on her knuckle. She sighed heavily.

'But, as I said the other day—it's probably not helpful to dredge up the past.'

Joe wasn't so sure. Already he could see evidence of how they'd both changed. When they were married, a conversation like this would have landed them square in the middle of another argument.

He had to admit he'd avoided over-thinking their past. It was easy in the Army to be completely distracted by the demands of an ever present, very real and life-threatening enemy. He'd lived from day to day, from task to task. It was simple—and necessary—to focus on the present and to block out his emotions, including any guilt regarding Ellie.

Now, it was hard to believe he'd been so single-minded. Some would call it pig-headed.

Selfish.

But had he anything more to offer Ellie now? He'd like to think that time and distance had honed the raw edges and given him maturity.

Watching him, Ellie gave an uneasy sigh, then pushed out of the couch and got to her feet. She walked to the window and peered out. 'It's stopped raining,' she said dully.

A kind of desperation touched Joe. She was walking away, changing the subject. And yet he had the feeling they'd been drawing close to something important. He'd even wondered if it was something they both wanted, but were too afraid to reach for.

He edged forward in his seat, his mind racing, trying to balance his gut instincts with cool reason.

At the same moment, Ellie spun away from the window. 'Oh, stuff it! I think I *do* need to talk about this. I mean, it's our only chance. Once you're gone—'

She lifted her hands as if she felt lost. Helpless.

Joe's chest tightened. This was a *huge* moment and he suddenly knew that he wanted to grab it with both hands. Even so, he felt nervous—as nervous as he had in Afghanistan crossing a field laced with landmines.

'I'm happy to talk,' he said carefully. 'I mean—we're in a kind of now-or-never limbo at the moment, so perhaps we should make the most of it.' He chanced a smile. 'And we do have the protection of a truce.'

Slowly, cautiously, Ellie returned his smile, and then she walked back to the sofa and sat at one end, straight-backed, lovely, but clearly nervous. 'Where should we start?'

Good question. 'I'm open.'

Ellie squinted her dark eyes as she gave this some thought. 'Maybe we could start with the whole Army thing. There's so much I don't really know about you, Joe. Not just what you've done as a soldier since we split. I never really understood why you wanted to join the Army in the first place—apart from a chance to escape.'

'Well, I was planning to join the Army before I met you.'

'Yes, I knew that. But why, when your family own a cattle property? Don't you like cattle work?'

'Sure. I like working on the land.' Joe knew he could say this honestly. He loved the physical demands, loved being at one with the elements, loved the toughness and practicality required of people in the bush. 'But with four older brothers, I had very little say in how things were run at home. So the idea of the Army was more an act of rebellion than anything.'

Ellie looked surprised.

'I was fed up with being bossed around by those brothers of mine. They were always giving me orders. Not just on the property either. They loved telling me what I should and shouldn't do with my life. I decided, if I was going to be bossed around, it may as well be for a damn good reason and not simply because I was the runt of the litter.'

'Some runt,' she said with a smile.

'That's how I felt.'

Her smile was sympathetic. 'There was an age gap between you and the rest of your brothers, wasn't there? What was it? Six years?'

'Almost seven. I think they hoped I'd stay at the homestead and be a mummy's boy, but I wasn't staying home when they were off having adventures. So I was always trailing after them like a bad smell, trying to keep up. Annoyed the hell out of them, of course.'

'Not great for the self-esteem.'

Joe gave a shrug. 'I eventually came into my own, but not until boarding school. By then, all my brothers had left and, as far as my classmates were concerned, I wasn't anyone's little brother. I was just Joe Madden.'

'Football star.'

'For a few years, yeah.'

'And the Army was a bigger and more exciting version of boarding school?'

This time Joe chuckled. 'You missed your calling. You should have been a shrink.'

But Ellie was frowning again, as if she was lost in thought. 'I *still* think the Army provided an excellent excuse to escape when our marriage got too rough.'

'You're probably right.' He fingered a loose thread

in the upholstery on his chair. 'Maybe it was something I had to get out of my system.'

'Is it out of your system now?'

That was a damn good question. 'I think so. I've certainly no ambition to become an old soldier.' Joe looked up and met her gaze. 'So what about you, Ellie?'

To his surprise, she looked suddenly trapped. 'How do you mean?'

'If we're spilling our guts, I thought you might have something about you and your family that we've never outed.'

'I was an only child,' she said quickly. Almost too quickly. 'No sibling issues for me.'

But the shutters had come down. Everything about her was instantly defensive.

Joe waited. Ellie had never really explained why she'd left home straight after high school and moved to Queensland. He knew her dad had died when she was young and her relationship with her mum was OK, but not close, certainly not as close as Angela would have liked. There were issues, he was sure.

'I thought we were talking about you and the Army,' she said stiffly.

Ohhh-kaaay. Closed door.

Joe wasn't prepared to push Ellie on this. Not today. 'So we're back to me.' He shrugged. 'So, what else would you like to know?'

'Are you glad you joined up?'

The question was loaded, and Joe did his best to skirt it. 'The Army has its good points and I've certainly gained new skills.' He smiled. 'And not all of them involve blowing things up.'

More relaxed again now, Ellie picked up a cushion

and hugged it to her chest. Joe told himself he could not possibly be jealous of a cushion.

'So do you feel OK after everything you've seen and done over there?'

'Are you asking if I have post-traumatic stress?'

'Well, you seem fine, but there's so much talk about it. I wondered.'

'Well, I certainly feel OK, and I came out with a clean psych test. Perhaps I was lucky.'

'I guess you were due some good luck.' Her expression was a little sad. 'Just the same, do you think being a soldier has changed you at all?'

Joe hesitated, remembering the rockiest days of their marriage and the times he'd retreated when he'd known Ellie needed him. He'd watched his wife sink deeper into despair and it had felt like a knife in his heart, but he'd had no idea how to help her. At the time, he'd been completely inadequate.

'I'd like to think I've changed,' he said. 'I've certainly had to shoulder some hefty responsibilities.'

Ellie nodded slowly. 'It shows. I think it's given you confidence. You seem much surer of yourself now.'

This assessment caught him by surprise, especially as the smile that accompanied it was warm and tender.

Careful, Ellie.

When she looked at him like that, he was back to thinking about rolling with her on that couch.

CHAPTER NINE

JOE HAD THAT look again.

The look stole Ellie's breath and sent heat licking low, making her uncross and recross her legs, making her think too much about his powerful body, hidden by that snowy white shirt and blue jeans. He had that look in his eyes that made her forget all the warnings she'd given herself and wish for things she had no right to wish for.

She sat up straighter, and Joe watched with an attentiveness that did nothing to ease the edgy distractedness of her thoughts.

Talk, Ellie. This conversation's been going well. Don't lose it now.

'So,' she said quickly before she lost her nerve, 'I guess we agree that our relationship might have been more successful if we'd taken things more slowly at the start. We might have understood each other better if we'd talked more. Been a bit more tolerant.'

Joe nodded, but then his eyes took on a wicked teasing gleam. 'Then again, I'm not sure it was possible for us to go slow.'

She felt her cheeks glow.

'The way I remember it, we were pretty damn impatient,' Joe went on, clearly ignoring her discomfort.

This was *not* a helpful contribution, even though it was true. Right from the start, they hadn't been able to keep their hands off each other.

'At least we're managing to behave ourselves now,' she said tightly.

'We're divorced, Ellie.'

Clunk.

'Yes. Of course.' But she felt winded, as if he'd carelessly tossed her high and then left her to fall.

She slumped back against the cushions and closed her eyes while she waited for her heartbeats to recede from a frantic gallop to an only slightly less frantic canter. When she opened her eyes again, Joe was still watching her, but his expression was serious now.

'Just so I'm clear,' he said quietly. 'You're not having second thoughts, are you? About the divorce? About us?'

Second thoughts?

No, surely not. The very idea made her panic. She had her future planned. Joe had his future planned. They had their separate lives planned.

She couldn't have regrets. There was no point in trying to turn the train wreck of their marriage into a fairy tale.

And yet…

Had Joe really opened a door?

Was *he* having second thoughts about their marriage? And their divorce?

He was looking a tad winded, and Ellie could well believe that he'd shocked himself with his question.

It was too much to take in, sitting down. She launched

off the sofa and onto her feet again, and began to pace while her mind spun like a crazy merry-go-round.

'Second thoughts?' she repeated shakily. 'I don't think so, Joe.'

And yet...

And yet...

Her sense of loss was a dull ache inside her, and every time she looked at Joe now the pain grew sharper.

'But I...I don't know for sure.' She shot him a quick, searching glance. 'What about you?'

His throat worked and he tried for a smile and missed. 'I was good with our settlement. But...but if you wanted to reconsider it—'

Ellie stopped pacing. *Oh, God. This was not supposed to happen.*

'It was all decided,' she whispered. 'I've filed for divorce. I've served you with the papers. You've signed them.'

'I know. I know. And don't panic, Ellie. Nothing has to change.'

'No.' She took a deep breath, and then another.

'Unless...' Joe added slowly, carefully. 'Unless we want it to change.'

Whoa!

He was opening up a choice.

He was actually making her an offer. A second chance to right their wrongs.

Ellie's heart soared high with hope, then hovered, trembling with fear, terrified of failure. How could they possibly make this work?

'It can't be wise, can it?'

'Does it feel unwise?'

'No.' She stared at him anxiously. 'I don't know.'

'I guess we can only trust our own judgement.'

'Trust. That's a biggie. And…and now there's Jacko to consider as well. I'd hate to stuff things up for him.'

'It's the last thing I'd want, Ellie.'

She was swamped by an urge to simply rush into Joe's arms, to have done with the what-ifs and the wherefores and to simply give in to her burning need to have his arms about her, his lips working the magic she could so well remember.

I have to be sensible.

More than any other time in her life, she had to be cautious and unimpulsive and prudent.

'How can we be sure we won't just make the same mistakes?' But, even as she asked this, she knew the answer. After everything she'd been through, there were no guarantees. From the point of conception, every stage of life was a calculated risk.

After four years in the Army, Joe would know this, too.

'I guess we could avoid our first mistake,' he said. 'We could try taking things slowly, spending time together, getting to know each other again.'

'Just talking? Just friends?'

'It's only a suggestion.' Joe was out of his chair now and he was pacing too, as if he was as restless as she was.

It wasn't a sitting-down kind of conversation.

'What about this job you have lined up?' Ellie challenged. 'Chasing pirates or poachers or whatever?'

'The agency probably wouldn't be thrilled if I pulled out at the last minute, but I'd be prepared to.'

Ellie reached the bookcase and turned. Half a room separated them now. 'So if we tried this, how would it

work? Would you be living here, at Karinya, and helping me with the cattle?'

'Yes, just as I was before, I guess.' He smiled at her.
'But hopefully without the arguments.'

'Or the sex.' Ellie's pacing came to an abrupt halt.

Her gaze met Joe's and she saw his eyes blaze with a
look of such fierce intensity that her breathing snagged.

It wasn't possible, was it?

She and Joe couldn't live together and simply be
friends. She was practically climbing the walls after
just a few days of having him here, touching close and
yet out of reach. And now they were planning to extend
this condition indefinitely.

As if they were both frozen by the prospect, they
stood, poised like opponents at Wimbledon, both as
tense as tripwires, both breathing unevenly, with the
stretch of carpet an unpassable gulf between them.
Their no-go zone…

Help.

All Ellie could think about was crossing that space,
rushing into Joe's arms and sealing her lips to his.
Winding her limbs around his tree trunk body. Kissing him senseless.

Say something, Joe. Break the spell.

He didn't move, didn't speak, and something inside
Ellie—most probably her willpower—snapped.

She flew across the carpet.

'I'm sorry,' she murmured half a second before her
lips locked with Joe's.

But Joe wasn't looking for an apology, not if the
hungry way he returned her kiss was any guide. He
pulled her close, held her close, keeping her exactly
where he wanted her, hard against him in all the right

places, while his lips and tongue worked his dazzling, dizzying magic.

He tasted of Christmas and champagne and all kinds of happiness, and Ellie was swooning at the long-remembered taste and smell and intensely masculine feel of him.

Her knees gave way, but fortunately her hands linked behind his neck provided a timely, but necessary anchor.

If there were warning voices shouting in her head, she didn't hear them. She was drowning in a whirlpool whipped to urgency by years of loneliness and heart-break and a longing she could no longer deny.

I'm sorry, Joe. I've been trying so hard to forget you, but I can't. I've missed you so much.

So, so much.

The hunger in his kisses was reassuring. Wrapped in his arms with their wild hearts beating together, she could feel the passion in him…both thrilling and com-forting, as if they'd both arrived at the same place and knew it was where they were meant to be.

Everything about Joe felt familiar yet even more ex-citing than before. Especially now when, in the smooth-est of manoeuvres that Ellie didn't stop to analyse, he swung her off her feet and onto the sofa.

Cushions tumbled as their bodies tangled, urgency ruling the day. Joe kissed her chin, her earlobe, her throat, and her skin leapt to life wherever he touched. In no time he was peeling down the neckline of her blouse, trailing downward kisses that grew hotter and hotter.

Ellie helped him with the buttons. The blouse fell away and Joe released a soft groan. In a haze of need, she might have groaned too. She wanted his touch. Wanted it more than air.

'Mum! Mamma!'

Oh, help.

They stilled as if they'd been shot. Hearts racing, they stared at each other in disbelief.

'Mummy!' came another imperious summons from the little bedroom down the hallway.

Ellie was panting slightly. She was straddling Joe, flushed and half-dressed.

Joe looked into her eyes and smiled, his eyes hinting at dismay warring with amusement. 'His master's voice,' he said softly.

A shaky sigh broke from Ellie.

'Mummee!' Jacko called again and the cot was rattling now.

Joe reached for her, a hand at her nape, easing her down towards him. He kissed her gently, taking his time to sip at her lower lip. 'Saved by our son,' he murmured.

Our son. Not the kid or the boy. *Our* son.

'I don't feel saved.'

'No, you feel damn sexy.' He skimmed broad hands over bare skin at her waist, inducing a delicious shiver. 'At least we've made interesting progress.'

Indeed. Already, as they eased apart, Ellie sensed a new light-heartedness in Joe.

But that wasn't supposed to happen.

'I'll get Jacko,' he offered, rising to his feet while she began to re-button her blouse.

'Thanks.'

A moment later, Ellie heard his cheerful greeting and Jacko's delighted crow in response. She went to the bathroom and found a hairbrush, studied her reflection in the mirror. Her skin was flushed and glowing, her hair a messy tangle.

They'd come so close…

So close.

But had they been taking an important step, as Joe hinted, or had they teetered on the brink of a huge mistake?

And, more to the point, if they went ahead with their plan for a second chance, could she make it work? Could she be a better partner now?

When she thought about the woman she used to be, too anxious and heartbroken and self-absorbed to see beyond her own problems, she cringed.

She wanted to be so much better.

Was fate pushing her to grab this new chance?

A freak of nature, a flooded river, had brought Joe back into her life, but, just now on the sofa, they'd been gripped by a passion that revealed a deeper truth. They couldn't deny the attraction was still there. Stronger than ever.

It was still hard to believe that they might retrieve their marriage. For so long Ellie had thought of herself as already divorced. It wouldn't be easy to start again. They'd both have to make big adjustments. Huge. But if Joe was willing…

She wanted to give it her very best shot.

Joe lifted Jacko from the cot and took him to the bathroom and then to the kitchen for a drink and a snack, but he was working on autopilot. His mind was on Ellie and the big step they'd just taken. The choice they'd made.

The choice *he'd* made.

Sure, impulsive physical need had played a part, just as it had when he'd first met Ellie. But when he'd married her he hadn't really had a choice. He'd made his girlfriend pregnant and he'd felt a strong obligation to 'do the right thing' by her.

Again, four years ago, when he was so clearly making Ellie unhappy, he'd felt obliged to set her free. He hadn't known any other way to handle their problems and at the time, he'd convinced himself he had no other choice, although, as Ellie had correctly pointed out, he'd also been escaping.

Today, however, he'd had choices.

He had a signed legal document setting him free and he had a job to go to, a safe escape route. He had plenty of options.

But he'd also learned, after only a few days here, that he and Ellie had both changed during their years apart. Sure, they'd been on vastly different journeys—there couldn't be two experiences more different than war and motherhood—but they'd both matured as a result.

And, of course, they now had Jacko. Within a matter of days Joe loved the boy with a depth that he'd never dreamed possible. As for Ellie...

He knew now that he'd never stopped loving Ellie. He'd walked away from her when it all got too difficult and he'd buried his pain beneath the façade of a hardened soldier, but the bare truth was—his feelings for her were still as tender and loving as they'd been at the start.

So, yeah, he had loads of choices now.

And today he'd chosen to stay.

With Jacko between them, they spent the afternoon taking a tour of inspection around Karinya. Ellie carted nutritional supplements to the new mothers and calves, and she showed off her investments to Joe—two new dams and a windmill pump—as well as her successful experiments with improved pastures.

'You've done an amazing job,' he kept saying over and over.

They visited his favourite haunts, including the old weathered timber stockyards and the horse paddock. Together, they leaned on the railings, feeding carrots and sugar cubes to the horses that came to greet them, while Jacko played at their feet with a toy dump truck, filling its tray back with small rocks and then tipping them out.

'I think I should apologise,' Ellie said, needing to give voice to the issue at the forefront of her thoughts. 'I can't believe we decided on a set of rules and I immediately went crazy and broke them.'

'Have you heard me complaining?' Joe asked with a smile.

'But we didn't stick to the plan we'd made five minutes earlier.'

'Maybe it wasn't a very good plan. Not very realistic, at any rate.' Covering her hand with his, Joe rubbed his thumb over her knuckles. 'Don't start worrying, OK?'

Ellie smiled. 'OK.' There was something so very reassuring about this new confidence of Joe's. And, if she wanted this to work, she had to learn to trust him, didn't she?

Back in the ute, they drove on. They checked the river height and found that it was going down. In another day or two it would be crossable. But there was no more talk of Joe leaving.

Instead, happy vibes arced between them. A delicious anticipation whispered in the afternoon air. As they drove back to the homestead, they shared smiles and gazes over the top of their son's snowy head, gazes that shimmered with hope and excited expectation.

For their evening meal, Joe carved the Christmas ham with great ceremony and they ate thick, delicious pink slices piled on sourdough bread and topped with spicy mango chutney. Dessert was a cheese platter, plus extra helpings of Christmas pudding, and there was another bottle of Joe's delicious wine.

After dinner, to Jacko's squealing delight, the three of them played hide and seek together in the lounge room. Then they piled onto the sofa, with Jacko on Joe's knee, and together they read his new picture books. Ellie and Joe made the appropriate animal noises—Joe was the lion, the cow and the bear, while Ellie was the monkey, the duck and the sheep—and Jacko copied them, of course, amidst giggles and gales of laughter.

While Joe supervised Jacko's bath time—a rather noisy affair involving submarines and dive-bombing planes—Ellie took care of the dishes and tidied the kitchen. They put Jacko to bed.

And then, at last, they were alone.

Ellie was a tad self-conscious as they settled in the lounge room, enjoying the last of the wine. She was on the sofa and Joe was in the armchair again, but she knew they shared expectations about the night ahead. She was plucking up the courage to raise the question of sleeping arrangements. Surely Joe wouldn't stay in Nina's room tonight? Was it up to her as his hostess to mention this?

Despite this minor tension, their mood was relaxed. Music played, low and mellow. The tree lights glowed. They talked about their little boy—about the miracle that he was and how cute and clever—even which boarding school he might attend in the distant future.

Then, almost as if he could hear them, a little voice called, 'Drink o' water, Mummy.'

With a roll of her eyes, Ellie put down her glass and went to the kitchen to fill Jacko's cup. When she took it in to him, he only wanted two sips.

'Nuff,' he said, shaking his head.

'This is just a try-on,' Ellie scolded gently. 'Now snuggle down.' She kissed him. 'Time for sleep. Night, night.'

Jacko snuggled, closed his eyes and looked angelic. Satisfied and pleased, Ellie returned to the lounge room.

'Where were we?' she said to Joe.

'I believe we were congratulating ourselves on our wonderful son.'

They laughed together softly, so as not to disturb him.

Then Jacko wailed again. Ellie waited for a bit, but the wailing grew louder and, when she went to his room, she saw that he'd thrown his teddy bear out of the cot. Of course, she picked it up and gave it back to him. 'No more nonsense. It's bedtime,' she said more sternly.

Back in the lounge room, Joe was flicking through a magazine. Ellie settled on the sofa once more, picked up her glass.

'Joe!' came an imperious summons from the bedroom. 'Joe! Joe!'

Ellie sighed. 'He's overexcited.'

'Too much hide and seek after dinner?'

'Possibly. This happens from time to time.'

'So how do you usually handle it?'

'Depends. Sometimes Nina—'

'Nina?'

'The nanny.'

'Oh, yes, I forgot about her. When's she due back?'

'After New Year. Anyway, sometimes we let Jacko cry and he just gives up after a bit.'

Joe frowned at this.

'It's acceptable parenting, Joe. It's called controlled crying. We've never let him cry for *very* long.'

He still looked disapproving. 'Perhaps I should go in there and try speaking to him sternly?'

'Like a sergeant major?' Ellie sent him an *as if* look.

'A little fatherly discipline.'

'Are you sure you know how to reprimand a two-year-old?'

'I can only try.'

She shrugged. 'At this time of night, anything's worth a try.' But, suddenly unsure, she added quickly, 'Don't be too hard on him, Joe.'

Despite her last minute doubts, Ellie's gaze, as she watched Joe leave the room, was one of pure lust and feminine admiration. She was prepared to admit it now—Joe Madden had always been the most attractive guy she'd ever met, and now he was hotter than ever.

It wasn't just the extra muscle power. There was a new confidence and inner strength in him that showed in the way he held himself. And it was there in his gorgeous smile. In his attitude, too. He'd certainly taken fatherhood in his stride.

Actually, this last surprised her. Back in the bad old days when they were having so much trouble starting their family, Ellie had always been worried that Joe's heart wasn't really in the project—that parenthood was more her goal than his. Heaven knew she'd accused him of this often enough in the past.

Now, she heard Jacko's delighted greeting as Joe reached him, and she listened with keen interest for the 'stern message' he planned to deliver.

She was steeled for the gruff voice, followed by Jacko's whimpering cry. Telling Jacko off wouldn't work, of course. Almost certainly, she would have to go in there and soothe her little boy.

The house remained hushed, however, and all Ellie heard was the low rumble of Joe speaking so quietly that she couldn't hear the words. And then silence.

The silence continued.

Ellie finished her wine and the CD came to an end. She didn't bother to replace it. She was too absorbed and curious about the lack of sound down the hallway.

Eventually, it got the better of her and she tiptoed to the door of Jacko's room.

In the glow of the night light, she saw Joe by the cot and Jacko lying on his tummy, eyes closed, his long lashes curling against his plump cheeks. Joe was patting his back gently and patiently.

Ellie smiled. So much for the firm fatherly reprimand.

Sensing her presence, Joe looked up and lifted his free hand to halt her. Then he touched a finger to his lips and the message was clear. *I'm in charge here and everything's under control.*

Fascinated, she propped a shoulder against the doorjamb and waited, while Joe continued his gentle patting regime with surprising tenderness and patience. It was hard to believe this big tough man had just returned from a war that involved blowing things up and quite probably killing his enemy.

After another minute or so, Joe lifted his hand carefully from Jacko's back. Ellie waited for the boy to do his usual trick of wriggling and squirming till the patting resumed.

But Jacko remained peaceful and still and, a moment or two later, Joe came out of the room.

His smile was just a tad smug.

Safely back in the lounge room, Ellie narrowed her eyes at him. 'So that was your stern father act, huh?'

Joe grinned. 'Worked a treat.'

'You old softie.'

'That's one thing I'm not.' He touched her elbow. 'Come here and I'll prove it.'

Heat rose through Ellie like a flame through paper. Without hesitation, Joe drew her in.

And just like that she was in his arms and he was kissing her, hauling her closer still. And, of course, his boast was accurate. There was nothing soft about this guy, apart from his lips. The rest was hard-packed manly muscle and bone from head to toe.

The house was silent as they kissed.

And the silence continued. The only sound was the far-off call of a curlew in the trees along the river.

Joe took Ellie by the hand and led her to the darkened doorway on the far side of the lounge room, and the question about the night's sleeping arrangements became irrelevant.

This was the bedroom he knew well, the room they'd once shared.

They didn't bother with lights. The glow of the

Christmas tree reached where they stood at the foot of the bed, as they shared another kiss, another embrace.

Now their kisses were long and leisurely and sweet. They'd been denied this for so long, never believing it could happen. But despite the four years' separation, they lingered now on the brink, confident and trusting, savouring the exquisite anticipation.

Joe kissed Ellie's neck and she kissed his rough jaw. His lips brushed over her lips, once, twice in teasing, tantalising, unhurried caresses.

He lifted her chin to trace her jaw line with his lips. 'I've missed you, Ellie.'

'Me too. I've missed you so much.' She hadn't admitted it before, but she wanted him to know. 'The whole time you were away, I was terrified you'd be killed. There'd be stories about Afghanistan on the news, and I always had to turn them off.'

Tears threatened, but she didn't want to cry. Instead she sought pleasure, easing his shirt from his jeans and slipping her hands beneath, rediscovering the texture of his skin, the hair on his chest.

Her hands dipped lower and a soft sound broke from Joe, and next moment he was undressing her and she was loosening his clothes as best she could.

She had a brief moment of panic. 'I'm not the same, Joe. Since the pregnancy and everything, things have—'

'Shh.' He silenced her with his kiss as his hands cupped her less than perky breasts. 'You're lovely, Ellie,' he murmured against her lips. 'Beautiful. I'm still crazy about every little part of you.'

He melted the last of her fears as he guided her to the bed—the bed they'd shared till four years ago. And now, still, they took their time, making love slowly, tenderly, with whispered endearments and heartbreaking thoroughness.

They knew each other so well, knew all the ways they longed to be touched and kissed and roused—a knowledge they alone shared—intimate truths that lay at the heart of their marriage.

This night wasn't just about sex and wanting—it was a time-honoured act of love, where past hurts could begin to heal and glimmers of hope for their future dawned.

Afterwards they lay close together, talking softly in the moon-silvered dark.

'Welcome home,' Ellie said.

She felt Joe's smile against her neck. 'It's good to be back.'

'We have to make it work this time.'

Gently he lifted a strand of hair from her cheek. 'We will, Ellie.'

She turned, admiring his strong profile limned by moonlight. 'I love the way you're so confident now.'

'Older and wiser perhaps…'

'That should apply to me too then.'

'I'm sure it does.'

Ellie suspected that she'd changed, too. She was also more confident, more willing to believe in a happy future. But was she prepared to trust?

I must. It's important…

'At least we no longer have the whole baby thing hanging over us.'

Joe shifted away slightly, as if he needed to see her face. 'I assume with everything you've been through that you're content with just one?'

'Oh heavens, yes. Aren't you?'

'Absolutely. I'm perfectly content with the three of us.' He chuckled. 'Anyway, I doubt we could improve on Jacko.'

Ellie smiled at the obvious pride in his voice, but of course she agreed. They couldn't hope for more than their cute little guy, even if they were able to, which they weren't.

'So we're OK not using precautions?' Joe asked.

'Well, yes, we must be, surely. Look how hard it was to get Jacko.' Ellie frowned. 'But I will check with the doctor next time I'm in town. Another pregnancy is the last thing I'd want now when we're starting over. I'm more than happy to close that chapter in my life.'

'That's fine by me.'

Unexpected relief flowed through Ellie. That particular ordeal was behind them. They'd been tested in the fire and were stronger now. 'So we should be OK, shouldn't we?'

'I reckon we should be very OK.'

As if to prove it, Joe kissed her again, deep and hard and long.

Melting fast, she wound her arms around him, and they made love again with a new sense of giddy freedom and joyful abandon.

CHAPTER TEN

BOXING DAY MORNING dawned. As always, Ellie woke early, and the first thing she saw was Joe lying beside her. She indulged in a few secret moments to drink in the sight of him, so dark and manly and downright hot, and her heart performed a little joyful jig.

She went to the kitchen and made tea and when she brought two steaming mugs back to bed Joe was awake.

'I can't lie around having tea in bed,' he protested. 'I've a cattle property to run.'

'Humour me, Joe. Just for today. It's a public holiday. I know that doesn't mean much out here, but let's pretend.'

Ellie opened the French windows onto the verandah and plumped up the pillows and they sat in bed together, looking out over Karinya's paddocks, where bright new tinges of green were already showing after the recent rains.

She clinked her tea mug against his. 'Here's to us.'

'To us,' he agreed, dropping a kiss on her brow.

'That's assuming you're still happy to stay.'

'Of course I am, Ellie.'

Joe shot her a wary sideways glance. 'You've got to trust me, you know. This won't work if you don't.'

'I know.' She was surprised he'd pinpointed the heart of her problem. She was learning to trust—to trust not just Joe, but herself, even to trust in their ability to face the unknown future. 'I'm sorry,' she said.

'And no more apologies. We could spend a lifetime apologising to each other, but we've got to put the past behind us.'

Ellie nodded and sipped at her tea. 'We're going to have to tell Jacko that you're his daddy.'

Joe looked so happy at this he brought tears to her eyes. She was quite sure he would have hugged her, if they hadn't been holding mugs of scalding tea.

After a while, she said, 'It wasn't all bad before, was it?'

Joe shook his head. 'To be honest, I have more good memories than bad ones.'

She settled deeper into the pillows, pleased. 'Do you have a favourite memory?'

'Sure,' he said with gratifying promptness. 'It would have to be that day you brought dinner out to the Low-mead paddock.'

'Really?'

'Yeah. I'd had a hell of a time, trying to fix that bore. It took me hours and hours in the blazing heat. And, just as I finally got on top of it, you turned up with a big smile and all this fabulous food.'

Ellie felt a little glow inside, just watching the way Joe smiled at the memory.

'You brought me soap and a towel,' he said. 'And, while I was cleaning up, you set up the picnic table and chairs under a tree. There was a red checked tablecloth and you'd cooked up this fabulous curry, and we had chilled wine, and caramel rum pie for dessert.'

'So it's true, after all?' She gave him a playful dig with her elbow.

'What's that?'

'The way to a man's heart is through his stomach.'

Joe chuckled. 'Guess it must be.' He picked up her hand, threaded his fingers with hers. 'That day's a standout because it was so spontaneous.'

'Spontaneous for you. I'd had it all planned for days.'

'A brilliant surprise. We were so relaxed and happy.'

'We were,' she agreed.

'So what's your favourite good memory?'

'Oh, I think it has to be the night we almost slept in the car park.'

'But ended up in the bridal suite?'

'Yes. It was just such fabulous fun.'

'Especially as we'd never had a proper honeymoon. We'll have to go there again some time.'

Ellie lifted a sceptical eyebrow. 'Do you think they'd welcome Jacko?'

'My mother would babysit.'

'Well, yes, that would be nice.' But Ellie's chest tightened at the mention of Joe's mother. She was reminded of her mother. She drew a quick calming breath. 'I suppose we're going to have to tell our families, aren't we?'

'About us?'

'Yes.'

'My folks will be delighted.'

'Mine won't.'

For the first time that morning, Joe frowned.

'It's OK.' She kissed his lovely stubbled jaw. 'Mum's going to have to cop it sweet. If she doesn't, I'm not going to let it bother me.'

'Promise?'

'Promise.'

* * *

The transition into their new lifestyle was surprisingly smooth. The river levels went down and neighbours who were travelling to Charters Towers offered to drive Joe's hire car.

Joe rang to resign from his new position patrolling the Southern Ocean. At New Year, Joe and Ellie both rang their families with their news and, as they'd predicted, Joe's parents were delighted.

'Joe, darling, I'm so relieved,' his mother cried. 'I've been praying for this.' She was tearful on the phone, but she was laughing and excited through her tears. 'Just wait till I tell your father. He'll be thrilled. As you know, we're dying to meet Jacko. And to see Ellie again. Do you think you'll be able to visit us soon? But if it's too difficult, perhaps we could visit you? We have so many extra hands to help here. It would be easier for us to get away.'

Before Ellie could ring her mother, there was a call from Nina, the nanny.

'Ellie, I'm so sorry to leave you in the lurch, but I've just had the most amazing job offer. It's my dream—a position at the Cairns Post.'

Ellie knew Nina had studied journalism and that the nanny job had only ever been a fill-in. 'Don't worry,' she said with a serenity that surprised her. 'My husband's back from the Army, so we'll manage between us.'

She hadn't told Nina about her plans to divorce Joe, so the girl accepted his return as a perfectly normal and lovely surprise.

Of course, Ellie had been looking forward to having a nanny so that she could be free to join Joe in the outdoor work that she enjoyed so much, but Joe was much keener to share both the housework and the yard work than he'd been in the past, so she knew that she'd spoken the truth. They'd sort something out between them.

They'd arrived at a new calmness, a new sense of closeness and solidarity. It truly did feel as if they'd been through a long and painful trial and come out the other side stronger. And, as a reward, it seemed they'd been granted their fairy tale ending, and Ellie was beginning to trust that it really could last this time.

Although her phone call to her mother tested her newfound confidence.

'Oh, Ellie, I knew it! You're as weak as water when it comes to that man.' Her mother's voice was shrill with dismay. 'I don't expect it will be very long before he leaves you again.'

Ellie made an effort to argue in Joe's defence, but her mother showed no signs of relenting.

'Do you really think you're helping me, Mum, by getting stuck into Joe every chance you have?'

Her mother spluttered. 'I'm only thinking of you, dear.'

'I don't think so.'

'But Ellie—'

'You've been down on Joe ever since you met him.' Actually, that wasn't quite true. Her mum had been suitably charmed by Joe the first time she'd met him. It was only later, around the time of their wedding, that her attitude seemed to have soured. Ellie had never understood why.

'It's not just my opinion, Ellie. Harold warned me about Joe.'

'Harold?'

'Yes. He's learned so much from local politics and he's a very astute judge of human character. But you've always been so sure you know better. I don't suppose you'll visit us now, will you?'

'Well, I—'

'We'll just have to come and visit you then.' This was announced snappily before her mother hung up.

Ellie wasn't given an option. Her mother and Harold were coming, steamrollering their way into her home.

The very thought made her feel fragile and nervous. She tried to shrug it off. She told herself that, with Joe on her side now, she was strong enough for anything.

She almost believed this until the morning she realised that her period was two weeks late.

CHAPTER ELEVEN

SHE COULDN'T BE pregnant, surely?

The sudden fear that gripped Ellie was all too familiar. She was remembering the miscarriage that had started the downhill spiral and had ultimately wrecked their marriage.

Even the memories of Jacko's safe delivery couldn't calm her. Everything from Jacko's conception to his birth had been carefully controlled under strict clinical supervision. Ellie had spent most of the nine months of her pregnancy in Townsville while a manager took care of the cattle and Karinya.

An unplanned pregnancy now would bring to the surface all her old anxieties, all the tension and worry about another possible miscarriage or ongoing complications.

The last thing she wanted was to go through that again. Not now she had Jacko, and she and Joe were so happily reconciled.

Everything was going so well. Joe was genuinely pleased to be back here, to be with her and to be working Karinya. Only last night he'd told her this again.

'After growing up on a cattle property, I can't help feeling attached to the land—to the red dirt and the mulga. I'm scratching my head now, wondering how on earth I thought I'd be happy floating around in the Southern Ocean without you and Jacko.'

But would Joe still be happy if their old problems surfaced?

Ellie was aware of the irony of her new dilemma—she'd spent so many years longing for a baby, and now she was dismayed by the prospect. She and Joe had negotiated their new future together based on the understanding that their fertility and pregnancy issues were behind them.

They were starting a new life—just the three of them.

I can't be pregnant. Not with my record. It must be just out of kilter cycles.

She hunted around at the back of the medicine cabinet and found a pregnancy testing kit—years old, but never opened. Fingers crossed, it would still work.

She was so nervous she thought she might throw up as she waited for the result to show. She closed her eyes, not brave enough to watch what was happening to the stick, and she prayed that two coloured lines would *not* appear.

I can't be pregnant. I can't.

She allowed longer than the allotted time, just to be sure, and then she opened her eyes the tiniest crack, and peeked nervously at the tiny screen.

Two lines.

Oh, my God. Two strong, thick, no-doubt-about-it lines.

This couldn't be happening. Sweat broke out on her forehead, her arms, her back.

She stared at the lines in a disbelieving daze. She knew she *should* feel happy about this, but she could only feel shocked and scared. And foolish.

Pregnancy would land her right back where she and Joe fell off the rails. They would be reliving that horror stretch. They'd have to go through all that uncertainty again.

Why on earth had she been so confident that this couldn't happen?

How could I have been such a fool?

Her hands were shaking as she wrapped the testing stick in a tissue and hid it in the rubbish bin. She put the second stick back in its box in the cupboard. She might try again in a few days' time, just to double-check, to make sure this wasn't a crazy mistake. Until then, she wouldn't tell Joe. She *couldn't* tell Joe.

There was no need to upset him unnecessarily, especially when his parents were due to visit them at the end of the week.

Stay Zen, Ellie.

She nailed on a smile, knowing that her major challenge now was to make sure that neither Joe nor Jacko could sense how tense she was.

Over the next few days, Ellie thought she managed quite well, but there was still no sign of her period. She tried again, and the second testing stick showed another pair of very strong lines.

Her tension mounted. Joe's parents would be arriving at the weekend and she'd been looking forward to their visit. She hoped they would see for themselves how happy she and Joe were now, and she'd been in a frenzy of preparations, setting up an extra bed in the spare room, cleaning and polishing, baking cakes and slices.

Now, she was going to have to tell Joe about the pregnancy before they arrived, and she really had no idea how he'd react. In the near future, she would need to see a doctor, too. That thought made her even more anxious.

On the night before the Maddens were due, Ellie's stomach was churning as she went to say goodnight to Jacko. Joe was reading him his favourite picture books—they'd been taking it in turns lately—but she'd spent longer than usual in the kitchen tonight, putting the final touches to her baking.

It was time to call a halt to the reading or Jacko would be over-excited.

She'd thought Joe was reading the books on the sofa, but the lounge room was empty. There was a light in the bedroom—no voices though, no growling lions or gibbering monkeys. Surprised, Ellie crossed quickly to the bedroom doorway.

The sight she found there stole her breath.

Her husband and son were sound asleep, lying together on top of the quilt. Joe had one arm stretched out and Jacko was huddled close, sheltered by his shoulder.

They looked so peaceful, so close. Father and son…

There was something so silently strong and protective about this simple scene. It touched a chord deep within her.

In the past few weeks she'd been growing more and more confident that, whatever happened, Joe was here to stay. Now, watching him sleeping beside his son, she felt a strong new soul-deep level of certainty.

With Joe she could face the future. They had everything they'd ever wanted right now, and they could cope with this pregnancy together, whatever the outcome.

I'll definitely tell him about the baby tonight, she decided. She would run a nice relaxing bath and, when she came to bed, she would wake Joe gently and tell him about the pregnancy. She would tell him so calmly that he'd know she was OK, that their marriage—no matter what happened—was going to be OK…

Ellie was smiling as she tiptoed away. The only dark cloud on her horizon was the prospect of Harold arriving with her mother in a fortnight's time. But she wouldn't think about him tonight, wouldn't let him spoil her calm and upbeat mood.

She ran a lovely warm bath, lit a rose-scented candle and placed it on a stool in the corner of the bathroom. She turned out the main light and the room was pretty in the soft glow of candlelight. Deliberately, she made herself relax and lie back, eyes closed, breathing slowly, deeply and evenly, in and out.

She pictured herself serenely and confidently telling Joe her news—not too excited and not at all anxious. She would be positive and optimistic, taking this new pregnancy in her stride.

The candle scents and the soft light were soothing. She sank a little lower into the warm, welcoming water. No matter what happened in the next few weeks, she would do everything to remain calm. For Joe. She would—

The phone rang in the kitchen.

Ellie sat up quickly. Joe was asleep. She wondered if it had woken him, or whether she should clamber out of the bath and run, dripping, through the house.

Then she heard Joe's footsteps crossing the lounge room and going down the hall. Heard his voice.

'Hello, Angela.'

Her mother.

Whoosh. Ellie sank beneath the water, incredibly relieved that Joe was dealing with this call. She couldn't handle a conversation with her mum tonight. It would only wind her up again, wiping out the Zen.

She certainly didn't want to think about two weeks of Harold in her house—and with only one bathroom. How many times might he accidentally open the door?

This ghastly thought wouldn't go away. It wrecked Ellie's peace and brought her sitting up so abruptly that water sloshed over the side of the bath. How on earth could she kid herself that baths were relaxing?

Without warning and totally against her will, she was reliving those nights when Harold came in. The images were still disgustingly vivid in her memory.

Harold's leer. His teeth flashing in his red face as he grinned at her. His eyes bulging as he stared at her breasts.

Ellie shuddered and squirmed, her skin crept and her relaxation was obliterated in a flash. It was useless to continue lying in the bath with memories of her stepfather intruding. She stood quickly and scrambled over the side, not caring about the dripping water. She pulled the plug and the bathwater began to gurgle noisily down the plughole and along the old-fashioned plumbing.

As she reached for a towel, she thought she heard another sound beyond the gush of the disappearing water—the faint creak of the bathroom door opening. *Creepy Harold.*

She spun around.

Irrational fear exploded in her chest.

A shadowy male figure hovered in the doorway.

'Get out!' she screamed in a hot streak of panic. '*Get out!*' Her reaction was visceral, erupting from a place beyond logic. Eyes tightly shut, she screamed again. 'You monster. Leave me alone!'

'For God's sake, Ellie.'

She was so gripped by blinding panic it took a moment to come to her senses.

Joe?

Joe was standing at the door?

Of course it was Joe.

And he was staring at her in horror, as if she'd turned into a multi-headed, fire-breathing monster.

I'm sorry.

Ellie was panting and too breathless to get the words out at first. She tried again. 'I'm sorry, Joe, I—'

But he didn't wait for her apology. He took another glaring look at her, gave a furious shake of his head, then whirled around and left her, slamming the door behind him.

Appalled, shaken, Ellie sank onto the edge of the bath.

She couldn't believe she'd reacted like a maniac in front of Joe, as if she was terrified of her husband, the man she loved. It wasn't as if they hadn't shared the bathroom before. Only last week they'd had all kinds of steamy fun making love in the shower.

And she couldn't believe this had happened tonight of all nights, when she'd been trying her hardest to remain calm.

Clearly, she was as tense as a loaded mouse trap.

The look on Joe's face had said it all. She'd seen his stark despair, his disappointment and disgust.

She wanted to rush after him, but common sense prevailed. She would have a much better chance of offering a calm, rational explanation if she wasn't dripping wet and wrapped in a towel. Hastily she dried her body, her arms and legs and roughly towel-dried her hair.

Her silk kimono was hanging on a hook behind the door and she grabbed it quickly, thrusting her arms into the loose sleeves and tying the knot at the waist. As she dragged a comb through her wet hair, her reflection looked pale, almost haggard.

Too bad. She didn't have time to fuss about her appearance. She had to find Joe. The way he'd looked at her just now had frightened her badly.

It was as if he'd wanted to put as much distance between them as possible, as if he was certain their marriage was doomed, as if he'd already left her.

She didn't find him in the lounge room, or the kitchen, or the study, or their bedroom.

Had he left already? Taken off into the night?

Fearing the worst, Ellie hurried out onto the dark front veranda. Joe wasn't standing at the railing as she'd hoped.

Then she saw a shape on the front steps. She felt a brief flutter of relief until she realised that Joe was sitting slumped forward, as if defeated, with his head in his hands.

He looked shattered.

Her tough, highly trained, Special Forces soldier was sunk in total despair.

I've done this to him.

Ellie could feel her heart breaking.

She pressed her hand against the agonising ache in her chest. Now, more clearly than ever, she was aware of the depth of her love for Joe. These past few weeks had been the happiest in her life. The two of them were conscious of how close they'd come to losing each other and each new day together had felt precious. They'd even been laughing again, the way they had when they first met. And with Jacko joining in the fun, their lives had been so joyous. So complete.

Or had it all been a fragile mirage?

Had this bitter end always been waiting for them, hovering just around the corner?

After her hysterics in the bathroom, how could she possibly tell Joe about the pregnancy? How could she expect him to believe she'd cope with it calmly?

How could he have any faith in her?

Ellie was almost afraid to disturb him now, but she knew she had no choice. She had to try to apologise and to explain. Perhaps she even had to finally tell him about Harold.

Wasn't it time for courage at last?

Speaking to Joe was the first step.

Her legs were unsteady as she moved forward, her bare feet silent on the veranda floorboards.

'Joe?' she said softly.

His head jerked up. Instantly, he glared at her. 'What the hell's going on, Ellie?'

'Joe, I'm so sorry.'

Already he'd sprung to his feet, as agile as a panther. But his face was white in the moonlight. 'What's got into you?' He threw up his hands. 'What was that all about in there?'

'I'm sorry. It wasn't a reaction to you, Joe. Please believe me. I didn't know it was you.'

His scowl was derisive. 'Who else would it be, for God's sake? You saw me. I was standing right in front of you and you kept screaming. I'm your husband, damn it, not an axe-murderer. I thought—'

He shook his head and his lip curled in disgust. 'I

thought we were going to be OK, and then you go and pull a crazy stunt like that.'

'It wasn't a stunt.'

'What was it, then?' His eyes were fierce. 'You must have been truly terrified. Of what? Me? Am I supposed to find that reassuring?'

'I thought… For a moment, I thought…' Ellie swallowed the rising lump of fear that filled her throat. 'I can't explain unless I tell you…' The fear was stifling. 'There's…there's something I should have told you years ago.'

Joe stared at her, his blue eyes narrowed now—puzzled and mistrustful.

Ellie knew he must be wondering why she still had an apparently important issue that she hadn't shared with him. It probably made no sense at all after the soul-searching depth of their recent conversations.

'So, what is it?' he asked cautiously.

Despite the trembling in her stomach, Ellie came down the steps till she was next to him.

'It's Harold,' she said.

'Your stepfather?'

Ellie nodded.

Joe was frowning. '*He* freaks you out?'

'Yes.' It was all she could manage.

For long, nerve-racking seconds, Joe stared at her. She could see a muscle jerking in his jaw, betraying his tension, and she could see his thoughts whirring as he put two and two together. She saw the moment when understanding dawned.

He swore softly. 'That's why you left home so young?'

'I had to get away.'

Joe swore again with extra venom. He stood, glaring off into the black silent night, and when he turned to Ellie again, his eyes were still harsh, still uncertain.

'You've never breathed a word of this.'

'I know. I always meant to.'

'Why? Why couldn't you tell me?'

'I tried, but it was unbelievably hard. I felt so ashamed. And I'd already tried to tell my mother and she wouldn't believe me, so I thought I should just try to forget it, to put it all behind me.'

'Oh, Ellie.' Joe reached for her then. He took her hands, folded them in his, and then he slipped his arm around her shoulders and drew her close and his warm lips brushed her forehead. He sighed, and she felt his breath feather gently against her cheek.

It was the most wonderfully comforting sensation. Ellie dropped her head against his shoulder, savouring his strength. It felt so good to have offloaded this at last. And Joe understood. She should have known he would. She should have trusted him...

Then Joe said, 'Tell me now.'

Instinctively, she flinched. 'But you've already guessed.'

'My imagination's working overtime. I want to know the real story.'

'You might think I'm making a whole lot of fuss about nothing.'

'Nothing? After you almost clawed my eyes out to-night?'

She gave a defensive little shrug. 'I wasn't that bad.'

'Bad enough. And, whatever happened, I know it's affected you—it still affects you after all these years.' He gave her shoulder an encouraging rub. 'I'm not going to doubt you, Ellie.'

She knew this was true. Joe wasn't like her mother; she'd been blinkered and so impressed with her new role as the mayor's wife that she hadn't wanted to hear anything bad about Harold.

Joe, on the other hand, was genuinely worried—about her.

And so she told him.

They sat together on the wooden step, looking out over the dark, silent Karinya paddocks, where the only sound was the occasional soft lowing of a cow. Ellie's kimono fell open, exposing her knees, but she didn't worry about covering them, and she told Joe her story, starting with some of the things he already knew, like her father's death just before her thirteenth birthday, and how her mum had sold their farm and moved into town, marrying Harold Fowler eighteen months later.

'But, right from the start, Harold gave me the creeps,' she admitted.

She went on to explain how he'd just patted her at first, but over the next couple of years his attention had become more and more leering and suggestive, and then he'd come into the bathroom without knocking, choosing nights when her mother wasn't home.

She explained how she'd tried unsuccessfully to tell her mother.

'I knew then that if I stayed at home, the situation would have only got worse.' Ellie shuddered. 'And tonight I was thinking about Harold coming to stay here for two whole weeks. I don't suppose he'd dare to do anything stupid out here, but I was lying in the bath tonight, remembering, and wondering how on earth I would cope, and then the bathroom door opened and… and I freaked.'

Joe had listened to everything without interrupting, but now he said, 'Actually, he's not.'

Ellie frowned. 'Pardon?'

'Harold's not coming here. That's what I was coming in to tell you. Your mother phoned. She sounded a bit upset, but she usually does when she's talking to me. She was ringing to tell you that she's coming out here on her own. Harold's too busy to get away, tied up with council meetings or something.'

Ellie let out a loud huff of disbelief.

'And it's just as well he's not coming,' Joe said, clenching his fists on his knees. 'I might have felt obliged to take him outside and read him his horoscope.'

She almost smiled at this. 'I wonder if he guessed.'

'I reckon he knows I'm not his biggest fan. I haven't liked to say too much to you, but I've never taken to that guy.'

'And I should have told you about this long ago.'

Joe shrugged, then he looked at her for long thoughtful seconds before he spoke. 'It's interesting that you're not hung up about sex.'

Ellie gave him a shy smile. 'Not with you, at any rate.'

'Thank God.'

'But I think I probably have trust issues. I'm always expecting to be disappointed.'

'You've had your share of disappointments.'

'But I've reacted badly too. It probably sounds crazy, but I'm wondering if my father dying had an effect as well as Harold. I was always scared you were going to leave me.'

'And then I did leave.'

'And who could blame you?' Ellie's throat ached

as she looked away, remembering all the times she'd lashed out at Joe, blaming him unfairly, even though he couldn't possibly have been responsible for all her disappointments. She'd never really known where that unreasonable anger had sprung from. 'I guess I should have had some kind of counselling.'

'It's not too late.'

'No, but I already feel better, just having told you.'

Joe drew her in for another hug and, with her head against his shoulder, she closed her eyes, absorbing his warmth, his strength, his love.

Quietly, almost gently, he asked, 'So, while we're here, I guess I should ask if there's anything else you need to get off your chest?'

Oh.

Of course there was.

Ellie's nervousness shot to the surface again and she sat up straight, pulling away from him. She drew a deep breath. 'Actually, yes, I'm afraid there's something else quite important.' Her throat tightened and she swallowed, trying to ease her nervousness. 'There's another reason I've been tense, although I'm sure I'm going to be OK.'

Of course he looked worried, but he was trying to hide it. 'You're not sick, are you?'

'No, no. I'm fine. But—' Ellie dragged a quick steadying breath '—according to *two* home tests, I'm…I mean *we*…are…'

His face was in shadow so she couldn't see his expression, but she knew he was staring at her. Staring hard.

'You're *pregnant*?' he asked so softly it was almost a whisper, an incredulous whisper.

'I'm afraid it looks that way, if the home tests are accurate. They're a bit out of date, but the lines were very clear.'

This confession was met by a troubling silence. Ellie hugged her knees, not daring to guess what Joe might be thinking.

At last she had to ask, 'Are you OK, Joe?'

'Yeah, I'm OK, but I'm worried about you. How do *you* feel about this?'

It was a much better response than she'd feared.

'I'm getting used to it. Slowly. It was a horrible shock at first. I was so sure I was safe.'

'You had me convinced it couldn't happen.'

'I know. I'd convinced myself.' She hugged her knees more tightly still.

'How long have you known?'

'A few days. Since Monday. I hope you don't mind that I kept it to myself. I didn't want to bother you if it was a false alarm.'

Joe was staring at her again, and it was some time before he spoke. 'Wow.'

'Wow?'

'Yeah. I'm seriously impressed, Ellie.'

This was the last—the very last—reaction she'd expected.

'You've been worrying,' he said. 'I know you must have been. I know what a big deal another pregnancy is for you, and yet all week I had no idea you were worried about a thing. You've just carried on calmly, getting ready for my parents' visit as if nothing was the matter.'

'Well, I made a decision, you see. I'm going to stay calm about this pregnancy, whatever happens.'

Joe was smiling as he slipped his arm around her again. 'Good for you.'

Relieved beyond belief, Ellie leaned in and pressed a kiss to the underside of his jaw. 'I'll be upset if I lose another baby, of course I will, but you're the most important thing in my life now. You and Jacko. I've learned my lesson. I'm not going to let anything spoil what I already have.'

Reaching for Joe's hand, she pressed her lips to his knuckles. She still couldn't get enough of touching and kissing him.

'I love you, Ellie Madden,' he murmured against her hair.

'I know it's hard to believe from the way I behaved, but I've never really stopped loving you.'

'I can't believe I nearly let you go.'

'I can't believe I pushed you away.'

A hush fell over them and Ellie guessed they were both thinking how close they'd come to losing each other permanently.

'But we're going to be fine now,' Joe said.

'We are,' she agreed with absolute certainty.

'And I hope, for your sake, that this pregnancy's a breeze, Ellie, but, whatever happens, I promise I'll be there for you.'

Joe touched her cheek, turning her face to his. 'This time, and for ever, I'll be with you every step of the way.'

He sealed his promise with a kiss and it was, without doubt, their happiest, most heartfelt kiss ever.

EPILOGUE

SUNLIGHT STREAMED THROUGH stained glass windows onto massive urns of white lilies and gladioli and carnations, the legacy of a big Townsville society wedding that had been held in the church on the previous day.

This morning, after the main service, a smaller group gathered around the font. Most of the Madden family were present, including Joe's parents. One of his brothers had been required to stay back to look after the property, but the other three were present, plus their wives and a flock of Joe's nephews and nieces.

Ellie's mother, Angela, was there too, smiling and looking genuinely happy for the first time in many months.

The past year had been an extremely distressing and difficult ordeal for Angela, but her separation from Harold and their subsequent divorce were finally behind her.

Now she was already settled in Townsville in a beautifully appointed penthouse apartment with stunning views of Cleveland Bay and Magnetic Island. After the christening, all the gathered friends and family were going back there today for a celebratory barbecue lunch on the rooftop terrace.

The new apartment was in Angela's name, but the mortgage was her ex-husband's responsibility. Of course, she'd taken him to the cleaners. After suffering unbearable public humiliation when gossip about his harassment of several young women had spread like wildfire through their country town, it was the least Angela could do—especially when she'd realised, to her horror, that the accusations her daughter had made all those years ago were true.

But all that was history now and today's gathering was an extremely happy occasion. Ellie looked radiant in a rose-pink linen dress that showed off her newly slim figure. In her arms, plump baby Will slept like a dream, blissfully unaware that he was wearing a long, intricately smocked christening gown edged with handmade lace that had been worn by members of the Madden family for over a century.

Will's older brother Jacko couldn't understand why a boy had been dressed in girl's clothes, although Jacko had learned quite quickly that babies were strange creatures who slept too much and cried a lot and demanded far more than their fair share of attention.

Today, however, Jacko was also in the limelight, as he was being christened alongside baby Will. Ellie had been too busy when Jacko was a baby to think of such things as christenings. These days, however, she was taking every aspect of motherhood in her stride.

There had only been one scary incident during the early months of this pregnancy when Joe had rushed her in to the hospital in Charters Towers, but, fortunately, it had been a false alarm. After a few days, she'd been allowed home again and, after that, everything had gone smoothly.

Will was an easy baby, who liked to sleep and eat and smile. His birth had not caused any dramas. He'd arrived just before dawn on a beautiful September morning, and Joe was with Ellie for every precious, amazing moment.

And now Joe's mother held Jacko's hand as the minister stepped forward.

Joe caught Ellie's eye and they both smiled. They'd taken a very roundabout way to reach this point, but the rough and rugged journey had been worth it. They knew there'd be more bends in the road ahead, but that was OK as they'd be travelling together. Always.

* * * * *

THE FIREFIGHTER TO HEAL HER HEART

ANNIE O'NEILL

This book is first and foremost dedicated to all of those who volunteer for the South Australian Fire Service. You are all heroes and heroines in my eyes. I would also like to send a special nod (and a glass of wine) to my fabulous sister-in-law who has been an incredible source of encouragement to me. Lots of love to you, Kymberley.

xo Annie O'

CHAPTER ONE

"So, DO YOU think we should practice a tiger or a lion roar?"

Liesel was finding it difficult not to laugh as she knelt on the barnyard's baked red earth, eye to eye with the tearful seven-year-old. This hadn't turned out to be the farm visit Devlin had been dreaming of. Or her, for that matter. She'd been nabbed by a harried teacher to come along on the school farm visit as a "responsible adult." The promise of some spring sunshine had won out over the nagging in her head about knuckling down to fill out the school's immunization requirements. The "responsible adult" moniker had made her laugh at the time but now, as she kept Devlin still in the ominously named cattle crush, she knew her nurse's credentials could come in handy.

How Devlin had managed to stick his head through the metal bars designed to keep cows restrained was beyond her. His penchant for showing off might have been the trouble. Now he was paying the price. All of the students had howled with laughter before being shuttled off to help feed the orphan lambs. The farmer, Mr. Jones, hadn't been very quiet with his use of the word *guillotine* when he realized the CFS was going to have to be called. Thank goodness the word was unlikely to be in Devlin's vocabulary. Yet.

If she could just cheer the gloomy-faced boy up a bit as they waited for a CFS crew to arrive, she was sure all would be well. The Country Fire Service dealt with car accidents all the time so would be used to extracting people from steel structures. The thought made her shiver. Blocking out the disturbing images, Liesel gave Devlin's pitch-black crew cut a good scrub with her hand. "Not to worry, Dev, it could be worse. You could be stuck in here with a girl!"

She laughed as Devlin screwed up his young face at the idea of being that close to a girl.

"I could think of worse things."

Liesel shaded her green eyes, squinting hard against the late-afternoon sun to see who was attached to the made-for-late-night-radio voice. Since she'd lost Eric, it took a lot to get her to respond to a man on a primal level—but the rich drawl she'd just heard sent a wave of shivery delight down her spine despite the heat of the day.

Her eyes worked fast to adjust to the glare—quickly turning the silhouetted six-foot-something male into a poster boy for South Australia's volunteer fire service. A thick shock of sandy blond hair had become a sexy tousled by-product of the red helmet he was putting on the ground as he knelt beside her—a pair of bright blue eyes securely fixed on Devlin. Golden stubble outlined his well-defined face. She normally wasn't a fan—but on this guy it looked more Rugged Bachelor than Unkempt Slob. Despite herself, her eyes swept down the golden hairs of his toned forearm and spied a ring-free hand. Not everyone wore a ring, but no ring was a pretty good indication…

"How long have you been caged up in here, mate?"

Devlin flicked his long-lashed eyes up to Liesel.

"Miss, it's been about three hours, hasn't it?"

Liesel threw her head back and laughed. "Hardly, Devlin—I think it's closer to fifteen minutes."

"All right, Dev—is it all right if I call you Dev? Or should I say Dare Devlin?" He paused for Devlin's grin—a show of acceptance of the new nickname—and continued, "My name's Jack and we're going to get you out of here as soon as possible." He turned, putting a hand on Liesel's shoulder, lips parting to reveal a crooked smile. *Uh-oh... that's a knee-weakener.*

"Is it all right if I call you Miss?" He laughed good-naturedly at her startled expression then stood up, putting a hand under Liesel's elbow to help her to her feet as he rose.

Crikey. And he's got manners.

"Miss is great." She tried to force her lips into a casual smile as she silently raced through a quick-fire series of questions. Had her hair seen the right side of a brush recently? Had she unscrewed the lid on her mascara that morning? Then used it? Had her fair skin and freckles already had their daily allotment of sunshine? All too aware of the arrows of heat beginning to shoot across her cheeks, she grew wide-eyed as she spluttered on, "You can feel free to call me Liesel—I mean, Miss Adler. Or Nurse Adler. I'm the school nurse. Registered."

For crying out loud—the man didn't ask for your CV, Liesel!

Jack dropped a slow wink in her direction, simultaneously giving Devlin a soft chuck under the chin. "I think Miss Adler will do perfectly."

Her heart did a quick-fire yo-yo trip across her rib cage as she dared to look up into his smiling eyes. They were an awfully nice shade of turquoise.

Wait a minute. Did her lashes just flutter? *Get a hold of yourself, Liesel.*

Her eyes dropped back to Devlin, who was looking up at her with a pained expression as he tried to wrangle himself free from his head-locked position.

Clenching her hands into tight fists, she shut her eyes. Just as suddenly as her heart had soared at Jack's sexy wink, it plummeted with a painful twist. Here was this small boy she was supposed to be caring for and she was acting like a love-struck teen. Images of Eric flashed past her closed eyes.

Eric.

Her behavior had been disloyal to him—to his memory. She knew the day for moving on would come at some point—soon even—but this couldn't be the moment. Could it?

"Miss Adler?"

"Yes, sorry." Liesel forced her voice back to the soothing nurse tone she used with the children but kept her eyes fixed on her charge. "What do you need to do to get this little man free?"

Jack was going to have to give himself a ripper of a talking to when he got back to the station. *He wasn't here to flirt.* Or wink, for that matter. Winking was reserved for little old ladies and four-year-olds who needed cheering up, not for cute-as-they-come school nurses. He wouldn't mind running his fingers through a few of those corkscrew red curls of hers. From the shine glinting off of them, they'd feel about as soft as the dark green silk top she was wearing. She wasn't even in a uniform, but his imagination could certainly fill in the— *Whoa! Don't even go there, Jack.*

Ladies were meant to be off the radar, whether or not they were standing right in front of you looking as petite, cat-eyed and creamy-skinned as they came.

Jack heard himself clear his throat a bit too violently as he gathered equipment from the back of the crew truck.

Gear. Work. Much safer terrain.

He was here to help the little boy and from the looks of the heavy-gauge steel, he would need more than a bit of dishwashing soap to get him free. Poor kid. He wouldn't be Dare Devlining for a while, from the mortified look on his face. He'd have to keep an eye on his progress and see if he'd be a candidate for the Country Fire Service cadets in a few years. With the right training, a spitfire youngster could very easily turn into a hero.

Come to think of it, their station could also do with some volunteer nurses on the force. He'd only been at the Murray Valley posting for a few weeks. His assignment was a Class A rescue mission. Its volunteer forces needed some bolstering. Big-time. The lads at the station had told him the school nurse had been someone's granny up until recently so he hadn't even thought of bringing the new one into the loop as regards the station. Now that he'd met Liesel?

Easy there, cowboy.

Then again, she *was* a nurse. He wondered if…

Focus, man.

Jack pushed himself back into action mode.

"I'm going to put some earplugs in your lugholes, all right, mate?" Jack knelt down by Devlin, feeling a little too aware of Liesel's presence behind him. "This thing's a bit loud. It's called a hydraulic spreader. Basically a big set of automated pliers." Devlin looked at him dubiously as he continued, "I'm going to pull these bars a couple of centimeters wider and unless you grow some more brains between now and then, you should be able to get that noggin of yours free and Mr. Jones can have his crush back for the cattle. What do you say to that?"

As Devlin's forlorn face flooded with relief, Liesel felt herself choking back another giggle. This guy was good. He had such a relaxed way with Devlin that any fears she may have had about having to call the boy's parents to explain to them that their son was going to have to spend the night in a barnyard vanished.

Thoughts of her own little boy flitted through her mind.

She had imagined the moments he would have spent with his father countless times. Moments like this—well, not quite like this—watching Jack interact with Devlin tore at her heart.

It was still difficult reconciling the fact that her little Liam would not have a single memory of his father. Then again, she silently chastised herself, it wasn't as if falling in love with a ski patroller had been a safe bet. Hazards had been a day-to-day reality with his job. As a trauma nurse in a ski medical clinic she had seen the aftermath of the daily dangers he'd faced.

And now? Now it was taking life day by day in a quiet country town. Her job as a school nurse wasn't crisis free—but skinned knees and the odd sprain were safer territory. Better on her frayed nerves. Not to mention the fact that Liam got free childcare in the school crèche, making her nurse's salary stretch a little bit further.

Surviving the past couple of years had worked by sticking to the day-by-day principle. Trauma centers, extreme sports, high-octane thrill-seeking? All relegated to a no-go zone. Winking, blue-eyed firemen certainly didn't belong on the safe list.

"You might want to pop a pair of these in as well if you're going to hold the little fella's hand while I crank up the pliers."

Startled, Liesel stared uncomprehendingly at the orange foam orbs Jack held in front of her. "Sorry! I was miles away."

"No kidding." His eyes held hers in a questioning gaze. Not accusative, just curious. "It wasn't hard to miss."

Telling him the truth wasn't an option. Neither was acknowledging the tingles working their way up her arm after he'd handed her the earplugs. For crying out loud! She was behaving as if she'd never spoken to an attractive man before. For the first year after she'd lost Eric being with another man hadn't even occurred to her. Nine months later it had all been about Liam. Now, three years later... *Was this really going to be the day?*

"I was just thinking about whether or not I should take a picture for his parents or if it's best to just leave it to the imagination."

Jack unleashed another relaxed smile as he bent to start the small generator for his pliers. "I think this is one best left to the imagination!" He signaled for her to put her earplugs in then checked Devlin's were securely in place before pulling the cord on the generator. With one sharp tug it roared to life.

Curiosity overcame nerves as Liesel watched Jack pick up the enormous pair of pliers attached to the hydraulic hose. He indicated she should shield Devlin's face with her hands as he slipped the pliers between the steel bars. In less than a minute the bars were gently pried apart and the little boy effortlessly pulled out his head, shooting out of the crush at high speed. Above the din she could hear him calling to the other students about his great escape.

Laughing, Liesel turned back to Jack, who was expertly returning the bars to their original position. If Mr. Jones hadn't already seen Devlin's shenanigans gone wrong, he would have never known they were there.

After snapping the generator off, the peaceful cadence of the countryside once again took over.

"Well, thank you so much." Liesel resisted looking too deeply into the blue eyes trained on her. She was in serious danger of mooning. And swooning. She really needed to get a grip. "I'm sorry to have wasted your time on something that wasn't a real emergency."

"What?" Jack stepped back in mock horror. "That wasn't a real emergency? I thought I'd got myself a humdinger of a job there."

Despite herself, Liesel felt drawn to his easygoing

nature. Never mind the man was gorgeous—he also seemed to inhabit an infectious sense of fun. She hadn't felt carefree in—well, in a long time, and it was something she missed.

"You know what I mean." She swatted at the air between them. "It wasn't like it was a bushfire or a car crash." She suddenly found herself unable to maintain eye contact. Firemen—especially men who volunteered to go into hazardous situations—were definitely in the no-go zone.

His voice turned serious. "Of course I do—but we take all of our callouts seriously and I, for one, would hate to think anyone would hesitate to call us if we could help."

She looked up into those amazing blue eyes of his as if to confirm that the words he spoke were genuine.

"Truly," he reiterated solidly, as though mind reading the few threads of doubt tugging at her conscience.

"Well, I know one little fellow who will be dining off your heroics for weeks."

Jack leaned back against the cattle crush and nodded appraisingly at her. "So, you think I'm a hero, do you?"

A flush of heat rushed up her throat as he waited for her answer.

"Of course not! I mean, you definitely were to Devlin—"

Jack's easy laughter stopped her inane flow of apologies.

"Don't worry, Miss Adler. I'm always out for a free compliment if I can get one." He tilted his head in her direction, capturing her attention with another one of those winks. *Resist, Liesel. Resist.*

"There is one way you can repay the Country Fire Service if you feel you owe us one."

Liesel crooked her chin up at him, curiosity getting the better of her.

"Murray Valley needs more volunteers. Big-time. A nurse would be a great addition to our local crew."

Liesel felt herself physically recoil from the suggestion. *Not a chance.*

She didn't do hazardous things anymore. Not with a son to look after. Not after the loss she'd suffered.

Jack knew in an instant he'd overstepped the mark. Her gentle, sunny personality vanished the moment he'd made his suggestion. There was definitely something painfully private she was keeping close to her chest. Fair enough. It wasn't as if he didn't have his own secrets. Secrets he kept to make his life easier, more honest. Or was that an oxymoron? Keeping secrets to stay honest.

"Liesel! Quit flirting with the handsome fireman," a female voice called from across the farmyard. "We've got to get the kids back to school for pickup!"

Jack and Liesel instantly widened the space between them, staring stricken-faced in the direction of the voice. Liesel looked absolutely mortified and Jack hadn't felt so caught out since he'd been found snogging the headmaster's daughter behind the bike shed when he was thirteen. As if by design, he and Liesel simultaneously looked back at each other, saw their mutual expressions of dismay and immediately burst into unrestrained guffaws.

"Sorry, I didn't mean to look so disgusted! I mean, no—not disgusted." He waved away the choice of words as if the gesture would erase them. "It's not that you repel me or anything—"

"I think you'd better quit while you're ahead!" Liesel laughed, wiping away invisible tears from her eyes. She threw a quick glance over her shoulder toward the growing hubbub of children. "I had better go."

Jack felt a tug of resistance. *So soon?* "Right. Yeah, of

course." He stepped forward and offered a hand. "Nice doing business with you, Miss Adler."

What a first-class dill!

Liesel's green eyes flashed up at him, unsurprisingly bemused. He'd really gone in for the bad conversational hat trick. *Nice doing business with you?*

She slipped her petite hand into his and offered him a quick shake of thanks. The delicacy of her fingers instantly made him feel protective of her. Not his usual response to a woman. Normally he wanted to protect himself from whatever she might want from him. Time. Commitment. Less time at the fire station. Too much history in that department had made him wary. But this one, Miss Liesel Adler, something about her told him she wanted nothing more than to stand on her two feet.

"See you around." Liesel threw the words in her wake as she accelerated her brisk walk into a jog to rejoin the group.

Jack watched her retreat round the corner toward the school bus and spoke to the empty barnyard. "I certainly hope so."

It was all Liesel could do to keep the hot burn of embarrassment from her cheeks as she rejoined the group.

"Got an eye for a man in uniform, have you, you naughty thing?" Cassie Monroe—or Miss Monroe to the students—raised her eyebrows up and gave her lips a tell-me-more twist. Her friend and colleague didn't do subtle.

"Hardly!" Liesel shot back at her colleague, a bit more spiritedly than she'd intended.

"Did you get his number?" Cassie continued, as if Liesel hadn't said a thing.

Liesel sent her a meaningful glare. A glare that she hoped said, *Stop talking right now!*

"You're going to see him again, right?"

Nope. Guess the glare hadn't worked.

"I hardly think it's appropriate—"

"Anything's appropriate," Cassie interrupted, "when you're trying to get back on the horse again."

"I'm not trying to get on anything—horsey or otherwise." This conversation was definitely not going in the right direction.

"Liesel." Cassie fixed her with a loving glare, hands planted on her shoulders. "It's time to get back out there and you're the only one who doesn't know it."

"Come along, children." Liesel actively avoided responding. "Let's start getting on the bus. Everyone sure they haven't left anything behind? Rickie—have you got your backpack?"

She felt Cassie sidle up beside her and heard a whisper in her ear. "You're not going to get away with the silent treatment this time, my dear." She felt her arm receive a good solid pinch. "After school. Playground. I want details about the hot new fireman."

Rubbing away the sting of Cassie's pinch, Liesel couldn't help but grin back at her friend. They had only known each other since the beginning of term, when Liesel had taken up her new contract. Cassie's thirteen-year-old son appeared at the nurses' station a bit too frequently—the only plus side being that the two women had become pretty well acquainted. A couple of girlie nights in, a few tips about where to shop, a detailed who's who at the school and Cassie had already proved to be a great friend.

Liesel hadn't known a soul out here in wine country and meeting a fellow single mum, even if Cassie's son was much older than her own, had taken the edge off the anxiety she'd felt at making the decision to move away from her parents' house in Adelaide.

In reality, there had been no other option. A disastrous fortnight at the city's biggest A and E department had proved crisis management was no longer her forte. The other staff had known her situation and had hovered over her, making her feel more paranoid and edgy than confident and comfortable. The two-week tenure had culminated in a disastrous incident where she'd completely frozen over a patient with a gory chainsaw injury. Unacceptable. She'd fired herself before the bosses had had a chance to do it for her.

She'd made the move to Engleton and it just had to work. She didn't have the energy, or the money, for more change. Small-town life and a job she could do without turning into a bundle of nerves were meant to put an end to chaos. To the memories. And maybe, just maybe, one day she and Liam would be more than a family of two.

In truth, she had been pleasantly surprised to discover her new posting as a school nurse was less calm and more "commotion" than she'd originally thought it might be. Mundane had been her goal but, as usual these days, she found she hadn't quite made the right call. Apart from the requisite paperwork, it was great fun to spend time with the children, even if she interacted with most of them when they weren't at their best.

She still had to force herself to take each case as it came, but the occasional heart-racer—a broken collarbone, a deep cut to the forehead, a pencil stabbed into an unsuspecting student's arm—had all been little teasers reawakening the Liesel who'd spent over five years thriving off the high-stakes charge of saving lives. It was a life she thought she'd needed to lay to rest. But now she felt as though it was her personal mission to provide the children with a safe haven in the school. Everyone deserved that when they were in pain—to feel secure.

It was why she had moved back home after giving birth to Liam. Being on the mountain—the mountain that had taken Eric's life—had been just too much. His parents had been amazing, more supportive than she could have ever imagined, and knowing Liam wouldn't be able to see his paternal grandparents as often as they wished made the decision even harder. They did their best to make her feel a part of their own family, but when her own parents had flown over to see her and meet Liam she'd known in an instant where she belonged. Home. Australia. Where the hot sun and burnt landscape provided no memories of the snowcapped mountains where her heart had been ripped from her chest three short years ago.

Liesel skipped up the steps of the bus and grinned at the sight of the children jockeying for the "top spots." Nothing had changed from when she was a kid. Front seats and backseats were still the most popular and now the mayhem of fifteen children organizing themselves in the middle rows played out in front of her.

The seven-year-olds had clearly had a wonderful time at the farm. Some carefully held eggs in Mr. Jones's distinctive red cartons in their laps. A gaggle of children were plastering their faces to the windows to catch final glimpses of the sheep and cattle. Others were talking about helping feed the orphaned lambs, and it was just about impossible not to hear Devlin already bragging about how he'd helped the fireman pull apart the iron bars with his own hands to get free of the crush. A quick glimpse toward the barn and she could just see him swinging into the cab of his truck. Yum. Talk about eye candy!

Liesel felt Cassie sending her a knowing look as Jack's name was bandied about by the children. She sent her friend a smirk and didn't bother to hide her grin.

This was good. She didn't feel she was just convincing herself now. It *was* good. Being around the children all day reminded her of life's endless possibilities. A year ago she could only see dead ends. Now? Now she was ready to slowly start carving out a new life for herself and Liam.

The last thing in the world she wanted for her son was to have his life curtailed by her grief. It had taken every ounce of energy she'd possessed, but when her parents had offered her use of their holiday let—their "retirement fund"—for the first few months she spent out here in Engleton, she'd gratefully accepted. She'd have to move out when the summer holidays came, but that was a bridge to cross in a few months. It was as if fate had been giving her a gentle nudge. *Go on*, it had said, *take a chance*.

Liesel sank into a seat near the driver, a little sigh slipping through her lips. For her son, she would take chances.

This was Jack's favorite stretch of road along the Murray Valley and he'd missed it. No doubt about it. Four years was a long time to stay away from home. There'd been phone calls, but a clean break had been called for and he had made it easy for everyone by packing a bag and leaving.

Intuitively, Jack guided the truck through the sloping hills that spilled into a wide river basin. The land was thick with spring vines unfurling new leaves and clutches of miniature grapes. Next year's wine.

He glanced at the cloudless sky, knowing his background had built in a need to check the weather at regular intervals. His father had done it instinctively and now—well, the apple hadn't fallen too far from the tree. Just a bit farther than usual.

As the moments ticked past he was surprised to see he'd managed to get to the end of the valley without even noticing. It didn't take a brain surgeon for Jack to know he'd been distracted by a certain freckly nose. Or was it the wild spray of deep auburn curls? They certainly didn't detract from anything. A collection of distinctively beautiful parts to make up one heck of a whole. Even with his eyes wide open he could picture those sexy feline green eyes that a certain school nurse had kept tilting up at him underneath a long set of lashes. Liesel was definitely on a par with just about any adorable-one-minute-and-knee-bucklingly-sexy-the-next movie star he could think of.

Meeting a beautiful woman had been the last thing on his mind when he'd received his transfer notice to move back to the Murray River Valley. Confronting his demons had his plate piled pretty high as it was.

He leaned his head back against the truck's headrest, one arm navigating the vehicle along the wide country road dividing the vast tracts of vineyards. The cab briefly filled with a bark of laughter as Jack ruefully acknowledged he knew this road so well he could probably close his eyes and daydream all he wanted about Engleton's new school nurse. As if on cue, his left hand automatically flicked on the indicator and his foot eased off the accelerator before he'd even looked to the right to acknowledge the arched gateway he'd been through thousands of times.

River's Bend Winery.

His family's legacy.

His father's, more specifically. John Granville Keller, locally known as Granville due to his father before him having carried the same name.

He caught movement out of the corner of his eye, a clutch of tourists stepping out onto the veranda of the modern wine-tasting center. He'd seen the plans but had never seen the real thing. It looked good. Becca had done well.

As if thinking about her was strong enough to draw her to him, he saw a familiar blonde figure emerge from the group on the veranda. He slowed the truck to a stop, just remembering to slip the gear lever into Park before jumping out and giving his sister a good old-fashioned bear hug and swing round.

"Hey, there, stranger. I like the new threads! Fireman blue suits you."

Good old Becca. He could count on her for not giving him a case of the guilts. That was his father's specialty.

"You're looking good, sis! And so's your new tasting center." They both turned to give it an appraising look. The sleek modern lines were beautifully crafted to fit in with the lush riverscape surrounding them. He couldn't wait to have a good nosey round—and snag a chilled bottle of the unoaked chardonnay Becca had been bragging about in her emails.

"It beats that old shack you were so fond of." He felt his sister give him a good solid jab in the ribs. He gave her a playful jostle in return before turning her to face him, serious this time.

"How are you? Really? Are you good?"

"Really good, Jack. Just missing you. Staying for tea?" She turned her hundred-watt smile on for him and he couldn't resist pulling her into another deep hug.

"Not today." She pulled back from the hug with a frown.

He tapped the brim of his CFS cap. "Duty calls!"

It might have been true—but it was an excuse he'd used all too often for the past few years. They'd spoken on the phone a lot, emails, texts—but the real thing was something he missed. Staying away from his family had been harder than he had thought—but if he was ever going to prove to his father that he could amount to something then complete focus was necessary.

Thank heavens Becca was such a star. She knew everything there was to know about River's Bend—the crops, the land, their impressive output and, more important, she showed a business acumen that would've been as natural a match to the Australian Securities Exchange. He was proud to call her his kid sister, even though the ponytails and plaster-covered knees were a thing of the past.

"You know you're always welcome. No need to wait for an invitation."

"I know, Bec. I know." He let her go and made a little show of wiping away some invisible dust on her shoulders. "Right, well. Best get on to see Old Man River, then."

"Go gently with him, Jack." His sister's voice was loving but held a genuine note of caution. "It's not been easy for him the past few years."

"I wasn't the one who forced me to choose between a life in the CFS or the farm." He instantly regretted his words when he saw the shots of pain in his sister's eyes and tried to lighten the atmosphere with a playful boxing move. "At least you came out the winner—running a gold-star winery!"

"This was never about winning or losing, Jack."

"I know." He pulled one of her hands into his. "I'm sorry, that was a low blow. You've done an amazing job here, sis. Far better than I would have. I mean it."

He gave her a contrite smile. "Don't worry, Bec. I'm an older and wiser version of 'that wild Keller boy.'" He did a spot-on imitation of the town's former roving police officer and enjoyed his sister's smile at the likeness.

He didn't have a record. No. But he did have a history. Nothing horrible, just the usual teenager-gone-off-the-rails sort of stuff that happened when…when stuff happened.

He climbed into the truck, threw a wave at his sister and eased the truck into first gear. "We'll get that dinner soon, I promise!"

Good ol' Becca. She really was her father's daughter, growing up steeped in the station's quirks and customs. Stubborn as a mule and born to work the land. As a little girl, she was always being retrieved by one of the farmhands from among the vines, where she would spend hours painstakingly setting up her own "wine-tasting" sessions for her dolls. His traditional father had just presumed Jack would take over the business and that his sunny-faced daughter would marry well and be content to enjoy River's Bend from the sidelines.

As a team, they would've made quite a dynamic duo. But life hadn't panned out that way. The winery was her calling and, after his mother's death, the CFS had been his. Too bad his father hadn't seen things that way.

Jack began taking deep, slow breaths. He'd need all the reserves of calm he had to get down the long track past the sleek tasting room, the outbuildings that made up the actual winery, and down the slope into the curved drive fronting the stone expanse of the Keller family home. He may not have spent the past four years here but it was definitely home.

The sprawling three hundred hectares encompassed so much. The eucalyptus-rich expanse of river land he had escaped to as a boy on hot summer days. The exquisitely manicured gardens and orchard where he and Becca had played hide-and-seek. The wooded site near the bridge where they'd spread his mother's ashes after the fateful out-of-control fire so many painful years ago. The new barn built over the burn site as if it would erase the fact Ava Keller had died there. The same barn where he'd had the final, gut-wrenching fight with his father about choosing the fire service over a life on the land.

He stopped for a minute and let himself take in a delicious lungful of the blossoming vines. Coming home was tougher than he had thought. He'd spent virtually every day here until he was twenty-five. He hadn't thought jumping between a life as a CFS volunteer and his duties at River's Bend had been such a wayward existence. But his father had—and had forced him to make his choice.

And he had. He was genuinely committed to the fire service and all it stood for out here in the country. The people out here relied on volunteers to help fight the annual bushfires, pry them out of cars, even rescue the odd kitten—or little boy, as in today's case. Now he was in a position to make it even better. Without this service people would die. As his mother had. Keeping the local station on the map was essential.

Jack slowed the truck to a stop on the hard, iron-rich earth in front of the house, his father already walking out onto the front veranda as if four years hadn't passed and he'd been expecting his son to turn up about now.

Jack hated the look of disappointment creasing his father's face when he saw the uniform.

He would make his father proud. He would understand. One day. He just had to hang on to his principles. Hang on tightly to all he knew was true.

CHAPTER TWO

"I'VE GOT TO hand it to you, Kev. This one's a real corker."
Liesel snapped off her protective gloves and popped them
in the bin.

"Thanks, miss!"

"I should've known you'd take it as a compliment."
Liesel sent the brand-new teen an admonishing glare, al-
beit with a twinkle in her eye. "A black eye and a sprained
wrist on your birthday hardly give you bragging rights."
She secured the brace on his arm before reaching into the
cupboard behind her for a chemical ice pack.

"They are when you finally popped Diggy Reynolds a
good one on the nose. You couldn't have asked for a better present, miss."

Liesel winced. She'd seen Diggy first. It had been an
impressive nosebleed, but thankfully not a break. Deviated septums weren't killers—but they sure did hurt. She'd
have to talk to Cassie about the incident. Again. Kev's file
was now officially the fattest in her cabinet.

Liesel gave Kev her best "harrumph" as she twisted the
ice pack, felt the coolness flood through the packet and
gently laid it across his wrist. The thirteen-year-old knew
just as well as she did that she had a soft spot for him. Even
if he was permanently in trouble. She was pretty sure an
absent father was the cause, but she was hoping Cassie had

things in hand. The counseling training she'd had in Adelaide was setting off all of the alarm bells that Kev was a troublemaker in training.

"Look, you make sure you keep that wrist iced for the next few days, otherwise I'll tell your mother on you."

"Tell your mother what, Kevin Alexander Monroe?"

Cassie's head popped out from around the corner of Liesel's nurses' station, lips pursed, eyebrows raised. Liesel quickly sent Kevin a look indicating it was up to him now and then wheeled her chair out of the way as Cassie entered.

"What is it this time, bud?" Her tone was sharp, but Cassie's face spoke of the volumes of love she felt for her son. "I've got a class to start in five minutes and a hot date with a fireman—so you had better tell me that this week's injury doesn't need a trip to the CMC."

Liesel's attention level shot straight up and, disturbingly, into the a-little-bit-jealous territory as an image of a certain sandy-haired fireman flitted through her mind. Trying her best to quell the heroic poses he was enacting in her imagination, she smiled up at her friend. "A date? You didn't tell me."

"Now, now, my little woodland fairy friend." Cassie laughed, openly pleased she'd piqued Liesel's interest. "We've *both* got a date with a fireman so don't look so envious."

Liesel felt her nose crinkle—her go-to *what are you talking about?* expression.

"Uh-oh, Miss Adler," Kev broke in warily. "You're Mum's latest double-dating victim. Better beware!"

"Right, you two." Liesel stood up briskly, wanting to put an end to the conversation as soon as humanly possible. "Time's up. I've got an assembly to prepare for." She shuffled them both out of the nurse's office and shut the door behind her with a satisfying click.

Discussing her love life, or lack of one, in front of the students, let alone the son of her new—her only—friend here in Engleton wasn't on the agenda. She leaned heavily against the door, allowing a slow breath to escape her lips. A breath she hoped carried away some of the ache she felt whenever she confronted the idea of moving on.

Yes. She'd loved Eric with all of her heart, an over-the-moon-and-back-again young woman's heart, but she'd never even got the chance to have her wedding day, let alone share the birth of her son. Now, at the ripe old age of twenty-eight, Liesel had a daily wrestling match with the feeling that she was "finished" in the romance department.

It had all happened so fast. A whirlwind love affair in an American ski resort. The spontaneous proposal. Their surprise pregnancy. Losing Eric. Never having the family that she had only just begun to imagine.

She started at the *tap-tap-tap* against the door.

"I know you're in there, Liesel. I can hear you breathing."

Despite herself, Liesel giggled. Being friends with Cassie gave her little glimpses back to the "old Liesel." The free-spirited young woman she used to be.

Cracking open the door, she allowed her friend access to one of her eyes. "Friend or foe?"

"*Friend*, you noodle! C'mon," she pleaded. "Open up!"

Liesel pulled open the door while simultaneously grabbing a light jumper from the hook on the wall. "Make it fast. I'm afraid I've got to get going down to the gym for an assembly. The principal just told me about it fifteen minutes ago."

"Cool your rockets. I'm heading the same way."

"Your class is coming?"

"You could put it that way." Cassie adopted her best nonchalant voice. "Or you could say that my class is coming to your date."

Liesel stopped in her tracks.

"Cassie Monroe! What have you done?"

"Oh-h-h-h…" Her friend was fastidiously avoiding eye contact now. "It might have been me who volunteered you to help with a little demonstration."

"What *demonstration*?"

"The first-aid demo for the first, second and third years. It was meant to be a ladders demonstration, but…" Cassie used her best cheerleader voice.

"But what?"

"Now, that, I don't know exactly. All I know is it has turned into a first-aid demo."

"And who exactly is leading today's first-aid demo?"

"Oh, I think he might have a familiar face."

Liesel felt her body go rigid as Cassie pushed open the door to the gym. Smack-dab in the center of the room a certain sandy-haired fireman was kneeling on the floor, setting up his kit. Seeing Jack again had the same effect on her nervous system as it did on the no-longer-dormant butterflies in her tummy. They were going crazy.

"Oh, no, you don't!" Cassie caught her arm as Liesel tried to turn and leave. "You're the Murray River Valley school nurse and I don't think there is anyone better placed to help our local CFS crew inspire young minds."

"But—"

"Nope. I don't want to hear it." Cassie gave her a quick hug and a push. "Now, go and put on a good show for my class. They just might be the future doctors of Engleton. Back in a tinkle!"

Liesel watched as her friend hastily retreated down the school corridor. If there was one thing she definitely knew about Cassie, she was persistent.

Jack first caught a glimpse of the familiar auburn curls through the gym door. As Liesel virtually hurtled through it, he felt bushwhacked anew by her fresh-faced beauty. Her petite features instantly made him feel like a klutzy brontosaurus who'd been charged with protecting a tiny and exquisitely beautiful tropical bird. His modus operandi at these gigs was usually big and loud, but something about her made him want to ratchet things down a notch.

"Are you the set of helping hands I was promised?"

"I'm afraid so."

Jack took on board the microscopic flinch as she made eye contact with him. What had provoked that?

"Apologies for the last-minute setup. The CFS are trying to do as much outreach in the local schools as we can and after we met the other day I realized we hadn't done a demonstration here in ages." *Too obvious?*

She squinted up at him, waiting for more information.

"I'm trying to score a few more points locally before I turn in my outreach stats to the big boys in Adelaide." *Too macho. Definitely too macho.*

"What exactly are we meant to be doing today? I heard a rumor it was going to be snakes and ladders." Liesel crossed her fingers behind her back, hoping that demonstrating anything involving body contact was off the agenda. She was beginning to feel a little giddy in Jack's presence and feeling that way—particularly in front of the student body—was definitely not in the rulebooks.

Jack rose to his full height, arms spreading out in front of him as if preparing to sell his wares to Liesel. "Ahh. Well, HQ decided today was the day all the ladders would be checked out by one of their techs. Safety-first bureaucracy, and all that." He gave her a knowing look and she couldn't help but nod along. The world of school nurses was weighed down with thick ledgers of mind-numbing paperwork. It was little wonder his was, too.

"This is what we're going to do today." He waved an

arm across everything he'd been laying out on the gym floor. "It's what you find inside a proper first-aid kit—one you'd find at a school, in a restaurant, the science lab. I know these kids are too little to reach one, let alone use it, but we can try and make it fun." His eyes twinkled down at hers and if she wasn't mistaken she saw the beginnings of a wink form, reconsider, then withdraw. *Shame.* Her butterflies were just about ready for another whirl round her tummy.

Liesel knew her eyes were meant to be following Jack's to take in the array of splints, plasters, bandages, wipes and protective glasses—a deluxe edition of first-aid kits. Instead, they were working their way from one of his long-fingered hands along his golden-haired forearm— she had a weakness for a well-defined forearm. Tanned, well-toned, his definitely measured up. Her eyes slid up and over the biceps filling his short-sleeved CFS T-shirt to a set of awfully broad shoulders—

"Like what you see?"

Heat instantly spread across her cheeks. *Obviously.* She hadn't ogled anyone from such close range in years. Three years, to be exact. A twist of guilt knotted up her butter-flies and as she looked up at him she realized in an instant he was referring to the contents of the first-aid kit.

Doubly embarrassing.

Even if he hadn't seen her do an ocular tiptoe up his arms and on to the expanse of his shoulders, he would be sure to spy the flush of embarrassment continuing to heat her cheeks. *Say something, you idiot!*

"It's great. You've really got the full Monty here."

She clapped a hand over her mouth. The full Monty! Her brain did a whiz-bang dress and undress of the un-suspecting man in front of her and before she could stop it, Liesel felt herself succumbing to a full-blown case of the nervous giggles.

* * *

Jack had no idea what Liesel was finding so funny but was glad to see, whatever it was, that it brought a happy glint to those kitty-cat eyes of hers. He took a swipe at his chin. Maybe he still had some egg yolk on there from this morning's egg and bacon roll.

"I'm sorry." Liesel spoke through her fingers, actively trying to stifle her laughter. "I don't know what's got into me this morning." She cleared her throat and gave her feet a little stomp on the gym floor, as if the motion would add some sobriety to the moment. It worked. For a second. As soon as their eyes met again she burst into another peal of laughter that was about as infectious as they came.

Feeling at an utter loss as to what would have caused it, Jack was relieved to see a flow of students start to make their way into the big gymnasium. He bent his head in their direction and stage-whispered, "Quit your laughing, Miss Adler. You'll take away my tough-guy image."

Hardly. She didn't know a single thing about Brigade Captain Jack Keller, but there was little to nothing that would diminish from the all-man mojo he was exuding.

Liesel took herself off to a corner to choke down a few more mortified giggles as the students made their way in. Being a few dozen meters away from him made it easier to spy on him. Well, not spy really…assess. Jack had clearly thought out the presentation more than he'd let on and was soon directing the children according to age toward floor seats or the stands.

He was good with them. A natural. He started off the talk with a few jokes that immediately captivated the children's attention. Liesel had to admit it, if there was anyone who could get this boisterous group of young kids interested in first-aid training and the CFS cadets, Jack Keller was the man for the job.

* * *

"All right, Miss Adler, time for you to come over here and for us to find out just how smart you are!"

Liesel did her best *who, me?* double take before realizing all eyes in the gym were focused on her and Jack was genuinely waiting for her to join him. The old Liesel would've loved being center stage, playing the jester to his brigade captain. The new Liesel? Not so sure about being in the limelight anymore.

Twenty minutes later Liesel realized she shouldn't have worried a bit. Jack Keller wasn't out to embarrass her—or anyone, for that matter. He really struck her as one of those genuinely kind guys who just wanted to help.

He had devised a really clever game where he would call out the name of an item in the first-aid kit and then he and the children would count how many seconds it took her to find it. Then, when she had found it, he would equate the time it took her to find it with what would have been happening to the patient while they were waiting. The children loved it and at the same time were learning how important it was to get help quickly in an emergency. They were putty in his hands and Jack seemed to be having just as much fun as the students.

"Right. I think it's time to pull out the big guns." Liesel watched as Jack's head turned a quick right, left and back again. Whatever it was he was looking for clearly wasn't there. Liesel thought she might be mistaken…but was he looking embarrassed?

"Right. We've just come onto the CPR part of our demonstration and it appears my good friend Resusci Annie decided to cop out for this particular trip." He scanned the room, his eyes coming to rest on Liesel, complete with that cockeyed smile of his. *Oh, no.* She was in trouble now.

"Who thinks Miss Adler should come and stand in for my dum—my good friend Resusci Annie?"

Jack knew he was going out on a limb here, but he might as well find out now whether or not Liesel gave as good as she got. She'd been great in participating in his game and seemed to know how to play along with him to maximize the learning potential for the children.

The whoops and hollers of the kids were all the confirmation Jack needed to usher a blushing Liesel to the center of the gym floor. He had to remind himself the blushing wasn't for him—it was for the children. Right? Either way, the flush on her cheeks was having a nice effect on his ego.

"Who'd like to see what it looks like when someone faints or passes out?"

Another cheer filled the gym and Liesel gave Jack a sidelong *thanks a lot, pal* look before performing one of the most melodramatic faints he had ever seen.

Score one to Liesel.

Oh-h-h-h, he's close. Really, really close. Not safe territory!

Jack was right in the middle of explaining the need to check for breathing when Liesel became a little too aware of him kneeling next to her. Then leaning over her. Then whispering in her ear, his soft breath an indicator as to just how close his lips were. His very, very kissable lips. Had her lips just quivered? *Please, say that didn't just happen.*

"I'm going to touch you, touch your head, is that all right?" She tried her best to nod slowly, maintaining the illusion of being unconscious. It was just as well she was lying on the floor. With her eyes closed. The effect of that low voice on her central nervous system seemed to get more results on her than a defibrillator. She felt one of those big capable hands of his gently touch her forehead. It was strange to her that she didn't feel vulnerable. Everything about this man seemed capable, safe. But he was close. Too close. She had to lift her head. *Now.*

"So, to check for breath you just want to lean over and—"

"Oh!"

Jack's mouth swept across hers as if by design. She found her lips breezing across his and meeting his stubbled cheek in virtually the same movement. It was softer than she had thought it would be. Not that she'd thought about it. Much.

His warm scent, a delicious sunbaked salty-sweet combo, filled her nostrils, her body's responsiveness quickly shooting to code red. Cheers and squeals of laughter pealed from the children. Liesel instinctively began to pull back as if she'd been set alight. In a lightning-fast move, she pushed herself away from Jack and up into a seating position. A thousand thoughts clamored for attention as she tried to put together what had just happened.

"That's one way to give the kiss of life, children. Not necessarily approved by the Red Cross, but nevertheless…" She could see him smiling at the children but was more aware of the questions flying through his blue eyes as he locked onto her own.

It's such a good thing I'm sitting down already.

I want to kiss him. For real.

No, you don't!

Yes. Yes, I do.

In front of half the school? And forget about Eric?

Eric.

Liesel was sure you could see her heart beating through her light summer top. Jack extended a hand to help her up. She didn't dare accept it.

"I think we should wait until Captain Keller comes back fully prepared to explore this lifesaving method." She pushed herself up and looked at her watch-free wrist as if willing a timepiece to appear. The not-so-artful dodge.

*First-class confirmation that I am not ready for this. It
seems my body is—but not the rest of me.*

"Looks like I've got to get going." She glanced in
Jack's direction but didn't dare meet his eyes. It would've
been too easy to call her bluff. "I'm afraid I've got to run.
Thanks for the presentation."

She must have looked like a terrified rabbit the way she
was hot-footing it out of the gym, but she needed to get
out of there. Away from Jack Keller.

Those milliseconds of intimate contact had wiped away
the rest of the world for a moment and that wasn't how
things needed to be right now. She was a single mum. She
had responsibilities. Responsibilities that included putting
forward a positive example for the children here at the
Murray Valley School.

Heart thumping, she closed the door to her office. It was
the perfect sanctuary. A quiet place to process what had
just happened. If anything had happened at all.

Her mouth went dry as she realized the whole incident
was down to her lifting up her head when she hadn't been
meant to. It had all been a mistake and from Jack's perspective she'd just behaved like a first-class lunatic. In
the blur of the moment she had just assumed he'd felt the
same charge of emotion that had flooded through her as
their lips had brushed together. Liesel scrubbed her fingers
through her hair. Terrific! Now he knew without a shadow
of a doubt the impact his touch had on her.

Oh, this was not good. She collapsed her head onto
her crossed arms, fervently wishing her desk could absorb her into the woodwork. This was Class A Embarrassment Central.

"Am I going to have to check for breath again?"

Liesel bolted upright, curls flying everywhere and
hands unsure where to come to rest at the sound of the
voice that had awakened her senses as if she'd been Sleep-

ing Beauty. Disheveled Sleeping Nutcase was more like it. Could this day get any worse?

Hands firmly planted on her hips, Liesel tried to adopt a casual air, as if she was always almost kissing someone during first-aid demonstrations. "I'm good. Very good. Everything's good here."

If erratic heart rate and jangling nerves were a picture of perfection.

She forced herself to make eye contact with Jack, prepared for the derision he no doubt would have for her ridiculous behavior. What she saw instead was an oasis of calm. A gentle smile played on his lips, little crinkles appearing at the edges of those blue-as-the-sky eyes of his. He leaned casually against the door frame of her office as if he'd been born to fill it, and everything about him said, *Relax. You're safe with me.*

"Glad to hear it. Sorry it was all a bit of a mess today. Organization is generally a bit more of a strong point. I'd like to make it up you—to the school, I mean." He shifted his feet slightly, his smile still as warm as the spring sunshine.

"Sure, that'd be great." Liesel winced. Had she sounded too eager? This wasn't really playing it cool. Or safe. "I mean…I'm sure the children would absolutely love it."

"You know," he continued, seemingly unaware of her internal battle for a bit more personal strength, "it would really be great if you could come down to the station sometime and throw some ideas around. Now that I know you're not—"

He stopped abruptly, almost looking bashful. It was cute. Supercute.

"Not what?"

"The fellas told me you were a granny on the verge of retirement."

"That would've been my predecessor, Mrs. Heissen."

She could feel his eyes run up and down her body to doubly confirm she was the opposite of an aging grandmother. The examination wasn't helping her maintain any sort of cool, calm and collected demeanor. His eyes landed on hers. Ping! Crystal-blue perfection.

"I feel I've really missed a trick, not introducing myself to you when I got my transfer here."

"Sorry, I've got an appointment to get to." *Liar.*

She took another glance at her invisible watch. She'd already made enough of a fool of herself.

"Fair enough, but don't think I'm going to give up easily."

She raised her eyebrows at him. Give up on *what* exactly?

"This is a small town and come fire season we genuinely could do with all the help we can get."

Aha. He's still recruiting. Wrong bark, wrong tree, mate.

"I'm sorry, but I'm afraid I just wouldn't have much to offer in the way of free time."

He carried on as if she hadn't said a word. "Not to mention the fact I've only been in town a few weeks and haven't yet found the perfect chocolate milk shake in the area. I'm on a quest. Care to join me?"

Oh. Well, that was quite a different suggestion. Although just as dangerous, given that it meant spending time alone with Jack Keller.

"That sounds like a laudable quest, Captain Keller—"

"Jack."

"Jack." She said the name deliberately before continuing, "I'd really like to help, but—"

"Great. That's settled, then. Things are pretty hectic over at the station for the rest of the week and I've got to get down to Adelaide for a weekend's training session—sometime next week?"

"Sure."

The word leaped past her lips before she'd had a chance to rein it in. Hadn't she just told herself that time spent with Jack Keller was a bad idea?

Jack was still grinning as he lifted the last bits of gear into the station truck. He was feeling remarkably cheery. And a little bit guilty. He was pleased his made-up quest for the perfect chocolate milk shake had worked in convincing Liesel to go out with him. That was a white lie he could live with. The one giving his gut a good kicking was the part about being new in town. Technically, it was true. He *was* new in town if you discounted the first twenty-five years of his life. If you forgot about those and just focused on the past four he'd been away and the man he'd become during those years...then, yes, technically he was new in town.

He was focused. Driven. Making a decision to be a full-timer for the CFS had added the sorely needed rod to his spine. Gone were the days of the noncommitted heir to River's Bend. His father no longer had to put up with experimental fields of hops for a microbrew, escapee pigs destined for air-dried sausage or a pair of Clydesdale horses clearly not meant for work in the forty-degree heat. All well-intentioned ideas with no real follow-through. Now his life was about tangible results. A new Jack Keller was definitely in town.

He coasted down the school drive and pulled out onto the highway, doing his best to surrender his doubts to the beautiful afternoon.

Nope. It was no good.

Everything was too familiar. The road, the tiny cluster of shops, who ran them, the clumps of gum and eucalyptus trees shading this house or that. If he was going to see Liesel again, he was going to have to come clean—at some point.

Truth be told, it would be nice to date someone who didn't have a clue about his history. Someone who just liked plain ol' Jack the fireman.

He gave a little snort. *Date!* He hadn't dated anyone properly in years. Girls in Engleton had always had their eye on the River's Bend prize, while in Adelaide during training there just hadn't been enough time. Or just not the right women. Or maybe for once he just wanted to see something through and prove to his father he had it in him to talk the walk. Or walk the talk. Or whatever that saying was.

Liesel definitely had something that spoke to him. Too bad the timing was shambolic.

He pulled the truck into the station-house drive, smiling at the sight of a couple of volunteers washing down one of the big rigs. It had just received a whopper of an upgrade thanks to a ten-grand anonymous donation. All of the guys had sworn ignorance and he believed them. They had an angel out there and he, for one, was grateful. The volunteers were great guys. He was just getting to know them, but already they had him knee-deep in barbecue invitations and bursting with ideas for fund-raising drives.

They'd make a success of this station. He was sure of it. The big guns over in Adelaide had given him a year to turn around the waning number of volunteers and poor track record on incident attendance. It would mean a lot of hard work, being on call 24/7 and his 100 percent dedication. He pressed his lips together as if to strengthen his resolve and scrubbed a hand through his hair.

He'd been kidding himself back at the school. He barely had time to grab a meal for himself, let alone complicate his life with a milk shake quest and a beautiful woman.

Short, sharp shock it was, then. Who was going to feel the pain the most, though, was up in the air.

CHAPTER THREE

"No-o-o-o!" Liesel did her best to squelch a few choice words as she wrestled with the steering wheel, the *thud-thud-thud* coming from her swerving car the unmistakable sound of a flat tire.

A quick glance in the rearview mirror showed that Liam, strapped into his car seat, was snoozing away, blissfully unaware of his mother's battle for control with the vehicle. At least one of them was relaxed! She pulled over as quickly and as safely as she could, a glance at the dashboard clock confirming what she already knew. They'd be late. Getting to Adelaide in an hour with a flat tire to fix was out of the question. Not to mention the fact her adrenaline was running at full pelt. Another reminder she didn't—couldn't—do high octane anymore. Just the few seconds it had taken to pull the car over had been more than enough to set her heart racing. Her hands shook as she put the car into Park and rested her head on the steering wheel to collect herself, before getting out to assess the damage.

"That was a well-controlled skid, Miss Adler. I didn't have you pegged for a rally driver."

Liesel nearly jumped out of her seat at the sound of the male voice—the exact same male voice attached to the exact same pair of lips that had been doing reruns in her head since yesterday afternoon.

"Hello again." Liesel managed a feeble wave through her open car window, heart still racing but for a completely different reason now. "Fancy meeting you here."

"It's one of the perks of living in a small town."

Mmm...he wasn't kidding. Then again, these run-ins were beginning to accrue quite a high count of embarrassment in her camp. Why couldn't he ever see her when she was doing something normal? Or, even better, laudable? Not that it mattered. Not really.

"I hope you weren't racing off to find a chocolate shake without me."

"At nine in the morning?" She couldn't help but laugh. "Even *I'm* not that keen!"

"Shall we take a look at your car?"

"I'm sure it's just a flat—I'll be fine." Liesel ran her fingers through her tousled hair. This guy sure had a knack for showing up when her hair and a comb were distant strangers.

"Oh, I never had any doubt about that."

Liesel felt herself being appraised by him and wished for the second time in as many seconds that she'd looked in the mirror that morning and perhaps even bothered to pop on a bit of lip gloss after brushing her hair. She was only going to housesit for her parents so hadn't bothered with the whole dolling-up routine.

Who was she kidding? Dolling up had been the last thing on her agenda for the past three years. Yet under Jack's gaze she suddenly felt the need to look her best. No. Not "the need"... No, that wasn't it. She *wanted* to look good. For him to like what he saw. And the collateral wake of feelings that went along with that little revelation was throwing her nerves into a right old jumble.

"First things first, Miss Adler." He squatted down so

his head was level with hers, a long index finger reaching out to pull a couple of wayward curls out of her eyes. "Any bumps or bruises?"

Liesel shook her head, praying he hadn't noticed the lightning bolt shooting down her spine at his touch. It was obvious he hadn't done it as a flirtatious move—she'd made the same gesture along Liam's forehead countless times. Although somehow she didn't think her two-year-old got butterflies in his stomach when she did it.

"Would you like me to take a look at your car?" Jack pressed, standing up with a nod toward the back of her car.

Not really. Basking in that crooked beam of a grin of yours is working pretty well for me.

Rescuing damsels in distress had to be his true calling. Seriously.

He had already proved he was good with schoolboys in distress, and from the spray of goose pimples shivering up her arms in the morning sun he wasn't going far wrong with the damsel part, either.

"That'd be great." Liesel made her decision, clicking the door open and hoping it would signal to Jack that she needed a bit of space. Close proximity to this guy was unnerving. In a good way. *Far too good.*

She got out of the car and joined him at the offending rear tire.

"Looks like I won't be getting to Adelaide anytime soon."

"I'm afraid you won't be getting to Adelaide at all with that. It looks like a cracked tire wall—not just a flat."

Liesel stood in silence, her mind working through all the possibilities. She'd promised to look after her parents' "replacement child," Moxy, the toy poodle, while they spent a weekend with her sister in Melbourne. Their neighbors were a bit too elderly for the walks and if anything went wrong—well, she was hoping nothing would go wrong.

Their train left in just a couple of hours and after all their amazing support she couldn't let them down.

"I'm headed to Adelaide."

"Are you staying long?"

"Overnight." Liesel looked up at the sky in frustration. She had to sort this out. "I'm meant to be house-sitting for my parents."

"Why don't you catch a ride with me? I'm doing a weekend course with the Metropolitan Fire Service. I'm not heading back until late Sunday afternoon. Would that work for you?"

Jack let the words hang between them in the fresh morning air. They were out there before he'd had a chance to really think about what would happen if she said yes. But seeing the stricken look on Liesel's face had instinctively made him offer his help.

"Oh, I couldn't let you do that."

"Why not? I've got a perfectly good truck with a spare seat."

"That's really kind of you, but…" Her mind raced, knowing there was a lot he didn't know about her, a lot she wasn't ready to share. "I don't even know your full name."

"Officially it's Brigade Captain John G. Keller, but given that we're both technically state employees—meaning we're colleagues—I'd say you should still just call me Jack. And I'm warning you now—" he waggled a finger at her "—you'll *never* get to know what the *G* stands for!"

There was that laugh again. A smiling Liesel was definitely better than the one who'd looked utterly panicked when he'd arrived. He wasn't sure what it was about this woman, but being around her brought out a deep need to protect her. Not to mention a whole slew of other things he'd already decided were not options for him. Like finding out what it would be like to really kiss those ruby-red lips of hers.

Lust aside, he reasoned with himself as he held open her car door, as one of the few salaried members of the CFS he was a civil servant. It was his job to help.

Shaking away the idea his protective impulses were anything more than a fireman's gut reaction to any human in distress, he gestured toward the truck. "Grab your stuff and hop in, Miss Adler."

"Oh, no, really. I couldn't accept." Her eyes darted to the backseat of her car. "It's not just me."

Jack's eyebrows shot up at his oversight. "Right, well, who have we got back here? You have a dog?" He tipped his head so he could get a glimpse of the backseat passenger.

Liesel moved in between him and the car as if by instinct. "He's my son."

"And what a good-looking little fellow he is." Jack peeped over her shoulder, trying his best to give her a relaxed smile.

He sure hadn't seen that one coming.

He felt sucker punched. Liesel was taken. She wasn't wearing a wedding ring and certainly didn't have a mumsy aura about her—but a son was a pretty good indicator she wasn't available. True, he hadn't considered dating someone with children before, but—honestly? He hadn't even considered *dating* in a long time. It might take a little while to shake off the effect she had on him but—big picture—it was probably just as well she was off the market.

"Should we give his dad a ring and have him come collect you two?"

Ice flooded Liesel's veins. She still hadn't found a way to tell people about Liam's dad. Not without wanting to cry or subjecting the other person to huge waves of embarrassment.

"No, it's just us, I'm afraid."

She felt Jack's hand rest lightly on her shoulder. It was all she could do not to press into the warm comfort of it. Lean into the strength he offered.

"Not to worry," Jack said gently. "Guess it's a good thing I showed up. Let's get you two packed up and hit the road."

As if in a daze, Liesel followed Jack's lead. She was so grateful to him for not prying. Not asking more. Just a few short years ago she'd been a girl who loved to hash out emotional affairs in minute detail, but keeping things neutral was her survival mode now. In fact, accepting a ride from a virtual stranger was a leap out of her current comfort zone, but it wasn't as if she had a lot of choice. Her parents were expecting her and what harm could come of it? They were both state employees. Colleagues. *Right?*

Jack gave her the number of a local towing company, who, after a quick chat, agreed to pick up the car and drop it at the school on Monday morning when they had finished. Everything fell into place like a well-laid plan. Living in a small town definitely had its advantages.

As she spoke to her parents to let them know about her change of plans she watched as Jack expertly unclipped Liam's travel seat, a single muscled arm smoothly moving him from car to truck before securing all of the appropriate buckles in his backseat with barely a flutter from her son's sleeping lashes. She grabbed the enormous tote bag she'd hurriedly packed moments before they had left the house. It contained more of Liam's things than her own. Looking after herself had come a distant second over the past two years and this morning had been no different.

"You're going to have to forgive the mess, I'm afraid." Jack sent an apologetic glance toward the front cab of the truck. "Regulation dictates we keep it free of excess materials, but regulation doesn't take into account a man's hunger when on call twenty-four hours a day!"

"Don't worry about it." Liesel found herself strangely relieved to see the jumble of empty soft-drink cans and tomato-ketchup packets lying about the cab. It took the superhero edge off, making him the tiniest bit more human.

"Here, let me take that for you."

She felt her mega-sized tote being lifted out of her hands as if it didn't weigh a thing and watched as Jack deposited it in the backseat on top of what looked like a regulation issue CFS duffel.

"It's not all mine, I promise." She scrunched her face at the memory of going through Liam's room at high speed this morning, covering every single option for what her son might or might not need for the next forty-eight hours. She liked to be prepared. Some would say overprepared, but this morning's tire disaster was proof you just couldn't plan for everything. Not even a run-in with a handsome fireman who'd danced in and out of her subconscious last night.

"Right!" Jack smiled across at her as she climbed into the front of the cab. "Where are we headed, Miss Adler?"

"The Northern Hills, if that's all right. Near the Kangaroo Creek Reservoir."

"No problem. The station where we're doing the training is just across the reservoir from you, at Houghton. You all buckled up?"

Uncertainty flickered through her eyes as he spoke and Jack tutted when he saw her glancing at the door handle, as if second-guessing her decision to accept a lift into town.

"Don't worry, love. I don't bite. You're getting a certified rescue." Turning off the jokey voice, he continued, "If you like, I can call it in to the station. Just so we're all on the up-and-up." He reached for the in-cab radio.

"It's all right. Sorry, sorry. It's just been a bit of a mad dash this morning and now with the tire—"

"Even better that you're catching a ride, then. Not good to be behind a wheel when you're stressed. Just sit back and enjoy the ride."

Much to her surprise, Liesel found herself doing just that. Conversation with Jack was easy and after a few more "Miss Adlers" she managed to convince him to call her Liesel. Despite her initial reservations in riding along with him, she found her trust in this man deepening as the kilometers glided past.

"Will you and the little fella be hitting the town tonight? There are some nice places around where you are."

Liesel laughed at the idea of going out. She couldn't remember the last time she'd been out for dinner, let alone feeling as if she was "out on the town."

"Hardly. It's just going to be me, Liam and some Saturday-night television, I'm afraid. All very boring."

"Why don't you let me take you out?"

Liesel caught her breath at the words, eyes widened in surprise.

"Both of you, I mean. Training stops at five. We could go for an early tea and I'll get you back before the little man's bedtime."

Liesel checked her instinct to immediately say no. The butterflies soaring round her tummy were already clinking icy glasses of Pinot Grigio on a restaurant patio with him. The scared, desperate-to-be-wrapped-in-cotton-wool side? Firemen were still in the no-go zone. For her son.

"Thanks, but I don't think we should. The whole reason we're going to Adelaide is to look after Mum and Dad's cherished poodle." She found herself embellishing the task, detailing for him the great attention to detail her parents lavished on Moxy.

"Sounds like they should have called her Cleopatra or the Queen of Sheba."

Liesel laughed in agreement, treating herself to another

sidelong glance at Jack. He was a good guy and the fact he wasn't pushing her was something to appreciate. Actually, it went beyond that. For the first time in ages Liesel was enjoying the simple pleasure of having a normal conversation.

Normal.

She'd been craving that sensation for a long time now. Since Eric had died it was hard to know what normal was. Hard to know when someone wasn't treating her like a bereaved single mum or just as her old self—footloose, worry-free, globe-trotting, fun-loving Liesel.

If someone had told her she'd find "normal" sitting in the cab of a pickup next to a ridiculously fit fireman in the heart of Australia's wine country, she would have laughed herself silly.

She leaned against the window, hoping he couldn't tell she was looking at him through her dark sunglasses. Again.

No doubt about it. He was gorgeous, of the good old-fashioned hunky fireman variety. He probably had girls hitting on him all the time. She was guessing her permanently rumpled appearance made her "friend" material rather than a possible girlfriend. Not that she had imagined dating him. Or kissing those full lips of his, or rubbing a cheek along that silky-soft stubble lining his face before stealing another cheeky kiss… *Liesel! Stop it!*

She pressed her lips together. Hard.

"C'mon." She heard Jack's teasing voice from the other side of the cab. "It'll be fun. We could even start our chocolate shake quest early. I know a place Liam would love."

"Sorry, Jack." Liesel fixed her gaze straight ahead. "I really think we ought to stay in."

Jack gave his head a quick shake. She sure was making asking her out difficult. And given the fact he wasn't on the hunt for a girlfriend, it was pretty weird he was pushing so hard. No. That wasn't true. He knew exactly why he was pushing so hard. He wanted to get to know her. Plain and simple.

His let his fingers run round the leather steering wheel, before glancing in the rearview mirror at Liesel's peacefully sleeping son. A son. He'd hardly thought about having a girlfriend, let alone a wife. Children, future heirs to the Keller dynasty? They were all wisps of cloud in his imagination. There was nothing plain and simple about his life right now and, from the looks of things, not in Liesel's, either.

He should let it go. Leave Liesel in peace to have her quiet night by the television. They drove on in silence, each seemingly absorbed in their own thoughts.

"What's that?" Jack's eyes darted around the cab at the sound of a popular sixties tune coming from the footwell.

"It's my ringtone, sorry." Liesel dug furiously in her bag to end the blaring tones, glancing back anxiously at Liam, whose eyes only blinked open and closed quickly before he drifted back to sleep.

"Bit of a hippie, are you?"

"Used to be." Liesel glanced up at him, a flicker of mischief flashing across her feline eyes before she pushed the "accept" button on her phone. "Hello?"

Jack glanced across, unable to hear the words of the caller, but the high-octane delivery and Liesel's raised eyebrows indicated it wasn't a pleasure call.

"Cassie, I need you to slow down. How big is the burn?"

Jack's attention level shot up a few notches. Burns went with fires. He tapped Liesel's arm, gesturing that he could turn around if she needed. She shook her head, clearly focused on the caller's rapid-fire explanation.

"We've got to establish the depth of the burn, all right?"

Jack was impressed with the calm in her voice. She had initially struck him as quite a timorous, shy little thing, but the steady, capable voice he heard now showed him a whole other side to the enigmatic Miss Liesel Adler.

"Is it just red and glistening or are there any blisters?"

Jack pulled the truck onto the hard shoulder. Liesel shot him a quick look of gratitude. It was fleeting, but just the grateful glimpse from those expressive eyes puffed up his pride a bit. He wasn't sure how she did it, but he wanted to make sure he earned the gratitude her look had expressed.

"Have you put anything on it yet, Cassie?"

Cassie. The name rang a bell. One of the teachers up at the Murray Valley School?

"It doesn't sound too bad, Cass—but if I were you I'd make sure you give it a good clean and then wrap it loosely in a light bandage. You need to be careful not to pop the blisters." She paused and Jack smiled as her soothing voice turned into that of a strict schoolteacher. "Tell Kev he is, under no circumstances, to pick them open. No gaming devices if he does, and I don't care if he's thirteen and knows everything."

She paused to listen and offered Jack an apologetic smile. "All right, Cass? Call me if there are any problems, or take him straight to the clinic if it gets infected. Speak soon."

"Everything all right?"

"Sorry, yes. I didn't mean to delay us. It's my friend Cassandra Monroe—up at the school?" She raised her eyebrows in question and he nodded—he did know Cassandra. And her son, Kevin. He'd heard through a couple of the guys at the station that the boy had become a bit of a tearaway since his dad had left town a year or so ago. One to put on his cadet recruits list. Being a cadet had given him focus—now he was trying to pay it forward.

"He's one of the most accident-prone kids I think I've ever met. This time it's a mishap with the grill pan."

Jack's eyes opened wider. "Is he trying to become a chef?"

"Hardly!" Liesel gave a hoot of laughter, her fingers flying to cover her mouth as she glanced back to make sure her son was still asleep. "Cheese on toast," she whispered, her attention now fully captured by Liam.

They both watched him in silence, the previous conversation forgotten.

Jack had never been one to coo over babies, but he had to admit Liesel's toddler was a handsome little chap. It was incredible to him how trusting the boy looked, deeply and comfortably asleep in his car seat as if he hadn't a care in the world. Building his own family was something he had always imagined happening one day. He cleared his throat. Getting broody was *not* on today's agenda.

"Shall we hit the road again?"

Liesel flicked through the TV channels, finding it difficult to believe the hundred-plus channels her parents received contained absolutely nothing worth watching. It would have to be a cooking show. Maybe that would inspire her to get something to eat. Liam had nibbled at her uninspired offerings before ultimately abandoning them for a game of tug-of-war with Moxy the Wonder Poodle, leaving Liesel with her own listlessness to contend with.

It didn't take a brainiac to figure out she had no attention span because of some not-so-idle daydreams about dining with a certain fireman. Too bad she couldn't take her advice as easily as she dispensed it. The number of times she'd encouraged Cassie to shake off a bad date and to keep on trying! Now here she was turning down a date—no, not even a date really, a casual dinner with the first man to stir feelings in her that she thought had died with Eric.

She flicked the channels again. Doughnut-making.

Nope. Still not as interesting as thinking about Jack. About that one, perfectly still moment when his strong hand had held her—well, held her shoulder, at any rate. Or back in the gym when just the brush of his lips had—

Stop. It. Now.

She looked across the room at her son, happily sharing his teddy bear with the poodle.

Liam. He was who she needed to focus on. Not Jack.

A knock at the door pulled her out of her reverie.

She jumped up from the sofa, tightening up the drawstring to her tracksuit bottoms as she went to the door. One of the neighbors must have popped round.

"I couldn't resist." Two enormous chocolate shakes worked their way round the door frame.

Most decidedly *not* a neighbor.

Jack handed her the ice-cold drinks, his wrists weighed down with two very full bags of takeaway from a local rotisserie.

"Hope you haven't eaten yet."

How he'd divined roast chicken was one of her favorites she'd never know. Liesel felt a smile creeping onto her lips.

Was this another little nudge from fate?

Or a supersize push?

CHAPTER FOUR

"YOU'RE MAKING IT very difficult to resist your charms."

"You think I'm charming now, do you?"

Jack scooped out the final dollop of potato salad for Liesel then leaned back in his patio chair, highly aware of feeling a bit too eager for her response.

She made a noncommittal noise, took a huge forkful of potato salad to her lips, smiled coquettishly, then devoured it in one go. He watched as the tip of her tongue captured the last miniature dot of mayonnaise resting on her upper lip.

And another point to Liesel for winning sexiest eater of takeaway rotisserie!

There was no keeping an appreciative smile under wraps. From where he sat, Jack felt he'd come out the true winner. A genuinely relaxing evening with a woman he could get used to spending a lot more time with. Not to mention her son. Talk about an infectious laugh.

He had to admit to being shocked by the fact Liesel had a child, but as the idea grew on him, and having seen them interact like the natural twosome they were, it would now seem strange to imagine her without him. Liesel never mentioned the father but Jack was pretty certain that was a topic better left for her to bring up. The boy was a testament to his mother—fun-loving and relaxed. Just a happy little toddler enjoying life, the way it should be.

Jack rested his chin on a temple of fingertips. With the sun behind him, he had the perfect position to enjoy watching the remains of the sun dance through Liesel's auburn curls. It was all too easy to imagine slipping his fingers through her hair, brushing a thumb along the soft down of her cheek before drawing her in closer to him for a...

He shifted. He was staring, a move unlikely to be found in the rulebook for *playing it cool*. He pulled a hand through his own hair and tried to turn the gesture into a casual stretch. Nope. No good. He was just succeeding in looking like an idiot.

"If you consider this morning's heroics—"

"A hero *and* charming," Liesel interrupted with a burble of laughter. "This is a red-letter day for Captain Keller, isn't it, Liam?"

The two-year-old, tightly curled in his mother's lap, responded by snuggling in even deeper and emitting a little boy-sized snore.

"Clearly my charms aren't working on your son."

"I guess you're going to have to try a bit harder." Liesel cocked an eyebrow with a playful smirk, and then just as quickly averted her gaze. *Had he seen a glint of flirtation there?* Good.

"That is a challenge I will happily accept." Jack pushed back his chair and started collecting what remained of the takeaway. The milk shakes were long gone. Scored seven out of ten. "Why don't you get the little man to bed and I'll sort these things out?"

Liesel accepted his offer with a silent smile. Jack watched her slip through the patio doors into the comfortable bungalow her parents had moved into a decade earlier—a downsize, apparently, after their daughters had moved out of the original family home. It had a nice family feel about it. Loved and lived-in. The same feeling River's Bend had had before his mum had died.

He dragged a hand through his blond thatch again, giving his scalp a bit of a knead as if it would stop the memories from shifting into high gear.

Jack turned his attention to the handful of scraps left on the picnic table. Chicken? Gone. Potato salad? The tiniest smudge of mayonnaise lurked in the corner of the takeaway container. Veggies? *Nada.* They'd made mincemeat of the "family meal" he'd ordered. Demolished the lot.

Scrubbing at his chin, he realized anyone looking over the fence would've seen the three of them as just that—a family. Not really what he'd had in mind when his eyes had first lit on Liesel in the barnyard the other day, but he had to admit, learning she had a son hadn't detracted from his response to her. She brought out the all-male side of him in a big way. He'd been showing off for the past couple of hours and there was no doubt in his mind if any of the lads from down the station had seen him being used as a jungle gym by a poodle and a two-year-old with an insatiable desire for "More!" then the ribbing would have been long-lived.

The entire evening had been fun. Good old-fashioned fun. And he knew he'd come back for more. If Liesel was up for it.

Pulling the light blue duvet over her son's shoulders and tucking his favorite cuddly tiger under his arm, Liesel couldn't stop herself from lingering a bit over her son. His cheeks were still flushed from a full evening of chase with Moxy, enough airplane rides from Jack to last a lifetime and another first, eating grilled vegetables. She didn't know why she hadn't thought of barbecuing them before. Cranking up the barbecue for just the two of them had seemed excessive. She'd have to reconsider. Liam had devoured a pile of veg that normally would have been ignored whether they were diced, sliced or shaped into flying saucers.

Her lips slipped into an easy smile. Jack definitely knew how to tantalize the right things into a young boy's tummy.

Who was she kidding? He knew how to tantalize *her*, too. The number of times she had caught her gaze lingering on his hands, wondering how it would feel if he slid his fingers along her hip, round to the small of her back… She looked back down at her son. She'd have to squelch those feelings for now. No matter how irresistibly tingly an effect he had on her, Liam had to stay her priority. She couldn't stop her smile from broadening. At the very least, knowing Jack would be an asset to the weight loss she'd suffered over the past couple of years.

She and Liam had attacked Jack's takeaway like a pair of starving wolves. And Liam had already had his tea! It was as if Jack's presence had given them both an extra jolt of energy, reminding her that life did have its footloose and fancy-free moments. She giggled a little.

Fancy-free was for sure. With his unerring ability to catch her at her worst, she had given up worrying about the fact that her couch-potato outfit hardly flattered her petite figure. She was just having fun with a new friend—right? Well, a new friend who flirted, gave her goose pimples from ten meters away and lit up her tummy like a lava lamp for the first time in—well, a very long time.

Liesel's fingers ran through the fine waves of her son's blond hair. From the looks of things, it didn't seem as though he'd share her thick, corkscrew curls. It was definitely Eric's hair.

Her stomach clenched. Eric. Her son's father. Her first love. And had she really just spent the past couple of hours flirting with another man as if he had never existed?

Her body gave her the answer before her mind dared confirm it.

Yes.

Liesel felt her lips thin as she tried to press away the fact that not only had she kept Eric and their history out of the conversation with Jack, but she hadn't even thought about him. They'd been having so much fun and the time had flown by. How could she have let this happen? She needed to knock some sense into herself—and she definitely needed to give herself a good mental talking-to.

Tipping back her head, she closed her eyes as tears prickled at her lashes.

Would it ever end? The guilt? The need to hold on to the past knowing full well the only way to give her son a future was to let go? And how much? Were there guidelines? How much of the past could she let go of before safely moving on?

"Liesel, you need to come now."

Jack's low voice sounded urgent. He was halfway back down the corridor before she'd swatted away the stray tears he hopefully hadn't spied trickling down her cheeks.

"What's going on?"

"Your parents' neighbor has just had a nasty fall on her back patio. Pretty sure it's her hip but she's nonresponsive. Her husband's with her now. I'm going to call an ambulance but the first aid required is beyond my terrain. See you there in a few minutes?" Jack grabbed the wall phone, not waiting for an answer.

Instinct took over. Liesel bolted out of the back door and through the adjoining gate between her parents' and the Daleses' backyards. The two sets of parents were longtime friends; they'd known each other long before their children had been born and had moved next door to each other for this very reason—to be there if they ever needed help.

Liesel's heart lurched into her throat at the sight of Mrs.

Dales sprawled on the hard tiles of their patio, a small pool of blood forming along the slate stone beneath her head. Mr. Dales looked up at her, eyes stricken with panic. "What do I do? She's barely conscious."

This was exactly the sort of situation Liesel had been trained to deal with. Extreme trauma. And exactly the type of scenario she'd been actively avoiding since she'd frozen in the Adelaide trauma unit.

She had a duty of care. And her head was spinning.

She had a duty of care.

Her instinct was to run and curl up in Jack's arms, hands pressed against her ears, blocking it all out. She'd feel safe in his arms.

She had a duty of care.

He was here. Close by. She could do this without freezing. Steeling herself, Liesel stepped forward, placing as reassuring a hand as she could on the elderly man's shoulder. It had worked for her when Jack had done it so she hoped it had the same calming effect on her neighbor.

"You're doing a great job, Mr. Dales. My friend is ringing for help." She let herself feel the invisible squeeze on her own shoulder.

"Would you run into the kitchen for me and grab some clean towels, ice and some warm water? Don't try and get it all in one trip, all right?" He nodded wordlessly and disappeared into the kitchen as she knelt, turning her full focus onto Mrs. Dales. Her fingers automatically dropped to the woman's slender wrist to check for a pulse. Her skin was deathly pale and she was now unconscious. A sharp trauma could cause that. Liesel knelt closer, tipping her cheek to the side to check for breathing. The faintest of breaths stirred the fine hairs on her cheek. Uneven. Slight. But breathing.

Thank you. Thank you. Thank you.

As if on autopilot, Liesel started working her way

through a mental checklist she hadn't used for a long time. She wouldn't move Mrs. Dales at all. That would be a job for the SAAS team when the ambos arrived. They would have neck braces, immobilization backboards, the lot. Her job now was to stabilize Mrs. Dales as best she could. The possibility of a break bordering on a key arterial route was often lethal. The slightest of movements could cause paralysis if the break was in the neck or spine. Equally, a sudden movement could loosen a blood clot, sending it on a fatal path, ultimately blocking the blood supply to the brain.

Liesel scrunched her eyelids together as tightly as she could, a heavy exhalation gushing past her lips. It felt as if she was short-circuiting.

Breathe. Focus. Jack thinks you can do this. You know you can do this.

Liesel opened her eyes, blocking out everything but Mrs. Dales. From the placement of her legs and her sprawled arms, it was clear she had taken quite a fall. Broken hip, leg, back, arm, wrist—one or all of them were possibilities. Intrascapular fractures, breaks along key arterial routes of the neck, were also a possibility. Much more likely in a woman than a man, but from the placement of Mrs. Dales's body, she guessed it was more likely to be a hip injury than anything else.

She'd encountered quite a few broken hips during her tenure on the slopes, young people usually—daredevil skiers losing a game of chicken with a pine tree or suchlike. They were extreme traumas but youth was on their side.

For the elderly? Life wasn't as kind. Particularly with someone who was suffering from osteoarthritis—an affliction shared by both Mr. and Mrs. Dales. Her parents had laughingly told her about how their lives were reduced to swapping notes about medications over the garden fence. It was no laughing matter now.

The elderly were highly susceptible to these types of

injuries and Liesel knew more than most that a broken hip for someone in their seventies could easily result in death. If not today, the chances of it happening over the next year were high. Too high.

It was the cut to the head that needed immediate attention. Head injuries always bled heavily but weren't necessarily as bad as they looked. Infection could be the real problem.

Liesel made a quick scan of the patio. A plate of raw sausages was strewn over the crisscross of slate and stone tiles. The squared edge of the barbecue side tray was just to their left. A small stain of red and a couple of white hairs on the corner betrayed its status as the culprit for the head wound. Liesel's instinct was to stem the blood flow as quickly as possible but, well aware her hands weren't sanitary, was relieved to see Mr. Dales appear alongside her with a pile of immaculately clean dishcloths.

"We were just going to cook a few sausages and she—" Mr. Dales stopped as if just describing how the accident had happened would make the situation worse.

"Thanks, Mr. Dales. These are exactly what we need." Liesel gave his arm a gentle squeeze, before pressing a cloth to the wound, using another to carefully dab at the trickle of blood running down Mrs. Dales's face. "Would you mind going to your medicine cabinet? Any gauze bandages, antiseptic—anything like that would be a great help."

He nodded silently, his softly jowled cheeks betraying a slight tremble.

Liesel stemmed the flow of blood as best she could. It was not too long a cut, about seven centimeters, but it was jagged and had been lacerated by the aluminum of the barbecue side tray, which probably contained an untold number of germs. She had to get some antiseptic in there before applying a bandage. The cut most likely required a couple of butterfly stitches or adhesive strips. Again, things she didn't have to hand.

Liesel felt her heart rate begin to speed up again. She wanted order, precision and calm. Without all the appropriate kit to hand, how was she going to help Mrs. Dales to the best of her ability? The buzz began in her ears again.

Stop it, Liesel. Stop it! The old you wouldn't be freaking out like this! You'd improvise and make the best of a bad situation. Focus, focus, focus.

"Ambos should be here in under ten."

Liesel's eyes shot up at the sound of Jack's voice. There it was. The injection of calm she needed.

"Don't worry." He pulled Liam's baby monitor out of the back pocket of his worn jeans and waggled it between his thumb and forefinger as he opened the clasp of the gate between them with the other hand. "I've got you covered."

She believed him. Right here, right now, kneeling on the patio in an old pair of sweats and an oversize T-shirt, hands mechanically swabbing away at the blood on Mrs. Dale's forehead, she believed him. And she was grateful for the strength emanating from him because it was taking every single teeny-tiny morsel of concentration she possessed to keep her cool.

"What can I do to help?" Jack crossed the lawn to the patio in two long-legged strides—poised for action.

Liesel blew a fine stream of air past her lips. She wasn't going to let him hear her voice shake.

"There's not too much more to do until the ambulance arrives. Without proper immobilization, I think it's too dangerous to move her." Just hearing her old voice say the words as she connected with those pure blue eyes of his and—*ba-bump ba-bump*—her heartbeat began to steady itself.

"You're the expert." He gave her a mini-salute of respect.

"Hardly." Liesel shook away the compliment. "I haven't been around this sort of injury in a while."

"Looks like you're doing all right from where I'm standing."

He was good. Almost too good. Could fate have sent him to help restore her confidence in life? In living?

She heard a low buzzing and followed Jack's hand as it automatically slipped the beeper off his belt loop and pulled it up for inspection. His change of demeanor was instantaneous.

"Liesel, I've got to get this. House fire in the hills at the back of a small estate bordering on dry bushland."

Her head didn't turn. Was she angry? Focused? *C'mon! Give me something to work with here!*

Leaving wasn't his style—but fighting fires was. Jack winced, simultaneously scanning the yard as if one of the blossoming rosebushes would offer him a solution. On call was on call. He was already wasting precious seconds. The longer a fire burnt, the more harm came of it. He had to go.

Mr. Dales came through the patio doors, using both of his hands to carry a wicker basket overflowing with multicolored medicine tubes, bandages and cotton swabs.

"Anything here of use? How is she?"

"That's great, Mr. Dales, thank you. She's still unconscious, but she's got a steady pulse. Not long now." Liesel's voice was tight, her eye line fastidiously restricted to her patient and the basket of first-aid items.

Jack stayed static, his impulse to help Liesel overriding his professional duty. It was an entirely new feeling. He knew his behavior was entirely personal. Professionally? Lingering wasn't an option.

Mrs. Dales was in good hands. He watched as Liesel's slender fingers swept through the basket brought by Mr. Dales. Were they shaking or just hurried? Maybe he should wait until the ambulance arrived.

"Go on, I'll be all right."

She flicked her eyes up at him. Her voice was solid. He guessed he had his answer. He had to go.

As she heard Jack's truck pull away from the curb, Liesel let Jack's words run through her mind in a loop. He was right. She knew how to do this. It was scary, especially on her own, but she could do it. She let her fingers slip down to Mrs. Dales's wrist, a religious check on her pulse rate. Liesel held her breath and waited.

One.

Two.

Where was it?

Her fingers flew to Mrs. Dales's neck, just below her chin.

Where was the pulse?

She knelt directly over the elderly woman, fingers moving from the papery-soft skin of her wrist to the same position on her forehead where Jack had touched her just a few days previously at the first-aid demonstration.

She shifted her cheek to feel and listen for breath. "Mrs. Dales?"

There was nothing.

"Mrs. Dales?" It was all she could do to keep the panic out of her voice. She could sense Mr. Dales approaching. They'd been married just shy of fifty years. The same as her parents. The couples were going to share a golden wedding anniversary cruise to New Zealand via the South Pole in a few months. A group of adventurers, they'd told her, smiles spreading across their faces at the thought of everything life still held in store for them. The type of future she hoped for herself one day.

No, no, no, no. She wove her fingers together, intuitively beginning to perform the perfectly timed compressions essential to bringing back breath. Bringing back life.

In the distance she thought she could hear— Yes! She could hear the faint sound of an ambulance siren. *I can do this. I can do this.*

Jack's conscience gnawed at him. He'd been flat out for the past seven hours and hadn't had a moment to call Liesel to check on how things had gone with her neighbor. With the moon ready to make its descent and the sun teasing at the horizon, he was pretty sure a phone call would be an unwelcome intrusion. Liesel was one tough cookie, but she had looked as white as a ghost when he'd left. Not to mention seeming none too impressed with him when he'd announced he had to race back to the station. She worked in the public sector—surely she knew it wasn't personal.

Attend a fire or stay with a medical emergency he couldn't assist on, with an ambulance en route?

These were the types of decisions he had to make all the time now. Staff numbers were short. Decisions had to be made. Prioritizing crises—the bureaucracy of fighting fires.

"Drink this before you drop off, Jack. It'll do your muscles wonders."

Jack put up his hand and caught the flying bottle of colored liquid. "This one of your magic vitamin drinks, Chief?"

"Precisely, mate." Jack's commanding officer sank onto the bunk beside him and began to peel off his socks. "Get that down you and you'll feel better than new."

"Better than that house we just doused at any rate."

"I've never seen a place go up so quickly. Like it was made of kindling or something." The regional chief officer shook his head. "Such a shame."

Jack shook his head in agreement as he bent over his knees to unlace his leather boots. It never ceased to amaze him how quickly a house could be reduced to a pile of ashes.

"How was your date?" His boss jigged his eyebrows up and down for effect.

"Sorry, mate?" Jack thought he'd been discreet about nipping out of the station for a bit.

"I saw how quickly you hightailed it out of here earlier. Never seen anyone go for a quick bite to eat 'with a mate' with such well-combed hair." He reached across the space between bunks and gave Jack a light punch on the arm. "Looks like love-'em-and-leave-'em Casanova Keller is back on the scene!"

"Hardly!" He winced away the moniker from his training days. Liesel was in an entirely different category from the girls he used to date. If you could call two or three nights maximum dating.

"Was she worth getting a reprimand for?"

"Reprimand?" Jack felt his forehead crinkle in consternation. He'd arrived at the station before the callout.

"I'm just joshing you, mate, but you'd better watch it. The higher-ups are getting more strict about personal lives taking precedence over station business. Especially when we're short on staff and belts are being tightened. It wouldn't take much for them to close down Murray Valley in the blink of an eye."

"They said I had a year."

"They say a lot of things."

Jack sat back in his bunk, stuffing a pillow between his head and the wall.

When he was working he liked to be entirely focused. That's why his cavalier approach to "dating" during his training days had earned him the Casanova nickname. The theory was, if he didn't get serious with anyone then he could keep his eye on the prize—running his own station. The fact that his assignment was in his hometown only doubled the stakes.

The station and its success was his main aim right now. It had to receive his full attention. Failure was, quite simply, not an option.

He could hear his father's voice as clearly as if he were sitting next to him, *"You have always been an either-or fellow, haven't you, Jack?"*

He'd been right.

Either he joined the rugby team or he joined the Aussie rules team.

Rugby.

Either he put Engleton Station on the map or he turned down the posting.

Map.

Either he accepted responsibility for his mother's death the day of the fire or he—

No. That hadn't been his fault. That's what the facts said anyway. Too bad his father didn't see things the same way. If he hadn't run round the back of the barn, outside his mother's sight, she might not have entered the barn. Then again, she might have. She'd loved the horses as much as he had. It had been their secret meeting point. If ever Jack had been escaping another how-to-run-the-winery lesson from his father, his mum had known exactly where he'd be. The stables. He hadn't ridden a horse once since then. Or discovered the love his sister had for running River's Bend.

Either he ran the winery his father's way, turning his back on the CFS, or he left River's Bend, leaving his sister to pick up the reins.

Even that seemed to be going wrong.

Seeing Liesel had been a bad idea. He was 100 percent certain he had not been 100 percent focused tonight. He just couldn't keep his thoughts away from Liesel. What it would be like to run his fingers through her hair. Tasting her, touching her, falling into a first-class sensory overload. Having Liesel in his life simply wasn't going to work if he couldn't focus.

"Earth to Jack."

"Yeah, mate—sorry?" Jack tried to snap himself back into the room.

"Who is she?"

"Who?"

"The girl—the woman—you're mooning over. I haven't seen such a dopey expression on your face in—well, ever." The chief tugged a blanket over his shoulders, appearing visibly amused with himself for having hit all the right buttons.

"She's not— It's not what you think. She's a nurse I'm trying to persuade to volunteer down at the station. Just putting in a bit of personal time with her to talk her through how it all works."

Yeah, right! Who's going to buy that load of malarkey?

"Don't worry, mate." The chief stuck a ringed finger out from under the khaki blanket and wiggled it in front of Jack's dumbstruck face.

Obviously not the chief.

"Twenty-two years in February. She made us get married on Valentine's Day so I wouldn't forget the anniversary."

"Clever." No way he was going to contribute more to this conversation. Holes were getting dug everywhere and he didn't have the energy to dig himself out.

"That she is, mate. That she is." The chief rolled over toward the wall, throwing a few words over his shoulder as he went. "Just make sure your girl can handle your lifestyle—because the fire service is in your blood. That's one thing about you she won't be able to change."

Jack pulled his unlaced boots off and tugged on a fresh T-shirt but his guaranteed shut-eye from a few minutes ago was off the radar now. From a casual night out to advice on long-term wedded bliss. *Thanks a million, Chief!*

CHAPTER FIVE

IT HAD BEEN four days and…Liesel flicked her eyes up to the office wall clock clicking away the slow-motion seconds…ten and a bit hours since Jack had dropped her and Liam off and she hadn't heard a peep since. Despite her best efforts, each time the phone rang, her entire body responded with a whoosh of adrenaline and an accelerated heartbeat.

A huge chunk of her wanted to shake off her concerns and ring him or at least drop him a thank-you note—to just go for it and see what sparks might fly between them. Maybe even have a good old-fashioned snog!

The other part? Not quite ready to part with her fears over his chosen profession. If she was truly being sensible, Jack Keller wasn't an option in the romance department. She didn't want to date. Didn't want to hang out. She wanted to fall madly in love and start a proper family with someone. How did you put all of that in a greeting card?

Maybe she should just choose the teenager way of dealing with it and blank him. Out of sight, out of mind—problem solved!

She tipped her chin up and closed her eyes to try it out. A vision of Jack in his formfitting CFS T-shirt tangoed past her closed lids. He moved in closer, took her face in his big man hands and lowered his mouth to—

Hmm. That plan might need some work.

"What's got you so blue?"

Cassie's high-beam smile failed to lighten her mood. Liesel pointed at a stack of paperwork on her desk.

"More data entry." She made a stab at returning the toothy grin still shining away at her from the doorway. "The joys of nursing!"

"Not enough excitement for you out here in the back of Bourke, Miss Adler?" Cassie waggled a reproachful finger at Liesel then placed it on the side of her nose, her face settling into a reflective pose. "Or could it be there hasn't been enough action with the local fire department?"

Liesel scrunched up a scrap of paper and threw it at her friend, trying her best to laugh away the accusation. "Don't be ridiculous." *Was she that easy to read?*

Cassie's attention shifted abruptly from Liesel to someone behind her. "What are you doing out of class, mate? I hope it wasn't another fight." Liesel couldn't make out the mystery boy's muttered response. "Are you all right, love?"

Liesel shot out of her chair. Cassie's tone was not good. Neither was the scene playing out in front of her office door.

"Kev? Kev, what's going on, love?"

Cassie was on the floor, kneeling by her ashen-faced son, who was doubled up in obvious agony. Cassie's face was wreathed in terror. Liesel felt the familiar coils of fear start to constrict her own breathing. She knew part of her job was to provide calm in a situation like this, to embody common sense and active pragmatism, but seeing Kev gasping for breath was overreaching the parameters of her remit of scraped knees and brushing a few tears away. It wasn't outside her training, though. And there was no time to lose.

"What's going on? He doesn't have asthma!" Cassie's

voice was low but the tone screamed volumes. Kev needed help. "Call an ambulance, Cass. Now."

Liesel dropped to her knees, fingers flying to Kev's carotid artery to check his pulse. It was racing and anyone could see he was barely getting any breath with each painful attempt to inhale. She placed hands lightly on either side of his chest. One definitely responded more than the other as he fought for breath. Collapsed lung. It had to be.

Primary spontaneous pneumothorax.

Liesel had seen it before. When a fast-growing, lanky teen like Kev had yet another growth spurt not all of the organs had a chance to catch up and occasionally a tiny tear in the outer part of the lung allowed air to escape, which would then get trapped between the lung and the chest wall.

"Hurts…" Kev wheezed the word out.

"I know. You're going to be all right. We're going to patch you up but you're going to have to stay as calm as possible to help slow your breathing down. I think you're just working on one lung right now, okay, Kev?"

Kev's eyes flew wide open, a sheen of sweat visibly breaking out on his forehead. Liesel wanted to bite her tongue the moment the words were out. She was there to calm him down, not distress him more.

The truth of the matter was this was a dangerous situation and, without help arriving soon, any number of problems could arise. His heart rate was fast and if it went over one hundred and thirty-five beats a minute Kev could quickly begin to suffer from tachyarrhythmia. He was young, but even a teenager needed a steady flow of blood and oxygen to the heart and body. Without it, permanent tissue damage to the heart and brain could begin to occur in as little as three to four minutes. Next came the kidneys—

"He's on his way."

"Who?"

"Jack Keller. The closest proper ambo is an hour's drive away."

"What?"

"The hospital always uses the CFS when they don't have anyone around."

"We'd be just as well driving to the hospital ourselves, then. What is it, about twenty minutes away?"

"More. He said he's bringing the station's paramedic SUV. It's part of the Community Emergency Response Unit and we can put on the lights and siren. He'll get us there faster."

Liesel sat back on her heels, mind racing. If Kev did, in fact, have a collapsed lung, he must have waited some time to come to her for help. He would've felt some tugging in his chest, tightening, possibly a whoosh of air and further tightening until the condition began presenting itself as it was now. Very seriously.

She locked eyes with Cassie. "We've got to keep Kev as calm as possible. Technically, as a school nurse, I am not allowed to administer aid to him but, in the same vein, I have a duty of care to help him if there is no one around to do so. I believe there's air in his pleural space—"

"What's that? I don't know what you're talking about, Liesel!"

"It's air trapped outside his lung by the chest wall." She gave Cassie a moment to steady her own breathing and blink back some tears. "We're going to get through this, all right?"

"That's right, Cassie, you couldn't ask for a better trauma nurse. I've seen this one in action."

And there he was. Brigade Captain Jack Keller. Filling the doorway with his six-foot-something good looks. Capable, calm, ready for action and completely off-limits.

* * *

"Is the gurney locked in?"

"Securely." Jack gave Liesel a quick nod and glanced at Cassie. "You're going to want to buckle up for this, Cass. All right?" Without waiting for an answer, he closed the back door of the enormous SUV, quickly jumped in the front, threw a few switches, and, lights in full swing, they shot past the school principal, who was soberly waving them off.

"What's our ETA?"

Liesel was grateful she didn't have to shout over any sirens. The roads were relatively clear out here and the lights on their own should give other drivers ample warning.

"Ten to fifteen minutes, traffic pending. Are you going to be all right?" Jack's eyes were firmly on the road but Liesel knew his mind was on the patient. It wasn't looking good. Kev was presenting all the signs of a tension pneumothorax, a life-threatening condition. This was different from a spontaneous pneumothorax, which often occurred when just sitting or resting. Kevin had managed to tell them he'd been out on play break with the other students when the pain had started.

She looked down at him, an oxygen mask secured loosely to his mouth. There were no telltale signs he'd been in another fight. That would've been her first guess. His last set of black eyes had faded and he showed no other external injuries.

She gave the elastic band a small tug, ensuring Kev could get maximum airflow. The large SUV was kitted out to the nines for emergency medical scenarios, just the sort of vehicle she would've wanted if she'd— Nope. Not going there. At the very least she could thank her lucky stars they hadn't attempted the drive on their own. Avoiding face time with Jack wasn't worth risking Kev's life. The teen was definitely going to need more assistance than she could offer and the oxygen tank was vital. She knew they'd be safe in Jack's hands. Whatever her personal feelings were, he was a professional you could depend on.

When they arrived at hospital, she was certain Kev would need immediate attention—specifically, a needle aspiration. Liesel had only witnessed it being done, had assisted. It was generally a doctor's job to insert the needle into the chest cavity in order to release the trapped air. Some doctors preferred to use tubing in the chest but research she'd seen in her nurses' journal had proven it to be more traumatic for the patient and generally increased the hospital stay. She hoped the Murray Valley Hospital was up to date on that front, for Kevin's sake.

"Do you think it was the other kids? The ones from last time?"

"Sorry, Cass?"

"Do you think he was roughed up by those lads again?"

Liesel shook her head at her friend, confused. "I don't think this has anything to do with a fight. Besides, I thought it was the other way round."

Cassie huffed out a solitary "Ha!" before letting her head fall into her hands.

"What's going on Cassie?"

"They're bullying *him*, Liesel." Cassie's eyes were filled with anguish as she continued. "He puts on such a brave face, trying to be the man of our family, but the boys are relentless. I told him to be bigger, better than they are by not fighting back, but if I've put him in danger…" A ragged sob filled the closed space in the back of the SUV.

Liesel reached over Kev and squeezed her friend's shoulder. "You don't know that. Let's wait until we hear the whole story."

Returning her focus to Kevin, Liesel's eyes shot wide open, alarm bells ringing dangerously. Kev's chest had become distended and after a quick check she confirmed his trachea had deviated to the opposite side of the collapsed lung. This was a sign ER teams usually only found when examining X-rays. But Jack was thin enough that she could see the shift of location despite the fact it was located behind the sternum. She pulled off Kevin's oxygen mask and checked for breath. They didn't have time to wait anymore.

"Jack. Pull over."

He didn't wait to hear it a second time.

"What do you need?"

"I am going to have to aspirate Kevin's chest. The risk of the car hitting a bump while I'm inserting the needle is too high." She heard him snap back the seat belt and pull open his door as she signaled to Cassie that she would be best out of the car while she did it.

"I want to stay here."

"Please, Cassie—you'll be right outside the car. Just give us a few minutes. It's all we need." Liesel felt horrible as she made her friend climb out of the back of the SUV, but this was a first-time procedure for her and Kevin's life depended on it. She needed absolute focus. Jack was in her place before she'd taken in Cassie's absence.

"What can I do?"

Liesel was already pulling on gloves and protective face- and eyewear, which had been easily visible in the vehicle's storage boxes.

"Can you find a fourteen-gauge over the needle catheter that's about three to six centimetres long?"

"Give me a minute."

"We don't have a minute."

"I'm here to help, Liesel. Not hinder." His voice was quiet, reassuring. He handed her the needle catheter with hands already sheathed in the precautionary blue gloves. One glimpse into his clear eyes and she knew it was true. Knew Jack's presence added to her confidence. He was the one her mind had leaped to when she'd needed confidence with Mrs. Dales. And he was here for her again. She felt a charge of the old Liesel flash through her. She could do this.

Liesel made a lightning-fast scan of the storage boxes. She couldn't see any devices for creating a one-way valve, an essential part of the procedure. She'd have to use an EMS trick Eric had taught her. She grabbed a protective glove and ripped off a finger, quickly inserting the IV catheter into the sterile nitrile.

"Is there any saline solution?"

"Just over here." They had a rhythm now, a cadence to their work. Fluid, swift, focused.

Liesel pulled a ten-millimeter syringe out of its sterile packaging, quickly drawing five millimeters of the saline into it. Here, on the side of the road with traffic passing by, she couldn't be sure she'd hear the gush of escaping air when she inserted the catheter needle into Kevin's chest. If—*when*—she hit the right spot, the air would create bubbles in the saline, giving her a visible indicator she had done the job properly.

"Can you cut open Kevin's T-shirt, please?" She would need full access to his chest. Inserting the needle in exactly the right spot was vital. The midclavicular line. Inserting it into the medial sternal or axillary lines could only worsen an already bleak scenario.

"Stay with us, Kev. We're going to help you, mate."

Jack's rich voice was like a soothing tonic in the charged atmosphere of the SUV. She knew the words were meant for Kevin, but they were just what she needed as she palpated her fingers downward from the teen's collarbone to his third rib. There was no messing this up. She held the loose "finger" of glove over the needle, having wiped antiseptic over the midclavicular line she'd marked with a pen. She needed to direct the needle into the intercostal space just above the third rib and nowhere else.

She glanced up at Jack, his eyes the only thing visible above the protective face mask he'd pulled on. She could see the confidence in them as he nodded at her. She felt a charge of readiness and pulled herself into a strong-seated position.

Poising the IV needle over the small "X," she held her breath, steadied her hand and inserted it through his skin with a quick, sure movement. Almost instantaneously the fluid in the syringe began to bubble. It wasn't over yet, but they had won the first major battle. She lifted her eyes up to Jack's questioning gaze, only trusting herself to answer him with an affirmative nod.

She waited until the bubbling stopped then withdrew the needle, leaving the "finger" of glove in the puncture wound to act as an exit valve until they got to the hospital. She disposed of the needle in the sharps box attached to the wall of the cab and quickly taped the blue glove finger into place. It wasn't pretty—but it was functional and that's what counted.

"Can I look?" Cassie's head peeped round the corner of the back door.

Jack's long legs unfolded themselves from the back of the vehicle to make room. Liesel resecured the pure-flow oxygen mask to Kevin's mouth and, out of the corner of her eye, saw that Jack had folded the worried mother in his arms.

"He's going to be all right, Cassie. I'm sure of it. Why don't you jump in the back again and we can get your boy to Valley Medical?" She could hear the relief and conviction in Jack's voice that Cassie's son would be all right. If there was some way she could tap into his confidence and let it refill her own depleted resources, she would do it in an instant.

The women rode in focused silence in the back of the vehicle, each holding one of Kevin's hands, after Jack gave them a seven-minute ETA.

Liesel caught Jack's eye every now and again in the rearview mirror. She'd tried to stop herself from looking, but found she couldn't help herself. What was she, seventeen again?

It seemed ridiculous, but Liesel felt as though she was drawing new stores of confidence and positive energy each time their eyes locked. The surges of certainty she felt about her nursing skills when she was with Jack were exactly what she'd been missing at the A and E unit. It felt amazing. Was this what change felt like?

Liesel suddenly felt like turning a thousand thoughts into action. Finding a permanent home for herself and her son. No more relying on her mother and father. She wanted to push the limits on her nursing skills, really find out what she was capable of. Maybe even reconsider Jack's offer to go down to the CFS? At the very least, she knew she wanted to explore whatever it was that was zinging between her and Jack. A glimpse, a light touch, a brushing of lips… She pressed her eyes shut, the memory of their aborted attempt at displaying CPR pinging front and center in her mind's eye.

Her body felt as though it was awakening after a long, long winter. Her loose cotton top made of eyelet fabric played over her skin, bringing out a shiver of heightened awareness. When she had pulled on the royal-blue top that morning, the last thing in the world it had seemed was sexy, but now, fully aware of Jack's glances back into the cabin of the vehicle, it suddenly felt sensual. The tiny holes in the fabric exposing miniature flashes of skin. Had he noticed? Her eyes pinged wide open. She really wanted him to notice. She felt like dancing. And kissing. Was he feeling the same way? Or was she just hallucinating this entire "thing" between them?

Her eyes intuitively flickered to the vehicle's rearview mirror. There they were. Those bright blue eyes. Watchful. Assured. And giving her a long, slow wink.

Jack loved moments like these. The successful handover to the emergency department. A moment to know you'd done your job and done it well.

Cassie was at the reception area, giving her son's details, and the emergency department doctor was giving Kevin a once-over before shifting him onto a hospital gurney.

"Looks like you saved this young fellow's life. How long have you been an emergency medical responder?"

"I'm not." Jack shook his head regretfully. "I started the training in Adelaide, then got a transfer before I could complete it."

"Then how did you learn this trick?" The doctor pointed at the tip of the rubber glove, still doing its job in Kevin's chest.

Jack shifted his eyes from the ED doctor's approving gaze to Liesel. He tipped his head in her direction. "It was this talented young woman here."

"Impressive." He nodded approvingly at Liesel then called behind him for a couple of medics to help with a transfer. "Have you been in the Country Fire Service long?"

Jack watched Liesel stiffen at the question then try to laugh off her reaction. "Not me. I'm just the school nurse."

"But where'd you learn that technique? I've seen it on the internet, but only from North American sources."

Liesel went quiet for a moment, her fingers playing along the rail of Kevin's gurney. "Someone from America taught me."

Jack didn't know who that someone was, but from the change of her tone they had been pretty important to her. He'd heard she'd worked in America through Cassie, but had she also left her heart there? He hoped not. He knew a relationship was the last thing he needed right now, but logic didn't stop him from hoping Liesel was available. If he were a finger-crossing man, he'd be doing it right now.

"You've got a lot of valuable training behind you for a school nurse. We could easily use you here at the Valley Med or on the EMR team. Blimey, I'm surprised Jack here hasn't recruited you yet."

"Believe me, I have tried. She's rebuffed my every advance." He leaned against a nearby pillar, crossing his arms over his chest and hoping he looked more casual than keen. Because he was more than keen. On a number of levels.

"Did that include convincing this young man to detach a lung for you?" The doctor grinned down at his new patient, who, to Jack's surprise, gave him a half-wilted thumbs-up.

"Deal's a deal, mate." Jack played along. "You're guaranteed a spot on the cadet force as soon as you're up and running."

At that Liesel nearly choked. She knew it was a fiction, but still! Besides, the reminder of Eric had served its purpose. She was giving this sort of stuff a wide berth for a reason. Right?

"I appreciate the effort, Kev, but I could've saved you the trouble. If I wanted to be recruited, I would be in uniform already. Keep it low level next time, all right?"

"He's all checked in." Cassie breathlessly appeared by her son's hospital gurney.

"Right! Let's get to an exam room, see about getting this glove out of Kevin's chest and try to reinflate that lung." The doctor gave Jack and Liesel a final nod of thanks before wheeling the gurney down the hall.

* * *

If he had thought he'd stood a chance to get her into the CFS before, Jack was hearing loud and clear that she wasn't interested. What was stopping her, exactly? She obviously had the skills and her crisis management was top rate. He watched as Liesel's feline eyes followed Kev's gurney through to the double doors leading to the surgery department. Pure class. And seemingly intent on turning him down.

She was clearly talented. What was holding her back? Was it worth one final push? He'd have to test the waters with care.

He shook his head. What was wrong with him? Was he doing this for the station or for himself? Both, definitely—but the fact that he kept pursuing her was a pretty big clue that the scales were definitely weighted in one direction. If he recruited her, then he was guaranteed to see her all the time and that was an idea he liked the sound of. A lot. Then again, if relationships were off-limits, having her in his crew would be like having the best bottle of wine in the world uncorked in front of him and being told he couldn't have any.

He tried to shrug off the maze of conflicting thoughts. Fine wine, he concluded, was worth waiting for.

"I guess I'd better get you back to school, miss." Jack unfolded his arms, pushing himself away from the pillar with his foot.

"We're back to 'miss,' are we? After all we've been through?" He could tell she'd been going for a jokey tone, but there was more meaning behind the light words and her bright smile.

"Liesel." His voice had gone deeper than he'd anticipated and the space separating them suddenly seemed minute. He could smell the wildflower freshness of her skin as the whir of activity surrounding them seemed to still to a slow-motion hush. In seconds he could be holding her in his arms, willing whatever made her so very sad to go away. He watched as a soft flush rose to her cheeks and as suddenly as the moment had come between them, it flashed away.

Liesel glanced at her watchless wrist, laughed and then scanned the room for a clock.

"It's just past four," Jack interrupted, even though her search for a clock had given him more time to drink her in.

"I think I've missed the final bell." Liesel threw him a *yikes* expression and shrugged.

"Good." Jack scooped up her small hand and tucked it into the crook of his arm. "That means I can take you out for a congratulatory milk shake."

"I really should get back…"

She wavered just enough to give him the confidence to have another go.

"C'mon, we can pick up a couple of shakes and I'll show you my favorite spot on the river."

He could see she was tempted. Even though he saw the hints of that pinky blush coloring her cheeks again. He could guarantee that if she really knew what he was thinking, her color would definitely deepen. Him, Liesel, a warm spring evening down by the river. Anything could happen…

"I've got to pick up Liam."

Jack stopped in his tracks. Liam! Of course. He was an idiot to forget. "Where is he? We could pick up the little man and bring him along."

"Really?"

Jack nodded his head in the affirmative, loving it when he saw the sparkle in her eye. If just a fraction of that was for him—

"You're sure you wouldn't mind? He's just at the school nursery. The latest they can keep him is four-thirty."

"I guess we'd better hit the road, then."

Liesel felt as if she was floating on a big, bouncy cloud of happiness. She tried to wipe the dreamy expression off her face as she tucked in Liam but as she replayed the evening's picnic down by the river, keeping the smile off her lips proved impossible.

She pulled the door to her sleeping son's room shut and began to tiptoe back to the veranda. Jack had insisted on waiting out there, settling into a cushioned deck chair to "keep an eye on the river," even though she'd insisted he was welcome to come in.

"It wouldn't be proper," he'd said, as if he were a character in an English costume drama. Old-fashioned manners, straight-up-her-alley good looks… He'd even wiped a dab of mustard off her chin after a particularly greedy mouthful of artisan sausage. Who knew a tiny gesture could get her all shivery?

It was absolutely ridiculous how she reacted to his slightest touch and how spending time with him seemed to blur the rest of the world into a fuzzy haze. Considering she'd had just about every single one of her danger-zone buttons pushed that day, it was a wonder she hadn't just accepted his last-minute offer to opt out of the picnic, be dropped off at home and crawl into bed with Liam curled up beside her and a hot mug of chamomile tea.

It appeared Jack knew her better than she knew herself. A picnic by the river, her son whooping it up with all the kookaburras before devouring his tea, not to mention a first-rate chocolate milk shake to recharge her batteries. Maybe it was as simple as having a couple of hours off not to think about Kevin and the high anxiety she'd felt as she'd dealt with his collapsed lung.

As she looked back on the afternoon, she was beginning to see that instead of feeling a terror that she'd stepped into hostile territory by reverting to her trauma nurse days, she should feel confident and proud of what she had done. This was twice now that she'd been forced out of her comfort zone and had found herself...comfortable. And, truthfully, she hadn't been *forced* out of her comfort zone. She just hadn't fled—which had been her default position up to now. She was a good nurse and using her skills came naturally. Kevin could have died if it hadn't been for her quick diagnosis and treatment. A technique she wouldn't have known about if it hadn't been for Eric.

She pressed her eyes shut, willing herself to have the strength to always love Eric but somehow move forward. She knew she had to. Not just for Liam but for herself. It was just a question of *when*.

Ha! So much easier thought than done.

She opened her eyes again, quietly making her way into the kitchen to drop off Liam's nighttime bottle. She turned in the growing darkness of the kitchen, eyes adjusting to the remains of the evening's light.

She could see Jack's silhouette through the screen door. He'd hitched a hip up onto the veranda's railing, his long back supported against a post, looking as happy as could be, while the sun set beyond him among the tangle of gum and eucalyptus trees.

If time were her plaything she would've stayed there for ages. Just looking at him made her feel all zingy with feminine response. Not bad for a five-meter gap. She had never seen someone who looked more comfortable in their own skin. He stretched an arm across his body, pulling his knee up along the railing. The movement cinched up the T-shirt, which didn't do a very good job of disguising his well-defined biceps. Her eyes ran along the broad spread of his shoulders and slipped up to his face. As if he felt her watching him, he turned and met her gaze. She felt herself soften, a warm swirl of heat gathering in her belly.

"This is an amazing place you've got here."

"I wish it were mine." Liesel pushed the screen door open, praying he hadn't seen how much she'd been ogling him.

"It's my parents' place. They bought it a few years ago to be their retirement fund." Jack raised a curious eyebrow. "You know, a holiday cottage for people wanting to spend some time out in wine country, or enjoy the river."

"Wise move. They sound like good folk."

"They're great. I can't imagine what I…what we—I mean, Liam and I—would've done without them these past few years."

"Oh?"

Jack raised an interested eyebrow. Liesel wavered. They were having such a lovely evening. She didn't want to go there. She didn't want to rehash recent history when all of the sudden the future seemed like something she could begin to imagine.

"They're brilliant grandparents!" *Good dodge, Liesel!* She shifted her gaze away from Jack's. "Anyhow, we need to move on come summer so they can collect their holiday rent—but I can't tell you how grateful I am for their generosity." Liesel smiled warmly.

Before Eric, before Liam, she'd been the opposite of a planner. She'd traveled all around the world, seeking out youthful thrills, pushing her nursing skills to the limit and scraping the bottom of her savings account to make ends meet.

It was hard not to feel wistful about the young woman she had been not so long ago. Young, brave, ready to make a difference. Undefeatable. So much had changed.

"They say you don't choose your family, but it seems

your parents did a pretty good job of endowing you with their sensibilities. You're lucky to be so close."

Was that a hint of sadness in his eyes? Or the setting sun? Hard to tell, but something flashed there.

"They do a mean yabby bake. My parents."

Jack swung round, planting both feet solidly on the wooden floor. "Do they now? That sounds like a bit of a challenge."

"I thought you were a city boy." Liesel accepted the dare, relieved just to be having fun again. "What do you know about a good old-fashioned yabby bake?"

"I've spent a bit of time on the river."

"Oh, yeah?" Liesel dismissed the second twitch of darkness she thought she saw flash across his eyes.

"Yeah. I live on a houseboat."

"Seriously? I always wondered what type of person lived on a houseboat."

"Well, you're looking at a Class A example."

Liesel couldn't help but give a snort of laughter. She doubted there was anyone alive who could make living on a houseboat seem sexier than Jack.

"You doubting my status as Old Man Murray River?"

"You bet I am."

"Then you'd better prove it to me."

Liesel merrily crossed the veranda toward him, hand extended. "I bet you I can out-yabby you any day of the week."

Jack rose to his full height, reaching out a large hand to meet her much smaller one. A crackle of electricity zigzagged up her arm and played across her chest as their fingers connected.

"Winner picks the prize?"

Had his voice gone husky? Liesel's eyes met his. The deep lake blue of them was so inviting she felt as if she could dive straight in. If she could stop the world right now, she would.

"Within reason." Her voice was barely a whisper.

"What kind of man do you take me for?" He closed the space between them with a deliberate step. The honeysuckle breeze wove between them, almost tangibly filling in the ever-decreasing pockets of space. Liesel felt her breath quicken. Her eyes flicked to his chest. Still gorgeous, but safer than his eyes.

"A pretty nice one." *Lame! That was pathetic, Liesel!*

"That's a relief." Jack reversed his stride, still holding her hand as he sat back down on the veranda railing. She found herself willingly responding to the gentle tug on her arm and stepped into the opening between his legs. She and Jack were at an easy eye level. Tiny crinkles appeared round his eyes as his face softened with a slow smile. Her fingertips twitched with a desire to trace along them. The air between them felt alive with the pleasurable tension of sexual attraction. Her gaze dropped to his lips. She felt another ribbon of heat tease its way through her, swirling in slow undulations below her waist.

A parrot called in the distance. A burst of laughter sounded from across the river. A family playing a board game? It was all a blur. The only thing Liesel was fully aware of was Jack. It was all she could do not to slip a hand, both hands, into that thick blond hair of his. Explore it with her fingertips then draw them down along his neck, thumbs grazing the strong angles of his jaw before feeling her way toward the well-defined spread of shoulders.

Her eyes flickered back to his. She felt her lips part, her tongue wetting her bottom lip then retreating, unprepared to make the first move. She hadn't done this for a long time. Standing here, in the thickening silence, everything felt incredibly new. A first-time experience. A sudden longing flooded her entire body. A desire to move forward, to experience new things. Jack's bright blue eyes sought—what was it, permission? She didn't know what hers were saying in return, but as her back made the smallest of arches toward him, as if being tugged in his direction, he tipped his head down and, oh, so gently rested his forehead on hers.

They stood like that for a moment, as if each of them was trying to let their mind catch up with what their body was calling out for.

He was so close. *So perfectly close.*

Liesel felt Jack's fingers unwrap themselves from around her hand then slip one by one onto her waist. It was all she could do not to roll her hip toward him and whisper, "More." She felt his breath on her cheek. A physical ache began to pulse through her. As if reading her mind, Jack's fingers guided her in closer, her hips grazing the sides of his parted thighs. The fabric of her skirt suddenly felt incredibly thin, hot sparks of heat on her hips and thighs teasing at her very core.

Her back arched instinctively more fully toward him as, in a single fluid moment, his lips met hers. She drew in a breath and began to tentatively explore. His full lips moved in complete synchronicity with her own. Soft, curious, intimate. She didn't know how, but he tasted like the beach.

Any doubts she'd had about kissing Jack slipped through the floorboards as if she had shed an overheavy winter coat. All she could feel now was Jack. His lips tasting, teasing her own, not into submission but into a sensual communion. He spread the fingers of a broad hand across the small of her back, the other slipping up her spine, his thumb shifting along the delicate curve of her neck until it came to rest in the shallow hollow at its peak, where his fingers tangled themselves among the curls at the back of her head.

She felt tiny in his arms, delicate, safe. Her breasts

grazed lightly across his chest, her nipples responding with a lightning-quick response. She felt her hips push into his hands as he wrapped his fingers round them, firmly holding her in place. Unable to resist, she pressed into him, her lips seeking more, her fingers finally able to thread themselves through that deliciously thick, sun-bleached hair of his. She had to stop herself from tipping back her head and letting out a full-throated laugh of delight. She was kissing Jack Keller! It was better than she had let herself imagine. He smelled amazing—like burnt-sugar caramel—he tasted sexier and she wanted more.

Jack had to resist the urge to scoop Liesel up in his arms, carry her into her bedroom and have his incredibly wicked way with her. As each moment passed, resisting was becoming a greater challenge.

A low moan escaped his lips as he felt her breasts sweep against the thin cotton of his T-shirt. There was little doubt her body was responding to his touch. If she were to press in much closer, Liesel would be just as aware of the effect she was having on him. A full-blooded, inescapably male response to her incredibly sexy figure.

Her slim waist? Perfect for tracing with an index finger. He felt his thumb graze the underside of her breast and her body tipping toward him at the sensation. He buried his head in the crook of her neck and shoulder, as pure white as the driven snow, fighting the urge to relieve her top of its bright red buttons.

Willpower, Jack. She's worth the wait.

He couldn't resist tracing his lips along the creamy length of her neck, his teeth taking a cheeky tug at her earlobe as his hands made a slow-motion journey from her collarbone, down her sides to her hips. As he kissed her, he could feel a low groan of satisfaction vibrate along her throat, a soft rush of air crossing her kiss-swollen lips.

He drew both his hands along her back, his fingers tracing upward as he teased more soft kisses out of her. Suddenly unable to resist his body's desire for more, he pulled his thumbs along her jawline, drawing her even closer to him, daring her to meet the passionate intimacy of the kisses he wanted to give her. His teeth tugged softly at her lower lip. He took a deep breath of her sun-warmed meadowy scent, tongue tracing the deep red contours of her rosebud mouth. Her tongue met his in teasing little suggestions that she could give as well as receive. He felt her small fingers slip away from his hair, her fingertips playing along his time-enhanced five o'clock shadow. He tipped his chin up as first her lips then her tongue teased its way down his throat toward his Adam's apple. He heard himself respond with a deep moan of carnal approval.

Crikey. She was really bringing out the caveman in him. And he liked it. Jack captured both sides of her face in his hands and held her back for a moment, eyes caught in each other's gaze, each of them taking deep lungfuls of river air. Did she want him as badly as he wanted her? This could go further—much further. Her eyelids quickly shifted from a sexy feline smolder to a wide-eyed question. It was then that he felt the beeper buzzing against his leather belt.

Fire. He had to go.

CHAPTER SIX

GIVING A GRIN and a wave to Jack as he headed off to the fire had taken incredible willpower. Liesel knew she had only just managed a halfhearted attempt to look cheerful at best.

She flipped the security hook onto the screen door and let herself sink back into the deep sofa cushions. Evening over!

Her fingers lifted to her lips. She could still feel the heat in them, the tiniest of pulses waiting, wanting more. Who was she kidding? Her whole body was virtually vibrating with desire for the man. Desire unfulfilled and, from the looks of things, likely to stay that way. She tipped her head back against the headrest, willing herself not to cry.

You are bigger and better than this. It's what he does for a living so just...just...just what?

Get over it?

Hard to do.

Don't see him ever again?

Possible, but not easy, considering the local population head count.

Suck it up and see where this goes, even though it's facing all your fears at once?

And we're back to "get over it."

Her fingers dangled over the edge of the sofa and grazed

the surface of the telephone. Cassie! She would know what to do. Bless her, the poor woman had been left high and dry by a no-goodnik husband a couple of years earlier and she had hit the dating train—such as it was out here—as if it was the last caboose out of town. She was always positive, open to new ideas and didn't seem to get knocked back when things didn't work out. "Aim high and stay true!" Her familiar motto rang in Liesel's ears as she dialed her friend's number.

"And how can I help you tonight, Miss Adler?" Liesel laughed at her friend's greeting. She always forgot about caller ID.

"Hey, Cass, I'm in a bit of a bind. I just…um…" How should she put this exactly?

"I knew it! I knew it would be today!" Cassie interjected.

"Knew what?"

"You kissed the fireman!"

"Are you sure Kev doesn't mind?"

"Are you kidding? He is living the life of Riley up at Murray General. He's their star patient." Cassie dipped her finger into the cookie-dough bowl and took a swirl of the mixture onto her finger as if it were icing. "Plus, he's got the promise of some of your delicious baking first thing tomorrow. We both love it that you bake when you're upset."

Liesel couldn't help sticking her tongue out at her friend.

"Besides, he gets a whole hospital full of doctors to make sure he doesn't go all crazy deflating-lung boy on me again." Cassie concluded her statement by licking the remains of the dough off her finger with a wide smile of satisfaction.

Liesel laughed, happy to see her friend back in good spirits after the day's extreme stresses. Talk about wrenching! She was surprised Cassie looked as energetic as she did.

"This is a ripper of a recipe, Liesel. The boys are going to love these."

Liesel felt an awkward twist in her stomach. It was just one large blond-haired man she cared about. And that was going to have to stop. Cue: more baking!

"I was thinking of doing a batch of my pecan cinnamon rolls, as well. Those are good anytime of day so it doesn't matter when they get back. I could just drop them off tonight and they could heat them up whenever." Baking for Jack was one thing. Seeing him when she didn't really know where she stood? That was a whole other kettle of fish.

"You know, I was chatting with Jack the other day—"

Liesel's eyes shot up and she felt herself tense. *Oops. There goes my poker face.*

"About *Kevin*," Cassie emphasized heavily, unable to keep the amused grin off her face. "For their CFS cadets thing. I thought it might help give him some confidence. Anyhow, it came up that they are still looking for volunteers."

"No." Liesel's response was solid. "I told you, now that I have Liam, it's just not an option. He's already lost one parent to—"

"I know." Cassie laid a hand on Liesel's arm, steadying her frenzied stirring. "I wasn't talking about going out and fighting fires, you dill. I was talking about the odd shift, cooking for the boys when they come back from a job. You know, make 'em all feel like heroes with your fluffy cinnamon rolls."

Liesel shot her a reluctant look and shook her head. She knew she was being petulant but how was she going to make it clear that she just did not want this in her life? She wanted Liam to have a father again one day—and a guy who went out and fought fires for a living? Not going to work.

"Do you want to see him again? It's not like you've had a fight. He got a call to work." Cassie pressed on. "Do you want a relationship with Jack or not?"

Liesel's nose began to tease her with the telltale prickle and she forced herself to retrain her eyes on the well-beaten cookie dough. It had had enough of a beating and so had she. Cassie had a point. It wasn't as if he'd kissed and fled the scene. He'd held her and caressed her and unleashed a heated swell of sexy feelings she hadn't experienced in a long time. But she still had to play it a little cool. Right?

"Who wouldn't?" Or not so cool. She pulled baking sheets out of the cupboard, actively trying to avoid eye contact with Cassie.

"I really like him. I can't even begin to explain to you how nice—more than nice—it was to be with him. And tonight…"

"Tonight?" Cassie tried to gently tease more out of her.

"Tonight, when we kissed, it was— Oh, I don't know— this is going to sound nuts."

"Takes one to know one," Cassie shot back, encouraging her to continue.

Liesel sent her a teary grin, wiped at her eyes with the back of her hand and began spooning lumps of cookie dough onto her baking trays.

"Tonight, when we kissed, it was as if the universe was saying to me, 'It's all right to move on. You'll always love Eric and the times you had, but it's all right to move on. Especially with a guy like this.' And then Jack's beeper went off and I knew he was going to a fire and all of the sudden the universe was saying exactly the opposite!"

"I think you're giving the universe too much credit."

"Yeah? Well, look where it got me last time I didn't listen!"

Liesel snapped out the words, slapped the tray into the oven, clapped the door shut and began on a second batch. It was all she could do not to scowl at the fluffy combination of butter, flour, eggs, chocolate chips and dark brown sugar. Her love life, or lack of one, might be a disaster, but if she had anything to do with it, the whole of Engleton would be enjoying fresh cookies in the morning.

"Liesel." Cassie softly broke into the silence. "I am listening harder than I ever have. I almost lost my boy today. My son would've died if it hadn't been for you. *That* puts things in perspective."

Tears sprang to Liesel's eyes afresh. How could she have been so thoughtless? She turned to her friend, ashamed of her petulant behavior. Ditching the cookie-dough spoon, she threw her arms around her friend in a big bear hug. "I'm so sorry, Cass. That was a horrible thing for me to say."

Cassie returned the hug with a big squeeze then held her friend out at arm's length. "Look, I can't tell you what to do with your life. But from where I'm standing, you've been itching to get back to the business of *living* for a while and, as far as I can make out, the universe—if that's what's talking to you—is saying here's a perfect chance. Jack couldn't be more gorgeous, he obviously fancies you and, yes, he has a dangerous job. But that's what you're drawn to, Liesel, men who live on the high-octane side of life. It's who *you* are, as well. I saw you today."

Liesel's eyebrows shot up. "I was just doing my job."

"It's a lot more than a job to you. It's your passion—and you like to push it to the limit. I saw the pride in your face when your rubber glove valvey thing worked. You saved my boy and not everyone could have done it. Face it, love, life with an IT guy just wouldn't cut it for you."

Liesel couldn't help but giggle. The local computer genius had tried to ask her out a couple of times, but her gut instinct had said, *I don't think so*, in the blink of an eye. Despite everything, she knew she was more adrenaline junkie than computer geek. She embraced Cassie again, this time with a happy laugh. It was pointless to try and contradict her friend. Cassie had her down to a T.

Jack was bone-tired. He leaned his head against the cool tiles of the shower, grateful to feel the jets of water shooting down his back. They'd been twenty minutes late to the fire. Twenty minutes late meant an easily containable bushfire had nearly spread out of control. Luckily, the wind had been on their side this time. Next time? Luck shouldn't play a role at the CFS. If he hadn't been with Liesel—

"Hey, Cap'n! Get a move on. Breakfast is here!" The shout came over the shoulder-height shower curtain.

"What?" He quickly rinsed the soap off his face. "We don't have anyone scheduled on today."

"Looks like one of the Jack Keller fan club has come to the rescue once again! Hurry up, mate, or I'll eat yours, as well."

"What are you talking about, Nate?" Jack pushed aside the shower curtain, wrapping a towel round his waist.

"Don't play bashful, Captain. Surely you know—"

"Know what?" Jack cut him off, pretty sure he knew what was coming.

"Hey, don't get me wrong." Nate's voice went serious. "We all appreciate how hard it must be to be Ol' Man Gran—I mean, Granville Keller's son. It's a lot of weight to take on your shoulders."

"Right." Jack tried to keep from clenching his jaw. "What was the fan club crack about, then?"

"Nothing, mate. Honestly." Nate raised his hands in surrender. "Us married blokes think it's great you've got the ladies flocking over to cook for us after a big fire, that's all."

Jack tilted his head in the direction of the dining hall. "You best get out there, then."

He toweled off quickly, his hunger diminishing by the second. So the boys saw him as Granville's son before they saw him as captain, did they? He wondered if they still imagined him in short trousers. Was he going to have to prove to his father and the entire population of Engleton that he had grown up and was making something of himself?

He squared himself up, ready to play it cool to whoever the woman was who'd shown up to cook breakfast. He hoped she had a thick skin because today wasn't his day—and if TLC was what she was after, it didn't look as if it was going to be hers, either.

"Smelled so good, I couldn't wait for a shower."

"Please—" Liesel gestured at the laden trestle table just outside the kitchen hutch "—help yourself to as much as you like."

She grinned as the soot-covered man accepted a plate of fresh-off-the-grill eggy bread with a side of bacon. She couldn't help but shoot an anxious look over his shoulder to see if a certain someone had entered the dining hall.

At the very least, she knew her stress baking had come up trumps. Cassie had taken Liam to the hospital to visit Kev so she had been free to chop, dice, bake and scramble in the station's catering-sized kitchen.

Steaming cinnamon rolls, eggy bread, a huge bowl of fresh fruit and a platter of scrambled eggs surrounded by thick-sliced, locally made bacon were all being demolished by the crew. They'd been out all night and were obviously famished.

Liesel gave a chagrined chuckle at the empty kitchen. Cassie may have railroaded her into serving up breakfast to the exhausted volunteers, but she could see from the smiles on their faces she had done the right thing. She hadn't met a lot of people in Engleton these past few months, but it was easy to see these men were part of a proper community. It looked fun out there, all the laughing and gentle joshing despite the obvious fatigue they all felt. Like family.

She couldn't help but wonder what Jack would think of her efforts, if he was there at all. She hadn't seen a single golden whisker since the crew had returned. A little shiver tickled its way down her spine as her fingertips remembered tracing along Jack's soft shadow of stubble.

Before Cassie had come over and knocked some "straight talk" into her, Liesel had been ready to give up the ghost on pursuing a romance with Jack. Stupid or not, she didn't need her innermost fears thrown in her face every time the man's beeper went off.

Yes, she really, really liked him. More than a lot. And so did her son. And Jack seemed to like him, too. Something she didn't take lightly.

In between making batches of baked goods she'd sat down and thought about it. Hard.

Eric had always said she had one shot at "being Liesel" so she'd better make the most of it. She knew she wasn't going to be able to shrug off the past in one fell swoop, but step by step, day by day...

From the snippets of conversation floating through the kitchen hatch, it was clear it had been a tough night but one when no one had been hurt.

Thank you, universe!

An unexpected sexual charge surged through him when Jack laid eyes on Liesel, looking so natural in the stationhouse kitchen. Her clingy sundress didn't help calm his body's response, either. Every fiber in his body wanted to vault through the kitchen hatch, pull the shutters down, lift her up to the counter, dispense of her flimsy dress and begin to kiss and caress her the way he'd wanted to last night.

He tried shrugging off the heated sensations. One thing was for sure. His response to her told him everything he needed to know. If the station was going to work, Liesel was too big a distraction to be in his life right now.

She turned around and spied him, those emerald-green eyes of hers bright with expectation—with hope.

"This is a surprise."

"A nice one, I hope." Her lashes dropped, hiding her expressive eyes, a light pink flush playing along the curves of her cheekbones. *Strewth.* She was about as beautiful as you could get.

"What are you doing here?" *Open mouth, insert enormous boot.*

"I thought I'd see what the CFS was about—but if you'd rather…"

She wasn't flushing with pleasure anymore.

"It's not really the best—"

"You're right," she hurriedly backpedaled. "I shouldn't have come. This was a bad idea."

"No. It's not that. The guys are loving it." He shot a glance over her shoulder then lowered his voice. "Look, I'm sorry about last night—"

"Oh. I see." Her voice was level but were her cheeks flushing a deeper red? Liesel moved as if to turn away.

"Not the…before. The after." This was not going well. *C'mon, Jack. Man up!* "This isn't really the best place for you to be right now."

If he could wipe the hurt from her eyes he would, but he had to get her out of there and clear his head. His gut churned with an overwhelming need to keep Liesel as far away from all of this as possible—the dirt, ash, smoke, fire. As strongly as he'd hoped to get her involved in the station, he now felt a more powerful drive to ensure she was as far away as possible. The thought of putting her in harm's way, of coming into contact with the danger that automatically came with the job, his job? *No.* Not a chance. He didn't think he could bear it if anything happened to her.

Was this how his father felt every time he heard the sirens? How he'd felt after he'd lost his wife? Powerless? Well, Jack had the power and the position to say no. No to all of it. Even if it did feel like stopping one of the best things that had come into his life.

He shot a look at the volunteers, all hard workers who could do with even more support. Liesel was the answer to a professional prayer. But her presence tore at his focus. Not professional.

Lack of focus cost lives.

Lack of focus meant the station would close, endangering the lives and homes of a lot of locals. After losing his mother because there hadn't been enough hands on deck, there was no chance he'd see that happen again. See someone go through the grief his family had endured. His father in particular.

He had to make a choice.

"You have always been an either-or fellow, haven't you, Jack?"

His father's voice rang in his head. A persistent chiseling away at his ability to make the right decision.

He felt as if his heart was being ripped in half.

"Sorry, Liesel, I've got to run."

Liesel inhaled sharply as if all the air had been sucked out of her. She stood stock-still, staring out into the dining hall at the receding back of Jack Keller, certain she looked little short of a first-class idiot.

What had just happened? She couldn't have misread his signals. Could she?

Suddenly feeling acutely aware of the glances being thrown her way, she wondered what she must look like to all of them. A fire station groupie hoping to bring a smile to the lips of the big hunky firemen? Well, fire*man*. And from the way Jack just spoke to her, she'd just been summarily dismissed.

Talk about humiliating! Were there boundaries she was supposed to have known about? Was she supposed to be a secret? The idea made her feel sick.

She watched dumbly as he threw a quick glance over his shoulder and without so much as a smile grabbed a cold drink from the dining hall and left the room.

Liesel felt her cheeks flame up, not with embarrassment this time but anger.

How dare he treat her like that? How *dare* he?

She hadn't been the one popping round with chocolate milk shakes, suggesting spontaneous picnics, pushing her to her professional limits and back again. She hadn't been the one pulling him into her arms and giving her just about the most perfect set of kisses and knee-weakening caresses she could have ever imagined. How *dare* he dismiss her like this?

Liesel curtly turned her back on the dining room and surveyed the kitchen. It looked as if the breakfast fairy had exploded in there.

Fine.

If he didn't want her around, it jolly well wouldn't look as if she'd been anywhere near his precious fire station. Just like a fireman to blow hot and cold. The irony would've made her laugh if she hadn't been so cross. The counter began to appear in moments. Then gleamed. The cupboards? Scrubbed inside and out.

Despite her Herculean efforts, scrubbing Mr. Tall-Blond-and-Way-Too-Handsome out of the kitchen was proving hard. Far too hard. Little thoughts niggled away in her mind. None of Jack's behavior that morning rang true with the man she'd been spending time with. It was well and truly out of character. Or was it? What did she really know about Brigade Captain Jack Keller? She could just howl with fury! It wasn't as if she was falling for the guy or something.

Oh.

Wait a minute.

Was she falling for him?

Hardly. He couldn't have made that much of an impact with his perfectly winning personality, supersexy kisses and too-good-to-be-true good looks. She scrubbed at the long-neglected corners of the refrigerator, certain that steam was pouring out of her ears. The *nerve* of that man!

She had finally thought she was taking massive strides forward. Finally feeling brave enough to move forward with her and Liam's lives—moving out of the fragile egg-shell existence they'd been living. It really was a good thing she couldn't scream in here because she was building up to a proper old-fashioned tizzy.

How *dare* he treat her as if she was some sort of love-sick puppy, desperate for his attention? Lovesick puppy. There it was again. This wasn't looking good.

"Wow, you can do mine next if you like!"

Cassie's voice was a welcome extinguisher to her over-heated thoughts.

"Oh, what happened to *you*? Jack not show up for your big breakfast bonanza? Or did he hate your cooking?"

Liesel knew it was meant to be a joke but it didn't feel anywhere close to being funny. She sat back on her heels, trying to slow her thoughts to a lower gear before respond-ing to Cassie. From the looks of things her friend was al-ready reading her like a well-thumbed book.

"Here's someone who can cheer you up!" Cassie swung Liam's car seat into view, complete with her son, the most committed nap-taker in the southern hemisphere. She felt her body soften, the anger slip away.

"Ohh, it's Liam the Super-Sleeper!" she stage-whispered, before nuzzling her face against the crook of his neck. He smelled like a new beginning. This little guy was the light of her life. He was who she was living for, fighting her demons for. And she couldn't let herself forget that. Not for a second.

"Li-e-se-e-l…" Her friend drew out her name as if it had several syllables. "What's going on?"

"It appears the bushfire wasn't the only fire that was put out last night." Liesel threw a crinkly browed glance in the direction of the dining room.

Cassie lowered herself to the floor alongside Liesel and Liam.

"Spill it."

"C'mon, let's get out of here!" Liesel grabbed her friend's hand. "I've got a better idea."

Jack hit the empty country road, his feet taking full-length strides, temples throbbing with a grade-A headache and thoughts running at full speed. He knew he should be trying to catch up on his sleep but he had to physically work the stresses out of his system.

He couldn't believe he'd just blown Liesel off like a casual fling—and the moment he'd left the station he'd known she meant more to him than that. A lot more.

Up until now it had been easy—too easy—to keep women at arm's length. Throughout his teens he'd never trusted anyone because he'd never known if they'd liked him or if they'd liked John Granville Keller III, heir apparent to River's Bend Winery. As he refocused his energies into making something of himself at the CFS, relationships were the last thing on his mind. Making good on his silent vow to his mother was key to ensure more people didn't die because there wasn't a fire service.

Not that his decision had helped things with his father. Far from it. Granville Sr. had been a changed man after his wife had died. Utterly grief-stricken at the loss of his true love. Jack hadn't understood it at the time, but he was getting a firsthand glimpse into what it was like to lose someone you cared for. The look on Liesel's face after he'd made it clear she wasn't welcome? Awful. It was as close as anything had come to the moment Jack had told his father he'd chosen the CFS over the winery. His father had taken his decision to leave as a full-frontal blow to the legacy his son was meant to have accepted like a golden mantle.

Jack kicked up his speed.

Why couldn't things be easy? When he'd been in Adelaide, he'd been driven—as though his divided energies had finally found a home base. He had been right to have chosen the CFS over running the winery. Becca was amazing at steering River's Bend into the future while he, on the other hand, had been born to fight fires. And then along had come Liesel. Delicate and strong, cream-skinned and flame-haired Liesel, forcing him to confront his either-or existence. He'd made a choice that morning and it didn't feel right.

He forced himself to sprint, enjoying feeling his lungs strain, his legs burn, his arms pump against the warm spring air. When he couldn't take it anymore he stopped, hands falling to his knees so he could catch his breath. When he looked up he started with surprise at seeing where his body had automatically taken him: River's Bend.

Home was where the heart was? There was definitely something to that. Until he fixed things on this front, he didn't know how much good he'd be as a boyfriend to Liesel. *Boyfriend?* Yeah, right. He choked out a laugh. As if she'd let him anywhere near her after his performance that morning. Looked as if his habit of burning bridges was getting even better.

It was the most extraordinary feeling. Being in the hospital. Just wandering the halls was like visiting an old friend.

Liesel had left Liam and Cassie chatting away with a very animated Kevin showing a newfound confidence now that he had a top-of-the-range personal injury story.

She had to smile as he told his mother and the new shift nurse about how all the doctors had deemed his the "coolest pneumothorax" solution they'd ever seen.

Now, strolling the corridors, she could hear snippets of conversation floating from patient rooms, drifting above the high desks of the nurses' stations, snapping rapid-fire from doctor to doctor. All the talk, the hospital banter, had once filled her up like high-octane fuel. It had also been exactly what she'd been avoiding like the plague for the past three years. What had she been so afraid of?

Today it felt like a dose of the perfect medicine. The simple truth was the hospital was familiar terrain and had never failed to assure her she had chosen the right profession. There were so many people to help and to care for—and she knew she was good at it. Working at the school was great, but the electric atmosphere of an emergency department had always been more her style.

Maybe this would be a better place to start putting her fears behind her. A hospital was every bit as much of a community as a fire station. She'd even seen the notice boards filled to the brim with Harvest Festival notices, film nights, exercise classes, all sorts—all promises of things to come once the patients had healed.

All those things were out there for her, too. But had *she* healed?

Realistically, things wouldn't—couldn't—work with Jack. Her main priority was her son and Jack's was the station. He obviously wanted to compartmentalize things in his life—and that was the last thing she wanted. At the very least, she should just enjoy the fact that a deeply gorgeous man had found her attractive enough to pursue—at least for a little while. Despite everything, the grief, the rebuilding, today's supersize disaster, she was still a woman. A desirable one. Which was a good feeling. And if she was going to try to lavish everything with icing, Jack had helped rekindle her passion for medicine. So maybe…

She took a big breath and pushed through the double doors into the ED waiting room. She eagle-eyed a corner seat that would be perfect for surreptitiously watching the action. She glanced at the wall clock. Fifteen minutes. She'd give herself fifteen minutes.

CHAPTER SEVEN

"EXCUSE ME, MISS?"

Liesel didn't have to turn around to identify the young male voice.

"What is it?" She swung around to face Kevin, thankful that she'd bitten back the *this time* she had been going to tease the teenager with. "Wow! Look at you!"

It was probably the first time she'd seen Kevin look shy. And clean-cut. And a part of her felt like begging him to change back to the ragamuffin kid who was in her nurse's office a bit too frequently.

"What do you think of my new threads?" Kevin put on a pose as Liesel took in his immaculate new Country Fire Service Cadets uniform.

"I think you look fantastic!" She didn't have to like the uniform, did she? It seemed ridiculous to admit, but complimenting the uniform was just a bit too close to complimenting a certain Captain Jack Keller. Or Captain Persona Non Grata, as she liked to think of him these days.

"I hate to be a party pooper—but has your doctor approved this?"

"He already said I have to wait to do the ladder training."

When had Kev seen Jack? She'd seen neither hide nor hair of him for five days. Not that she was going to admit to anyone she was missing him. At least her house had benefited. It was sparkling clean. If she could have spring-cleaned her own son, she would have.

As if reading her thoughts, Kevin continued, "Jack came to see me at the hospital after work. He said he's been really busy and would like it if I could be his second in command. You know, in charge of the clipboard, checking all the cadets in and out, that sort of thing, until I'm ready to begin training. Be, you know, like a manager."

Oh. So Jack had thought of everything. And Kevin looked so very proud. The first time she'd seen him this confident in ages.

"So what can I help you with, mate?"

"Mum says would it be all right if you took me to cadets this evening, please? She's got parent-teacher conferences tonight and has to prepare."

"Oh, did she, now?" Liesel raised a suspicious eyebrow.

"Yeah." Kevin looked back at her blankly. He obviously didn't see the thoughts whirling round her head at turbo speed or know his mother's fine-tuned ability for setting Liesel up on dates she had no interest in going on. *And* on the day a seven-year-old had vomited all over her top. Perfect.

"She didn't say anything else?" There had to be more to this than met the eye.

"I don't think so," Kev replied hesitantly, already accustomed to his teenage brain letting him down in the messenger department. His eyes shot up to the ceiling, as if that would help, then returned to Liesel. He gave her a small *I don't know what you're talking about* shrug.

Typical teenager.

Why didn't you tap your mother for the real *reason behind this trip?*

Five ludicrously long days had passed since that ridiculous morning in the fire station and not a peep from Mr.

Hot-and-Not-So-Nice. Guess it was time to start up more tutorials at the school of hard knocks.

She tried unsuccessfully to shake away the sensation of being in Jack's arms.

How could she? Kissing him had made her feel incredibly, beautifully, wonderfully alive.

And had she heard *anything* from him?

Nada. Zilch. Nothing.

She'd recapped the morning at the station again and again as the hours had turned into days. Jack didn't seem the type of man to kiss and run, but, for all she knew, he could have disappeared off the end of the earth and she'd be none the wiser.

Cassie had tried playing Twenty Questions with her—or more like Twenty Excuses of Captain Keller.

"Fire season's kicking into full throttle."

"The man has a phone."

"So do you."

"He blew me off when he last saw me."

"Is that what really happened or is that what you think happened?"

"I'm a girl—I know these things."

"Are you still in high school?"

"Doesn't matter how old you are, a blow-off is a blow-off." Then she had stuck her tongue out at Cassie. It had seemed the right thing to do.

"He's very busy recruiting for the station." Cassie had returned the gesture.

"And he suddenly doesn't need nurses anymore?"

"Yeah, because you were chomping at the bit to take him up on that offer!"

Good point.

Liesel had tried out some of her own.

"He doesn't want a premade family."

"Don't be stupid. You said he had an amazing time with Liam."

"He made a mistake and thinks I'm ugly."

"As I said, don't be stupid. Look in the mirror!"

"He's just not interested."

And Cassie hadn't had anything to say to that. How could she? It wasn't as if either of them had a hotline to Jack and his thought processes.

Served her right. She knew falling for—no, not falling for, just having a crush on…or whatever it was—a guy in the fire service was definitely not for her, and Jack Keller was in the fire service, so out of sight…out of mind?

She felt the wind fall out of her self-righteous sails—he was definitely not out of mind.

"Are you all right, miss?" Kev's voice snapped her out of her reverie.

"Of course! Just having a little daydream!" *A rotten one.*

She scooped up her keys from her desk and grabbed her handbag. Better get it over and done with. "Ready to go?"

Jack recognized the car as it pulled into the station and felt an instant shot of remorse. He was overdue, long overdue, in apologizing to Liesel for his stupid behavior. There was no excuse—well, there were excuses but none that made up for pulling her into his arms, sharing mind-blowing kisses with her and then virtually writing her off the next day at the station. And the one hundred and seventeen or so hours since then. He was going to have to do some serious backpedaling.

He strode toward the car, intent on making things up to her.

"Kev! You sure look sharp, mate."

Was that Liesel already sticking the car into reverse? Wasn't she even going to say hello?

He grabbed hold of the passenger-side door before Kevin could slam it shut.

"Hey, Liesel. How are you going?" *Lame. Lame and pathetic. And cowardly.*

"Late to pick up Liam. Do you mind?" Her head tipped toward the door he was holding open, clearly not interested in chitchat. *And she's back in the ring!*

"Liesel, hang on a second." He held on to the car door, despite the fact he could feel her moving the vehicle slowly back down the sloping station drive. "Blimey, what happened there? Are you all right?"

"What do you mean?" He watched her turn bright red as she took in what he'd pointed out—a huge stain covering most of her body-hugging blue top.

"Work."

She's not really giving away much, is she? Or does she think I'm just staring at her breasts? Which is exactly what I'm doing. Stop it, Jack!

"What happened?"

"Too much chocolate birthday cake for one of the youngsters."

"Crikey. Not really a job perk, is it?"

Her face showed she was doing anything but enjoying his stab at casual banter.

"Sorry. I'm late and I'm not going to let my son down. He likes consistency." And another hit! A palpable hit! *Suck it up, Jack. She's in the right here.*

"I owe you an apology."

"You don't owe me anything."

Her eyes flicked up to his and he felt the same electric jolt of attraction he had the very first time he'd laid eyes on her. Feisty, gorgeous and trying her best to run him over.

"I do, Liesel. An apology and an explanation." A clutch of cadets gathered outside the station house were openly watching as his walk turned into a jog as he tried to hang on to the car door. He looked like a stalker. *Way to lead by example, Jack!*

"I was a jerk. Please. Just give me a few minutes to explain."

Her car shook from the quick application of brakes.

Good! She was softening. No more playing hard to get. He closed the passenger door he'd been hanging on to, leaned down and stuck his head through the window. Perhaps a wry grin would put things on a better note...

"Listen to me, Captain Keller. I don't play games. Never have, never will. And I will not let some daredevil fireman wreak havoc with my life or, more important, my son's. So *back off*."

Ouch. He wasn't entirely sure how she made a clenched jaw and words bit out through gritted teeth appealing, but it was just about all he could do not to jump into the car with her and prove the last thing he was was a fly-by-night. Wrestling with priorities? Absolutely. Game player? Not anymore.

"Liesel, please." He couldn't help a moment's distraction by some poorly timed laughter from the boys. "Give me a chance?"

"I'm sorry, Jack, I have to keep my priorities in order and being treated like a hanger-on is most definitely not one of them. Please let go of the car. I have to collect my son."

Jack took a quick glimpse up at the cadets and waved them toward the ladder tower, where they'd be running drills. "Get yourselves a bottle of water from the cool box, boys. I'll be with you in a second."

He dipped his head back into Liesel's car window. "Liesel, I know I don't deserve it, but let me explain." Her expression remained neutral. "Over dinner?" He saw her tip her chin up ready to make an excuse but before she could start he jumped in, "I'll make it for you—at yours—once the little man's gone to bed."

She narrowed her eyes, clearly reluctant to agree. She sure did make mad look good. Really good.

"I make a mean lemon tart."

He saw her lips twitch a bit.

Was that a smile she was fighting? He hoped so.

"C'mon. Say yes. Fighting with you is no fun."

"Is that what we're doing, Captain?" She quirked an eyebrow at him.

"Not if I have anything to say about it." He thought he would plunge forward and take her lack of a refusal as a yes. Just about as tentative a yes as you could get but he was pretty sure if—or *when*—he showed up at her house tonight he wouldn't get the door slammed in his face.

As she glanced in the rearview mirror, Liesel was surprised she didn't see steam coming out of her ears. And goofy cartoon love hearts. How mortifying. Covered in a child's vomit and trying to play it cool? Disasterville! Or was it? Did she have a date with Jack tonight? It seemed like it, didn't it?

Even so, Cassie should count herself lucky she was in parent-teacher conferences or they would most assuredly be having words. Sharp ones.

And Jack Keller? She didn't know whether to close her heart for good or let the cartoon lovebirds swirling around her carry on with their chirping.

Tonight! Her heart skipped a beat. *Traitor!*

She drummed her fingers along the top of the steering wheel. What was there left to be angry about?

I know, she thought facetiously: *child abuse!* How dare Cassie use her own son to get her within spitting distance of the one man in the whole of Australia who had her every nerve end smarting with embarrassment. And frustration.

Not to mention a healthy dollop of regret that things hadn't taken a fairy-tale course.

Then again, lots of bad things happened in fairy tales—evil witches, danger-filled woods, charming wolves dressed in sheep's clothing…

These days the dangerous bits of the old-fashioned stories were edited out. But this was real life. No director. No editor. Just good old-fashioned making it through day by day.

If she hadn't known better, Liesel would have sworn all the blood in her body was churning its way up to a storm-force hurricane. Hurricane Liesel! It had a nice ring to it.

Common sense was telling her to cut Jack out of the picture. Kissing him had unearthed a big fat pile of psychological laundry she could hardly begin to sort through, let alone press, fold and put away in the attic. If only she really could stuff all her feelings in the cupboard and close the door. That'd be the life!

Being angry with Jack had been easy when she hadn't seen him. The second those bright blue eyes of his had met hers? Putty.

She flicked on the radio for the five-minute drive back to the day care to pick up Liam. A little smile played across her lips as she imagined her son running toward her and jumping into her arms as he did every day at pickup. He was getting more handsome every day and—curiously—more of an amalgam of herself and Eric. The first year or so he had almost exclusively looked like Eric and now he was definitely a product of the two of them.

Her thoughts shifted a bit too quickly back to the dangerously blue eyes and thick thatch of blond hair her fingers had itched to run through just a few short days ago. The stubble outlining that pair of cheekbones a model would be happy to sport. Tanned forearms propped on her car's window frame. Well-defined muscles nicely visible as they went taut and then relaxed beneath a light spray of blond arm hair. The man was gorgeous.

She'd let Jack make her dinner but would play it cool. He'd just be a nice bit of fireman eye candy she could enjoy from time to time. From now on they'd be friends.

Her eyes flicked down to the car clock.

Four twenty-seven.

Liam went down at seven.

Two and a half hours. And three minutes.

Not that she was counting. Or worried about if she had time to take a shower, not smell like little kid puke and tame her curls in some way. This time Jack was going to know what he was missing. She wasn't some naive country school nurse he could play mind games with. She'd traveled the world and worked on some of the most difficult trauma cases a person could imagine, for heaven's sake! Frankly, he could come over and apologize until the cows came home, but this time she would stay strong—remain immune to his sexy, firemanly charms.

She was woman!

"Hear me roar!" she shouted out into the car, unconcerned if anyone saw her. She cranked up the pop music on the radio for good measure. "Roaaaarr! Take that, Captain Keller! Let's see you take on the she-lion tonight!"

Jack felt his shopping basket getting heavier by the minute. He knew he couldn't buy his way back into Liesel's good books but he sure could try to cook his way there. Lemons… Where did they keep the lemons in this place?

"Why, Captain Keller, what a surprise, meeting you here."

Jack looked up and saw Cassie Monroe sending him a Cheshire-cat grin over a pile of artisan bread.

"G'day, Cassie. How are things?" He felt like a character in a soap opera. Mysterious but charming. He hoped.

"Good. Good." She nodded along with the words. "Haven't seen you around much."

The words were loaded with meaning and he knew what they were saying.

You treated my friend poorly. Really poorly. And us girls stick together.

"It's been mad at the station." It was true, but even as the words left his lips he knew they sounded weak.

"Right, of course. Fire season." Cassie nodded along with an earnest expression. "I guess you fire blokes don't use telephones during the high season for safety reasons?" Her facial expression read like a triumphant picture book.

"Cease-fire! I'm on a rescue mission tonight!" Jack lifted up his basket for Cassie to inspect. He was relieved to see her nod approvingly at the collection of fresh groceries. He was going for a lemon and asparagus risotto, roasted tomatoes, all topped with a nice bit of grilled fish.

She gave a sniff of approval. "At least you didn't pick up a packet of snags for the barbie." She went on tiptoe to make a more detailed inspection. "If my ex-husband had cooked this well, he might have stood more of a chance." She laughed good-naturedly, the tension of their previous banter dispersed into the early-evening air of the open-walled farm shop.

"Hopefully Liesel's ex wasn't up to much in the kitchen. I might know my ingredients but I—" Jack stopped in midflow, acutely aware Cassie had shifted into yet another mode: protective mother hen. She threw a furtive look over each of her shoulders before joining him on his side of the bread display.

"Has she not told you?" Her voice was low, concerned.

"Told me what?"

"About her ex?"

"Not a word. I thought Liesel had a don't-ask-don't-tell sort of thing going on."

Cassie fixed him with a serious glare. He could practically hear the invisible seconds ticking past. What was going on? He'd just presumed it was a loser boyfriend or husband who'd cut town when a kid had arrived on the scene, so he hadn't pressed for details. His only thought had been that the guy must've been an idiot to let her go. Not to mention Liam. He was up there on the cute-kid meter.

"Cassie," he gently prodded. "What is it? If it will help me make things up to Liesel for being a first-class berk you've got to tell me. As I said, I'm on a rescue mission here."

She motioned him over to a quiet corner of the country store.

"This didn't come from me, but if you really want to make things work then you need to know the truth. I'm doing this for Liesel's good because I can tell you this— that girl is her own worst enemy."

Cassie fixed him with a burn-holes-through-your-head glare. He nodded, not interested in the politics of her confession, just the content.

"You'll have to ask her yourself."

"What?"

"You want Liesel in your life? You earn her trust—and then you'll win her confidence." Cassie was well into her mama-bear role now.

"Can't you even give me a hint?" *Youch. If looks could kill.*

"Ball's in your court, Jack. Time to kick up your game a notch."

"Are you sure I can't show you around?"

Jack shooed Liesel away from the kitchen, handing her a cool glass of what looked like very fancy wine in the process. "Positive. You just go get yourself settled out there on the veranda and enjoy the sunset. Before you know it, dinner will be served!"

More time to wonder what on earth was going on with this chameleon of a man. *Thanks for nothing!*

Her fingers played across her lips. Lips a bit too keen to pick up the action from the last time she'd been out on the veranda with a certain someone. Maybe gnawing on them would put them off. Kissing was *not* on the agenda tonight.

Her teeth released her lips. No good. Pillar of strength or not, Jack still sent her tummy's butterflies into a tailspin.

She chanced another peek into the kitchen. It struck her how at home he looked in her kitchen. She could hear him humming quietly to himself. Steadily chopping, frying, cleaning as he went—what a plus! He had changed from his uniform into a faded pair of jeans that hung loosely off his hips. Maybe he was hiding a secret past as a jet-setting jeans model. He looked just a bit too good.

His trim waist was visible above the wooden counter-tops, swiveling here and there to hunt for a pan in a cup-board, a knife in a drawer. The broad reach of his shoulders extended farther as he stretched to pull a pair of plates down from a shelf. This was like chef porn. Or something. She really needed to get a grip.

At the very least, she had to congratulate herself for agreeing to let Jack work his way back into her good books. She was well and truly intent on making a life for herself and Liam here in Engleton and, like it or not, Jack was part of the small-town package.

She took another sip of the delicious wine. It was quite unlike anything she'd had before. "This wine is great, Jack. How did you hear about it?"

"I just keep my ear to the ground. I know a thing or two about wine."

"Well, color me impressed—this is great. It's local, right? You sure I can't give you a hand?"

"You bet. It won't be long now."

Jack didn't feel right withholding information from her. It officially bugged him now that she didn't know everything about him. He would get there. She'd know his whole story one day—when he had everything in place. Sorting things out with his father was just another bridge to cross and he wouldn't be ready to go there until he had Engleton CFS station firmly placed on the map and his father's stamp of approval.

He looked up from his chopping, the gentle curves of Liesel's silhouette just visible through the screen door, backlit by the final rays of the day's sunshine. It was all too easy to imagine running a hand along the soft swoop from her waist to her hip and he felt his body respond. It would take less than a second to cross the room, pull her into his arms and kiss her as deeply and completely as if the world were about to end.

Actions spoke louder than words?

Most of the time. But that wasn't what tonight was about. It was about respect. And a healthy slice of humble pie.

"Why don't you come on in? Dinner's just about ready."

He should have been focusing on his risotto, but found watching Liesel cross the room, fingers playing through her auburn curls, a better option.

"That's not a burning smell, is it?" She wrinkled up her nose and tilted her head, trying to pinpoint the source.

Jack looked down and realized the risotto was the culprit. Staring doe-eyed at Liesel hadn't done it any favors.

"Is that smoke?"

"Oh, no! The fish!" Jack whirled around to look in the

grill. He reached in to pull out the grill pan, realizing too late he didn't have an oven glove on.

"Ow-w-w!"

"What happened?" Liesel was by his side in an instant.

"The fish!"

"What about your hand?"

"Burnt." He held it up for her to inspect.

"Whoops." Liesel's voice held a barely contained giggle. "I'll just grab some ice for— Is that pot meant to be boiling over?"

Jack whirled around, burnt hand cupped in his good one, only to find his asparagus turning to mush in a sea of frothy, boiling green water.

"Go." Liesel was handing him a tea towel filled with ice and pointing to the veranda.

"But—your dinner."

"I think we can agree this might not be the night for me to sample your home cooking."

That had better be a twinkle in her eyes.

"Here, take this. It'll help dull the pain." Liesel went to the fridge and pulled out the bottle of wine he'd brought and poured a few healthy glugs into a glass.

He gratefully took the glass, feeling the chilled wine cool the red mark already rising on his hand. He lingered a moment, watching as she swiftly and efficiently switched off the oven, the stove, the grill, and removed all the burning and boiling kitchenware from the offending heat sources.

"Would you believe this isn't really the fine-dining evening I'd envisaged for us?"

He watched the smile on her face grow even larger. Had he noticed how full her lips were before?

"Maybe not, but it's been pretty fun watching a fireman incinerate every single course of a meal."

"You know—" he sidled up to her, hoping he looked

like a sexy cowboy "—not every man can turn a meal into a three-fire alert."

She gave him her best *wow, I'm impressed* face then rummaged through a kitchen drawer next to the phone until she found what she was looking for. Triumphantly holding up a colorful piece of paper, she waggled it in the air between them.

"Pizza?"

CHAPTER EIGHT

"Yum. That was just what the doctor ordered." Liesel lay back on the sofa, hands appreciatively rubbing her full belly. Pepperoni always hit the spot.

"You mean you didn't fancy a beautiful asparagus risotto with river trout tonight?"

"Uhh…" She eyed him dubiously. "I'm not entirely sure how to answer that."

"How about like this?" Jack leaned toward her on the sofa, looking very much as if he was going to kiss her. Her body reacted as though she'd just been filled with recharged batteries. Everything was tingling. Everything wanted to say yes.

She felt herself stiffen.

"Sorry, Jack. I…I can't."

He pulled back, a freshly bandaged hand raised in a gesture of surrender. "That's cool. I just thought you might like to know you've got a bit of pizza left over for later just here." He wiggled a finger by the edge of his own mouth, signifying she was wearing a face snack.

Sexy, Liesel. That's the way to play it. Turn a man down for a kiss he wasn't going to give you.

"Sorry, I thought—"

"I know." Jack shook his head, more at himself than at her. "I did—I do want to kiss you. I just covered like a bloke. Don't worry. Your face is still the same beautiful picture of perfection it always is."

"Hardly!" Liesel tried to laugh away the compliment while simultaneously swiping at her cheek. He was right. There was nothing there.

She looked across at him, suddenly aware of how quiet he'd gone.

"What? What is it?"

"I mean it, Liesel."

"What, about the pizza?"

"No, you silly thing—about how beautiful you are."

Oh, no! You're not meant to make me feel pretty—like a woman again! We're supposed to be friends!

"I'd say right back at you but that's not really what a bloke wants to hear, is it?"

"Liesel, I'm being serious." She could see it in his eyes—but the only way to survive this was to carry on playing the fool. Or was it time to take a breath and act like a grown-up?

"So am I, Jack." He nodded for her to continue. She felt like squirming or, better yet, running away and pretending none of this was happening. But that wasn't who she was now. She was a grown woman and a mother. *Bite the bullet, Liesel!*

"Look—I don't know how much you're going to like this but I need to let you know where I stand. For myself and for Liam."

He leaned back against the sofa cushions, brows raised and wearing an open expression that invited her to continue. Lordy, he was sexy. He didn't make a "friends' night" easy in any way.

"Okay—here it goes. I've felt as though there has been something between us—at least, there seemed to be a few days ago." Then the words began to pour out. "It's obvious the fire department is your priority. You and me—and whatever we are or aren't—it's clearly something you don't have room for in your life. I don't want you to think of me or Liam as things competing for your attention—something you have to choose between."

"You're right, the station *is* my priority right now."

Liesel felt her heart sink. That had ended more quickly than she'd thought.

"But," he continued, a hand slipping over to rest on her knee, "once I've got it secured on the map, I don't want to look up and find you're not there."

Liesel gulped. Hard. She watched as Jack's eyes implored her to believe him. Holy cow! What was he saying exactly? He wanted her to wait for him? But that meant being put on hold. No. That wasn't right, either. They'd be better off deciding on a friendship now. A really sexy, hormone-fueled, abstemious friendship. With benefits?

"I think…" He gathered her hands in his, a thumb skimming along her wrist. "I think there's something else that's frightening you. I know I work crazy hours and the lifestyle is a bit nuts—but you're no stranger to that world. You're a strong, amazing woman. I've never met anyone like you. It's one of the reasons I'm over here incinerating dinners, trying to get back into your good books! I know I'm not ideal boyfriend material but would you be willing to give it a go?"

Ping! Ping! Ping! He was hitting all the marks. You bet there were other things that frightened her.

Him dying, for example. That was the best example— no need to continue.

"I don't know, Jack. It's just not what I imagined. Waiting around for someone."

"Are you saying I'm just anyone?"

He put on just about the most gorgeous hurt expression a man could muster.

Boyfriend material?

He wasn't hanging up his fireman's hat—but wasn't pulling his punches, either. He wanted her in his life. Could that be enough to risk loving him? Risk losing him?

"I just think it's a lot to ask of someone." *You're dodging the real issues here, Liesel!*

"C'mon, love." His voice was all low and sexy now. He was playing emotional hardball. "I've felt the sparks between us, too."

Liesel allowed a cheeky smile to begin to creep onto her lips. *Boyfriend material.* It made her skin all shivery. In a good way.

What was Liesel's smile suggesting? Three seconds ago he'd felt like an onion—freshly relieved of a new layer. Exposed and on his way to the frying pan. She'd called a spade a spade. But that thick-lashed twinkling set of emerald eyes looking up at him… His fingertips were itching to pull that cute little body of hers closer to him. Really close.

"It would be much easier to believe what you said if you found a way not to give me the cold shoulder for showing up at the station with a tray of cinnamon rolls."

"I was a pretty big jerk the other day, wasn't I?"

He watched as Liesel's smile grew toothy. This whole bare-bones thing was a bit less painful than he'd thought.

"You were a super-big jerk."

"Anything I could do to make up for it?"

She put her best coy face on. Those cat eyes of hers did their magic. Stirrings of a distinctly male nature were coming to the fore and he hoped she was experiencing the same lusty call.

"Oh…" She planted a finger at the side of her rosebud mouth. "I could think of a thing or two."

Jack didn't need any more prompting. From the saucy look in Liesel's eyes he knew it was time to let actions speak louder than words. He cared for Liesel. Deeply. If she was willing to try things with him despite his commitment to his job, he would do his red-blooded best to thank her.

Pushing himself forward on the sofa, he started planting soft kisses on Liesel's neck. From the way she tilted it toward her shoulder he knew he was on the right track. "How's this? Any closer to working my way back into your good books?"

"A little." The words might've been bland but her voice had purred them. He took them as a cue to continue. They might have things to work on, but if access to Liesel's creamy smooth neck was the payoff, he was going to be a rich man.

A sigh escaped Liesel's lips as Jack brushed his lips along her forehead, her cheeks, each touch sending a warm flush of pleasure straight through to her very core. His fingers teased their way along her jawline, drawing her chin toward his expectant lips. She felt her breath catch in her throat until Jack sealed the moment with the most tender of kisses. A kiss that soon turned hungry, more demanding.

Caution, playing it safe, fear—all of them faded into the background as the need to respond to Jack's kisses consumed her. Liesel pulled herself up onto her knees, still kissing him, teasing, nibbling, her hands beginning a tentative exploration of his chest. Through the cotton top she could feel his nipples harden. She couldn't resist giving them a playful swirl and tweak before moving on, exploring him, his body. His perfectly sexy body. A wash of pure animal lust rushed through her, turning thoughts into mush and physical contact into explosions of pleasure. Thank God Liam was a good sleeper. She could feel a moan of pleasure rolling through her throat.

She wanted him. She wanted Jack more than she could have imagined possible. Her hands slipped below his waist, onto his thighs and round the back for a cheeky squeeze of that jeans-perfect bum of his. He felt so good!

So male. Everything shifted into primal responses. The touching, the soft moans of pleasure meeting in midair between them. She pressed her breasts against his chest, unable to resist nestling into his neck. Jack's scent flooding her senses, heat passing between them as if they were unclothed.

Why were they wearing clothes? Everything was in the way now. His shirt, hers. His jeans, her skirt. An urge to rip the buttons off his shirt shot through her fingers. As her hands continued to explore there was no doubt Jack was feeling the same way she was. A strong arm slipped round her waist while another possessively slipped below her hips. In a single swoop Jack pulled her legs up around his waist and was carrying her toward the bedroom. "You ready for this?" His voice was urgent, full of need.

"More than I thought possible!"

If Liesel could've made her legs more like a human pretzel she would have. It was still early morning—the perfect time for a sexy snuggle. She nestled into the human spoon Jack had wrapped round her and wove her legs between his. The night of lovemaking had gone beyond anything she'd imagined. He had, by turns, been passionate, gentle, insatiable, patient. She felt like a first-class sex kitten.

Thank goodness she wasn't facing him. Just thinking about the fact that his beeper or radio could go off at any moment brought a salty sting to her eyes. She clamped them shut. Making love with Jack had dug just about the biggest hole she could've imagined. Here they were, not even twenty-four hours into trying out the boyfriend-girlfriend thing and already she was nervous about him being called out.

This wasn't going to work. The painful twist in her heart was proof she was going to have to break things off. Now. If it was going to be painful today, it would be even more so in a week, a month, a year, when Jack might or might not have things the way he wanted them. If she'd learned anything, it was that life didn't wait around for things to be perfect.

This? Lying in Jack's arms? It was pretty close to as perfect as a girl could get. So she'd just have to cherish this memory and move on.

Jack obviously needed to focus on the station and having her moping around was hardly going to help things. Not that moping was her style. Thanks to him, she was seeing more clearly than ever that she might have been hasty in vowing never to work in the trauma wards again. She thrived on it as much as Jack was charged by putting out a fire or rescuing someone. They each had their calling. But for right now? Her main calling was to roll over and see what sort of early-morning kisses she could elicit out of a sleepy Jack Keller. She teased and nibbled at his lips and from the press of his hips against hers, both their thoughts were clearly headed in the same direction.

The sound of the telltale buzz of his mobile phone brought a distinct moan of displeasure from Jack. Despite her vow to try and chill, Liesel stiffened. Could she really do this?

Jack reached across Liesel's shoulder and grabbed his phone from the side of the bed, where they'd hastily discarded their clothes the night before. He took a glimpse at the screen. A text.

How about coming to River's Bend tonight? Casual barbie. Dad's coming. I forbid you to say no. Love Bec.

Great. A fence-mending night. Jack knew it was long overdue but he wasn't quite ready. Not to mention the fact he still had to tell Liesel his family lived just down the road. He pulled a hand through his hair and flicked the phone back onto the jumble of clothes. Something was bound to come up. As much as he hated letting her down, he'd let his sister know his excuse in an hour or so. But for now he had some more kissing to— "What's up, buttercup?"

Liesel was actively wriggling her way out of his arms. She'd spent the entire night getting about as close as a woman could to a man and now she was beating a retreat?

"Was that the station?"

"No." Jack felt himself drawl the word to try and buy some thinking time. He knew they hadn't gone deep and dirty in terms of discussing their lives last night, but Liesel was obviously worked up about the station. He tried to pull her back into his arms but she pushed herself up to a cross-legged position and folded her arms solidly across her chest.

"Is there something more than me prioritizing the station that bugs you?"

"How about everything?" Liesel tried her best to laugh off the comment, but knew her raw voice betrayed that it came from a very real place. All of it was scary! His job, how he prioritized it over everything else, how he didn't want to include her in it and, most important, the real possibility he could be injured or worse. That about covered it.

The salty sting of tears began to threaten. *No!* She pulled her hands from his and scrunched them into fists. She wasn't going to succumb.

"Let's try and break it down. What's really bugging you?"

I'm falling in love you with you, you idiot.

"Look, it's just not going to work, is it? Us. Me waiting. I'm hardly going to spend a year pining while you run off and act the hero."

The words tasted acrid. That was what Eric had always done—acted the hero. And if he had, just that once, been sensible, thought of her—he might be alive.

Jack pressed his hands down as if to calm her. "I'm not asking you to do that. Not at all. You know me better than that, don't you?"

She could feel herself bite away a response. She thought she knew him—knew his character—but there were a lot of gaps.

"I'm not entirely sure what I'm asking, or how we can make this work…but I think it's worth it—the wait." He dropped her one of those hard-to-resist winks. "We've got sparks, baby!"

Obviously! But it's such a big risk!

Jack slipped out from under the sheet and pulled on a T-shirt and boxers then sat down solidly opposite her on the bed. It was a good move because having this discussion with a naked Jack Keller was taking a boatload of concentration.

"You say you're scared—so let's break it down. Just start with one thing and we'll go through all of them." Jack looked around the bedroom. "You got a pen and paper? We could make a list if you want."

Despite herself, she smiled, appreciative of his gesture of trying to make it a more comfortable atmosphere for her. She loved lists. How he knew her so well after such a short time was beyond her. She reached over to the bedside and pulled on a long T-shirt. *May as well make this even.*

"I think I already got one in here." She tapped her head.

"Okay, shoot. Number one?"

"Number one…" Lordy. All her reasons jostled for pole position. "Number one—your job scares me."

He nodded. It was no secret firefighters lost their lives in Australia—hell, everywhere—every year.

"I'm not going to change jobs. I can't do that." The words could've sounded belligerent, but coming from Jack they were just the truth. The fire service was part of him, she knew that instinctively.

"I know. I'm not asking you to. It's just that…" She bit her lip. If she told Jack the real reason behind her hesitancy he might just agree it was too big a hurdle to leap and they should call it quits. But that was what she wanted anyhow, right?

Wrong. Right now she wasn't entirely sure what she wanted. She took a big breath, swallowed her tears and began, "Liam's father died in a terrible accident. He was a ski patroller and I knew he faced danger every day, but we were young—we took risks. I just didn't ever imagine his risks having such permanent repercussions. The same week he died I found out I was pregnant with Liam and—well, I don't think I need to say how awful the next year was. But in so many ways it was great! Liam was such a happy baby—he brings me so much joy. I moved back to Australia and my family could not have been more amazing in supporting me." She shook her head in wonder. "I don't know if I could have dealt with Eric's loss as well if I hadn't had them."

Her hands flew to her eyes. Staunching the flow of tears just wasn't working. But she wanted, needed, to get the rest of her story out. Jack needed to know why this was all so difficult for her.

"When I met you, I… It was nice."

He raised his eyebrows.

She smirked back at him, despite herself. Fine. They were telling the truth here, right?

"Better than nice. But with your job and everything it—" She had to stop. She didn't want to sob, didn't want to lose it. This was all part of growing up, moving on, taking charge of her life. She squeezed her eyes shut and blew a slow breath between her lips, willing herself to stay strong. Lashes flecked with tears, she finally braved opening them and there he was, steady and solid as ever, Jack and his bighearted smile.

"Liesel, I'm so sorry. I wish I'd known." He moved a hand up to her cheek, brushing a few curls behind her ear. It was strange how being touched by him when she was telling him about Eric didn't seem like any sort of betrayal. It was crazy! She and Jack were sitting in bed after a mind-blowing night of hot sex and she was telling him all about her dead ex-fiancé. And it felt okay. She certainly hadn't anticipated that. Had she moved further ahead in the emotional stakes department with Jack than she'd thought?

Taking advantage of Liesel's faraway thoughts, Jack jumped in. "You're right about me, you know," he began, then quickly qualified, "to an extent."

"That sounds ominous."

"It's not meant to." His voice softened. "Look, I didn't join the fire service because of a great calling to be macho and fight against Mother Nature's fiery wrath. She's a powerful force and I can assure you I take every precaution available to me. I want to live as much as the next guy." And he meant it. Looking into Liesel's eyes, her emotions laid bare before him, he knew in his heart he would do everything in his power to stay safe for her.

"Then why? Why do you do it?"

"The truth?"

"Yeah. That's what we're doing here, isn't it?" Liesel couldn't keep a bite of punchiness from her voice. It wasn't as if she had just bared her soul to him or anything!

"I joined because my mother died in a horrible barn fire when I was a kid and while everyone around me was doing everything in their power to put the fire out, I ran round the back of the barn to see if I could get my pony out. My mother ran in front. I'll never know if she was going in for me, the horses or both. Either way, my idiot move…" He cleared his throat and punched some air back into the pillows before continuing. "Since then, I'd always thought if I'd known what to do—had had some training—she would still be alive today."

Liesel's mouth went dry, her fingers covering her lips as she nodded at him to carry on. Jack knew loss as well as she did. Horrible, gut-wrenching, life-changing loss.

"Surely, though, the CFS was there."

"That's just it!" Passion ignited his words. "They weren't! There weren't enough volunteers, or they were out doing something else—I don't know. It doesn't matter now—they just weren't there."

"And you're trying to make up for it by running the Engleton CFS station?"

"In part. I can never make up for it. Not in my father's eyes."

"What does that mean?"

"He blames me. Holds me responsible for her death."

"What? Surely not. You said you were only a boy."

"She went into the barn and I wasn't there to stop her."

"You can't think he blames *you* for that, though?"

His father had been in a rage when he'd joined the CFS cadets straight after his mother's funeral. He'd never seen him so angry. Asked him straight-out what good he thought learning about fires would do him now—now that the damage had been done. It hadn't been an outright accusation. But it had been enough. "It's complicated. But losing my mother—well, he's never been the same. His grief consumed him. I swore I wouldn't let that happen to anyone else if I could help it."

Those clear blue eyes of his tore at her. How Jack spoke

about all this without crying was beyond her. It explained his drive, his ambition with the CFS. She reached across and gave one of his hands a squeeze. "If what I've seen is anything to go by, I know you'll do your best."

"That's kind of you, Liesel, but my best doesn't seem to stretch far enough. If I was proper boyfriend material, I'd find something else to do—something that didn't scare the daylights out of you."

"I can't imagine you giving up the CFS."

"Nor can I." Jack hung his head, shaking it as if he was trying to find a way out of the situation.

A fug of gloom hung between them as Liesel's upper teeth gripped her lower lip then shot it out again, her thoughts fighting for order. Being in the CFS was every bit a part of Jack as nursing was in her. She couldn't believe for a second he'd ask her to give up nursing, so she could hardly ask him to give up his profession. Cassie had already called her kettle black anyhow. Accountants and IT guys weren't her style. Men on the front line, helping people in times of need, were. And that was Jack to a T.

The truth was, he had a lot of irons in the fire and she just couldn't risk putting herself and Liam through the heartache of another loss. She pressed her hands onto her face, hoping it would help silence the roar of blood rushing through her ears.

Friends only?

They had such a connection!

She peeked at him through her fingers. Just a glimpse of that tousled blond hair and her tummy went all fizzy. She couldn't believe how powerful an effect he had on her, and now she'd have to give it all up?

She sucked in a sharp breath, held it, then made her decision.

If only he didn't smell so good! And feel so good. And—

Stop. Giving up Jack Keller was going to be a mammoth task, but she had to find the strength to do it.

"It sounds a lot to me like we've both got some demons to tackle."

"You're not wrong there, love."

Love. Boyfriend material. He was making this tough!

"So-o-o—it's probably best that we call whatever this is a day and just be friends."

If she'd slapped him, he couldn't have felt a more vicious sting. It was all Jack could do not to give her a disbelieving double take.

"Are you kidding me?" He gestured at the rumpled sheets, their discarded clothes, himself. "After last night? You want to just be friends?"

"No. I want to be a lot more than friends—but I just don't think it's possible. Not for me. Not for Liam."

"Liam?" He stopped before he stuck his foot in it. Of course the little boy factored into this whole thing. Whatever it was. *Nothing*, from the looks of things. He felt as if he was splitting in two. "I think Liam's great! You can't doubt the fact that I care for him, would look after him." *And you. I'd look after* you.

"I believe you—I do." She pulled her gaze away from his, obviously as unhappy as he was but determined to stick to her guns. "I just have to make sure he has someone in his life who will be there for him. And I— We—" She stopped, visibly wrestling with her words. "We need someone in our lives whose life is straightforward, who we can rely on."

He felt his nerve endings go dull with sadness. Sadness that she was right. She had the same clarity his father did. She saw him for what he was: a man on a self-imposed mission. And until he saw that mission through, he wasn't the man she wanted—or needed—in her life.

"And I'm not that guy."

"Not right now, Jack. I wish to God you were, but you're not."

"Friends?" He put out a hand, wishing it was to caress her but knowing the best he would get was a handshake.

"Friends."

CHAPTER NINE

"YOU GOING TO the Harvest Festival?"

Cassie was using her teasing voice. The one that was saying one thing and meaning another. Since the great unsaid involved Jack, Liesel didn't feel like playing. The past few weeks of "just being friends" had been tough. She had feelings for him. Big, huge, undeflatable feelings, and this whole being sensible thing was turning out to be harder than she'd thought. Particularly when anytime her thoughts veered in a certain tall, blond and incredibly gorgeous direction her insides turned into happyville. What a disaster.

"That's the plan."

"Planning to meet up with any special friends?"

Liesel suddenly felt the hairs on the back of her neck stand on end.

"Sorry, Cass. Did you catch that? Do you mind…?" She gestured at the radio playing on her friend's kitchen counter.

"What?" Her friend flicked the volume up a notch and leaned in to hear the announcer.

"That's right, folks. In case you haven't heard, you'll want to avoid the high street in Engleton. Looks like one of the vintners is out of luck as a lorry has lost its entire load and taken out quite a few other vehicles—"

"Switch it off."

"I thought you wanted to hear it."

No. This could not be history repeating itself.

"Jack was just heading into Engleton. He messaged me to see if I wanted to meet him for milk shakes."

"Ooh! Still keeping in touch with Mr. Pants-on-Fire, are we?"

"Cass, you're not hearing me!" Liesel heard her voice rising. "He could be in that crash!" Panic was setting in. This was exactly what had happened with Eric. Exactly how she had learned he was in trouble that day. Had her pulse raced this fast? Had her heart lodged as high in her throat? She couldn't remember. All that mattered now was that Jack could be in trouble and she could help. This time she wasn't going to stand by and wait to hear what was happening. She was going to be there.

Jack hadn't lost consciousness but the past few seconds had played out as if they'd been hours.

He'd pulled into traffic behind a large truck hauling grapes from the harvest and remembered thinking the heavy vehicle was taking the corner into town a bit fast for such a huge load, and then—jackknife. He'd pulled the emergency brake and whipped the wheel round in a one-hundred-and-eighty-degree safety turn—but he'd had to pull in sharply to avoid oncoming traffic and had tipped his truck. The passenger side of the truck had seen better days, but he was all right.

Jack unclipped his belt, bracing himself as he did. He'd have to climb out of the cab. His truck was on its side but he was unharmed. He'd had a narrow escape. From the sounds coming through his open window, not everyone had been so lucky.

"He'll be fine with us." Cassie held Liam on her hip and gave Liesel a grim smile. "Go."

Liesel swept her son's fringe aside and gave him a quick smooch on the forehead. He was why she was doing this. There was no chance she was going to raise him to believe you had to be fearful of life. Life was about making the most of it—the good and the bad. Even if it did make your blood run cold with fear at times. Jack had given her strength to face her fears and conquer them.

"Just friends" or not—it was her turn to help.

"Mr. Jones, it's Jack—Jack Keller. Can you hear me?"

The front of the farmer's truck might as well have not even existed—it had crumpled into nothing. The haulage truck must have caught it head-on from the looks of things, and now Mr. Jones's legs were trapped in the lower cavity of his cab. His air bag may have saved his life, he had a pulse, but Jack wasn't so sure about his legs.

"Help! Over here!"

The call was thin, a child's.

Jack looked up from the unconscious form of Mr. Jones to the car on the other side of the haulage truck, a blue estate car. Flames were shooting through the sides of the bonnet. And they weren't taking their time about growing.

He felt something wet on his face and swatted it away. The sky was as blue as they came today—it couldn't be rain.

"Help!" The child's cry came again.

"What do you need me to do?"

Liesel. It was the salve he needed to bring order to the blur of chaos threatening to engulf him.

"You came!"

"Of course I came. That's what friends do, right?" Worry threaded through her eyes, but so did something else. Something stronger than the friendship they had shaken hands on those two long months ago.

"Liesel… I'm sorry, I…" He scanned the crash site.

This wasn't the time. "Can you stay with Mr. Jones? I've got to run—"

He watched as Liesel's face turned a ghostly shade of white.

"Jack, your forehead." Her voice wavered as she spoke and he watched her physically regroup before continuing. "You've got to get that seen to before you do anything."

He lifted his hand to his forehead again, the smear of blood on his palm helping him to connect the dots.

No. Children in burning cars came first.

Liesel's mind went into overdrive.

Head wounds bled a lot. Common knowledge. It didn't necessarily mean he was concussed, but Jack had definitely looked confused when he'd seen her.

Her eyes made a quick scan of the scene, as if she were making an incident report. They were both trained in mass casualty management, but if Jack had been concussed during the crash he definitely should not be taking part in the rescue efforts. But timing was just as crucial. Seconds counted in a scenario like this.

Establishing scores for each of the cases needed to come automatically, otherwise lives could be lost.

Extreme cases first, secondaries put into order in a temporary triage unit until additional support arrived. Jack needed to be on that list and he… *Where was he?* He had been standing there just a second ago.

Flames leaped from the car on the far side of the haulage truck. She saw a figure running toward the vehicle—a familiar athletic figure.

"My mummy's stuck! Please can you help?" A little girl tugged at Liesel's arm, pulling her in the direction of Engleton's general store, now an open cavity. The haulage truck must have sideswiped the brick structure, taking the entire storefront along with it. Liesel shot a backward glance toward Jack, but thick smoke blocked her view. Her heart leaped to her throat. If she wanted any more proof that he was the wrong man to fall in love with, she had it right here in front of her. *Love?* Her skin began to feel clammy, the buzz of indecision drowning out her thoughts.

The insistent tug of little fingers on her hand brought her round. Her teeth clenched in frustration. This was the nature of their work—hers and Jack's—their individual callings. It wasn't about being a hero; it was about saving lives, and right now lives were at stake. Clarity hit her like a lightning bolt. This was precisely why Jack felt he couldn't have her in his life. Love made you lose focus and lives were lost.

"Where's your mum, sweetheart?"

"In here." The little girl tugged her across a pile of bricks and a cascade of tinned food that must've been on display at the front of the store.

A man staggered over the pile of debris, heading toward the street, holding an arm close to his chest. From the limp manner in which it hung, there was little doubt it had been broken. At least the bone hadn't pierced through the skin. Infection was often a compound fracture's worst enemy. She turned toward him to offer help.

"Over here." She felt the sharp tug on her hand again. Right away Liesel saw the girl's mother prostrate, face down on the floor, lower limbs trapped under a tall grocery shelving unit. She immediately dropped to the floor.

Liesel's fingers instinctively located the woman's pulse along the side of her throat. Thready. The woman was lucky she and her daughter hadn't been directly under the shelving. They could've been killed in an instant. Even so, it wasn't looking good.

"I can't feel anything." The woman's voice was hardly a whisper.

"Don't move your head, it's very important." She lowered her own head to be as close to the floor as possible.

"My name is Liesel. I'm a nurse. We're going to get you out of here, all right?" As she said the words she felt her strength grow. She was a nurse and she knew how to help. This was what she'd been trained for. She was prepared for this.

"What's your name?"

"Marilyn."

"Marilyn, that's a beautiful name." Liesel took in the pool of blood forming around the woman's head. Could be a head injury or, more likely, a broken nose. She threw a quick look over her shoulder toward the woman's daughter. She shouldn't see this. "Darling, do you mind doing me a favor?" The little girl nodded, desperate to be of some use. Liesel's eyes tore across the front of the store. Astonishingly, the structure of the building seemed sound. "Do you see that fire extinguisher there? I need you to find an adult outside to help carry it to the fireman, all right?"

"Which one?"

Jack. He needs it.

"There's only one out there now, darling, all right?" *My Jack.* "You're a clever girl. Can you do that for me?" Liesel knew it was heavy—too heavy for a little girl. If she couldn't find anyone to help, she'd have to drag it.

Liesel tilted her head up to listen for the telltale whine of sirens. Someone surely would have responded by now. They had to know at the station, if the call had gone out on regular radio, right?

Then again, the local CFS was made up of volunteers, except for Jack and he was already here. Her heart twisted with a need to ensure he was all right. She clenched her eyes shut.

Focus, Liesel.

"Marilyn, I'm going to try to shift these shelves, all right?"

"I can't feel anything—I can't move."

"As little movement as possible is a good thing right now." Liesel prayed her words wouldn't have any lasting impact. Worst-case scenario? The woman could end up a paraplegic. Best case? Some nasty bruising.

If she'd had time to cross all her fingers, she would have, but right now she needed to relieve the pressure off Marilyn's spine.

Liesel scanned the shop to see if there was anyone left in the building who could help. Deserted. The man with the broken arm must have been the last one out of the store. The unit wasn't massively heavy, but she was petite and it would take some effort. The longer the shelves pressed into Marilyn's body, the more profound her injury could be. One false move…

She grounded her feet as best she could at the corner of the unit. Her hands gripped the sides of the shelves, stomach muscles tightened, and with a big inhalation of breath she began to lift.

Jack barely took the time to register the figure of the young boy at the side of the road. He knew the lad wouldn't leave with his mother trapped in the car. He wouldn't have, either. The side of the car had been struck by the swing of the second haulage trailer, landing the vehicle perilously close to the milk bar's oil storage tank. The door wouldn't budge and neither would her ankle. Flames soared from the bonnet of the car to the wooden veranda.

The look of terror on the woman's face tore at him.

He either had to get that fire extinguished or get her out—but he didn't have his tools. Half of the town was out at work. His crew hadn't arrived yet. She wasn't going anywhere.

"In the back." The words came out as a ragged half scream.

"Where?" Through the fear, Jack could see she was telling him something. Emergency kit. Many people carried aerosol-style fire extinguishers these days. That had to be what she was telling him.

He bolted to the back of the car, thankfully unharmed by the crash, and popped the rear door open. A small puppy lay cowering in the corner on top of a couple of wool blankets. The family pet. The poor woman's car was on fire and she was worried about their family pet. The selflessness of the move doubled his drive.

The vehicle was lodged in the veranda of the local milk bar and already the beams along the tin veranda roof were aflame.

Jack swiftly lifted the dog in his arms, turning to bring him to the little boy. His eyes widened in amazement at the sight of the boy helping a young girl of around seven years old drag a huge fire extinguisher across the road toward him.

"Good work, guys." He handed over the puppy, simultaneously signaling for them to run back to the far side of the road. He spread the blankets for the boy's mother, helping her to cover herself before he lifted up the fire extinguisher. If the flames got much hotter, the blankets would protect her somewhat. From there, he went into autopilot to extinguish the flames coming from the car bonnet. He needed to sever the connection between them and the burning storefront.

A lone teenage employee came hurtling through the front door with two jugs of water.

"No! Get out of there, mate. Don't throw that water!"

Water and oil didn't mix. Ever. There was no guarantee the flames crackling up along the veranda beams hadn't caught their fair share of oil from one of the vehicles caught up in the incident. His eyes snapped to the pin on the fire extinguisher, with a built-in triple check it was the right type. Dry powder was best. Everything slipped into slow motion. The teenager moved across the patio toward the flames. Jack tore to the front of the vehicle, slamming the gearshift into Neutral, willing himself to have the strength to move the car. There was no time to get the woman out.

"Cover your face with the blanket!"

The woman in the car looked terrified as he pressed onto the frame of the burning car with his back and shoulder and began to push. This was mind over matter. He had to move the car away from the storefront. He didn't care what it took, but he was damned if he was going to let another little boy lose his mother to a stupid fire. Not on his watch.

He saw it first. Then heard it.

The teenager had ignored him and had thrown the jugs of water onto the flames.

Liesel collapsed on top of the shelving as the unit fell away from the woman with a crash. The force of what must have been an explosion outside the store had sent her flying. Or was it adrenaline? Or both?

Jack was out there.

She scrabbled to her feet, fighting the urge to run out onto the street. She needed to make sure Marilyn was stabilized.

Where was Marilyn's daughter? Liesel's gut clenched, knowing she had been the one to send the child out into the street—the scene of an accident. She'd thought getting her out of the building had been a good thing.

Where was Jack?

A swell of nausea turned her stomach.

She heard voices shouting. It was impossible to distin-

guish one from another. A small girl appeared in the doorway. Marilyn's daughter.

She looked shocked, but she was alive. Liesel heaved a
sigh a relief. Thank God.

The wail of sirens filled the air as Marilyn's daughter
ran toward her. Liesel held her in a tight embrace. The
noises outdoors became more distinguishable. The guys
were here. The CFS. Whatever had happened in that explosion could be dealt with now. If anything had happened
to Jack...

*No. It was one night only. Nothing more. They were just
friends now. But you could still love a friend, right? Just
not be in love with them.*

"Marilyn, can you hear the sirens?" She released the
woman's daughter from their hug and knelt down on the
floor. "Marilyn?"

No response.

Liesel moved her hand to the woman's lips. A soft
breath tickled her fingers. She was breathing. Okay. Good.
"What's your name, hun?"

"Kirsty."

"Okay, Kirsty. I need your help again. Could you please
hunt down some frozen peas for me? As many as possible."

Help was coming. But she needed to tend to Marilyn
up until she was officially handed over to the emergency
services. Each moment that passed meant more swelling
around the damaged areas of her spinal cord. There was no
chance she could conduct therapeutic hypothermia properly but a few tactically placed bags of peas would help.
As soon as a crew arrived she would see if they had any
methylprednisolone. The steroids could help reduce in-
flammation.

Her eyes shot to the open front of the shop. Where were
the guys? Her view was blocked by one of the haulage

truck trailers. The sirens had stopped and a steady hum of activity had replaced the eerie silence after the explosion.

Would anyone know they were in there? Or was what was happening outside so big they didn't have any spare resources? She couldn't believe how alone she felt. Not knowing… It was just like that day on the mountain.

Tough. She had to pull it together for Marilyn.

Liesel scanned the standing shelves of the shop for anything to help. Diapers. Not ideal, but it was an emergency. She grabbed a few packets of diapers using them as soft braces to keep Marilyn's neck in place. They weren't heavy enough. She needed something to weight them down.

"Is this enough?"

Kirsty's arms were stacked to her chin with frozen peas. Perfect. She could place them along Marilyn's spine—but she'd have to be incredibly careful. If the cold made her shift at all…

Don't panic, Liesel, you can do this.

"What do you need?"

The voice rolled through her like a longed-for drink of water. Her instinct was to run and jump into Jack's arms and smother him with kisses. His face was a smear of soot and blood, a small clot knotting up at his hairline—but he was alive! Her heart soared with relief. Jack was alive!

One night only. It was your choice.

There was work to do. This was what she had to do now. Pour her passion into her work. It was the only way. Her focus sharpened.

"We need a backboard. Possibly two."

Jack sent a questioning look. God, she loved those blue eyes of his. *Keep your eye on the ball, Liesel, not on the hot fireman you thought you might have lost.* The hot fireman who tugged at her every heartstring.

"We're going to have to roll her and I can't do it on my own. She's presenting possible neck or spine injuries."

"I'll get one of the lads to bring you a backboard and lend a hand."

As swiftly as he'd appeared, Jack vanished around the corner, still managing to leave in his wake that incredible sensation of confidence and strength he always seemed to infuse in her. He was a man who could handle a crisis. And he clearly trusted her to the same level. Professionally. And that was the only bond they would share from now on. Work. It'd take a while, but she could suck it up. Eventually.

Jack was so engrossed in supervising Mr. Jones's release from his truck that he jumped at the light touch on his arm.

"Sorry! I didn't mean to freak you out."

Liesel. A sight for sore eyes. "No worries. Looks like I've got a case of the jitters, eh?"

"A big strapping fireman like you? Unlikely!" Her eyes teased but he could see the concern creasing her brow. His fingers itched to smooth away the worry, kiss away the fear. But he needed to make sure Mr. Jones was all right first. The poor man had been knocked out by the impact of his air bag hitting him, but miraculously he hadn't received any leg injuries. From the look of the front of his truck, Jack would have sworn some sort of higher power must have been on watch. It had been demolished. The EMTs would take him to hospital for a once-over just in case. Sometimes a frontal blow from an air bag could cause a broken rib or, in some rare cases, a heart attack. The hospital would definitely need to run a few tests before sending him home.

"The EMTs have it covered. It's your turn now, pal. Move it!" Liesel crooked a finger at him, making the come-here-now gesture look more sexy than he was sure she'd intended.

Jack followed, presuming she was heading toward the

flashing ambulance lights just visible beyond the haulage truck. If he had a right to stop her from turning the corner he would. His gut clenched as she came to an abrupt halt, his eyes soberly following hers. The milk bar was a cinder shell, three of his guys still at work tamping out the smoldering remains. The half-burnt-out body of the estate car in front of it lay abandoned like a sun-dried carcass left for the scavengers.

"Were there—"

Her fingers flew to her throat as if the words were lodged there.

"No. No, there weren't. By the skin of our teeth there weren't."

He ground out the words, unwilling to tell her how close it had been. Death. He wasn't ready to hear the words spelling out the plain truth. She had been right to have backed off from him. Today had been dangerous. Too dangerous.

An understaffed station was to blame for all this. He could have easily been killed, along with several others. And now Liesel was staring at the proof that her worst nightmares could, in fact, have come true. Today.

"What happened?"

"The kid who worked at the milk bar tried to lend a hand—he threw water onto the fire coming from the car. The water reacted with some oil in the flames and, I know it's hard to believe, looking at this mess, we were actually incredibly lucky—" he scrubbed a sooty hand along his chin as Liesel stared at him dumbly in disbelief "—instead of igniting the burning vehicle, the flames were sucked into a fireball under the tin roof of the veranda. The milk-bar kid suffered his fair share of scrapes and bruises but is otherwise injury-free. Unbelievably lucky for such an incredibly foolish move."

He knew he sounded harsh and tried to soften his words. "He should have been educated. If we had more than one

donor angel, we could afford to hire someone else. A part-
timer, maybe, who could have come round town and taught
everyone and made sure the proper extinguishers were
in place."

"Donor angel?"

"Someone's sent in a couple of checks over the past
year. Big ones. It's been incredibly helpful, but the station was in very bad shape when I inherited it. Maybe if I
hadn't spent the last chunk on re-kitting out the truck…"

Liesel ached to see him in so much pain. It wasn't right
that he accept all the responsibility for what had happened
here. One man couldn't predict every accident that was
going to happen in what was an expansive rural area. It
just wasn't possible.

Jack turned to face her, his large hands taking hold of
her shoulders. His eyes seemed to be searching for some
sort of evidence that he couldn't have done more. "You
were right to worry, Liesel. I shouldn't have ever have
asked you to wait for me. At the rate I'm going, it could
take years for us to get the sort of support we need."

"Jack, I—"

"Shh…don't worry, darlin'. This is on me. It's too much
to ask, taking on all this." He nodded toward the smoldering high street then gave her shoulders a quick squeeze
before releasing them. "Still friends?"

"Of course." The words came out as a whisper, followed
by a silent *always* as he turned away from her.

Jack knew he was letting emotion cloud his logic. If only
he could give up his professional calling, make friends
with his father and go back to a nice, safe life at the winery. Then he'd be able to give Liesel the fairy-tale ending
she deserved.

If. There were so many ifs. He raked a hand through

his hair, a masculine stab at keeping emotion at bay. No good. It was still charging through him like a herd of wild elephants.

"Jack, if you ask me, I can't believe you did so much *good* work today. On your own, no less."

Liesel's voice broke through his rampaging thoughts.

"You think this is good?" He swept a hand along the small high street. It looked like a film set in a disaster movie. After the disaster.

Liesel took a step back, shocked at the harsh tone of his voice. This wasn't the Jack she knew. Today couldn't have changed him that much, could it? "I think the good really outweighs the bad here. Surely you can see that? There were no fatalities, right?"

He shook away her comment with a brusque wave of his hand. "Can you imagine what would've happened here if we weren't around? If the station didn't exist anymore? Today would've been a one hundred percent disaster. Can't you see that?"

Liesel felt herself suck in a deep breath. She wasn't going to use Eric as a cheap playing card to get ahead in this conversation—but Jack was alive, and so were all of the other casualties here. They were *alive*! There was no way she was going to let him call this situation a failure.

"I think I'm in a *very* good place to know when good outweighs bad." She put a hand on his arm, wishing she could stroke his face, wipe away some of the soot, hold him in her arms. "Jack, remember, I know more than most how bad a situation can get, and I for one am amazed and pleased with today's outcome."

"A mother almost died today, Liesel. Because of a care-less mistake. I almost got her killed because I took my eye off the ball for just a few seconds!"

The grief in his eyes went deeper than what was happening today. Much deeper.

"Jack, what are you *really* talking about?"

"I'm talking about my mum…" He raked a hand through his soot-laced hair. "I swore I wouldn't let this happen again."

"But you didn't! You saved her, you numpty!" The words may have been teasing, but Liesel's heart was in her throat. How awful for him. She wanted to hold him, soothe away the grief that was so clearly eating away at him, but saw he was too charged to be held, comforted.

"I didn't really lay any of your fears to rest, did I?"

"Not particularly." Her lips set and she shook her head sharply. "But let me tell you this right now—if I hadn't been so worried about you, I wouldn't have come out and helped the people I did. You've helped, Jack! Many people. That woman in the store could be paralyzed for life if I hadn't helped her—in the same way the woman in the car might not be hugging her son right now if it hadn't been for you."

Jack glanced over at the mother and son then looked back into Liesel's clear eyes, sparking with intention. "You were worried about me?"

"Of course I was! Can't you see I'm nuts about you and the whole reason your job makes me crazy is because I can't face the idea of losing you?"

"Come here, you." Jack pulled her in close to him, soot, filth and all, so she wouldn't see the tears in his eyes. Liesel was nuts about him! He hadn't wanted to admit it, but he'd been blindsided when she'd announced she just wanted to be friends after their very X-rated night together. And now she was saying their struggle to be friends hadn't been because of an absence of feeling but because of so *much* feeling.

Jack pulled his fingers through Liesel's hair and held her tight to his chest. He ached to kiss her. Tip that little chin of hers up and taste that strawberry-red mouth again and again. If she was nuts about him, he was positively cuckoo about her. Full steam ahead sparko. He was going to have to get some order in his life. Put things into a better place so he could make sure she had the life—and love— she deserved. Today was proof you couldn't change the past. But he did have something to say about the future.

First step, John Granville Keller. Mending fences with his father was a tall order, but essential to becoming the man he wanted to be for this woman he held in his arms. If healing old wounds couldn't be done, then Liesel was better off facing the future without him.

Liesel clapped her hands with a big laugh when Marilyn wiggled a toe on departure. The ambulance crew had the young mum safely strapped to a hard board, and if the toe wiggle was anything to go by, then any trauma she'd received on her spine might not be permanent. She crossed her fingers behind her back and gave a wink up into the heavens for good measure.

She reached out a hand to run down Jack's shoulder and just as quickly as he'd been so present with her, he was gone again. A few meters up the road, she could see his eyes trained on the burnt-out scene in front of them. It stung, but she knew it wasn't personal. At least she understood him now, knew his whole story. The CFS was Jack's life, whether or not he had a lovelorn school nurse on the scene.

And, sadly, he was right. Without the local station, the accident could have left far more destruction in its wake. Other emergency services were a good hour away. She chanced a look at his profile. He was an incredible man. Strong, passionate, committed. His drive to help was catching. He'd definitely reignited the flames of community service within her. But what would be enough for him to lay his own demons to rest? She knew talking it out over a bottle of wine was not really a "guy" thing but maybe someday…when the chances of them ending up naked in bed again weren't quite so high. A quick shake of the head was required to get that little picture out of her head before she approached him.

"Why don't I make us dinner tonight?" If he wanted to talk, she'd obviously listen, but something told her it might take a while. At the very least, he could chill out and let her be there for him.

He turned, slowly running a thumb along her jawline, as if tracing it gave him strength. "No, darlin', not tonight." He bent down and planted a soft kiss on her lips. A kiss so gentle she could've sworn she could float. A kiss so perfect it soared well out of "just friends" territory. Just as the whole world around her began to disappear he pulled back, nodding at the devastation of the high street. "I'm afraid I've got something else I have to do."

CHAPTER TEN

"HELLO, SON."

"Hey, Dad."

Scintillating start to a life-changing moment.

Jack covered his eyes, squinting against the late-afternoon sun to look up at his father, stationed at his usual post on the veranda. Rocking chair? Check. Steaming cup of coffee by his side? Check.

"What did I do to deserve the pleasure of Fire Brigade Captain Jack Keller all the way out here at our humble vineyards? Come to check our extinguishers?"

And we're off! Thanks for rubbing salt into the wound.

"C'mon, Dad, I was hoping we could have a talk."

His father's tone remained defensive. "Forgive me for being surprised, son. It's not like we've seen an awful lot of you since you've been back in the Valley."

"Fair enough." And it was.

Either-or. That was how he did things. And now the tactic was isolating him from everyone he cared about. If he didn't get his life in order he'd never be in a place where he could have—well, it all. Friends, family, loved ones… Liesel. Accident cleanup had kiboshed his plans to see his father straightaway and it was probably just as well. It had given him clarity. Perspective. And not just about his father—about Liesel, as well. In the days following the crash, it had become as clear as day to him that life with her as a friend was— It just wasn't good enough. He now understood firsthand how frightening it was to think of losing someone you loved in a dangerous situation.

He shook his head as he clumped up the steps and joined his father on the veranda. No wonder his father hated his life in the CFS—he was terrified of losing his son.

"This chair all right?" Jack pointed to the Adirondack-style chair next to his father.

"Suits me fine."

They were perfectly situated to look out on the sprawl of vines and outbuildings sloping down to the river's edge. It was beautiful. It was home. He wanted Liesel to see all this, love it as much as he did. He could sit here all day if…

"Well? Cat got your tongue? I need to get over to the shed and service the harvesters."

Jack took a sidelong look at his father. He wasn't really the mean old curmudgeon he was playing to Jack now. He was a good man. A traditional man who wanted the very best for his family, and he'd been dealt a raw deal.

It had been a long time ago, some twenty years now, when Jack's mother had died in the fire. She had been the love of his father's life. He'd never once hinted at remarrying. She had been his father's one and only and she was gone. Until now, Jack had felt he'd been on a quest to make up for it. And failing. Now he realized that by trying to make up for it he'd been making things worse. Only problem was, it had turned out his professional passion really was in the CFS. The trick was to find a balance.

He took a deep breath and lifted his chin in his father's direction.

"How's everything going with River's Bend?"

Not neutral territory, but it was a place to start.

"Your sister's keeping everything in order. Could do with a second pair of hands, though."

A compliment for Becca. That was a change. An insult for him. The usual.

"Dad, I want to talk to you about something. About the CFS."

"What about it?" His father's mouth thinned and his gaze stayed fixed on the horizon.

"I think I have a pretty good idea now why you're so dead set against me being in it."

"Oh, you think you've got it all figured out, do you?"

"No, but I've got a pretty good guess. I've done some soul-searching lately and I have a feeling my joining the CFS was about the cruelest thing I could have done to you after losing Mum."

He watched as his father registered what he was saying. The scowl on his father's face deepened then relaxed a hair.

"Dad, listen to me." He pulled his chair around so that he faced his father. When he felt he had his father's reluctant attention he continued, "We've got to lay this to rest. I know you think I'm full of extremes and that my world is black and white, but since Mum died…" He took a ragged inhalation and continued, "Since I ran round the barn that day, I swore I would dedicate my life to making it right. Turning inaction into action. And after years of hard work and training, it turns out I'm not just good at it but I love it. It's work I was born to."

"So what is it you want me to say? That I support you? I think you'll find I have been supporting you."

"By making me choose between the farm and the CFS?"

The scowl returned. "Am I meant to congratulate you for choosing a life in the CFS over the generations of hard work and development that went into creating all of this?" His broad hand indicated the hectares of old vines bursting with fruit. "All of this—" he punched each of the words out as if they were weapons "—ready and waiting for you on a silver platter."

His father stared at him glassy-eyed. Jack couldn't tell which way the conversation would go.

"I just want you to be safe, son!"

Jack reached across and took what was now an old man's hand in his and gave it a firm squeeze. God, he'd been an idiot. An idiot not to see a father's desire to keep what remained of his family safe and secure after such a horrible accident. It was the same thing Liesel had said. "What we need to figure out now is how you're going to forgive me. *If* you're going to forgive me."

Granville's eyes snapped to attention.

"Is that what you think? That I despise you?"

"It's been a little difficult to believe otherwise, Dad. The last thing I've felt here is welcome."

"Of course you're welcome. This is your inheritance! I wanted you and your sister to be able to raise your families here, just as your mother and I did, until…"

Jack flinched. At the rate he was going he would never have a family. He'd been sure he could have had a ready-made one with Liesel. One they could add to and make bigger and more rambunctious than the trio they could be now. If she would have him. He wasn't so sure he deserved her faith—her love.

He watched as his father's hand ran along the horizon. "Son, this is your history! My history and your grandfather's! And you just want to throw it all away on sorting out other people's problems. Putting out other fires that will never ever bring your mother back. Can't you see I didn't want that for you? A life reliving the horror of her death each and every single day? I wanted you to focus on the winery so you could let go of the past, have the future I'd built for you!"

"I would love to be part of the winery's future, Dad—but I can't give up the fire service."

"Well, it doesn't take a brainiac to figure that out." His father sat back in his chair.

Jack shot him an inquisitive look.

"Don't think I haven't heard about all your heroics on the radio. That's why I've sent those checks over to the CFS."

"What?"

"You don't think I'd just let my only son come back to rescue a two-bit fire station and not get some support from his old man?"

Now it was Jack's turn to swallow a heavy wave of emotion.

"That was you?"

"'Course it was! Who else do you think wants that place as well equipped as it can be? I'm not having you run round in a half-clapped-out tin pot! If my son's going to run a fire station, he's going to run a proper one. You're a Keller. We don't do things half-baked."

His father loved him. Had been there for him. Jack pulled his father out of his chair and hugged him. Tight.

"I don't know what to say, Dad. I really don't—other than thank you."

He felt the hug being returned. "Well, why don't you make your face a bit more of a familiar commodity out here in return?"

He was welcome at River's Bend. Could things really change in an instant? A life, a future here at the station was something he hadn't let himself consider. Jack's mind flooded with a wash of possibility. There was so much to consider he fell into a stunned silence.

His father gently pushed him out of the hug. "Why don't you go on in the kitchen and get something cold to drink, son? You look a bit parched. Clearing up that mess in town must be tough work."

"How d'you know?"

Granville pushed himself up out of his rocker and nodded his head in the direction of a radio sitting on the window ledge. Of course. What Granville Keller didn't know about Engleton wasn't worth knowing.

"Have a nosy in the fridge, too. After you get something to eat, maybe you can give me a hand with one of the harvesters. I've got to replace some old valves."

"That'd be great, Dad. I'd like that."

"So, you think they'd go for it?"

"We'll do everything we can!" The chirpy Murray Valley hospital rep gave Liesel a hug right there in the middle of the busy ED. "We need the Engleton CFS as much as you need us. We'd be delighted to help.

"That's great. I'll just jot down all of the details for you and we'll see you on Saturday night, then."

"Running a CFS recruitment stand doesn't sound like the most fun way to enjoy the Harvest Festival. Are you sure you're going to be able to do it all on your own?"

Liesel waved away the rep's concerned expression. "Don't worry, I've got a couple of spare pairs of hands in town to help and it's not as if I won't benefit from more people on the crew." *And Jack.*

She waved goodbye to the rep, scooped Liam up onto her hip and took a last look at the buzzing ED. Yup! It still gave her a buzz. Truth of the matter was, since the Great Grape Spill, as she'd been calling it, she hadn't been able to keep away from the hospital. She'd been popping by for the past week after school to check up on Marilyn, her patient from the crash. A full examination along with some dedicated rehab and she was going to be fine. She'd suffered a lot of bruising but no permanent damage. The same was true of the rest of the victims of the spill. Everyone who had sustained some sort of injury looked as if they'd come away from it largely unscathed.

Joke names aside, there were still a lot of serious issues to be dealt with. The wrecked shop, the burnt-out milk bar. Thank goodness the haulier was from a reputable company and had been fully insured. It might take a while for everything to come out of the wash, but once it did Engleton and her residents would be all right.

Especially if her plan worked.

She took a glance at the wall clock above Reception. Time to get a move on. She'd promised the volunteers down at the station some freshly baked muffins in exchange for keeping the recruitment stand at the Harvest Festival a secret from Jack. Just a few more days and he would know she was well and truly going to be there for him.

She didn't know if grand gestures were his thing—but it was time to show him she meant to battle her demons head-on. He had been open and honest with her about his life so it was time to lay her cards on the table. She loved Jack and wanted him to be in her and Liam's lives. Better to enjoy life day by day and as fully as possible than to live her life in fear. Fingers crossed, Jack still had room for her in his life.

"What are you doing down here?"

Not quite the greeting she'd been hoping for... He did look happy to see her, those blue eyes of his bright with surprise. It was hard to see him hold himself back from her when all she wanted to do was give him a hug and a kiss. Well, a lot more than that—but they *were* in public.

Liesel held up the plate of warm snickerdoodles in response. "Want one?"

"Love one." Jack took a cookie but kept his gaze fixed on Liesel. "How's the little man?"

"Well! He's well." *Missing you almost as much as I am.* "Busy! I never knew a two-year-old could have such a full social schedule." She laughed to fill the awkward silence. "I suspect you are, too."

"Not half!" Jack swept a hand through his hair. It took all her control not to do a follow-up caress. He looked tired. She hadn't seen him in over a fortnight and if she were a betting woman, she would've laid money on the fact he had been putting in twelve-hour-plus days. Maybe she should just tell him now she wanted to help, wanted to be there for him. Why keep it a secret?

"The high street is a mess. It's going to take a lot of work to get it back together, not to mention we're heading into peak fire season."

"Well, if anyone can make a bad situation good, you can."

"Jack! Mate!" one of the volunteers called out from the station house. Liesel watched as Jack's body went taut with attention. "Someone's just rung in a bushfire over at Cooper's Pass. Ready to saddle up?"

"Liesel…I'm sorry."

"Don't worry. I understand." She did, too. If there was a medical emergency she would've been running by now. Now wasn't the time to tell him he'd helped her find the strength to believe in love again. To believe taking risks— no matter how scary they were—was worth it. "I'll just pop these in the kitchen for when you lot get back. See you at the Harvest Festival?"

"I'd like that."

From the look in his eyes, she could tell he meant it. And that was enough to help her believe she was doing the right thing. At the very least, if Jack decided he only had time and energy for the CFS she would have been honest with him. Played her true hand. And honesty was vital.

"Mate, are you ready?"

"Sorry?" Jack looked up from the telephone receiver at the volunteer leaning into his office.

"It's getting on for seven o'clock. We got to get the rig ready for the festival."

Jack felt his forehead crinkle in confusion. "What are you talking about?"

"The rig, you know…" He watched as the volunteer clapped a hand over his mouth. "Forget I said anything. Uh…wheels up in ten minutes, all right, Captain?"

"Sure thing." Jack shook his head in confusion. The guys had all been a bit weird around him the past few days. He knew he wasn't a master at reading body language but it was hard to miss the sotto voce conversations, the side-long glances.

He pushed himself up from his desk and tried to shrug it off. The past forty-eight hours had been a whirlwind and there was no doubt he'd been in his own world for most of it. Ten minutes? Right. Better get a move on.

Liesel could hardly believe her eyes. River's Bend Winery was absolutely beautiful. It was hard to believe she'd lived in Engleton almost a year and hadn't been out to see this place yet—it was amazing. She and Liam stood hand in hand, trying their best not to gape at everything.

A few days after the crash River's Bend Winery had announced its decision to volunteer its tasting rooms as the location for the Harvest Festival, rather than it being held in the main street, where it had originally been sched-uled. By the looks of things, the winery had pulled out all the stops. Fairy lights swirled around a parade of gum trees leading up to the property. Bunting was strung along the veranda of the tasting room—an incredibly beautiful structure in its own right. A massive marquee, complete with an expansive dance floor, was floodlit and already thick with revelers.

The lawn had several huge vats with little staircases leading up to them where punters could kick off their shoes and enjoy a bit of their own winemaking. Local artisan cheese, sausage, bread and cured olive makers had set up a long stream of trestle tables and enormous washtubs filled with ice showed off wines from across the valley.

River's Bend management had made it clear one and all were welcome. So that was why she'd made the telephone call. If they were about community, they were about the CFS.

She gave Liam's hand a little tug. It was time they manned their stand—the Community Fire Service recruitment and baked goods stand. Her oven had been working overtime the past two days as she'd baked up more cookies, cupcakes and other delectables than she had in her entire life at one time. A few of the emergency staff at the hospital had said they'd share the roster with her to help raise money and recruit volunteers for the Engleton station.

It had taken all her powers of secret-keeping in order to not spill the beans to Jack. Being friends was tough, but watching him struggle was harder.

Her heart rate slipped up a notch when she saw him arrive amid a throng of firemen. They may have all been wearing the same uniforms, but no one filled it better than Jack Keller. In the slick black lines of the suit, he embodied the role of Engleton CFS Station's brigade captain. The commanding officers at HQ in Adelaide would've been impressed. She couldn't believe the pride she felt swelling within her. He was an amazing man. A small twist of pain began to tighten within her.

The time they had spent together over the past few months had filled her with such happiness. Her son had grown in confidence—and he wasn't the only one. She was a changed woman. She could feel it in her very core. Elements of the old Liesel had definitely come back—but the woman she was now? Fun, confident, a nurse, a mother. He'd made an impact. A big one.

"Are you the one in charge?"

An elegant gentleman approached her desk. She smoothed the skirt of her green dress and gave him her best smile of welcome.

"Absolutely. There are a variety of jobs down at the station—all volunteer, of course. Would you like to take a look?"

"No need, love. I think I might be a bit past running up and down ladders." He gave a rueful laugh and made a playful show of being a bit rickety. She laughed along with him, although she thought for a silver-haired man he looked pretty vital. And familiar. There was something about the way his eyes—

"The winery would like to make a donation, as well."

"Of course. Do you mean—"

"River's Bend." His eyes ran warmly around the premises. "This is our place and we'd like to put our continued support behind the CFS in the form of a memorial fund. I'm thinking somewhere in the neighborhood of ten thousand dollars. A month. I presume you'll take a check."

"Absolutely!" Liesel couldn't believe it. What an amazing start. She had hoped to have a good list going and at least a few dollars in the pot before Jack came—but this was even better than she could have imagined.

"My son works for the CFS but he's going to invest in his roots again."

"Oh?"

"Yes, he's thinking of moving back here, to the winery, to be with family."

"How lovely! You're a lucky man!"

"You bet I am. He's one in a million, my boy."

The gentleman looked so happy Liesel couldn't help but send him a wide congratulatory smile in response. She wondered which of the volunteers was his son. This gentleman seemed so familiar.

"Now, where do I sign?" The man lifted his pen in anticipation.

"Just here," Liesel spluttered, pulling the appropriate clipboard across the table toward him. "Just down here." She put her finger to the line where he should write his name. Just as quickly she was withdrawing it as if she'd been burnt by the words formed by the man's pen: John Granville Keller.

He noticed her sharp movement and looked up with a warm smile, eyes twinkling. Bright blue eyes.

"Liesel—"

She knew that voice. And there wasn't a chance in the world she was going to look at the uniformed man who had just approached the CFS stand. Not now. Not with shock turning her smile into a stupid fixed grin. Jack hadn't told her the truth. His whole story. She'd told him everything and despite their promise of friendship he'd still kept her compartmentalized. As if she was a dirty little secret to keep hidden away.

How could she not have seen it? She felt like such an idiot. And humiliated. She'd been so open with her own life, allowing Jack full, unfettered access to herself, her son. She had plans in motion to change her *life* for this man and he couldn't even tell her his father lived down the road? And that he was going to give up his all-important CFS? The very same CFS he had wanted to put her on hold for?

Blood was thicker than…than whatever feelings she'd

thought Jack had for her. She could feel her face burn with indignation.

Was she so off Jack's true radar that he had to keep her secret from his past? Apparently so. She forced herself to look up. She could do this. She could.

And there they were. Side by side. Father and son.

If Jack could have prevented her confusion, her pain, he would have. Correction. He could have, but he hadn't. So Jack did the next best thing he could think of…backpedal. Like crazy. "I see you've met my father."

"Yes, we've just met." Liesel had put on her best bubbly party voice but her eyes told another story. "He's going to make a very generous donation to the CFS. In the name of…"

She let the sentence hang for Mr. Keller to fill in.

"In the name of Ava Keller. It'll be an annual donation." He turned and clapped an arm along his son's shoulders. "Better than ad hoc. Your mother would've wanted it that way."

Jack rocked back on his heels. He knew he and his father had set the wheels of repairing old wounds in motion—but this was one heck of a gesture. He was truly touched. "Thanks, Dad." He pulled him into a strong hug. "I mean it."

"Well," Liesel began briskly, "it looks like you two have some catching up to do."

"Actually…" Jack broke in quickly. He had to stop any conjecturing Liesel might be doing right now. He could practically see the wheels whirling in her head. "We *all* have a lot of catching up to do." Jack reached out a hand, indicating he wanted her to join them.

Liesel tossed a quick look over her shoulder. Liam was happily playing away with a group of supervised toddlers. He looked happy, content. He was the one "man" she could rely on these days. Which was just as well, as it looked as if it would be just the two of them from now on. She just needed to get this over with, this whole horribly planned night, and then go about the near impossible task of putting Jack Keller out of her mind.

Liesel stiffened as Jack reached across and took her hand in his. His long fingers slipped through hers, instantly infusing her with that incredible feeling of warm protection she'd felt the very first time she'd met him. How could someone who made her feel so safe be such a master of deceit?

Relief flooded through her that she hadn't turned in her own CFS form yet. Maybe it wasn't too late to talk to the hospital about working there. Living closer would be a good idea, as well. Farther away from Jack.

Why had he kept all of this secret from her? Made a life decision to move on—away from everything she had thought he wanted to do? Had the whole CFS-is-my-life thing been a lie? Was it because she was a single mother? Or was he ashamed of her? As an heir to one of the region's most successful wineries, he could no doubt have chosen from a huge pool of adoring women.

She felt her mouth form into one of those crazy upside-down smiles. The good news was that if he was leaving the CFS to work at the winery, she wouldn't have to see him at the station when she encountered the team. He wasn't going to take away her newfound confidence on the nursing front. Not a chance. She felt the lines of her mouth grow firm with resolve.

See? There's a plus side to everything!

As she stomped reluctantly behind him, trying her best not to stare at that backside of his, she afforded herself a small snigger, grateful that Jack at least had the courtesy to bring her and his father to a quiet part of the sprawling lawn. Her humiliation wouldn't be completely public. Not to mention the fact that stomping in high heels was bloody difficult. She shot a glance back toward the toddler play-group at the sound of Liam's laughter. She could still see his little blond head happily at play. She'd been that happy just a handful of minutes ago.

Ignorance had been bliss.

"Just thought you'd like to keep an eye on the little guy."

Good old Jack! Thinking of everything again. Too bad I'm trying my best to squelch any feelings I have for you!

"Dad. Liesel." His eyes played between the two of them as if he was expecting them to start a sparring match. Or possibly use him as a punching bag. "You're the two most important people in my life and I think… I know I owe both of you an explanation."

Liesel and Granville opened their mouths simultane-ously to concur then muttered that the other should go ahead, their voices melding into a verbal jumble. They laughed nervously, turning to Jack in a joint appeal as if speech was no longer one of their skills.

Jack couldn't help but throw his head back and laugh. This was all a first-class disaster.

"Son, I don't really see what's going on here."

"Jack. You don't have to do this. I understand every-thing now and I'll just get going."

"No! That's just it." Jack raised his hands in a hold-it-for-a-minute pose before continuing. "Neither of you have the full picture…and the truth is I don't think I did until now."

Liesel looked at him uncomprehendingly. What was he going on about?

Jack turned to his father. "Dad, I love you and I would love to be part of life here at River's Bend again one day, but there are two pretty big conditions I have."

His father raised his forehead appraisingly and tipped his head, indicating Jack should go ahead and name them.

"One, Becca continues to run the winery and you use me as an ad hoc odd-job man. I will stay full-time with the CFS and continue to try and make it the best station in the region. From the looks of things—" he dropped a wink at Liesel "—there appear to be some new volunteers I hadn't counted on." He raised a hand as Liesel made a move to interject.

"In the meantime, I would love to help with the harvest and any other busy spells when Becca might need me. I promise you she won't be left alone. But I won't abandon the CFS. Do we have a deal?"

His father pushed his lips out, tentatively started to nod and then reconsidered. "I think I need to hear the other condition first."

Liesel cocked her head to the side. This was going to be interesting.

"Actually, Dad, I might need a bit of privacy for this one. Can you give us a minute?"

His father gave him a knowing nod and that all-too-familiar wink. "All right, son. I'll go get us a glass of something sparkling, shall I?"

"That'd be perfect." Jack waited a moment as his father worked his way back toward the booths before he turned to Liesel.

The wheels in her mind were spinning like mad to catch up with all this new information. How could Jack have kept all this from her? He had a whole family just sitting and waiting for him right here in River's Bend! A family he'd chosen to keep at arm's length until he sorted things out. Just as he'd done to her. Well, that just wasn't good enough. That wasn't love. That was... All thoughts disappeared as Jack turned the full force of his bright blue eyes directly onto her, clasping both of her hands in his, and began to speak. "What's more important to me, Liesel, more than the CFS, the winery—all of it—is you."

She drew in a swift breath. *What? Was this for real?*

"If my job has taught me anything, it's that life is so very precious and that you need to make the very most of it. I love you. I love you and I don't want to spend another day in my life without you. Liesel Adler, will you do me the honor of becoming my wife?"

Liesel's blood ran hot and cold.

"Is life so precious, then, that you keep your family hidden away from me? Or was it the other way round? You didn't want them to know about me?"

"No, that's not it at all," Jack protested, but she could see she'd hit a nerve.

"What about Liam?"

Jack laughed and squeezed her hands. "Well, I don't want to *marry* him, but I'd sure love it if you'd allow me to be the best father figure to him I can be—and maybe give him some brothers and sisters along the way."

"I don't know, Jack." Liesel tried to tug her hands free, her mind buzzing with too many thoughts. "This is a lot to take in. If you keep people you claim to love at a distance until you've got all your professional ducks in a row, then how can I know you'll be there for me, for my son, when we need you?" Liesel's eyes stung with the tears she'd been trying to keep at bay. The smile on Jack's face faded, his fingers keeping a firm grip on hers.

"I love you, Liesel. With everything in my heart. What would make you think I didn't?"

"Keeping your whole life a secret, for starters!"

"Not half!" Granville burst in, hands juggling three glasses of sparkling wine, the broad smile on his face betraying the stern words he was trying to impart. "How could you have kept this beautiful woman a secret from us for so long?"

"If she'll answer my question, we'll have the rest of our lives to explain."

Jack turned expectantly to Liesel, his eyes bright with anticipation. He loved her. He *loved* her. There was nothing to fight here—only a lifetime of happiness with the man she loved to gain.

Or more secrets to unravel. More time to wait until Jack decided he was truly ready to take part in a real family life. She couldn't live that way. All these conditions he kept putting on things! It shouldn't be like that. Love didn't work like that! It was big and powerful and overwhelming and exactly what she felt for Jack, but if he needed to live his life by a set of rules only he had access to—it just wasn't good enough.

"I'm sorry, Jack. I love you, too. You know I do, but I think in our case it's just not enough."

"What do you mean? I know I was late off the mark in telling you about my family but surely that's not a deal breaker?"

"You know my history, Jack, and you knew I didn't want any more mysteries. No more waiting, wondering. I just can't do this." She swiftly pulled her hands from his and ran as fast as she could across the lawn, stopping only to pull off her ridiculous heels so she could run faster. Chest heaving, she picked up Liam from the playgroup and wound her way through the buildup of cars to her own. She could hear Jack calling her name.

She needed to get out of there. Now.

Fumbling for her keys, she could hear Jack's voice getting closer.

Alone. She just wanted to be left alone. She and Liam had been doing perfectly fine before Jack Keller had come into their lives. The last thing she'd needed was to be railroaded this way or that by someone who, it had turned out, she barely knew. She quickly opened the side door and buckled Liam into his seat.

"Liesel, wait!" She could see Jack appearing from behind a truck and slammed the driver's door shut as if it would help stop the entire situation from happening. How could he have expected her to accept a marriage proposal from a man who only wanted her in one part of his life? The sidelines! Was he mad? Or was she crazy to have become involved with him in the first place?

"Liesel!" He was right by her window. Those dear eyes she adored were so close, silently pleading with her.

"I'm sorry, Jack." And she was.

Liesel put her foot on the gas pedal and pulled away from the manicured lawns, the beautifully decorated acreage, all of which could have been hers to enjoy if she'd just said one little word. She looked in the rearview mirror and saw Jack's silhouette against the fairy-lighted trees. Her gaze slipped down to her son, whose eyes were wide with bewilderment. She shifted the car up a gear and drove away.

"Have you gone completely stark-raving mad?"

Cassie stopped her from throwing yet another perfectly gorgeous floral bouquet into the rubbish bin.

"Hardly. I've got a son to look after and there is no chance I'm going to marry a liar."

"He's not a liar, Liesel. He's sorting out some issues."

"By keeping things secret from me. By partitioning me off. Hardly the foundation for a loving relationship." She handed the bouquet to her friend with a firmly set smile. "Here. You take it. I have to finish packing."

"You've got three weeks to pack and you still haven't found a new place yet."

"Common sense is not going to prevail right now, Cassie! I'm…" Liesel felt her voice about to break and she didn't want to give in to tears. Again. Her heart was absolutely broken and the only thing she had to rely on now was her own strength of character. That and the promise of a new job at the hospital come summertime. She had given notice at the school and just needed to set about finding somewhere for her and Liam to move into before her parents let out the house for the summer.

"Have you told your parents?"

"No."

"And that's different from what Jack did to you on what level?"

She turned to her friend, tears firmly swallowed. "It's incredibly different. He lied to me about his background, his present, his future, and then thought he could just drag Liam and me along whichever way his current mood took him. One minute he wants me in his life, the next he doesn't. Flip-flop! It's not acceptable. Not for me and definitely not for my son."

"Even if that future involves living on several hundred hectares of Murray Valley's finest winery with a blond hunk?"

"I fell in love with a plain old fireman."

"Ha! As if. And I seem to remember someone who was pretty dead set against falling in love with a man in a hazardous profession."

"People change."

"Exactly."

Cassie pulled her into a tight hug, flowers still in hand. The perfume of the wildflower bouquet filled Liesel with scented memories of being with Jack. Now she'd have to start hating flowers to boot. Terrific.

"Liesel, I know you're angry with him but you're obviously still in love with him."

Liesel stiffened. *So? Was that against the rules?*

"No one goes to this much effort to avoid someone they're indifferent to. I'm not asking you to forgive him this minute. I'm just saying maybe you owe him a second chance. A chance to explain himself. That's all he's asking for."

Liesel eased herself out of the hug and opened the back door of the house for her friend. She needed more alone time. "I don't know, Cass. Jack has done a pretty good job of burning his bridges."

"Just don't do anything you'll regret. Never is a long time to stay away from someone you love."

Liesel closed the door with a halfhearted wave and let herself slide to the floor. She propped her elbows on her knees and held up the card she'd managed to steal from the bouquet before Cassie left.

Poppies are red, cornflowers are blue, chocolate milk shakes mean nothing when I'm not with you.
I love you,
Jack

She tried to squelch the smile slipping to her lips and scrunched her fingers along her temple. Cassie would make a brilliant agony aunt. Of course she was still in love with Jack. Days were better knowing he'd be part of them. As things stood, days weren't very good right now.

Yes, she'd picked up the phone a dozen times and then hung up just as many after each bouquet had arrived. But she had her son to think about. He needed someone reliable in his life. Besides, she'd set the wheels in motion to move on. And that's what she was going to try and do. It wasn't running away—it was progress. At least that's what she'd keep telling herself. Maybe one day she'd actually believe it.

"She'll love it."

"You sure?" Jack grinned at his sister, a woman blessed with brains and good taste.

"Positive." She fiddled with his uniform collar for a minute then leaned back and returned the grin. "Who could resist my handsome big brother?"

"Liesel, apparently. I'm running out of silly rhymes!" He offered her a wry smile as he slipped the small box back into his pocket. He was on a mission. A long-term one if need be. Patience was something he was good at and he was determined to win Liesel back. If it took until he was as craggy and aged as some of their finest cellared wines, then so be it. After hearing through the town's very short grapevine that she'd handed in notice at the school and was accepting a job at the hospital, he needed to let her know he was in this for the long haul. He couldn't let her move on without trying again.

If he was really honest with himself, he knew she had every right to be angry. If he'd been in her shoes, he'd definitely need some cooling-down time. And a good old-fashioned apology.

So far he had sent a dozen bouquets. That made it twelve days since The Dark Night, including a Sunday when the florist had been closed and he'd had to improvise. He hadn't realized how difficult it was to make a bouquet. Thank God Becca had been around to help him. Being able to go to his family for help was incredible. They had his back—and he would need their support as he sorted out the cataclysmically large mess he'd made of things.

"So. Is that next on the agenda?" Becca tipped her head in the direction of his pocket.

"No, I've got something I hope will be a bit more persuasive in mind."

"More persuasive than Mum's vintage diamond-and-emerald ring?"

Jack rocked back on his heels and looked out of the tasting room toward the river. "Mmm…on a par, on a par."

* * *

Her office couldn't have sparkled more if it had been brand-new. Liesel popped the box of personal effects onto her immaculately clear desk, ready for her replacement. She'd already met the young woman, an Adelaide native like herself, and thought she'd be great. She would miss the children, but knew her new job at the hospital was a better fit. Leaving Engleton, that was going to be harder than she'd thought.

"Miss! Miss!" Kev appeared round the corner, urgently gesturing for her to join him.

She fell into a jog beside the teen, who had fully recovered from his collapsed lung. "What is it? Has someone been hurt?"

"You've got to come quickly, to the car park."

"What's going on, Kev?" Her brow crinkled with worry. A serious incident was not the way she was hoping to say goodbye to everyone on her last day at the school. She was hoping to leave everyone in good health. Then sneak away like the coward she was beginning to feel like. Dodging her problems wasn't usually her style. Oh, well. People changed.

"Just hurry!" Kev furrowed his brow in frustration, then broke into a run toward the double doors leading out to the back of the school.

She raced after him, heart pounding. There must be something really wrong.

The moment she burst through the doors she turned to go back in. Kev got there before her, blocking her entrance. "Miss," he cautioned with all of the gravitas a teen could muster, "my brigade captain needs to have a word."

And there he was, chocolate milk shakes in hand, as knee-weakeningly gorgeous as ever. Her dream come true, her worst nightmare. Jack Granville Keller III.

At least she knew what the *G* stood for now.

"Care for a ride in the country?" His too-kissable lips tipped up into a slow grin.

"I can't. I've got Liam."

"I've got Liam, actually." Cassie appeared beside her. "Kev and I are going to take him to the pictures."

"He's two." Liesel was grateful for the fleeting distraction from Jack's blue eyes. She'd missed them so much, the additional spark of life they seemed to give her.

"Going on three and he likes a good cartoon as much as the next person." Cassie dropped her a sassy wink before turning on her heel. "It starts any minute so we'd better get a move on."

"C'mon." She felt Jack's fingers thread through her own and give them a light squeeze before she'd realised he was beside her. She had to fight the instinct to return the squeeze. "Let's go for a ride."

"Jack, I really don't want to. It's my last day and I—"

He lifted a finger to her lips. "If you give me a chance, today could also be a day of firsts."

She resisted the urge to swat his hand away. She might be angry with him, but there was no need to be nasty. Besides, his finger against her lips was a teasing reminder of the sensual pleasures Jack had once released in her. Not that she wanted those anymore. Well, she did. But she *shouldn't* and that was going to have to be enough.

"On you go!" She felt Cassie give her a little shove. Looked as if she wasn't going to have much choice in the matter.

"A short one." She arched what she hoped was an assertive brow up at Jack. He gave her one of his crooked grins and all at once she was back in the barnyard, her body turning into a butterfly-filled lava lamp all over again. She retrieved her hand from Jack's and reluctantly followed him to the truck, where he'd placed the milk shakes in the beverage holders. For a man who thought of everything, he certainly had a knack for not explaining anything! Which was precisely the problem.

She chewed on her lips as he climbed into the cab and pulled the truck out of the school's car park just as they'd done dozens of times before over the course of their—whatever it had been. Friends didn't hide friends from their families. And she needed to remember that.

"Do you mind a little music?"

"Not at all." It would cover up the fact she couldn't think of a single lucid thing to say to him.

She watched as Jack flicked on the CD player then took in a sharp breath of surprise as the first song came on.

"This is—"

"Your favourite hippie music."

She couldn't help releasing a hint of a smile.

"Where are we going?"

"I'd thought of making it a secret, but figured we'd had enough of those." Liesel shot him a sharp look. Was he taking a dig at her or himself?

"River's Bend," he continued, his eyes trained on the road. "We're headed to River's Bend. I want you to see why I love it there and explain, if I can, what happened in the lead-up to the Harvest Festival."

"Jack, I just don't know. A lot has changed in my life."

"If you're talking about taking the job at the hospital, I heard." He saw her eyes widen in surprise.

"I have my sources!" Her cat eyes narrowed.

No more secrets.

"Cassie. Cassie told me. And I can't even tell you how proud I am of you. The hospital is lucky to have you. Truly." He placed a hand over hers and gave it a little squeeze.

"I know you don't owe me a thing, but I would do anything to win back your trust."

"It's not just my trust you need to earn, it's Liam's." A

surge of emotion shot through her like a lightning bolt. "I can't bring someone into his life who changes his mind on a whim about who he is and whether or not he wants us around." It was difficult to keep the hurt out of her voice, not to mention the anger, but she tried her best. Despite herself, she loved this man.

"Believe me, I know."

"But how could you?"

"Because I didn't think I had my father's trust all these years. And that hurt. A lot."

"You two seemed pretty chummy the other night." This time she knew she sounded unkind. And it felt wrong. Hurting Jack was the last thing she wanted to do.

"That's thanks to you, you know."

Uh, what was that? I thought I was being a jerk.

"Meeting you changed my life in ways I'd never imagined possible. At the very least, I owe you an enormous thank-you." He slapped the steering wheel gleefully. "Maybe you having a right old go at me. Blow off some steam. What do you say?" He was chuckling now, obviously delighted with the idea. "Do you fancy giving me a good old-fashioned telling off?"

"I don't really think that's necessary," she answered primly, before taking a sip of her chocolate milk shake. Delicious. A ten. Or was that Jack?

Quit softening my resolve, you...you picture of perfection!

He waggled his brows at her and spun out a toothy grin. "C'mon, darlin', you know you want to."

"Hardly. I'm more mature than you."

"That's what they say about girlies."

It was hard to stop the giggles from burbling forth. "Well, it's true." She pointed a decisive finger at him. "And I'm hardly a girlie."

Jack took his eyes off the road for a moment to appraise her. "No, darlin'. You are definitely all woman."

And *whoooosh*! There went the butterflies.

Jack turned the truck into the impressive entry gates of River's Bend. Her eyes scanned the seemingly endless rows of fruit-laden vines, the various winery buildings dotted along the left side of the drive and, as they wended their way along the dirt track, the classic country farmhouse sitting among a grove of gums. It was breathtaking. And off-limits. *Right?*

Jack clicked off the ignition and tipped his head in the direction of the trees. "C'mon. Let's take a walk."

Her resolve was softening by the second. And the seconds were flying past.

"Jack, I really don't think this is a good idea."

In a flash he was on the other side of the car, taking her hand in his. "I think you'll find it is. The future mistress of River's Bend really should know her way around the property, don't you think?"

Her fluttery tummy turned into a hard twist.

"No, Jack. I can't."

"Can't or won't?"

"Both. Not if you think compartmentalizing your life is a way to live. I've been through too much already. I'm not going to beg you to find out more secrets—nor am I going to sit around waiting for you to surprise me with another mind-blowingly huge plan for the future you 'forgot' to tell me."

"C'mon." He gave her hand another gentle tug, succeeding, this time, in guiding her round the side of the house into the sun-dappled woodland. They strolled for a few moments in silence, Liesel's head busy fighting the urge to turn into a pinball machine. When the thoughts settled a little, she still reached the same conclusion.

"Jack, I am so sorry for all you have been through, but you didn't trust that I would have been there for you."

"The way you trusted me with your history with Eric?"

Ouch. That hurt.

"That's not fair."

"Nor is keeping me in your bad books forever for the same mistake."

"It wasn't a mistake. It was…" Liesel hesitated, knowing Jack had made a legitimate point. "It was a tactical omission."

"Tactical omission?" Jack's eyes widened with disbelief. "Seriously?"

No. It was more than that.

"I thought I was waiting until I was ready to say goodbye to Eric."

Jack's expression softened. "Oh, darlin', you'll never say goodbye to him. He's the father of that great kid of yours. I was just hoping there was room in your heart for you to say hello to me."

Liesel felt tears prick at her eyes. She'd already said hello. Quite some time ago. And saying goodbye to Jack? It was proving near on impossible. Still. Her heels had been dug in, she might as well hash the whole thing out with him.

"It still would have been nice to find out you were a local boy and heir to a…to all of this before the Harvest Festival." She gestured at the beautiful woodland and expanse of riverfront that peeked through the bushes at the end of the path they'd been walking along.

"So you're telling me you would've gone for Jack the winery heir more than Jack the brigade captain?" His tone had turned brusque. He'd obviously had a lot of that growing up and it wasn't at all what she'd meant.

"No! Not in the slightest. I just felt like an idiot—everyone there knew who you were except me, the supposed object of your affection." She glared at him then felt her willpower weakening at the memory of him in his dress uniform. "Besides, I quite like Jack the fireman."

"Quite?" Jack's lips parted in a slow, sexy grin.

"A bit," she replied coyly, a finger working its way round one of her curls.

Obviously sensing he had some emotional purchase, she saw his confidence grow as he continued. It wasn't helping her resolve that a confident Jack was about as sexy as they made 'em.

"It would be an understatement to say the way things panned out at the Harvest Festival was the total opposite of how I wanted them to be."

"So I wasn't meant to find out anything at all?" Liesel stopped in her tracks, hands flying to her hips, chin quirked to the side. Sparks may actually have been shooting out of her eyes but she was too astonished to be sure. This was one heck of an apology! Resolve? Back into setcement land.

"No, you noodle, the total opposite. I wanted you to know everything about me, but with the crash and all, everything went pear-shaped. It was meant to be a Liesel dream night! There was supposed to be wine, delicious food, formal introductions to my family and me on a bended knee in front of the entire town with a beautiful ring and an accordion serenade."

Liesel couldn't help herself. She burst into hysterical laughter. "An accordion serenade?"

"Okay, maybe not the accordion serenade but everything else was true." Jack opened his arms wide, beckoning with his fingers that she should come in for one of his bear hugs. She wanted to, every pore in her body wanted to. But they still weren't quite there yet. She folded her arms as if they would help protect her from the answer to the next question.

"Are there more? More big things I need to know?"

"I once ate a worm on a dare from my sister then threw up in my dad's combine. It took him a week to clean it."

Liesel laughed softly, but kept her arms folded tightly across her chest. God, he made her laugh. She loved that about him.

Who was she kidding? She loved *him*. But she needed to know who the real "him" was. "Jack—be serious. I don't need a blow-by-blow account but a nice round nutshell version of the man I love would do before—"

"Before what? Wait!" His eyes went another notch up on the sky-blue barometer. "You love me?"

"Of course I do, you dill. Why do you think I was so upset?"

"Hang on. You said you needed a nutshell version of my life before—before what?"

"Before you can think about bending that knee of yours again." *Uh-oh.* She'd softened. *And we're back to putty!*

"Well, that, my darlin' redhead, is fair enough." He took a big breath and as he began to speak, ever so slowly began to lower one knee to the ground. "Nutshell version—I was born John Granville Keller the Third to Ava and Granville Keller. Lived an idyllic childhood here at River's Bend Winery with my sister, Becca. A fire, the details of which I have hashed over for the past twenty-odd years, took the life of my beloved mother and my father's true love. I blamed myself and, subsequently, thought my father hated me so I threw myself into a life of wild-child silliness that didn't really suit me until I eventually came to roost in the barracks of the CFS training HQ in Adelaide, where I found focus. Drive."

He took her hand in his and continued, his knee hovering inches above the ground. "I led a life of purposeful improvement with the fire service and active avoidance of my family and then one day—*pow!*—I met the most beautiful woman I have ever had the pleasure of laying my eyes on. She was smart, funny, has a cute-as-can-be kid who melts my heart every time I give him an airplane ride. She—her name is Liesel, by the way—gave me the strength to heal old wounds with my family and, more than anything…"

Liesel watched silently as Jack's knee met the ground and his hand slipped into his trouser pocket. He withdrew a small black box and flipped open the lid. "More than anything I wish she would agree to be my wife."

Her eyes widened at the sight of the glittering diamond flanked by two beautiful emeralds. It was the most gorgeous ring she had ever seen.

"Liesel Elizabeth Adler, will you please do me the honor of becoming my wife?"

If someone had told her your heart could actually get lodged in your throat, Liesel would've believed them at that moment. The man of her dreams was down on one knee, asking her to marry him, and she couldn't speak!

"Liesel?"

"There's just so much to process!" She knew she was just buying time—and she also knew what her heart was telling her.

"I'll do you one better, then. Would you agree to be my fiancée? I will give you a one-year warranty on any faults or problems you find with me." She raised a dubious eyebrow. "Within reason, of course."

"Well, that certainly is an interesting offer…"

"Liesel." His tone was insistent now. "Please, say something. Please, agree to spend your life with me."

Liesel dropped to her knees in front of him, wanting to look directly into those eyes of his when she answered. "Yes. Yes, I will, Brigade Captain Keller."

Jack threw back his head and let out a huge whoop. They were going to get married! Before she had a chance to take it in fully, Liesel felt Jack's hands slip along her waist, gently pulling her toward him. She couldn't believe a lifetime of butterflies and hot-blooded fireworks awaited her. And a man to rely on. Jack.

As his lips began to explore hers, she surrendered to the enjoyment of the sensual pleasures and promise of things to come as the future Mrs. Jack Keller.

* * * * *

WEDDING AT SUNDAY CREEK

LEAH MARTYN

For Claire, for professional insight
and delicious bubbly as we celebrate
the launch of my *twentieth* book for
Mills & Boon.

CHAPTER ONE

DR JACK CASSIDY, trauma surgeon, part-time explorer sometimes lover, stood away from the aeroplane, slowly absorbing the rich, bold colours of the Australian outback. And thought, unlike England, there was no elegant restraint out here. The colours were in-your-face heart-stopping and glorious.

He breathed in deeply, his eyes picking out the silhouettes of a family of kangaroos grazing in a nearby paddock. Big reds, he decided, feeling exhilarated by the sight. It felt good to be *home*. Added to that, he'd finally stepped away from the train wreck of a long-term relationship and felt freer than he had in months. Riding the upbeat feeling, he wheeled back towards the plane, where his luggage was waiting on the airstrip, and bent to pick up his bags.

The hospital was only a short walk away. He understood from his telephone interview that presently there was only one doctor at the Sunday Creek hospital, Dr Darcie Drummond. And that's where his knowledge of her began and ended. He just hoped Dr Drummond wasn't into role demarcation in the practice. If she expected him to just sit in his office and *administrate*, then she'd have to change her thinking.

Jack Cassidy intended to be a hands-on boss.

* * *

With the merest glance at her watch, Darcie decided it
was time to go home. The hospital would call her if she
was needed. Rolling her chair away from the desk, she
stood and moved across to the window, looking out.

It was still hazy towards the west and she knew the
grey bank of cloud in the sky was caused by intermit-
tent bush fires. Nothing to worry about, the locals had
assured her. It was the regular burning off of long grass
or bushfire fuel and the rural fire brigade would have
everything under control.

Darcie just hoped they did…

'Knock, knock.'

She spun round, several fronds of dark hair zipping
across her cheekbones as her gaze swivelled to the open
doorway. A man, easily six feet if she was any judge,
and someone she didn't recognise, lounged against the
doorframe.

Out of nowhere, every nerve in her body jumped to
attention. Darcie blinked, registering blue eyes, dark
hair, knife-edge cheekbones and a mouth that had her
instantly imagining fantasies that only existed in her
dreams. She swallowed dryly. 'Can I help you?'

'I sure hope so.' He gave a cool imitation of a smile.
'I'm your new medical director.'

He had to be kidding.

Darcie's disbelieving gaze ran over him. She wouldn't
have expected a suit and tie but this guy looked as though
he'd just come down from a Himalayan trek. He was
wearing combat trousers and a black T-shirt, his feet
enclosed in hiker's boots that came up over his ankles.

He didn't look like a senior doctor at all.

At least, not the ones she was used to.

'I came on the plane,' he enlightened her. 'You weren't expecting me?'

'No—I mean, yes. That is, we knew you were coming, we just didn't know when.'

He rumbled an admonishing *tsk*. 'Don't you read your emails? I sent my arrival details through a couple of days ago.'

Oh, help. This was going to sound totally lame. 'Our computer's anti-virus protection has turned a bit iffy lately. It's culling messages that should be coming through to the inbox. And a tree fell over some cables yesterday, bringing the internet down. We do the best we can…'

Jack caught her cut-glass English accent and frowned a bit. What kind of a hospital was she running here? Or *attempting* to run. Switching his gaze from her heated face to the sign on her door, he queried, 'You *are* Dr Darcie Drummond?'

Almost defensively, Darcie pulled back from the intensity of his gaze and cursed the zing of awareness that sizzled up her backbone. How totally inappropriate, she admonished herself. And grief! She'd forgotten his name! 'Yes, I'm Darcie Drummond.' Moving quickly from the window, she offered her hand.

'Jack Cassidy.' He took her hand, easily enfolding it within his own.

Darcie took her hand back, almost shocked at the warmth that travelled up her arm. 'You must think this is all terribly unprofessional,' she apologised.

One eyebrow quirked above Jack Cassidy's extraordinarily blue eyes. 'Thought of getting someone in to check your computer?'

Of course they had. 'We're rather isolated here,' she said thinly, as if that should explain everything. 'Technical help is never easy. You just have to wait until they get to you.'

He made a click of annoyance. 'The hospital should have priority. You should be out there, kicking butt.'

Darcie bristled. She knew whose butt she'd *like* to kick! And she was puzzled as well. She'd read Jack Cassidy's CV. That information *had* actually come through on her email. He'd been working in London for the past year. Surely he hadn't drifted so far from his Australian roots not to realise their rural hospitals were chronically under-resourced?

'I take it you do have running water?'

Darcie's hackles rose and refused to be tamped down. OK—he was taking the mick. She got that. But enough was enough. 'We draw water from the well outside,' she deadpanned.

Jack's smile unfolded lazily, his eyes crinkling at the corners. *Nice one, Dr Drummond.* He felt his pulse tick over. The lady had spirit. And she was a real looker. Working with her should prove…interesting.

He lowered himself onto the corner of her desk. 'I need to make a couple of phone calls, check in with the hospital board. Landline working OK?'

She sent him a cool look. 'Yes, it is.' She indicated the phone on her desk. 'Make your calls and then we'll see about getting you settled in.' With that, she turned and fled to the nurses' station.

And female solidarity.

Darcie palmed open the swing door and went through to the desk. 'He's here!'

Nurse manager Maggie Neville and RN Lauren Walker paused in mid-handover and looked up.

'Who?' Maggie queried.

Darcie hissed out the breath she'd been holding. 'The new MD.'

'Cassidy?' Maggie's voice rose a fraction. 'I didn't see anyone come through here.'

'He must have cut through the paddock and come in the back way,' Darcie said. 'He's in my office, now.'

'Oh, my stars!' Lauren's eyebrows disappeared into her blonde fringe. 'It must have been him I passed in the corridor. Big guy in combats, flinty eyes, *out there* sexy?'

Darcie nodded, her teeth meshing against her bottom lip. Lauren's description was OTT but Darcie supposed Jack Cassidy had come across as very…masculine.

Lauren snickered. 'I thought he must have been an actor come in for some treatment!'

Darcie and Maggie looked blank until Maggie asked, 'Why on earth would you think that?'

'Keep up, guys!' Lauren said, making a 'duh' face. 'There's a reality series being shot out at Pelican Springs station. The film crew and cast are living in a kind of tent city. I can't believe you didn't know.'

'All news to me,' Maggie said cryptically. She flicked a hand. 'With you in a minute, Darc. We're just finishing up the report.' Maggie went on to tell Lauren, 'Keep an eye on Trevor Banda, please. If that old coot is up and walking—'

'I'll threaten him with a cold shower,' Lauren promised cheerfully. She slid off the high stool. '*Ciao*, then. Have a nice weekend, Maggie.'

'Chance would be a fine thing,' Maggie muttered, before returning her attention to Darcie. 'So, we have a new boss at last. Someone to take the flak. What's he like?'

Absurdly good looking. Darcie gave a one-shouldered shrug. 'He seemed a bit…*strutty.*'

'You mean stroppy?'

'No…' Darcie sought to explain. 'Strutting his authority.'

'Throwing his weight around,' Maggie interpreted with a little huff. 'Well, we'll soon sort him out.'

'Maybe it's just me,' Darcie reconsidered, thinking she had possibly said more than she should about their new boss. 'He caught me unawares. I looked up and he was just…there.'

Maggie's look was as old as time. 'Six feet plus of sex on legs, was it? That's if we can believe Lauren.'

Darcie rolled her eyes and gave a shortened version of the missing email containing Jack Cassidy's arrival details. 'He didn't seem too impressed with us,' she added bluntly.

Maggie made a soft expletive. 'Don't you dare wear any of that rubbish, Darcie. You've been here. Done the hard yards when no other doctor would come outback. And how challenging was that for someone straight out of England!'

Darcie felt guilt a mile wide engulf her. Coming to work here had had nothing to do with altruism, or challenge. It had been expediency in its rawest form that had brought her to Sunday Creek.

She'd more or less picked a place on the map, somewhere Aaron, the man she'd been within days of marrying, would never find her. She knew him well enough to know he'd *never* connect her with working in the Australian outback.

It was that certainty that helped her sleep at night.

'I couldn't have managed any of it without you and the rest of the nurses,' Darcie apportioned fairly.

'That's why we make a good team,' Maggie asserted, picking up her bag and rummaging for her keys. 'I can hang about for a bit if you'd like me to,' she offered.

'No, Maggie, but thanks.' Darcie waved the other's offer away. 'Go home to your boys.' Maggie was the sole parent of two adolescent sons and spent her time juggling work, home and family. In the time Darcie had been here, she and Maggie had become friends and confidantes.

Although it was usually Maggie who confided and she who listened, Darcie had to admit. Somehow she couldn't slip into the confidences other women seemed to share as easily as the name of their hairdresser. 'I'll be fine,' she said now. 'And it'll be good to have a senior doctor about the place,' she added with a bravado she was far from feeling.

Jack was just putting the phone down when Darcie arrived back in her office. 'All squared away?' she asked, flicking him a hardly-there smile.

'Thanks.' He uncurled to his feet.

Taking a cursory look around her office, she moved to close one of the blinds.

'So, what are the living arrangements here?' Jack asked.

'The house for the MD is being refurbished at present, so you'll have to bunk in with the rest of us in the communal residence for now. At the moment, there's just me and one of the nurses.'

'That doesn't seem like a hardship,' he said, giving a slow smile and a nod of satisfaction.

Darcie felt nerves criss-cross in her stomach, resolving to have a word with the decorators and ask them to get a wriggle on. The sooner Cassidy was in a place of his own where he could strut his alpha maleness to his heart's content, the better. 'The flying doctors stay over sometimes too,' she added, making it sound like some kind of buffer. 'And now and again we have students from overseas who just want to observe how we administer medicine in the outback.'

He nodded, taking the information on board.

Darcie's gaze flew over him. She'd waited so long for another doctor. Now Jack Cassidy's arrival, the unexpectedness of it, seemed almost surreal. 'Do you have luggage?'

'There didn't seem anyone about so I stashed it in what looked like a utility room on the way through.'

'We've a small team of permanent nurses who are the backbone of the place.' Darcie willed a businesslike tone into her voice. 'Ancillary staff come and go a bit.'

He sent her a brooding look. 'So, it's you and the nurses most of the time, then?'

She nodded. 'The flying doctors are invaluable, of course.'

'Whoops—sorry.' Lauren jerked to a stop in the doorway.

'Lauren.' Darcie managed a brief smile. 'This is Dr Cassidy, our new MD.'

'Jack.' He held out his hand.

'Oh, hi.' Lauren was all smiles. 'You arrived on the plane and there was no one to meet you,' she lamented.

'There was a mix-up with emails,' Darcie interrupted shortly, fed up with the whole fiasco. 'Did you need me for something, Lauren?'

'Oh, yes. I wondered if you'd mind having a word with young Mitchell Anderson.'

A frown touched Darcie's forehead. 'I've signed his release. He's going home tomorrow. What seems to be the problem?'

'Oh, nothing about his physical care,' Lauren hastily amended. 'But he seems a bit…out of sorts for someone who's going home tomorrow.'

'I'll look in on him.' Darcie sent out a contained little smile.

'Thanks.' Lauren gave a little eye flutter aimed mostly at Jack. 'I'm heading back to the station. Yell if you need me.'

'What was your patient admitted for?' Jack asked, standing aside for Darcie to precede him out of the office.

'Snakebite.'

'You know, he may just need to talk the experience through.'

Darcie shrugged. 'I'm aware of that. I tried to find a bit of common ground and initiate a discussion about snakes and their habits. I knew Mitch would be able to tell me more than I could possibly know but he didn't respond. I'd actually never seen a case of snakebite,' she admitted candidly. 'But I know the drill now. Compression, head for the nearest hospital and hope like mad they have antivenin on hand.'

'Mmm.' A dry smile nipped Jack's mouth. 'Much more civilised than in the old days. They used to pack the bite puncture with gunpowder and light the fuse. You can imagine what that did to the affected part of the body,' he elaborated ghoulishly.

If he was hoping for her shocked reaction, he wasn't

going to get it. 'Pretty drastic,' she said calmly. 'I read about it in the local history section of the library.'

Jack flashed a white grin. Oh, she'd do, this one. Clever, cool and disarmingly sure of her ground as well.

It was a real turn-on.

Uh-oh. Mentally, he dived for cover. He'd just untangled his emotions from one relationship. He'd have to be insane to go looking for a replacement so quickly. But as they began to walk along the corridor towards the wards, the flower-fresh drift of her shampoo awakened his senses with a swift stab of want as incisive and sharp as the first cut of a scalpel.

CHAPTER TWO

JACK YANKED HIS thoughts up short with a barely discernible shake of his head. He needed to get back into professional mode and quickly. 'Give me the background on your patient.'

'Mitchell is sixteen.' Darcie spun her head to look at him and found herself staring into his eyes. They had the luminosity of an early morning seascape, she thought fancifully. She cleared her throat. 'He works on his parents' property about a hundred kilometres out. He was bitten on Monday last.'

'So he's been hospitalised all this week?'

'It seemed the best and safest option. I'm still getting my head around the distances folk have to travel out here. If I'd released him too early and he'd had a relapse and had to come back in—'

'So you erred on the side of caution. I'd have done the same. Where was he bitten?'

'On the calf muscle. Fortunately, he was near enough to the homestead to be found fairly quickly and he didn't panic. His parents were able to bring him straight in to the hospital.'

'You don't think he could possibly be suffering from some kind of PTSD?'

Darcie looked sceptical. 'That's a bit improbable, isn't it?'

'It can happen as a result of dog bites and shark attacks. How's he been sleeping?'

'Not all that well, actually. But I put it down to the strangeness of being in hospital for the first time.'

'Well, that's probably true. But there could be another reason why he's clammed up.' Jack's lips tweaked to a one-cornered grin. 'He's sixteen, Darcie. His testosterone has to be all over the place.'

Darcie's chin came up defensively. Same old sexist rubbish. 'Are you saying he's embarrassed around a female doctor? I was totally professional.'

'I'm sure you were.'

She swept a strand of hair behind her ear in agitation. 'Perhaps I should try talking to him again.'

'Why don't you let me?'

'You?'

'I'm on staff now,' he reminded her. 'And your Mitchell may just open up to another male. That's if you're agreeable?'

Darcie felt put on the spot. He'd given her the choice and she didn't want to be offside with him and appear pedantic. And he was, after all, the senior doctor here. 'Fine. Let's do it.'

Jack gave a nod of approval. 'Here's how we'll handle it, then.'

Mitchell was the only patient in the three-bed unit. Clad in sleep shorts and T-shirt, he was obviously bored, his gaze only intermittently on the television screen in front of him.

Following Jack's advice, Darcie went forward. 'Hi,

there, Mitchell.' Her greeting was low-key and cheerful. 'Just doing a final round.'

Colour stained the youth's face and he kept his gaze determinedly on the TV screen.

'This is Dr Cassidy.' Darcie whipped the blood-pressure cuff around the boy's arm and began to pump. 'He's going to be spending some time with us here in Sunday Creek.'

'Dr Drummond tells me you crash-tackled a snake recently, Mitch.' Casually, Jack parked himself on the end of the youngster's bed. 'What kind was it?'

The boy looked up sharply. 'A western brown. They're deadly.'

'They're different from an ordinary brown, then?'

Almost holding her breath, Darcie watched her young patient make faltering eye contact with Jack. 'The western is more highly coloured.'

Jack flicked a questioning hand. 'How's that?'

'These guys aren't brown at all,' Mitchell said knowledgeably. 'They're black with a really pale head and neck. They're evil-looking. The guy that got me was about a metre and a half long.'

'Hell's teeth…' Jack grimaced. 'That's about five feet.'

'Yeah, probably. I almost peed in my pants.'

'Well, lucky you didn't do that.' Jack's grin was slow and filled with male bonding. 'I heard you kept your cool pretty well.'

Mitch lifted a shoulder dismissively. 'Out here, you have to learn to take care of yourself from when you're a kid. Otherwise you're dead meat.'

Over their young patient's head, the doctors exchanged a guarded look. This response was just what they'd hoped for. And it seemed that once started, Mitch couldn't stop. Aided by Jack's subtle prompting, he re-laxed like a coiled spring unwinding as he continued to regale them with what had happened.

Finally Jack flicked a glance at his watch. 'So, it's home tomorrow?'

'Yeah.' Mitch's smile flashed briefly.

'What time are your parents coming, Mitchell?' Darcie clipped the medical chart back on the end of the bed.

'About ten. Uh—thanks for looking after me.' He rushed the words out, his gaze catching Darcie's for the briefest second before he dipped his head in embarrass-ment.

'You're welcome, Mitch.' Darcie sent him a warm smile. 'And better wear long trousers out in the paddocks from now on, hmm?'

'And don't go hassling any more snakes,' Jack joked, pulling himself unhurriedly upright. 'Stay cool, champ.' He butted the kid's fist with his own.

'No worries, Doc. See ya.'

'You bet.' Jack raised a one-fingered salute.

'Thanks,' Darcie said when they were out in corridor. 'You were right,' she added magnanimously.

'It's what's called getting a second opinion,' Jack de-flected quietly. 'I imagine they're a bit thin on the ground out here.'

'Awful to think I could have sent him home still all screwed up.'

'Let it go now.' Jack's tone was softly insistent. 'You've done a fine job. Physically, your patient is well again. He's young and resilient. He'd have sorted himself out—probably talked to his dad or a mate.'

She gave an off-centre smile. 'And we can't second-guess everything we do in medicine, can we?'

'Hell, no!' Jack pretended to shudder. 'If we did that, we'd all be barking mad. Now, do you need to check on any more patients?'

She shook her head. 'I'm only next door anyway if there's a problem.'

'Good.' In a faintly weary gesture he lifted his hands, running his fingers around his eye sockets and down over the roughness of new beard along his jaw. 'So, we can call it a day, then? I need a shower, a shave and a cold beer, in that order.'

'Oh, of course. I should have realised...' Darcie forced herself to take a dispassionate look at him. There was no mistaking the faint shadows beneath his eyes.

A sliver of raw awareness startled her. The fact that suddenly she wanted to reach up and smooth away those shadows, slowly and gently, startled her even more. Especially when she reminded herself that, for lots of reasons, her trust in men was still borderline.

The staff residence was next door to the hospital with a vacant block in between. Like the hospital, it was of weathered timber with wide verandas positioned to catch the morning sun and to offer shade during the hot summers.

'Here we are.' Darcie opened the gate and they went in, the heady scent of jasmine following them up the front path.

'Hello, who's this?' Jack asked, as a blue heeler cattle dog roused himself from under the steps and slowly came to meet them.

Darcie dimpled a smile. 'That's Capone.'

'Because…?' Jack bent and stroked the dog between his ears.

'He seems to get away with everything.'

Jack chuckled. 'Is that so, chum?' The dog's black button eyes looked back innocently. 'He's quite old, then?' Jack had seen the sprinkling of white hair mottling the dog's blue-grey coat. He went on stroking. 'What's his story?'

'Apparently, he belonged to one of the old-timers of the district.' Darcie recounted the information as she'd heard it. 'He died here at the hospital and his dog wouldn't leave, wouldn't eat and just hung around.'

'So the staff adopted him?'

'Something like that. Naturally, he couldn't be kept at the hospital so gradually they coaxed him over here and he's seems content enough to stay.'

'You're a great old boy, aren't you?' Jack gave a couple of hollow thumps to the bony ridge of the dog's shoulders. He was a sucker for cattle dogs. They'd had some beauties on the farm when he'd been growing up.

'Well, he seems to have taken to you.'

'Seems to.' Jack's expression softened for a moment.

Darcie took a shallow breath, all her nerve ends twanging. What a very compelling picture they made— a big man and his dog… She beat back the sudden urge to reach for her phone and take a picture. How absurd. How sentimental. Shooting her sensible thoughts back in place, she said briskly, 'Let's go in, shall we?

'There are six bedrooms, all quite large,' Darcie said as they made their along the wide hallway. 'Our funding allows for some domestic help. Meg McLeish keeps everything ticking over. She's a real gem.'

Jack managed a polite, 'Mmm.' He didn't need this kind of detail but it was a female thing. He got that.

'You should be comfortable in here.' Darcie opened the door on the freshness of lemon-scented furniture polish.

Jack's gaze tracked over the room, taking in the king-sized bed, fitted wardrobes and bedside tables. 'This is great, Darcie. Thanks. I'll manage from here.'

Darcie took a step back. Was he was trying to get rid of her? Tough. She hadn't finished. 'There's a linen cupboard at the end of the hall where you'll find sheets and towels. Sorry there's no en suite bathroom. I think the place was built long before they were in vogue. But there are two bathrooms for communal use.'

Jack plonked himself on the edge of the bed. 'Darcie—' he held down the thread of impatience '—it's all fine, thank you.'

'OK…' Her teeth bit softly into her bottom lip. 'I'll leave you to it, then.'

He looked up sharply with a frown. Had he offended her somehow? She'd tilted her chin in a gesture he was beginning to recognise. He pulled himself upright again. 'I'll just get cleaned up.' His mouth tweaked into a wry grin. 'I promise I'll be more sociable then.'

'Fine.' Darcie spread her hands in quick acceptance and began backing away. 'Come out to the kitchen when you're through and I'll find you that cold beer.'

Barely twenty minutes later Jack joined Darcie in the kitchen. She turned from the window. 'You were quick.' Her eyes flicked over him. Cleaned up and dressed in jeans and a pinstriped cotton shirt, he looked…well, more like a senior doctor should look, she concluded a bit

primly. Crossing to the fridge, she took out a beer from
a six-pack and handed it to him. 'You Aussies seem a bit
territorial about your brands. I hope you like this one.'

Jack barely noticed the label and twisting open the
top he took a long pull. 'Right at this moment I'd settle
for any brand as long as it was cold.' He hooked out a
chair. 'Are you joining me?'

She gave a stilted smile. 'I have a glass of wine here.'

'What do we do about meals?' Jack indicated she
should sit at the table with him.

'At the moment there's just Lauren and me.' Darcie
met his questioning look neutrally. 'So it's all been a bit
haphazard, depending what shifts she's on. We tend to
just grab something from the hospital kitchen. But now
you're here, perhaps we should get a better system going.
Do a regular shop.'

'Sounds good to me.' He rolled back his shoulders and
stretched. 'What about right now? I'm starved. What can
the fridge yield up?'

'There's some watermelon and fudge,' Darcie deadpanned.

'OK,' Jack said with studied calm. 'I see you've covered all the essential food groups.'

Her spontaneous laugh rippled out, the action bringing her whole face into vivid life.

Instinctively, Jack swayed forward, staring at the
sweet curve of her laughing mouth. And feeling something else. *Oh, good grief.* Instantly, he took control of
his wild thoughts, anchoring his feet more firmly under
the table.

Darcie tilted her head to one side. 'If we'd known you
were coming—'

'You'd have baked a cake,' Jack rejoined, sitting up straighter.

'Or cooked a roast.'

He chuckled. 'So, you're telling me there's nothing in the fridge we can make a meal with. No leftovers?'

She shook her head.

'A remnant of cheese? A couple of lonely eggs?'

'Sorry.'

'What about the pub, then? Food OK?'

'Pretty good. And it's steak night, if that's what you want to hear.'

'Excellent.' He downed the last of the beer and got to his feet. 'Let's go, then, Dr Drummond. I'm shouting dinner.'

'We'll take my vehicle,' Darcie said. 'It's a bit of a step up to the town centre.'

'What do I do about getting a vehicle?' Jack asked as they walked over to her car.

'The local Rotary Club bought a new Land Rover for the MD's use. It's presently garaged at the hospital. OK if we sort all that tomorrow?'

'Yup.' Jack opened the car door, sat down and leaned back against the headrest, deciding any further conversation about the practice could wait.

It was a typical country pub, Jack observed, with a bar, a billiard table and a scattering of tables and chairs.

'There's a beer garden through there.' Darcie indicated the softly lit outdoor area. 'We just have to order at the bar first.'

'So, what would you like to eat?' He guided her to the blackboard menu. 'Uh—big choice, I see,' he said dryly. 'Steak and vegetables or steak and chips and salad.'

'I'll have the steak and salad,' Darcie said. 'No chips.'

'You don't like chips?' Jack pretended outrage.

'I like chips,' she responded, 'just not with every-thing.'

They ordered and were told there might be a bit of a wait. 'Let's have a drink, then,' Jack said. 'Another wine?'

She shook her head. 'Mineral water, I think.'

'OK. Me as well. I don't want to fall asleep.'

Darcie sent him a cool look. Nice to know he found her conversation so scintillating. Being Friday evening, the beer garden was crowded. 'Most folk are friendly here,' she said, returning greetings from several of the locals.

'And you've made friends since you've been here?' Jack asked as they made their way to a vacant table.

'It's been good,' she evaded lightly. 'You're getting well looked over,' she added, taking the chair he held for her.

'I'd better behave myself, then.'

'Will that be difficult?'

'I'm not given to dancing on tables, if that's what you're worried about.'

Darcie propped her chin on her upturned hand. 'I've never actually seen anyone do that.'

'I tried it once.'

'Were you drunk?'

'Are you shocked?' Jack's teasing smile warmed the space between them. 'Final interviews were over and I knew they'd offer me a place on the surgical training programme.'

She raised an eyebrow. Oh, to have such confidence. But, then, she reasoned, Jack Cassidy seemed to be brim-

ming with it. She took a deep breath and decided to find
out more about this man who had literally dropped out
of the sky and was now to all intents and purposes her
boss. 'So—where have you come from today?'

His mouth tipped at the corner. 'You mean by the
way I was dressed?'

And his tan. 'Well, I didn't imagine you'd just arrived
from London.'

'No.' He picked up his glass unhurriedly and took
a mouthful of his drink. 'I've been trekking in New
Guinea for the past couple of weeks. I did part of the
Kokoda track. I always promised my grandfather I'd
walk it for him one day. His battalion was stationed there
in the Second World War.'

'So, it has some significance for Australians, then?'

He nodded. 'Our lads were heroes in all kinds of
ways. I got some good pics of the general area and managed to run off some film footage too. Next time I see
Pa, he'll be able to see how it is now, although it's many
years on, of course.'

Darcie felt her heartbeat quicken. She guessed this
was her opportunity to extend their personal relationship
a little further, ask about his family. But somehow it all
felt a bit…intimate. And he'd probably feel compelled
to reciprocate, enquire about her family. And as yet she
hadn't been able to go there in any depth—not even with
Maggie. While she was still cobbling her thoughts together, her attention was distracted by the sight of one
of the hotel staff making his way swiftly between tables,
almost running towards them. Darcie jumped to her feet.

'What's wrong?' Jack's head spun round, his eyes following her gaze. He sensed an emergency and shoved
his chair back as he stood. 'Do you know him?'

Darcie's eyes lit with concern. 'It's Warren Rowe. He's the manager—'

'Thank God you're here, Darcie.' Warren looked pale and shaken. 'The chef—young Nathan—he's had an electric shock. We need a doctor.'

'You've got two!' Jack turned urgently to Darcie. 'Grab your bag! I'll do what I can for the casualty.'

'How long has he been down?' Jack rapped out the question as the two men sped along the veranda to the kitchen.

'Not sure. Couple of minutes at most.' Warren palmed open the swing doors and jerked to a stop. He swallowed convulsively. 'It was the electric knife—'

Jack's breath hissed through his clenched teeth and in a few strides he was at the chef's side. The young man was glassily pale, blue around the lips and, worse, he was still gripping the electric knife that had obviously short-circuited and thrown him to the floor.

'I used an insulator and switched off the current at the power point,' Warren said helpfully. 'What do you need?'

'What emergency equipment do you have?' Jack had already kicked the knife away and begun CPR.

'Defibrillator and oxygen.'

'Grab them. We'll need both.'

'Oh, my God—Nathan!' Darcie burst in, her horrified look going to the young man on the floor. Dropping beside Jack, she shot open her medical case. 'Any response?'

'Not yet. Run the oxygen, please, Darcie. I need to get an airway in.'

'I can do CPR.' Warren dived in to help.

'Defib's charging.' Darcie watched as Jack positioned the tube carefully and attached it to the oxygen.

'Breathe,' he grated. 'Come on, sunshine. You can do it!'

Darcie bit her lips together. With sickening dread she waited for some movement from Nathan's chest. Waited. And watched as Jack checked for a pulse. Again and again. The nerves in Darcie's stomach tightened. 'Shocking?'

'Only option,' Jack said tersely. 'Everyone clear, please.'

Nathan's young, fit body jerked and fell. Darcie felt for a pulse and shook her head.

'Dammit! Shocking again. Clear, please.' Jack's controlled direction seemed to echo round the big old-fashioned kitchen.

Come on, Nathan. Come on! Darcie willed silently. And then…a faint jiggle that got stronger. 'We have output,' she confirmed, husky relief in her voice.

Jack's expression cleared. 'Good work. Now, let's get some fluids into this guy.' He looked up sharply. 'Has someone called an ambulance?'

'We're here, Doc.' Two paramedics stepped through with a stretcher.

Darcie looked up from inserting the cannula to receive the drip. 'Say hello to Dr Jack Cassidy, guys.' Relief was zinging through her and she gave rein to a muted smile. 'He's the new boss at the hospital—only been here a few hours.'

'And already saved a life, by the look of it. Zach Bayliss.' The senior paramedic held out his hand. 'My partner, Brett Carew.'

A flurry of handshakes ensued.

Nathan was loaded quickly. 'We'll see you across at the hospital, then, Doc?' Zach confirmed.

'We'll be over directly.' Jack turned to Warren. 'You should disconnect all power until it's been checked by the electrical authority. You might have other dodgy gear about the place.'

'Will do, Doc. Hell, I don't ever want to see a repetition of this...'

Jack looked around the kitchen. 'This will stuff up your meal preparation. Do you have a contingency plan?'

'We do. As it happens, we'd planned to put wood-fired pizzas on the menu tomorrow so we started up the brick oven for a trial run this afternoon. It's still going strong. We'll have a line of pizzas going in no time.'

Jack gave a rueful grin. 'You couldn't send a couple across to the residence, could you, mate? We still haven't have had dinner.'

'Yeah, absolutely. No worries.' Warren flicked a hand in compliance. 'On the house, of course. And thanks, Doc. Mighty job with Nathan.'

Jack waved away the thanks and they walked out together.

'Right to go, then?' Darcie had tidied up the medical debris and was waiting on the veranda.

Jack nodded and they went across to her car.

'Nathan didn't appear to have any fractures,' she said. 'But he must have landed with an almighty thump.'

'I'll check him thoroughly in Resus. Do you know if he has family to be notified?'

'Not sure. But Warren will have got onto that.'

Jack sent her a quick, narrow look. 'He said it was your initiative to have both the defib and oxygen located at the pub. Well done, Dr Drummond.'

'I was just being proactive.' Darcie shrugged away his praise. 'There's always a crowd in the pub at the week-ends. Accidents happen. The odd nasty punch-up. Even a couple of heart attacks while I've been here. Having the defibrillator and the oxygen on site seemed a no-brainer. And the staff at the pub all have first-aid knowledge.'

'Down to you as well?' Jack asked.

'And our nurse manager, Maggie Neville. You haven't met her yet.' Darcie gave a small chuckle. 'I think she could run the place if it came to it.'

'Good.' Jack stretched his legs out as far as they would go. 'Nice to have backup.'

A beat of silence.

'I was very glad to have *your* backup this evening, Jack.'

Jack felt an expectant throb in his veins. What was this? A tick of approval from the very reserved English doctor? And unless he was mistaken, her husky little compliment had come straight from her heart.

CHAPTER THREE

WHEN THEY PULLED into the hospital car park, Jack said, 'I can take over from here, Darcie. Go home. I'm sure you've more than earned a night off.'

She made a small face. 'If you're sure?'

'More than sure. I'm pulling rank, Doctor. You're officially off duty.'

'Thanks, then.' Darcie felt the weight of responsibility drop from her. 'I'd actually kill for a leisurely bath.'

'And dinner's on its way,' Jack confirmed, as he swung out of the car. 'Warren's sending over pizzas.'

Lauren stood with Jack as he made notations on Nathan's chart. 'How's he doing?' she asked quietly.

'He has entry and exit burns on his left hand and right foot. It's obviously been a serious shock. We'll need him on a heart monitor for the next little while.'

'He's coming round.' Lauren looked down at her watch to check the young man's pulse. 'You're in hospital, Nathan,' she said as Nathan's eyes opened. 'You've had an electric shock. This is Dr Cassidy.'

'Take it easy, Nathan.' Jack was calmly reassuring. 'This contraption here is helping you breathe.'

Nathan's eyes squeezed shut and then opened.

'Pulse is fine,' Lauren reported.

'In that case, I think we can extubate.' Jack explained to their patient what he was about to do. 'You're recovering well, Nathan, and there's an excellent chance you'll be able to breathe on your own.' He turned to Lauren. 'Stand by with the oxygen, please, but let's hope he won't need it.'

Lauren noticed the surgeon's hands were gentle. Mentally, she gave him a vote of approval. In her time she'd seen extubations carried out with all the finesse of pulling nails with a claw hammer.

'I want you to cough now, Nathan,' Jack said as the tube was fully removed. 'Go for it,' he added, as Nathan looked confused. 'You won't damage anything.'

Nathan coughed obligingly.

'OK, let's have a listen to your chest now.' Jack dipped his head, his face impassive in concentration. 'Good lad.' He gave a guarded smile. 'You're breathing well.

'Thanks, Doc.' Nathan's voice was rusty. 'Guess I've been lucky. When can I get out of here?'

'Not so fast, mate.' Jack raised a staying hand. 'You've had a hell of a whack to every part of your body. We'll need to monitor you for a couple of days.'

Nathan looked anxious. 'My job—'

'Is safe,' Jack said firmly. 'Warren will be in to see you about that tomorrow. In the meantime, I want you to just rest and let the nurses take care of you.'

'And we do that very well.' Lauren gave the young man a cheeky smile. 'Fluids as a matter of course, Doctor?'

'Please.' Jack continued writing on Nathan's chart. 'Call if there's a problem, Lauren. I'll be right over.'

'Will do. Good to have you on board, Jack,' Lauren said as they walked out.

Jack pocketed his pen and then turned to the nurse. 'What time do the shops come alive here in the mornings?'

'Depends what you need.' A small evocative smile nipped Lauren's mouth. 'There's a truckers' café that opens about five-thirty, supermarket and bakery about six, everything else around eight-thirty-ish.'

'Thanks for the heads-up.' Jack acknowledged the information with a curt nod and strode off.

'This is fantastic!' They were eating pizza straight from the box and Jack pulled out a long curl of melted cheese and began eating it with exaggerated relish. 'Why the look, Dr Drummond?' He gave a folded-in grin. 'You didn't expect us to stand on ceremony and set the table for dinner, did you?'

Darcie took her time answering, obviously enjoying her own slice of the delicious wood-fired pizza. 'I thought the present state of the fridge would have proved I'm no domestic goddess.'

'Who needs *them*?' Jack wound out another curl of cheese. 'Do you want the last piece?'

Darcie waved his offer away and got to her feet. 'I found some raspberry ripple ice cream in the freezer. Fancy some?'

Jack shook his head. 'No, thanks.'

'Cup of tea, then?'

'Any decent coffee going, by any chance?'

'There's some good instant. Near as we get can to the real stuff out here.'

'Perfect.' Jack got up from the table and moved across

to the sink to wash his hands. Drying them on a length of paper towel, he moved closer to look over her shoulder as she reached up to get mugs from the top cupboard. 'Turned out all right, then, didn't it?' His voice had a gruff quality. 'Our impromptu dinner, I mean.'

He was very close and Darcie felt warning signals clang all over her body. The zig-zag of awareness startled her, unnerved her. With her breathing shallower than usual, she said, 'It was great.' She took her time, placing the mugs carefully on the countertop as though they were fine china, instead of the cheerful, chunky variety from the supermarket.

'So, Darcie…' Jack about-turned, leaning against the bench of cupboards and folding his arms. 'Do you think we'll rub along all right?'

She blinked uncertainly. In just a few hours Jack Cassidy had brought a sense of stability and authority to the place, his presence like a rock she could hang onto for dear life.

Whoa, no! Those kinds of thoughts led to a road with no signposts and she wasn't going there. The water in the electric jug came to boiling point and she switched it off. 'We'd *better* rub along,' she replied, ignoring the flare of heat in his eyes and waving light-hearted banter like a flag. 'We're the only doctors for hundreds of miles. It won't do much for morale if either of us stomps off in a hissy fit.'

Jack gave a crack of laughter. 'Do male doctors have hissy fits?'

'Of course they do! Especially in theatres.' She made the coffee quickly and handed him his mug. 'They just call it something else.'

'Thanks.' Jack met her gaze and held it. She had the

most amazing eyes, he thought. They were hazel, coppery brown near the pupils, shading to dark green at the rims. And they were looking at him with a kind of vivid expectancy. 'I suppose men might have a rant,' he suggested.

'Or a tirade?'

'A meltdown?'

'Ten out of ten. That's an excellent analogy.' She smiled, holding it for a few seconds, letting it ripen on her face and then throwing in a tiny nose crinkle for good measure.

Hell. Jack felt the vibes of awareness hissing like a live wire between them. Enough to shift his newly achieved stable world off its hinges.

But only if he let it.

Lifting his coffee, he took a mouthful and winced, deciding he'd probably given his throat full-thickness burns. He had to break this proximity before he did something entirely out of character.

And kissed her.

'Uh…' His jaw worked a bit. 'Let's grab what's left of the evening and take our coffee outside to the courtyard.'

Darcie looked surprised but nevertheless picked up her mug and followed him. 'I'll just turn on the outside light,' she said. 'We don't want to break our necks in the dark.'

'There's plenty of moonlight.' Jack looked around him as they sat at the old wooden table. The smell of jasmine was in the air. It twisted around a trellis at least six feet high. 'I guess this place would have a few stories to tell,' he surmised.

'Probably.' Darcie took a careful mouthful of her coffee.

Tipping his head back Jack looked up, his gaze widening in awe at the canopy of stars, some of which looked close enough to touch, while myriad others were scattered like so much fairy dust in the swept enormous heavens. So very different from London. 'You're a long way from home, Darcie.'

Darcie tensed. She'd expected the question or something similar but not quite so soon. For a heartbeat she was tempted to lower her guard and tell him the plain, unvarnished truth. But to do that would make her feel vulnerable. And perhaps make *him* feel uncomfortable, or worse even—sorry for her. And she so did not want that from any man. 'This is Australia.' She feigned nonchalance with an accompanying little shrug. 'So I imagine I must be a long way from home. But this is *home* now.'

Jack heard the almost fierce assertiveness in her voice. OK, he wouldn't trespass. Darcie Drummond obviously had her ghosts, the same as he did. But he liked to think he'd laid his to rest. On the other hand, he had a feeling young Dr Drummond here appeared to be still running from hers.

'So, tell me a bit about Sunday Creek,' he said evenly. 'No GP here, I take it?'

'Not for a long time. Anyone with a medical problem comes to the hospital.'

'So we take each day as it comes, then?'

'Yes.' She smiled into the softness of the night. 'I've treated a few characters.'

He chuckled. 'It's the outback. Of course you have.' With subtlety, he pressed a little further, determined to get to know her better. 'Any one instance stand out?'

'Oh, yes.' She smiled, activating a tiny dimple be-

side her mouth. 'Pretty soon after I'd arrived here I had
a call out to one of the station properties. There'd been
an accident in the shearing shed. I was still at the stage
of being wide-eyed with wonder at the size and scope
of everything.'

'That figures.' Jack tilted his head, listening.

'When I stepped inside the shearing shed I was
thrown with the hive of activity. I'm sure I must have
stood there gaping, wondering where to go or whom I
should speak to. Then one of the men bellowed, "Ducks
on the pond!" and suddenly there was this deathly kind
of silence.'

Jack's laughter rippled.

Darcie pressed a finger to her lips, covering an upside-
down smile. 'You know what it means, of course?'

'Yep.' He shot her a wry half-grin. 'It's simply short-
hand for, "Mind your language, there's a lady present."'

'I had to ask Maggie when I got back to the hospital,' Darcie confessed. 'But the men were very kind to
me and, fortunately, the emergency was only a case of
a rather deep wound that needed suturing. I stayed for
morning tea in the shed. I think I managed OK,' she
added modestly.

'From the sound of it, I'd say you managed brilliantly.'
In the moonlight, Jack's gaze softened over her. She was
gutsy and no slouch as a doctor. He already had proof of
that. He wondered what her story was. And why she'd
felt the need to practise her skills so far from her roots.

Leaning back in his chair, he clasped his hands behind his head. 'I'll cover the weekend. I want you to
have a break.'

'Oh.' Darcie looked uncertain. 'Shouldn't I hand over
officially?'

'We can do that *officially* on Monday. Meanwhile, I'll get a feel for things in general, talk to a few faces.'

'I won't know what to do with myself...' The words were out before she could stop them.

'Have some fun,' Jack suggested. 'See your friends.'

He made it sound so simple—so normal. And it would look pathetic if she hung around the house for the entire weekend. Her brain quickly sorted through the possibilities. She supposed she did have a couple of friends she could visit—Louise and Max Alderton. They lived on a property, Willow Bend, only ten miles out. Louise was on the hospital board and somehow had sensed Darcie's need for a no-strings kind of friendship.

She could give Lou a call now. She'd still be up. See if it was OK to visit. Maybe they could go for a ride... 'OK. I'll do that. Thanks.'

Next morning, Darcie couldn't believe she'd slept in. If you called seven-thirty sleeping in, she thought wryly, sitting up to look out at the new day. The sun had risen, the temperature climbing already. Blocking a yawn, she stretched and threw herself out of bed. She had a holiday.

And she'd better remember there was a man in the house. Slipping into her short dressing gown, she sprinted along the hallway to the bathroom.

As she dressed, Darcie sensed something different about the place. A feeling of the house coming alive. And there was a delicious smell of grilling bacon coming from the kitchen.

And that could mean only one thing. Jack was up and around and amazingly he must be cooking breakfast. She hoped he'd made enough for two because she intended joining him.

As she made her way along the hallway to the kitchen, her newly found confidence began faltering. Perhaps she was being presumptuous. She didn't expect Jack to feed her. She really didn't.

But already her preconceived ideas about him had begun falling like skittles. He wasn't *strutty*—just competent. And from what she'd observed, he seemed straightforward and she liked that. If he'd only made breakfast for one, then he'd tell her so.

She paused at the kitchen door, ran her tongue around the seam of her lips and said, 'You're up early.'

Busy at the cooker top, Jack turned his head and gave her a casual 'Morning. How do you like your eggs?'

'Um…' Darcie's mouth opened and closed. 'Scrambled, I think.' She joined him at the stove. He was turning sausages and the bacon was set aside in the warming oven.

'Me too.' He gave her a quick smile. 'Will you do that while I watch these guys?'

'Yes, sure.' She looked around and saw a pile of groceries had been unloaded onto the benchtop. 'Have you been to the supermarket already?'

'I was awake early,' he said. 'Thought I'd do a quick swoop. I borrowed your car. I hope that's all right?'

'Of course.' Darcie searched for a bowl and began cracking the eggs. 'You must let Lauren and me pay for our share of the groceries.'

'We can talk about that later,' Jack dismissed. 'Tomatoes for you?'

'Yes, please.' Darcie's mouth began to water. All this home cooking was beginning to heighten her taste buds. 'And I'll make some toast. Did you get bread?'

'I did. The baker had his front door open a crack. I

gave him a shout, introduced myself and he obligingly sold me a couple of loaves.'

'That'll be Jai.' Darcie found the wholemeal loaf and hacked off a couple of slices. 'He and his wife, Nikki, relocated from Thailand. He makes gorgeous bread.'

Jack piled the cooked sausages onto a plate. 'Should we keep some of this food for Lauren?'

'Uh-uh. She'll sleep for ages. And she's vegetarian anyway.'

'Oh—OK. Good for her,' Jack said, though he sounded doubtful. 'We won't have continuous tofu to look forward to, will we?'

Darcie chuckled. 'Tofu is the new meat. But she's more a risotto person. Although she does a great grilled halloumi and courgette salad.'

'You mean zucchini? Well, that sounds all right, as long as there's a nice T-bone steak to go with it,' he said with wry humour. 'This is about ready. Should we tuck in?'

'I'll get the plates.'

'I hope it's up to scratch,' he said.

'Oh, it will be.' Darcie was adamant. 'You seem like an amazingly good cook.'

'I was reared on a cattle property,' Jack said, as they settled over their meal. 'We all had to learn to throw a meal together, especially at mustering time. If you were given kitchen duties, you had to have something ready to feed the troops or risk getting a kick up the backside. Sorry...' His mouth pulled down. 'That sounded a bit crass.'

'Not at all.' Darcie dismissed his apology. 'So, are there a lot of you in the family?'

'I'm the eldest of five. Two brothers, two sisters. I recall some pretty rowdy mealtimes.'

And he made it sound so warm and wonderful. Darcie felt the weight of her own solitary childhood sit heavily on her shoulders. Meals on your own didn't have much going for them. But that was her *old* life. She shook her head as if to clear the debris and firmly closed the lid on that particular Pandora's box. She drummed up a quick smile. 'So, happy childhood, then?'

'Mmm.' Jack hadn't missed the subtlety of her mood change or her quickly shuttered look. But he didn't want to be stepping on any of her private landmines. One thing he did know, he'd shut up about his happy childhood.

'So, what are your plans for today?' He'd already noticed her boots, jeans and soft white shirt.

'I'm going riding.' She filled him in about the Aldertons and Willow Bend. 'You'll probably meet Lou sooner rather than later. She's on the hospital board and a great innovator.'

'Excellent. As the sole MOs for the entire district, we need all the help we can get.'

They batted light conversation around for the rest of the meal.

'You'll find a set of keys for your use at the nurses' station,' Darcie said, as they finished breakfast and began clearing the table. 'Including those for your vehicle.'

'Thanks.' He bent and began stacking the dishwasher.

Darcie blinked a bit. Heavens, he really was housetrained. 'Natalie Britten will be the RN on duty and with a bit of luck a couple of our ancillary staff should turn up as well. There's a list of numbers to call if there are any staffing problems.'

'You like all your ducks in a row, don't you?'

Darcie's chin came up. 'We're running a hospital,' she countered. 'We have to make some effort for things to be orderly.'

'That wasn't my first impression.' He smiled then, a little half-smile that seemed to flicker on one side of his lips before settling into place.

'A tiny glitch.' Darcie shrugged away his comment. 'I think you enjoyed surprising us.'

'Perhaps I did.' He considered her for a long moment. 'Will you be home tonight?' Oh, good grief! He squirmed inwardly. He'd sounded like her *father*!

Darcie looked up warily. Was he enquiring whether she had a boyfriend who might be wanting to keep her out all night? Well, let him wonder about that. 'Yes, I'll be home. But I may be late.'

Jack closed the door on the dishwasher and stood against it. 'Have a good day, then.'

'I shall.' She hovered for a moment, pushing her hands into the back pockets of her jeans. 'Thanks for this, Jack. The day off, I mean.'

He shrugged. 'You're probably owed a zillion.'

'If there's an emergency…'

He sent her a dry look. 'If I need you, I'll call you. Now scoot.' He flicked his fingers in a shooing motion. 'Before I reassign you.'

She scooted.

Jack wandered out onto the veranda, the better to take in the vibe of his new surroundings. Leaning on the timber railings, he looked down at the wildly flowering red bottlebrush. The hardiest of the natives, it simply produced more and more blossoms, regardless of the vagaries of the seasons.

Raising his gaze, he looked out towards the horizon.

There was a ribbon of smoke-laden cloud along the ridge tops. So far it obviously wasn't a cause for concern. He hoped it stayed that way…

The clip of Darcie's footsteps along the veranda interrupted his train of thought. He swung round, a muscle tightening in his jaw, an instinct purely male sharpening every one of his senses. She'd gathered up her hair and tied it into a ponytail and she'd outlined her mouth with a sexy red lipstick.

His heart did a U-turn. His male antennae switched to high alert. Hell. This was right out of left field.

He fancied her.

Darcie stopped beside him, dangling her Akubra hat loosely between her fingers. 'Taking in the scenery?' Her quick smile sparkled white against the red lipstick.

'Just getting acquainted with the possibilities.' *And wasn't that the truth*.

'Good,' she said lightly, and proceeded down the steps. At the bottom she turned and looked back. 'Don't wait up.'

Cheeky monkey. Jack dipped his head to hide a burgeoning grin and countered, 'Don't fall off.'

Then, with something like wistfulness in his gaze, he watched as she reversed out of the driveway and took off.

His hands tightened their grip on the railings, some part of him wanting to rush after her, flag her down.

And spend the entire day with her.

CHAPTER FOUR

DARCIE HALF WOKE to the sound of knocking on her bedroom door. For a few seconds she struggled to open her eyes, calling groggily, 'Who is it?'

'It's Jack. Can you come to the door, please? We have an emergency.'

Jack? Jack…? Darcie closed her eyes again.

Hell, what was she doing? Jack glanced at his watch. He rapped on the door again. 'Wake up, Darcie! I need to speak to you!'

Jack! Oh, good grief! Darcie sat bolt upright as reality struck. Throwing herself out of bed, she padded over to the door. 'What time is it?' She blinked up at him.

'Five o'clock—' He stopped abruptly. She was pulling on a gown over a short ruby-red nightie, her breasts moving gently beneath the silk. *Hell.* His breath jagged in his throat. He stepped back and blinked. 'Uh—we have an emergency out where some kind of film is being shot. Do you know about it?'

'Not really. Lauren mentioned it. What's happened?'

'Apparently two of the actors have fallen into a disused well. The message the ambulance got was pretty garbled. But they've asked for medical backup. I'm sorry to disrupt your sleep-in but I think this needs both of us.'

'OK…' Darcie pushed the heavy fall of hair back from her cheek. 'Give me a few minutes.'

'I'll meet you out front. Don't mess about.'

Darcie made a face at the closing door. She pulled on jeans and T-shirt and pushing her feet into sturdy trainers she sprinted to the bathroom.

Armed with a couple of trauma kits from the hospital, they travelled in Jack's Land Rover. 'I've spoken to Mal Duffy, the police sergeant,' Jack said. 'He's given me directions to the site. It's about forty Ks.'

'So, apart from the ambulance, who's in on this jaunt?'

'The state emergency service.'

Darcie nodded. She was well acquainted with the SES and their dedicated volunteers. 'Mal heads up the local SES. Their vehicle with the rescue gear is kept at the police station but he'll have to try to get a team together. At this early hour on a Sunday, it could be difficult.'

Jack raised an eyebrow, seeming impressed with her local knowledge. 'In that case, we'll just have to wing it until they get there.'

'Why on earth would they be filming so early?' she wondered aloud.

'Maybe they wanted to catch a special effect with the light.'

She glanced at him sharply. 'You know something about making films, then?'

'Oh, yeah.' He gave a hard, discordant laugh. 'My *ex* is an actress.'

For a moment his words formed an uncomfortable silence between them. Darcie glanced at his profile but it told her nothing. Was he sad or mad or both? 'Ex-*wife*?'

'No.' He paused infinitesimally. 'We didn't get that

far. We'd been together for three years. But our jobs took us in different directions. In the end, the relationship proved unworkable.'

Of course, it hadn't helped that when he'd got to England, where Zoe had been filming, she'd found someone else. He swallowed the residue of bitterness. His ego had taken a hard kick, but life moved on. And thank heaven for that.

'I guess relationships are tricky at the best of times,' Darcie responded quietly. 'Do you have any idea what size this well might be?' She changed conversation lines tactfully.

'Going by my acquaintance with wells, I'd guess six by six in the old measurements.'

'So—the size of a small room,' she said consideringly.

Jack took his eyes off the road for a second to look at her. 'Any problems with confined spaces?'

'I've done a little caving...' Darcie recognised the flutter of uncertainty in her stomach. 'I don't know how that equates with going down into a well.'

'Only one way to find out,' Jack said. 'It'll be dark inside and there'll probably be rubble at the bottom. And I mean anything from rocks to old furniture. Usually, when a well is closed, some effort is extended to part fill the hole to make it less of a hazard. We'll need to look out for rats as well.'

'Rats?' Darcie suppressed a shudder. 'I hope they're dead ones and long gone.' A frown touched her forehead. 'It's daylight pretty early these days—how come they wouldn't have known the well was there?'

'I doubt it would have been used for years, and it's possible that some attempt would have been made to cover it over.'

'Well, whatever they did hasn't been good enough. Why wouldn't they build a roof or something?'

'A roof!' Jack hooted. 'You've still a lot to learn about life in the Australian bush, Darcie. Our graziers have to make the best use of their time to stay viable. They can't go around erecting a roof over every well they close. More than likely, they would have chucked some logs across the top. But with time they'll have become overgrown, which will have only served to camouflage the rotting wood beneath.'

'And there you have an accident waiting to happen,' Darcie concluded.

'By George, she's got it!'

Darcie gave an exaggerated eye roll. 'How much further, do you think?'

'Hmm…ten Ks possibly.'

'I hate this part of being a doctor out here,' she admitted candidly. 'Flying by the seat of your pants, not knowing what you'll find when you get there.'

'Comes with the territory, Darcie. You work as an outback doctor, you take on board the highs and lows.' And if she hadn't come to a realisation of that by now, then what the hell was she doing here?

'I understand all that, Jack,' she defended. 'It's just… medically, you can only do so much. And it's so *far* from everything.'

Jack felt his mood softening. 'Granted, we don't have the backup of a casualty department,' he conceded. 'So we make adjustments. In our heads as well as practically.' After a minute, he added, 'Whatever path we follow in life, we're probably conditioned by our backgrounds.'

'Perhaps we are.'

'I found working in London stressful.'

'Did you?' She sounded surprised.

'You bet. London is an amazing city, so many centuries of history, but I felt as isolated in the heart of its busyness as you possibly do here in these great open spaces. I'm human too, Doctor. Just like you…'

They turned to each other, eyes meeting. Seeing the slow warmth in his, Darcie's heart gave a little jiggle of recognition.

Suddenly, she felt a lift in her spirits, unexpectedly buoyed by his take on things. Perhaps they had, in quite different ways, quite a lot in common.

Within minutes they were at the location.

'OK, let's get cracking,' Jack snapped, as they alighted from the Land Rover. He moved to organise the gear they'd need, tossing Darcie one of the high-visibility vests the hospital had included.

Quickly, Darcie slid into the vest and secured the fastenings. 'We'd better find out who's in charge.'

'That looks like a site office.' Jack indicated the prefab building. 'We'll enquire there.'

A short, stocky man behind the desk shot to his feet as Jack rapped and stuck his head in. 'Blake Meadows,' he said, and held out his hand. 'I'm the film unit manager.' His gaze flicked to Darcie and back to Jack. 'You're the doctors?'

'Yes.' Jack made the introductions. 'What can you tell us?'

'Two of our young actors, Jessica and Lachlan, have fallen into the well. We've managed to gather a few details. Jess caught her arm on a piece of protruding metal on the way down.'

'So there's bleeding,' Darcie surmised.

The manager nodded. 'At the moment, she's been able to staunch it with her T-shirt.'

'And the other casualty?' Jack asked.

'Lachy hasn't been so fortunate.' Blake Meadows made a grimace. 'According to Jess, he landed on something hard—rocks maybe. Passed out. It's his leg...' He rubbed a hand across his face. 'If this gets out, we'll be in the news for all the wrong reasons. The company doesn't need this.'

'I don't imagine the young people needed it either.' Jack was tight-lipped. 'Can you direct us to the well?'

'I'll take you.' The manager hurried them from the office and towards an army-type Jeep parked nearby.

'We probably won't be able to do much until the SES gets here,' Jack said, as they scrambled aboard and took off.

'They should be right behind you,' Blake said. 'Frankly, I'm staggered with the promptness of everyone's response.'

Well, at least their attendance was appreciated, Darcie thought critically, hanging on for dear life as they rocked through the scrubby terrain towards the accident site.

To their surprise, Mal Duffy was already on the scene when they arrived. He greeted both doctors. 'Knew a short cut,' he explained in his slow drawl. 'This is my team for today. Meet Rod and Gez.'

With no time to waste, Mal and his team began erecting a tripod arrangement over the top of the well.

'Do we have any head torches?' Jack queried. 'It's going to be pretty dark down there.'

'Ah—unfortunately, we don't have any in stock,' Mal apologised. 'The lantern torches are high-powered and we'll place them to give you maximum light. Best we can do.'

'Put head torches on your list of priorities, then, please,' Jack countered thinly.

'Will do, Doc. Sorry for the glitch.'

'Has the air ambulance being notified?' Jack asked.

'CareFlight chopper is on its way,' Mal said. 'There's a helipad at Pelican Springs homestead. It's only about ten Ks from here. So once we get the casualties out, our ambos can shoot them across to meet the chopper.'

Jack's mouth compressed briefly. It all sounded straightforward enough but experience had taught him it probably wouldn't be. And if that was the case, then they'd just have to deal with any curve balls as they were thrown.

Mentally, Darcie began to prepare herself, watching as the SES team made their preparations.

'You OK?' Jack asked, shooting her a sideways glance.

'Fine.' She flicked a hand toward the SES team. 'I take it we're hooked up to this pulley thing and get lowered in?'

Jack nodded. 'We'll wear a safety harness. I'll drop in first and the SES guys will retrieve the rope and send you down. OK, looks like they're ready for us.'

Within seconds, Darcie found herself swinging down into the well. She gave a little gasp as she landed unevenly on some kind of rubble. Releasing herself from the guide rope, she began to take her bearings. It was darkish in the cavity, as Jack had predicted, and the place had a repulsive odour. 'Jack?'

'Right here.'

'Oh…' Darcie nudged in beside him, watching as he

aimed his torch across to the other side of the well, locating their patients. She heard the girl's subdued whimper and said quietly, 'I'll take Jessica.'

'Thanks. I'll see what's happening with Lachlan.'

Swinging the trauma pack from her shoulders, Darcie hunkered down beside the injured girl. 'Hi, Jess,' she said softly. 'I'm Darcie. I'm a doctor. Can you tell me where you're hurt?'

'It's my arm. I've been so scared...' Her teeth began chattering,

'And you're cold.' Darcie unfolded a space blanket from her supplies and tucked it around the girl. 'Did you hit your head at all?' she asked, beginning to test Jessica's neuro responses.

'No. I've done some stuntwork. I know how to fall safely. But Lachy's really hurt, I think.' She squeezed her eyes shut. 'Please...' she whispered on a sob. 'Can you get us out of here?'

Darcie felt put on her mettle. Quickly, she sifted through her options.

Both Jess's neuro responses and pulse were fine but she needed to be got out of this hell-hole and into the fresh air. 'I'll just need to check your arm, Jess.' Gently, Darcie removed the bloodstained T-shirt. She pursed her lips. Jess had a deep gash from the point of her shoulder to her mid upper arm. The site was already swelling and dark blue with bruising. It was still oozing blood. Thankfully, there was no artery involved.

OK. Mentally, Darcie squared her shoulders. She needed to show some initiative here. She took the girl's uninjured hand and held it. 'Jess, we have trained people waiting up top. I'm going to signal for one of them to come down with a retrieval harness and take you up.

The paramedics will take care of you until I can get up there and assess you properly. Is that OK?'

Jessica nodded. 'My arm's throbbing…'

'I'll give you something before you go. Do you feel sick at all?'

'Bit…'

Darcie nodded. 'I'll give you something to combat the nausea as well. You've been really brave, Jess,' Darcie said, shooting home the painkiller and anti-emetic. 'Now, let's get you up and out of here.'

It was all accomplished quickly and skilfully.

With Jessica safely out, Darcie concentrated on helping Jack with their other casualty. 'How's Lachlan?'

'Fractured NOF possibly. But we can't diagnose accurately without an MRI. His belly appears soft so it's safe to get a line in.'

'I think he's coming round.' Darcie felt a rush of relief.

'It's OK, Lachlan.' Jack's manner was calmly reassuring. 'You've fallen into a well, buddy. Knocked yourself out. I'm Jack and this is Darcie. We're doctors.'

Lachlan sucked air in through his lips. 'Leg…' he groaned. 'Pain's epic…'

'Yep. Hang in there, matey.' Jack gently lifted the youngster's head and applied the oxygen mask. 'Will you draw up morphine five and maxolon ten, please, Darcie? We don't want him throwing up on us. As soon as we get him stable, we'll follow with fifty of pethidine. That should get him through transportation to the hospital.'

Darcie shot home the injections quickly.

'Let's start splinting now,' Jack said. 'The sooner we get this lad out of here the better.'

Darcie's eyes were on high alert for any changes in Lachlan's condition as she watched Jack place the supportive splints between the young man's legs. 'Bandages now?'

'Nice thick ones,' Jack confirmed.

'This shouldn't have happened, should it?' Darcie said, working swiftly to bind Lachlan's injured leg to his good one.

'Not if the location scouts were on top of their game,' Jack agreed gruffly. 'I think I'll be having a word to the Workplace Health and Safety people.'

'Report them?' Darcie felt a lick of unease.

'Just doing my job, Darcie.' Jack was unequivocal. He looked at Lachlan's still form. 'Whack him with the pethidine now, please. I'll make my way back over to the opening and give the guys a shout for the stretcher.'

As Jack moved away from her peripheral vision, Darcie felt the cave-like atmosphere close in on her, her hearing fixed on every tiny sound. A fragment of leaf-like debris floated down and landed on her shoulder. She gave an involuntary shudder, shaking it off, feeling the nerves in her stomach crawl. The conditions in the well were awful.

Darcie pulled herself up with a jerk. This wasn't the time to start losing it. She had a seriously ill patient depending on her skills as a doctor. About to draw up the drug, she stopped and froze. In a second everything had changed. Lachlan was gulping, his eyes rolling back in his head, his colour ashen.

'Jack!' Darcie's cry echoed off the earthen walls. Instinctively, she ripped open Lachlan's shirt and began chest compressions.

'What's happened?' Jack's bulk dropped beside her.

'He's arrested!'

Jack's expletive scorched the air. He would have to intubate.

With the speed of light, he began zipping open sections of the trauma pack, gathering equipment. Centring himself for a second, he prepared to carry out the emergency procedure. And drew back sharply. He cursed under his breath. This wasn't going to work. He needed more light…

But there was none. He'd have to make do, feel his way.

Slowly, slowly, he passed the tube down Lachlan's trachea, attaching it to the oxygen. 'Now, breathe for me, Lachy,' he grated. 'Come on!' He waited a second and then checked the carotid pulse in the young man's neck.

Nothing.

'We'll have to defib him.' Jack reached for the life pack. 'We are *not* losing this one, Darcie.' Jack's voice roughened. 'I'm counting on you.'

Darcie's expression was intense. Every compression meant life for Lachlan. Her heart began to pound against the walls of her chest, her pulse thumping in her wrists and throat. She began feeling light-headed, perspiration patching wetly across her forehead and in the small of her back. 'Jack, hurry…'

'This is a bloody nightmare,' Jack hissed between clenched teeth. 'Be ready to take over the bag when I defib,' he snapped.

Darcie captured a rush of strength from somewhere. Whether Lachlan ever woke again could depend on their teamwork now.

'OK—do it!' Jack's command rang out.

Almost in slow motion Darcie reached out and took over the Air-Viva bag.

'And clear!'

Darcie dropped the bag and sprang back, willing the volts of electricity to do their work and kick-start Lachlan's heart.

A beat of silence.

'Jack?'

'Nothing. Let's go to two hundred. Clear!'

Darcie strove to keep panic at bay, aware only of its grip on her gut and the slow slide of sweat between her breasts.

'Start compressions again, Darcie.' Jack looked haunted. 'I'm giving him adrenaline.'

Darcie nodded, not capable of verbalising her reply.

Jack's mouth snapped into a thin line, his fingers curling round the mini-jet, which already contained the lifesaving drug. 'Come on, baby—do your job!' he implored, sending the needle neatly between Lachlan's ribs and into his heart. 'Clear!' He activated the charge.

A breathless hush as they waited.

Into the silence, the trace began bleeping and then shot into a steady rhythm. 'Yes…' Jack's relief was subdued.

Darcie slumped forward, her energy spent. She felt the threat of tears and held the heels of her hands against her eyes, gathering her composure. 'Oh, sweet heaven…'

Jack's arm came round her shoulders. 'Hey…'

'I'm OK…'

'You're not.' Jack turned her into his arms and held her.

Darcie allowed herself to be held, feeling the warmth of his body mingle with hers, melting into him, drawing strength from his strength and…the maleness of him. A need she hadn't known existed rose in her, but before she could wonder at its completeness she felt the swift stab of reality. She drew back sharply. What on earth had she been thinking of?

Lachlan was waking up, fear and confusion clouding his eyes.

'It's OK, Lachy.' Darcie beat back her own confusion. She took his hand and squeezed. 'You'll be fine.'

Jack swallowed, clearing the lump from his throat. He felt as though an invisible punch had landed in his solar plexus. She'd felt so right in his arms. And he'd so nearly kissed her. Taken that soft, beautiful mouth with his. And kissed her. Idiot. He drew in a quick, hard breath. 'Think a shot of midazolam is called for here, Dr Drummond?'

'I'd say so.' Darcie nodded, glad for the return to professionalism. The drug would act as a light anaesthetic and ease Lachy over the trauma of the next few hours. She turned away. 'Would you do it, please, Jack?' She wrapped her arms around her midriff, feeling hollowed out.

'Nice work, guys.' Zach Bayliss loomed out of the shadow, towing the collapsible stretcher. 'Could have been a whole different story, couldn't it?'

Darcie felt as though she'd been to hell and back. Swallowing hard on the tightness in her throat, she pulled herself upright. 'He's ready to move now, Zach. We've got him back into sinus rhythm but he'll have to be watched.'

'Understood, Doc.' Zach was a seasoned paramedic. He knew well the battle that had been fought here and, for the moment, won. 'Let's get this youngster on his way, then. If you're ready, Jack, on my count.'

In unison, they gently rolled Lachlan first on one

side then the other, sliding each section of the supporting plinth under him and snapping the pieces together.
A sturdy rope was attached to each end of the stretcher
and almost immediately it was being winched safely to
the top.

With Lachlan safely loaded into the ambulance, the
emergency crew gathered around. It had already been
decided Jess's care could be safely managed at Sunday
Creek hospital.

'Where do you want Lachy sent, Jack?' Zach gave
one last look inside the ambulance and closed the doors.

'The Royal in Brisbane is our best chance.' Jack was
already pulling out his mobile phone. 'I'll alert the head
of the trauma team, Nick Cavello. He'll coordinate everything from his end.'

'CareFlight chopper's landed at Pelican Springs.' Mal
Duffy joined the group.

'We'll take off, then.' Zach sketched a farewell wave.
'You're OK with Jess travelling with you and Jack, Darcie?'

'I've already settled her in the back seat,' Darcie confirmed. 'Take care of Lachy.'

'Will do.' Zach threw himself into the driver's seat
of the ambulance. 'Thanks, everyone,' he called, before
starting the engine. Within seconds, the emergency vehicle was being manoeuvred carefully away down the
bush track.

CHAPTER FIVE

'Just relax, Jess,' Darcie said, as they prepared for the trip back to Sunday Creek. 'We'll have you much more comfortable soon.'

'I'll try to minimise the bumps in the road.' Jack tried to inject some lightness into the situation and Jess gave a weak smile. 'Hang in there, kiddo,' he added gently. 'You're doing great.'

The return trip was covered mostly in silence as though each was busy with their own thoughts. As they reached the outskirts of the township, Jack said, 'It's still your day off, Darcie. I'll assume Jess's care if you like.'

'Thanks, but that's not necessary,' she answered firmly. 'Jess is my patient. I'd like to follow through.'

'Fine.' He glanced at her sharply with a frown. 'We'll need to debrief at some stage.'

Well, she knew that. Darcie rubbed at her collarbone through the thin material of her T-shirt. But if Jack had any thoughts of them *debriefing* about what had almost happened back there in the cave...

Soon they'd reached the hospital and Jack was reversing into the ambulance bay.

Dan Prentice, the hospital's only orderly, was waiting with a wheelchair and Jessica's transfer was made without fuss.

'Oh, hi, guys, you're back.' Natalie hurried forward.

'This is Jess, Nat.' Darcie kept her hand on her young patient's shoulder. 'Could you take her through to the treatment room, please? I'm just going to grab a quick shower and then I'll be back to suture Jess's arm.'

A quick shower meant just that. And years of practice meant Darcie had the logistics down pat. When she got back to the unit, Natalie had Jess ready in a gown, had drawn up lignocaine and opened the suture packs. 'Thanks, Nat. This all looks good.' Darcie gloved, pleased her patient was looking more relaxed. 'Little sting now, Jess,' she said, injecting the anaesthetic and infiltrating the wound. 'How's your tetanus status these days?'

'I had a top-up before I went on the film shoot.'

'Good.' Darcie smiled. 'That's one less jab we'll have to give you.' After several minutes she sought Jess's reaction and judged the anaesthetic had taken effect. 'Right, we're set to go. Nat, would you flush with normal saline, please? And, Jess, feel free to chill out, maybe have a little doze?'

Darcie's suturing was neat and painstakingly precise.

'You're so good at this,' Natalie murmured.

Darcie gave a half-laugh. 'I used to get hauled over the coals for being too slow.'

'I think suturing is an art,' Natalie maintained. 'In fact, everything about practising medicine is an art—at least, it should be.'

'Oh, if only that were true...'

Darcie inserted the final stitch. 'That's it.' She stripped off her gloves and stood back to enable Natalie to place a non-stick dressing over the wound. 'Jess, honey...' She roused her patient gently.

'Oh...' Jess's eyes fluttered open. She looked dazed for a second. 'Am I done?'

'Like a good roast.' Natalie chuckled. 'Dr Drummond's done a pretty fancy job with your stitches.'

'Thanks...' Jess blinked a bit. 'You've been really kind...' Two tears tracked down the youngster's cheeks and she wiped them away with the tips of her fingers.

Darcie pulled up a stool and sat down next to her patient. Poor kid. She'd been through a terrible ordeal. 'I want you put everything aside and just rest now, Jess. Think you can do that?'

Jessica bit her lip. 'I guess...'

'And I'd like to keep you here overnight.' And maybe for an extra one or two, Darcie thought. There could be residual effects from Jess's fall that would only become apparent later on. She gave her patient a reassuring smile. 'Now, can I call anyone for you—parents, perhaps?'

Jess shook her head. 'My parents live in Sydney. No need to alarm them. I'll call them when I'm up and around again. Mum would probably come racing out here and want to do my washing,' she added with a spark of humour. 'Where's Lachy?'

'We've sent him to Royal Brisbane. Dr Cassidy arranged that so I'm sure he'll get an update on Lachy's condition later today and let you know.' Darcie stood to her feet. 'Now, Nat will get you settled on the ward and I'll look in on you a bit later, all right? If you need a certificate for time off work, I'll take care of that as well.'

'I'm not going back there.' Jess shook her head firmly. 'They can shove their job.'

Mentally, Darcie stepped back. There was a raft of

separate issues here and after what had happened to her, Jessica was probably not in the right frame of mind to be making snap decisions about her job. Obviously, she needed to talk things through but that could wait. Darcie picked up the notes. 'Your arm will probably ache a bit after the anaesthetic wears off,' she told her patient. 'I'll write up some pain relief for you.'

'And don't be a martyr,' Natalie chimed in with a grin. 'Just yell if you need something.'

Jack was taking his time about things. He'd hauled the trauma packs through to the utility room, repacking them and replacing the items they'd used. They were now ready for the next emergency.

Strictly, it wasn't his responsibility, he conceded, but Sunday Creek wasn't a big city hospital and everyone had to pull their weight wherever it was needed. Even senior doctors. Besides, he admitted a bit ruefully, he'd wanted to be a hands-on boss. Well, now he had that here. In spades.

Job done, he went back to the residence, showered and changed and made his way back to do a ward round. There were only four patients and it wasn't an involved process. Returning the charts to the nurses' station, he paused for a moment and then looked at his watch. A second later, he was striding towards the treatment room. Pulling the curtain aside, he poked his head in. Nothing.

'Are you looking for me?'

Jack arched back. 'Darcie...' He blinked a bit. She stood there in pale blue scrubs, her hair twisted up into a topknot, her face scrubbed clean. She looked...wholesome and...gorgeous. He ordered his pulse to slow down. 'I wondered if you needed a hand.'

'All finished.' Darcie gave a guarded smile. 'We've put Jess on the little veranda ward. It's cool and quiet. Hopefully, she'll get some natural sleep.'

'Good.' He gave an approving nod. 'I was just on my way to get some food. Care to join me?'

'I'd kill for a cup of tea.'

Jack snorted. 'You need something more substantial than that, Dr Drummond. Come on.' He put out a hand in an ushering movement. 'Let's raid the hospital kitchen. They're bound to have a few scraps left over from breakfast.'

A short while later they were tucking into the crisp bacon and fluffy scrambled eggs Carole, the hospital's long-time cook, had whipped up.

'More toast, doctors?' Carole called from the servery window. 'I've made plenty.'

'Thanks, Carole. You're a star.' Darcie sent the older woman a warm smile and made to rise to her feet.

'I'll get it.' Jack's hand landed briefly on Darcie's forearm. 'Finish your food.'

Later, as they sat over big mugs of tea, Darcie said, 'I could sleep for a week.'

'Why don't you, then?' Jack saw her eyes were faintly shadowed. 'At least for the rest of today. I gave you the weekend off, if you recall.'

'I promised to look in on Jess later.'

Jack's mouth gave a mocking twist. 'I think I can just about manage that. Go home to bed, Darcie.'

'You mentioned a debrief.'

'That can wait.'

Darcie's heart began hammering. 'I'd...rather get it over with.'

A beat of silence.

OK. Jack drew in a long breath and let it go. It didn't need rocket science to fathom what was going on here. She was feeling guilty about what had happened in the well when, in reality, if there was any fault to be laid it was down to his actions, not her response. That he'd almost kissed her was beside the point. And she was wound up. He could imagine what her heartbeat was doing under the thin cotton of her scrubs.

And he was technically her boss. That point probably mattered to her. Plus they were sharing job space and home space. There was no room for awkwardness. He had to sort things. 'What happened was a pretty normal reaction,' he said evenly. 'Hell, we saved a life!'

She bit her lip. 'I…suppose.'

'It was just a hug, Darcie.'

Did he really believe that? Darcie fought for control of her wildly see-sawing heart. 'I…don't usually act that way with a senior colleague,' she countered, the set of her small chin almost defiant.

'But, then, I'd imagine you're not *usually* practising emergency medicine at the bottom of a stinking well, are you?'

'No.' She managed a small smile that was almost a grimace. He was spinning things to save her feelings. Well, if that's the way he wanted to play it… But he had to know she'd clung to him and he'd responded by holding her more tightly. He *had* to know that.

But it was his call. For now.

Jack laced his hands around his tea mug. 'If we'd won the lottery and I'd gathered you up in a hug, you wouldn't have thought it odd, would you?'

Her breath caught and fire flooded her cheeks. But

they hadn't won the lottery and it hadn't been *that* kind of hug.

And they both knew it.

She couldn't answer. Instead, she lifted a shoulder in a shrug. Jack Cassidy could make of it what he liked.

Darcie slept well into the afternoon. When she woke, she checked her phone for messages and found one from Maggie. She promptly called back.

'Hi, Maggie. What's up?'

'Can you come to my place for a barbecue this evening?'

'Um, yes, I probably could. Something special going on?'

'I wish I knew.' Maggie forced an off-key laugh. 'I've invited Sam Gibson.'

'The new vet in town,' Darcie said.

'I think I must be sick in the head to have started any of this.'

Darcie rearranged her pillows and made herself comfortable. Maggie was usually very much in charge but now she sounded rattled. 'So, what's with you and Sam?'

'He's come round for coffee a couple of times.'

'How did you meet?'

'We had to take our Staffy for his shot. It kind of went from there. He took the boys trail-bike riding yesterday so I thought I should ask him for a meal. A barbecue sounded, well, more casual, I suppose. Only I feel a bit weird just inviting Sam.'

Darcie chuckled. 'You want me there as a buffer?'

'I want you there as a friend! I'm so out of practice with this relationship stuff, Darc.'

'Oh, rubbish! You just need to chill out and enjoy this new friendship that's come your way. Flirt a bit.'

'Flirt!' Maggie squawked. 'How does one flirt again? Remind me. I vaguely remember something about fluttering eyelashes. If I did that, I'd look demented.'

'For heaven's sake, relax and go with the flow. If Sam asks you out on a date, accept nicely.'

'So says the woman who makes a career of not dating *anyone*.'

'I have so been on dates,' Darcie defended.

'Oh, when was that? I'll bet it was so long ago you can't even remember who you went out with.'

'I went out with one of the flying doctors only recently.'

'Brad Kitto?' Maggie dismissed. 'Fly in, fly out. Nice guy but he's a Canadian on a three months' exchange. How was that ever going to amount to anything?'

'OK, OK.' Darcie shrugged off a feeling of discomfort. She didn't need an inquiry into her dating habits, even from someone as well meaning as Maggie. 'But could I remind you this began as a discussion about your love life, not mine.'

'Point taken. So, will you come?'

'Of course…' Darcie gave an exaggerated sigh of acceptance.

'Oh, and invite the big guy.'

'Jack?' Darcie felt her mouth dry.

'Might be a nice chance for him to mix a bit with the locals. And I haven't met him yet.'

Darcie swallowed. She only hoped she and Jack could revert to being at ease with one another. Perhaps going out among a few friendly folk would help. That's if he agreed to it, of course. 'Well, I'll ask,' she said carefully, 'but he's quite likely pretty tired. We had a call-out at five this morning and he's been over at the hospital all day.'

'Mmm, I heard about the emergency from Karen Bayliss. By the way, I've invited her and Zach.'

'Oh, good. They're a nice couple. Would you like me to make a cake for dessert?'

'Oh, would you, Darce? I've spent most of the day trying to get my hair to look less like the ends of a straw broom.'

Darcie's soft laugh rippled. Maggie's colourful take on things always lightened her spirits. 'Shall I come round about five, then? Help you set up?'

'Thanks. And ask Jack,' Maggie reinforced, before she ended the call.

Jack was offhand when Darcie relayed Maggie's invitation.

'Sure. What time?'

'I'm going about five.'

Jack's mouth drew in as if he was considering his options.

'Is that too early for you?' Darcie's gaze was a little uncertain.

'Maybe a bit. Give me the address,' he added, his shoulder half-turned as if he was about to walk away. 'I'll follow on later.'

Information imparted, Darcie watched as he walked out of the kitchen as though he couldn't leave fast enough. As though he was distancing himself from her. Or from the situation they'd found themselves in. That was more likely, she decided.

Swiping up the scattering of flour from her baking,

she gave an impatient little tut. This unease was her fault. Why couldn't she have been cool about everything? Laughed it off as the adrenaline rush after having saved a life?

Because she couldn't.

Jack went back to his bedroom. He hated this…distance between them. And he didn't really feel like socialising. God, he just wanted sleep. But he had to show his face. Part of the job. Get to know the locals.

Ignoring what were probably house rules, he flung himself down on the patchwork quilt, boots and all, and stared at the ceiling.

Darcie Drummond.

She'd got to him. He snorted a self-derisive laugh. Perhaps he should just kiss her and get it out of his system. Get *her* out of his system. Yeah, like that was going to help. It would just muddy the atmosphere even further.

He pressed his fingers across his eyelids. He needed to lighten up.

It was early evening when Jack arrived at Maggie's place. The buzz of conversation interspersed with laughter and the mouth-watering smell of steaks cooking drew him along the side path and towards the back garden where he guessed the barbecue was happening.

Maggie saw him the moment he poked his head around the lattice screen. *Wow! Now, there was serious talent.* She smiled and went forward to greet him. 'Jack?' She rolled her eyes in a wry gesture. 'Of course you must be. I'm Maggie. Come and meet everyone.'

Maggie introduced Jack to Sam Gibson, who was

officiating at the barbecue. 'Welcome to Sunday Creek, Doc.' Sam's handshake was firm. 'I'm new here myself. Animal doctor,' he enlightened with a grin.

'We're bound to cross paths, then.' Jack laughed.

'But not instruments.' The dry irony in Sam's tone made Jack laugh again. It was going to be OK, he thought. He looked forward to relaxing and enjoying the down time.

'Zach you know, of course.' Maggie was pressing on in her role of hostess. 'And this is Karen, Zach's wife.'

'Hi.' Karen Bayliss gave a friendly little wave. 'And this is our daughter, Molly.' The pride in her voice was unmistakable as she tucked the baby onto her hip.

'How old is she?' Jack ran the tip of his finger along the plump little arm.

'Ten months.'

Jack's mouth crimped at the corners as the little one gave back a haughty look. He felt a twist inside him and the oddest feeling ripped through him. He could have been a father by now if things between him and Zoe had worked out. But for crying out loud! He was thirty-seven. As far as fertility went, he still had oceans of time to find the right woman to have a child with. He shook his head, wondering where the mad rush of introspection had come from.

'She's giving you *the look*,' Karen said with a chuckle.

'She's a princess,' Jack murmured. 'You're very lucky, Karen.'

'Yes, we know.' Karen sent a soft look at her husband. 'We'd almost given up hope when this one trotted into our lives. That's why we chose the name Molly. It means *longed-for* child.'

Out of nowhere, Jack felt drenched in emotion. Hell's bells. He blinked a bit, seizing the escape route with relief when Maggie said, 'And these are my sons, Josh and Ethan.'

'Hey, guys.' Jack shook hands with the two. 'I saw the trail bikes as I came through the carport. You ride a bit?'

'Yep,' Josh, the elder, said. 'Sam took us over to some tracks yesterday. It was awesome.'

'I like skateboarding best,' Ethan chimed in, sensing an interested audience in Jack.

'I used to do that when I was about your age,' Jack said. 'Do you have a bowl here?'

Ethan looked blank.

'Duh.' His brother dug him in the ribs. 'A skate bowl?'

Ethan coloured. 'I just use the concrete paths at the park. But some of the kids use the footpath outside the shops.'

'And you know you're not allowed to do that,' his mother intervened. 'It's illegal.'

'Yeah, I know, Mum.' Ethan gave Maggie a long-suffering look.

'Always good to obey the rules, champ.' Jack grinned, giving support to Maggie's parental role.

'Thanks,' she said, as the boys turned and went off about their own business. 'They're a challenge.'

'They seem like great kids, Maggie. Uh...' Jack raised an eyebrow in query. 'I've brought wine. Where can I stash it? Fridge?'

'Oh, yes.' For the first time Maggie noticed the carry bag he'd parked on the outdoor table. 'Sorry for rabbiting on. Just go up onto the deck. Kitchen's straight through. Darcie's there. She'll organise it for you.'

Head bent, Darcie was busy at the countertop. She

looked up, flustered when Jack walked in. 'Hi…' It was no more than a breath of sound.

He gave a tight smile. 'I brought some wine.' He hoisted the carry bag onto the bench. 'Maggie said you'd find a home for it.'

'Oh—OK.' Just looking at him caused a well of emotion to rise in her chest and lodge in her throat.

He was wearing faded jeans and a simple white polo shirt that showed the tanned strength of his upper arms. The arms that had held her with such caring. Such… tenderness.

She took in a breath that almost hurt and her gaze dropped to his mouth. Desire leached through her. The image of her leaning across the counter to kiss him sent her heart dancing a wild flutter in her chest. A jagged breath snatched at her throat. She didn't do this. Lust after men. And Jack was not some random male. He was a senior colleague. Her boss. She swallowed dryly. 'I'll find some space in the fridge.'

Jack's gaze stayed riveted to her. She was like a sprite in her black sleeveless top and long skirt that dipped round her ankles. He felt like jumping the counter that separated them, whirling her into a mad dance. And then slowly closing in on her so that their bodies were separated only by a whisper of air. And finally…

Darcie closed the fridge and turned back to face him. She gave him a smile that was gone before it could take shape. 'Have you met everyone?'

'Mmm, think so. Not too many faces to remember.'

'That's always a help.' She picked up a flat-bladed knife to finish off the frosting on her cake. 'Um, would you like a drink? Maggie left instructions for everyone to help themselves.'

'Thanks. I'll get something later.'

Jack propped himself against the countertop, leaning slightly towards her and catching the drift of her light-as-air shampoo for his trouble. 'Cake looks good.'

Tipping her head back, Darcie smiled. 'My contribution towards dessert. I once shared a flat with a pastry chef.' Darcie set the finished cake aside. 'She gave me a few tips along the way.'

'So chocolate cake is your signature dish?'

'It is.' She scooped out a tiny drizzle of frosting with the tip of her finger and pushed the bowl towards him, her gesture inviting him to help her lick the bowl.

He gave a huff of laughter. 'I haven't done this since I was about six.'

'Some catching up to do, then,' she suggested, and he chuckled.

'So, I guess you did this with your mother?' Jack asked.

She gave an off-key laugh. 'My mother doesn't cook. We had a housekeeper. I spent lots of time in the kitchen with her. My parents are history professors. Away on the lecturing circuit a lot. They missed most of my significant milestones when I was at school,' she added as a kind of resigned afterthought.

And wasn't that a crappy way to spend your childhood. 'Were you an only child?' Jack asked evenly.

'Mmm-hmm.' She dragged in a breath and let it out in a whoosh. 'Don't feel sorry for me, Jack.'

'Sorry for you is the last thing I feel,' he countered gruffly.

Their eyes locked and her tongue flicked a tiny dab of frosting from her bottom lip. Jack's throat closed uncomfortably. And for just a moment, a blink of time, there was a connection of shared awareness. Sharp. Intense.

'Hey, you two!' Maggie called, and suddenly their eye contact retracted as quickly as turning off a light switch.

CHAPTER SIX

MONDAY MORNING AND already the barbecue felt like a lifetime ago.

'Thanks for your input, Darcie.' Jack relaxed back in his chair, legs stretched out under his desk. They'd officially completed handover.

'If that's it, I'll do a ward round.' Darcie half rose.

'Hang on a minute.' He flicked a hand in a delaying motion. 'I've arranged for the theatre to be thoroughly cleaned and made sterile. I'm aware it's small but everything's there. If we can keep it ready for emergencies, it will save having to call out the flying doctors, which will in turn save them time and money.'

A beat of silence.

'You're the surgeon and the boss.' Darcie's gaze fluttered down and then up to meet his piercing blue eyes. 'It's obviously your call.'

'But?' Jack's dark brows rose interrogatively.

'We don't have much backup for major trauma.'

Jack all but rolled his eyes. Did she think he was a complete novice at this? He tapped his pen end to end on the desk. 'I'm talking relatively straightforward emergency procedures, Darcie, not heart transplants.'

Stung by his air of arrogance, Darcie said coolly,

'What about anaesthetics? I have a little knowledge but I'm not qualified.'

'I can guide you.'

Well, he obviously thought he had the answer to *everything*. But far from reassuring her, it only added to Darcie's uncertainty. 'I...just don't want us to start playing God every time there's an emergency and think we can automatically sort it here.'

'You don't like me taking over,' Jack interpreted flatly.

Darcie brushed a fingertip between her brows. That wasn't it at all. She wasn't making herself clear. But she'd woken with a headache that morning, her thoughts muddled, her concentration shot to pieces. And all because she couldn't seem to get a grip on her feelings about Jack. She felt very out of her depth but the last thing she needed was her personal feelings spilling over into their professional involvement.

A soft breath gusted from her mouth. Had it been only yesterday they'd been in cahoots like kids, licking frosting from a bowl?

'Didn't you sleep well?' Jack tilted his head, his eyes narrowing. The faint shadows were still there. Her light olive complexion was a dead giveaway.

She lifted her chin. Whether she slept well or not was none of his business.

For a second tension crackled between them, as brittle as spun sugar.

'Could we get back to the point?' Darcie said stiffly. 'I'm more than accepting of your appointment here, Dr Cassidy. The place needs a senior doctor. You're it. Obviously my protocols don't work for you, so change them!'

Jack clicked his tongue. 'It's about trying to get the

hospital up and running to its full potential, Darcie. So work with me here, please.'

He scrubbed a hand roughly across his cheekbones, reminding himself to get some eye drops. His eyes felt as though a ton of shell grit had been dumped there. *He* hadn't slept well. His thoughts had spun endlessly and always centred on this waif of a girl sitting opposite him.

But she wasn't a waif at all. That was just his protectiveness coming into play. And she wouldn't thank him for that. She was capable of taking care of herself. More than. OK. He'd better smarten up. 'Darcie, I need you on board with all these changes, otherwise nothing's going to work for us in any direction, is it?'

His plea came out low and persuasive and Darcie felt relief sweep through her. What he said made sense. They couldn't afford to be offside with one another. Professionally, they were doctors in isolation. It was simply down to her and Jack to make things work. Otherwise she'd have to leave. And she definitely didn't want that.

Where would she go?

'I guess we're both on a bit of a learning curve right now,' she admitted throatily.

'And medically it's been a draining couple of days.' Jack was more than willing to be conciliatory.

Darcie looked at him warily, meshing her teeth against her bottom lip. 'You'll have my support, Jack.'

He let out a long breath. 'Thank you.'

Darcie blinked a bit as he sent her a fence-mending kind of smile. *We'll be OK*, it seemed to imply. Well, she could live with that.

Rolling back his chair, he went to stand with his back against the window. 'The board will be here at eleven for a meeting.'

'Oh—OK.' Darcie rose. She flicked him a wide-eyed query. 'Do you want me there?'

'Silly question.' He paused deliberately, his eyes capturing hers, darkened by the slanting light from the window. 'Of course I *want* you.'

Darcie was still feeling the weight of Jack's parting words knocking against her chest as she finished her ward round.

She'd purposefully left Jessica until last.

'How are you feeling?'

Jess lifted her head from the glossy magazine she'd been reading. 'Much better, thanks.'

Darcie smiled. 'I can see that.' Jess was sitting in the easy chair beside her bed. The hospital gown was gone and she was dressed in a very cute pair of hot pink pyjamas.

'Are you going to release me, Dr Drummond?'

'Let's see what Dr Cassidy has to say, shall we?' Darcie plucked the chart from the end of the bed. She read Jack's notes swiftly. After an initial dose early yesterday afternoon, Jess had needed no further pain relief. Her neuro responses were normal and she'd slept well without a sedative. 'You've bounced back remarkably well, Jess.' Darcie replaced the chart. 'I guess I'm going to have to let you go.'

'Now?' Grinning, Jess threw her magazine aside. 'Cool.'

'Got time for a quick chat first?' Darcie propped herself on the edge of the bed. 'You're quite sure you don't want to go back to your job?'

'Quite sure.' Jess gave a small grimace. 'Too late anyway. I've already resigned and had a friend collect my stuff and bring it in.'

'No problem with contracts and things?'

'It was open-ended,' Jess explained. 'A get-out clause for both parties. They could get rid of me or vice versa.'

'It doesn't sound very secure.'

Jess flapped a hand. 'That's the business I'm in. It doesn't worry me.'

I must be getting old, then, Darcie decided. Because it would worry me. A lot. 'So, what are your plans?'

'Maggie checked to see if there were any flights out of Sunday Creek today. Apparently, one of the local graziers is flying his own plane to a conference in Brisbane this afternoon. He's kindly offered me a seat. I'll go and visit Lachy at the Royal. Then I'll head home to Sydney and start looking for a new job. There are a couple of films happening soon. I'll shoot my CV out. I'll be offered something,' she added with youthful confidence.

'So—obviously, you weren't happy with the film company at Pelican Springs?'

'They took short cuts with safety.' Jess was unequivocal. 'That doesn't work for me.'

Darcie looked thoughtful. So Jack had been right. But, of course, to make charges stick, you had to have people to back up your convictions. And if those same people needed their jobs…?

'I'm OK to go, then?'

Her patient's slightly anxious query jolted Darcie back to her role as Jessica's doctor. 'Just a couple of loose ends to tie up. I'll give you a note for your GP in Sydney and a script for some antibiotics just to be on the safe side. You'll probably be able to have the stitches out in a week or so. And I'll give you a leaflet explaining what's necessary for the care of your wound. This will be an essential part of its healing,' Darcie emphasised. 'Don't neglect it, Jess, all right?'

'I won't,' Jessica promised. 'Mum'll be on my case anyway. But that's what mums do, isn't it?' she added with a philosophical little shrug of her shoulders.

'Yes, I suppose they do.' Darcie's eyes were faintly wistful. She blew out a controlled breath. 'Now, I'll leave your paperwork at the nurses' station. See Maggie before you go. And, Jess, good luck with everything.'

'Oh, thanks, Dr Drummond.' Jess got to her feet, obviously keen to gather her things and get going. 'And thanks for looking after me,' she added with a very sweet smile.

'You're welcome and it's Darcie. We went through a lot together, didn't we?'

Jess nodded. 'I was never so pleased to see anyone as I was to see you at the bottom of that well…' The youngster suppressed a shiver. 'But we did good.'

Darcie smiled. 'Well, make sure you keep *doing good* when you leave here.' She went to the door. Pausing, as if a thought had just occurred to her, she turned back. 'Just to put your mind at ease, Jess, there should be minimal scarring on your arm. Well, nothing the camera will pick up.'

'I'm not a bit worried.' Happy, back in charge of her life, Jess grinned. 'Dr Cassidy said you did a brilliant job.'

Sunday morning, two weeks later, Darcie rose earlier than usual but it was obvious Jack had risen earlier still. She found him in the kitchen, his hands wrapped round a mug of tea. 'Morning,' she said, helping herself from the pot he'd made.

'Louise Alderton called last night,' Jack said. 'She invited us out to Willow Bend today. I accepted for both of us. I hope that's all right.'

A dimple appeared briefly as Darcie smiled. 'We're taking the day off, then?'

'We've earned it, don't you agree?'

'Well, you certainly have,' Darcie apportioned fairly. 'You've hardly drawn breath since you arrived.' But she wasn't about to question Jack's motives or his workload. He was the boss. He could do what he liked. 'A day out at Willow Bend sounds wonderful,' she said instead. 'What time do they want us?'

'As soon as we'd like. Max will yard a couple of horses for us. Fancy a ride with me?' His gaze lifted, straying momentarily to the sweet curve of her mouth.

'Should be fun,' she said lightly, but if she'd looked in the mirror at that moment she would have seen her flushed image reflecting a wide-eyed vulnerability.

They left for Willow Bend just after nine. As they drove, Darcie said, 'The colours are really something special out here, aren't they? The landscape seems so pure and clean and everything seems so incredibly *still*. The vastness takes my breath away.'

'You're not alone there,' Jack responded quietly, wondering whether this time away from the hospital confines would allow him to get to know her better. He wanted to. So much. But he couldn't rush her. He knew that as well. Perhaps they were destined never to be more than medical colleagues.

Perhaps today would be the day he'd find out.

* * *

'I've saddled the horses for you,' Max Alderton said. 'I hope you'll be happy with Hot Shot, Jack. He's fairly spirited.' They were sitting on the homestead veranda in comfortable wicker chairs, enjoying the morning tea Louise had prepared.

'Can't wait.' Jack's look was keen. 'Although it's been a while since I actually did any riding.'

'Hot Shot is a former racehorse,' Louise joined in. 'Nice mouth. Let him stretch out on the flats. Darcie will show you the trails we use.'

'I'll be riding Jewel as usual?' Darcie helped herself to a scone topped with jam and cream.

'Of course.' Louise smiled. 'I think she's missed you. You haven't been out for a while.'

Darcie lifted a shoulder. 'Busy at the hospital. Not that Jack's a slave-driver or anything.' She looked across at him and her breath caught in her throat. Those blue eyes were far too knowing. And suddenly she was afraid. Afraid of what seemed to be happening between them, and whether she wanted it or not.

After morning tea, Jack and Darcie made their way across to the horses. It was a beautiful day, not too hot, with a slight breeze.

A good day just to be alive, Jack thought a bit later, admiration flickering in his eyes as he watched Darcie swing lightly to her mare's saddle, her Akubra tipped rakishly forward and her hair cascading from under it to her shoulders. 'Where are we aiming for?' he asked, deftly circling his own mount to steady the frisky stallion.

Darcie flicked a hand towards a line of lacy willows.

'Louise and I usually cross the creek and head on up to the plateau. The view's amazing from there.'

They took off at a leisurely pace.

'Enjoying it?' Darcie asked after they'd been riding for a while.

'Fantastic.' Jack couldn't believe the sheer exhilaration he felt.

'Oh, Jack, look!' Darcie pointed to a mob of grey wallabies. Alerted to the presence of humans, the quaint little animals were suddenly all flying legs and tails, almost colliding with each other in their haste to leap away to the safety of the scrub.

'Silly beggars.' Jack laughed. Spurred on by the lightness of his mood, he gathered up the reins. 'Fancy a gallop?'

'You're on!' Darcie gave a whoop of delight and took up the challenge.

In perfect rhythm they took off across the paddock, their horses' hooves churning a wake of green through the tall grasses.

Leaving the flat country behind, they climbed higher and higher, until Darcie signalled she was about to stop and wheeled Jewel to a halt halfway up the slope. Her eyes alight with pleasure, she looked down. 'Isn't that something?' she said softly.

Jack reined in Hot Shot beside her, his gaze following hers to the expanse of the valley below, across the faint shimmer of the creek and beyond to the homestead nestling far away on the natural rise of the land.

'Yes, it is…' He closed his eyes, breathing in the woodsy tang of the morning air, tasting it, almost hearing it.

Watching him, Darcie took a long breath, loath to disturb what she perceived as a very private moment. She felt so in tune with him. So, what had happened? Had some fundamental change taken place within herself? And why suddenly today did *everything* about him seem to call to her? As if to clear her thoughts, she raised her gaze to the eastern rim of the cloudless sky. 'Should we head back now?'

'Uh…OK.' Jack blinked a bit, as if reconnecting with the world around him. 'Perhaps we could stop at the creek, spell the horses for a bit?'

The horses were surefooted, picking their way carefully down the track to the creek. Dismounting, Jack looped the reins around Hot Shot's neck, setting him free to graze.

Somewhat guardedly, Darcie followed his example. 'Are you sure they won't take off and leave us stranded?' she asked.

'Not when they have one another for company.' Bending down to the stream, he scooped up a handful of water and drank it thirstily.

'Is that safe?' Darcie bobbed down beside him, her head very close to his.

Jack scoffed a laugh. 'Of course it's safe, Darcie. It's running water! And see over there…' He pointed to where the creek trickled over some rocks. 'That's watercress. And it's lush and green, a sure sign there's no pollution.'

'If you say so, Dr Cassidy.'

Jack chuckled. 'Go on, try it,' he urged, and watched as she dipped her hand into the water and gingerly tasted it.

'It's quite nice.' She gave qualified approval.

'Quite nice?' Jack imitated her crisp little accent to a T. 'It's beautiful.'

She made a face. 'And you're the ultimate authority, I suppose. Jack—' She broke off, laughing. 'What do you think you're doing?'

'Nothing.' He grinned innocently, in the same instant showering her with a spray of water he'd scooped up from the creek.

Darcie shrieked. 'You are such rubbish!' Recklessly, she showered him back until it was a free-for-all battle between them.

'Enough!' Jack finally called a halt, the last of his ammunition slipping between his fingers in a silver rainbow of trickles.

'I'm drenched,' Darcie wailed, peeling her wet shirt away from the waistband of her jeans. 'And cold.'

'Poor baby.' Jack grinned, quite unabashed. 'Want me to warm you up?' He wasn't waiting for her answer. Instead, he reached out and gently drew her towards him, his intent obvious.

'Jack…?'

'Darcie…? Jack looked down at her. A stiff breeze had whipped up, separating tendrils of her hair from around her face and fluffing them out. She looked so vulnerable. And so desirable.

'Should we be doing this…?' Her voice faded to a whisper.

He made a dismissive sound in his throat. 'I've given up trying to find reasons why we shouldn't.'

Darcie swallowed; her heart tripped. He was bending towards her, the deep blue of his eyes capturing hers with an almost magnetic pull. And the sun felt intoxicatingly warm against her back. There was no urgency in the air.

Just a languid kind of sweetness.

Jack was so close to her now she could see the faint shadow across his jaw, the slight smudges under his eyes. Yet his face reflected a toughness, a strength.

'Sweet...' Jack took her face in his hands, his need materialising in the softest sigh before his mouth found hers. The kiss rolled through his blood and raw need slammed into him like nothing he had ever known. Her lips parted and her own longing seemed to match his, overwhelming him like the heady aroma of some dark heated wine.

Applying a barely-there pressure through his hands, he whispered the tips of his fingers down the sides of her throat, then in a sweep across her breastbone to her shoulders, gathering her in.

Darcie clung to him. And the kiss deepened, turned wrenching and wild. She felt a need inside her, an over-whelming need to be touched like this, held like this.

And *stroked* to the point of ecstasy by this man.

But it wasn't going to go that far. At least, not today. She felt Jack pulling back, breaking the kiss slowly, gently, his lips leaving a shivering sweetness like trails of insubstantial gossamer.

A long beat of silence while they collected them-selves.

'Oh, help...' Darcie turned away, sinking onto the ground and pulling her knees up to her chin. 'What was that all about, do you suppose?'

Jack settled beside her. 'Does there have to be a rea-son?' His voice was muted, slightly gravelly. 'We kissed. It's been waiting to happen almost since we met.'

Darcie inhaled a ragged little breath. 'I suppose...'

'I could say you were irresistible, if that will help.'

In a quick, protective movement, Darcie put her hand
to her mouth, feeling his kiss return in a wash of quivering nerve-ends. OK, they'd kissed, she owned. But as
a result had they opened another set of problems? And
where was any of it leading?

'Hey…' Jack turned her head a fraction, tipping her
chin up with a finger. 'Don't tell me you didn't enjoy it,
Darcie. Because I won't believe you.'

She breathed in and out, a soft little breath through
her slightly parted lips. 'It's not that.'

'What is it, then? Surely you know you can trust me.'

'I know…'

'Well, then…'

As if in a dream, she went with him as he gently lowered them to the grassy bank of the creek.

'Darcie…you're beautiful…' Jack buried his face in
her throat, his hand sliding beneath her shirt to roam
restlessly along her back and then to her midriff, half
circling her ribcage, driving upwards until his thumbs,
let free, began stroking the underswell of her breast.

With a passion she hardly knew she possessed,
Darcie took the initiative, opening her mouth on his,
tasting him all over again. And again.

How long they stayed wrapped in their own world
she had no idea, but when he drew back and they moved
apart to lie side by side, she could tell the sun had shifted,
shedding light on the face of the river gums. Her chest
lifted in a long steadying sigh. 'How long have we been
here?'

Jack shook his head. He felt poleaxed, set adrift without a lifeline. 'Does it matter?' When she didn't answer,
he turned to look at her. 'Are you OK?'

What was OK any more? Darcie wondered, pulling herself into a sitting position.

Jack half rose, leaning back on his elbows and surveying her. He didn't like what he saw. Her shoulders looked tightly held, almost shutting him out. 'Talk to me, Darcie.'

For answer, she plucked off a blade of grass and began shredding it. 'I don't know what to say...'

'About what?'

'This—us.'

Jack wrenched himself forward and sat next to her. He held up his hand as if to study it. 'Well, I'm real and as far as I know you're real. We're without ties and single. So where's the problem?' His dark brows hitched briefly. 'You *are* single, aren't you?'

'Yes!' There was a weight of feeling in her voice.

'So I'll ask again. What's the problem?'

She shook her head.

In the silence that followed, Jack reached across and took her hands, brought them to his mouth and kissed each palm. Then, while his eyes said, *Trust me*, he flattened them on his chest. The action brought Darcie very near the edge. Suddenly, without warning, she felt surrounded by him, his masculine strength and the wild pull he exerted on every one of her senses.

'Darcie...?'

'I was engaged, Jack.' Her voice was fainter than air.

'And?'

She swallowed dryly. 'I ran away and came to Australia.'

'So you broke it off. There's no shame in that. I'm sure you had your reasons.'

She pulled in a slow, painful breath. 'Oh, I did.'

Looping out an arm, he gathered her in. 'Going to tell me?' he pressed gently.

Darcie felt the weight of indecision weigh heavily. But if ever there was a time for honesty between them, then it was now. 'His name was Aaron,' she began slowly. 'He was a doctor where I worked at St Faith's in London. A bit older than I. We seemed well suited. We got along. He looked out for me. When he asked me to marry him, I didn't hesitate.'

'But later you began to second-guess your engagement,' Jack suggested quietly.

'Once he'd put the ring on my finger, he changed. Small ways at first so that I thought I'd been mistaken. But then…his caring turned into…control. Control in all kinds of bizarre ways…like how I wore my hair and make-up. He began choosing my clothes, insisting I wear what he'd bought…and that was just the beginning.'

Jack felt the tiny shudder go through her and swore under his breath. 'He wasn't physically abusive, was he?'

'Oh, no.' She shook her head decisively. 'I'd have been gone in two minutes. But, no…his behaviour was the problem. So…manipulative.'

'You did the right thing to get out.'

'You think so?'

'And fast.' Jack frowned a bit. 'What about your parents? Couldn't you have gone to them?'

She shook her head. 'My relationship with them is a bit complex. Sometimes I feel as though I don't know them at all. And they don't know me,' she added in a kind of quiet resignation.

Jack thought long and hard. Something was eating away at her. Whatever else, they couldn't leave things like this. 'Do you want to talk about it?' he offered.

'It goes without saying anything you tell me will be confidential.'

Darcie felt her mouth dry, her breathing become tight. 'Are you being my doctor here, Jack?'

'No, Darcie.' His voice was soft, intense. 'I'm trying to be your *friend*.' When she didn't respond, he took the initiative. Carefully. 'At what part of your growing up did you begin to feel alienated from your parents?'

'From when I was about twelve,' she faltered, after the longest pause.

'You mentioned a housekeeper so I'm guessing you weren't sent away to school?'

'No, but perhaps it would have been better. At least I'd have had company of my own age. I was lonely a lot of the time.'

Jack heard the pain in her voice and a silent oath lodged in his throat. 'Go on,' he encouraged gently, touching her lightly on the shoulder.

Darcie turned to look at him. It had been a feather touch of reassurance, and why it had the capacity to make her reassured she had no idea. But, unaccountably, it did. Words began to tumble out.

'My parents had reached the peak in their careers. They had invitations to speak all over the UK. In between speaking engagements they'd swoop home and gather me up like I was the most important thing in their lives. But in a few days they'd be gone again.'

'Pretty erratic parenting, then,' he said.

She tried a half-laugh. 'I guess you'd say so. And maybe...' she added, as if the thought had suddenly occurred to her, 'that's why I took Aaron at face value. He was always there for me. Something my parents hadn't been.'

'So, gravitating towards Aaron was a fairly natural reaction on your part,' Jack said. Cautious.

Darcie released her breath on a shuddering sigh. 'I think I was extremely gullible. So easily duped...'

'Hey, don't beat up on yourself. Foresight is a bit scarce on the ground when you really need it.' Concern showed in his gaze as it locked with hers. 'Did your parents ever get to meet Aaron?'

'Of course. We were engaged, planning a wedding. They liked him. If I'd tried telling them what I suspected about him, they'd have thought I was overreacting.'

'But they know where you are now? And reasons why you left England?'

'Yes.'

It seemed a long time until she continued. 'When I began to realise what my life would be like if I married Aaron, I knew I had to get away. I didn't trust myself to confront him because I knew how persuasive he could be. He'd have tried to talk me round.'

Jack rubbed a hand across his cheekbones. He couldn't bear the thought of her being the brunt of such subtle, despicable behaviour. 'Survival is an instinct,' he said quietly. 'So what did you do to survive?'

'I'd become friends with a doctor who'd come over to St Faith's on an exchange, an Aussie girl. When she left to continue her travels she told me if ever I found myself in Australia to let her know, and if I wanted a job she'd see if there was anything going in her old hospital in Brisbane. I called her and explained my difficulty. Within twenty-four hours I was on a flight. I left a note for Aaron, making sure he wouldn't get it until I was airborne.' She paused and then continued, 'I worked in

Brisbane for a couple of months but it wasn't the right fit for me.'

'You were still looking over your shoulder.'

She hesitated. 'Perhaps.'

Jack held her more closely. He could imagine her desperation. *Her fear...*

She turned up her face to his. 'I decided to do a bit of a job search on line. I saw the Sunday Creek vacancy...'

'And one year later, here you are.'

'Yes.' She took one slow breath and then a deeper one, feeling her lungs fill and stretch. It had been such a relief to tell Jack and have him believe in her.

He searched her face for an endless moment. 'Sometimes you look a bit...*haunted* for want of a better word. Do you worry that cretin will find you?'

'Not so much now. It's been ages and he'd never think I'd do something as bold as this.'

Jack snorted. 'He didn't know you very well, then, did he? You are one gutsy lady.'

'Me?'

His eyes caressed her tenderly. 'Yes, you, Darcie Drummond. Thank you for telling me. For trusting me with your confidence.'

Was what they'd done going to change things between them? Darcie wondered as they rode leisurely back to the homestead. It didn't have to, the sensible part of her reasoned. They could still be professional colleagues. But out of hours—what? Best friends? Friends with chemistry? Lovers? At the thought, butterflies rose and somersaulted in her stomach. Now, *that* was a bridge too far. Should she talk to Jack about how they'd handle things? Or not...?

Not, she decided, but her thoughts kept spinning this way and that.

Back at the stables, they unsaddled the horses and gave them a quick rub-down. 'Thank you for a lovely ride, sweetheart.' Darcie looped her arms around Jewel's neck and held her cheek to the mare's smooth coat.

'Are you talking to me?' Jack's mouth quirked into a crooked grin.

'Perhaps I was,' she said, and saw his eyes darken. 'Indirectly,' she added, and laughingly dodged the handful of chaff he threw at her.

CHAPTER SEVEN

IT WAS A week later when Darcie made her way along the corridor to Jack's office. They hadn't seen much of one another recently.

Jack had been away setting up what he called an outreach clinic. But at least he was at the hospital today and Darcie meant to make the most of it.

She knocked and popped her head in. 'Got a minute?'

'Good morning.' Jack heaved his chair away from the desk and beckoned her in. 'Haven't seen you much this week,' he said, as she took the chair opposite.

'No.' Her smile was quick and gone in a flash. She looked across at him. He looked serious and she wondered for the umpteenth time whether he was regretting their kisses and the shift even for a few hours from professional to personal. Maybe he hadn't thought about it at all.

The possibility left her feeling hollow inside.

'How are preparations for the clinic going?' she asked.

'So far, so good. The board members are enthusiastic and the owners of Warrawee station have offered space we can utilise. And it will be a central point and closer for some of the patients than having to travel in here to the hospital. Would you and Maggie have time to put your heads together and work out the basics of what we'll need for the start-up?'

'Of course.' Darcie looked enthusiastic. 'So—starting from scratch, we should think about furnishings for a treatment room and some kind of reception area? Bed, chairs, desk and so on. We can take patient files and laptop on the day. Maybe the whole area will need a lick of paint. And what about a water cooler, tea-making facilities…?'

'Hang on, Darcie.' Jack injected a note of caution. 'Let's just do the basics until we see whether patient numbers indicate it's viable. And it goes without saying all emergencies will still have to come here to the hospital.'

'I realise that. But I think a less clinical environment should work well for our indigenous folk, at least. Some of the elders in particular still have a fear of actual hospitals.'

'You've really got a handle on Sunday Creek and its people, haven't you?'

Darcie's gaze tangled with his as his gentle words soothed all the lonely places in her heart. Breaking eye contact, she said quietly, 'Everyone here has shown me the kind of respect a doctor can only dream about. And I've felt incredibly welcome.'

Jack rubbed absently at his jaw. 'You've obviously earned every bit of trust people have placed in you.'

Darcie coloured faintly, shrugging away his compliment. 'How often would you visualise running the clinic?'

'Perhaps every couple of weeks.' Jack's mouth turned down. 'Depends if folk warm to the idea.'

Darcie sent him an old-fashioned look. 'Establish it and they will come.'

'Let's hope so.'

'Am I going to get a turn or are you intending to keep it to yourself?'

His mouth puckered briefly. 'You may have a turn, Dr Drummond. Now…' Jack placed his hands palms down on the desk '…what did you want to see me about?'

'I'd like a second opinion about a patient, David Campion, age twenty-seven. He's an artist, lives fairly basically in a shack in the bush, according to Maggie. Rather eccentric, I suppose. He wanders in when life gets a bit beyond him.'

The leather creaked, as Jack leaned back in his chair. 'He's not using us as a hostel, is he?'

'No, I'd say not. He seems genuinely under the weather but I can't get a handle on whatever it is.'

'Drug use?'

'I've never detected any sign.'

Jack steepled his fingers under his chin. 'So, what does he live on—the sale of his paintings?'

'They're exceptional.' Darcie warmed to her subject. 'Wonderful outback images. He had a showing at the library not so long ago. I bought two of his smaller prints. They're on my bedroom wall.'

'Is that so…?' Jack's blue gaze ran across her face and down to where the open neck of her shirt ended in creamy shadow. 'I must look in some time.'

Darcie's heart revved at his cheeky remark. She moistened lips that had suddenly gone dry. Did he mean that? More to the point, did she want him to mean it? She swallowed. Was she brave enough to force the issue now, this minute? Go after what her heart was telling her she wanted, needed?

Jack hadn't missed her startled look, or the way her gaze fluttered down. Then back. He gave himself a mental kick. He shouldn't go around making facetious remarks like the one he'd just made. Look into her bedroom? What the hell had he been thinking of? But the remarks had just…slipped out. *Darcie.* Every time he looked at her, he came alive inside.

Wanting her.

But she was vulnerable.

So he shouldn't rush things.

It took him barely seconds to come to that conclusion. 'We'll talk soon, Darcie…'

Darcie caught her breath. The promise in his words was like a husky whisper over her skin, warming her.

For a second she looked at him like a deer caught in the headlights. She waited until her body regained its centre. Then she nodded. She knew what he meant. No explanations were needed.

Abruptly, Jack pulled his feet back and stood. 'Let's have a look at your patient, then, shall we?'

Jack's examination of David Campion was thorough. He ran his stethoscope over the man's chest and back, his mouth tightening. 'Cough for me now, please, David. And again. You've a few rattles in there. When did you last eat?' Folding his stethoscope, he parked himself on the end of the treatment couch.

'Dunno.' David shrugged his thin shoulders. 'Haven't felt hungry.'

'I'm going to keep you in.' Decisively, Jack began scribbling on the chart. 'You've a chest infection. We'll try to zap it before it turns nasty. I'd like to run a few tests as well, see if we can turn anything else up. Is that OK with you?'

The man blinked owlishly. 'I guess so.'

'We'll get you settled in the ward shortly, David.' Darcie sent her patient an encouraging smile. 'It was good you came in today.'

'A word, please, Darcie.' Jack clicked his pen shut and slid it into his shirt pocket. He stepped outside the cubicle and pulled the screens closed. 'Ask Maggie to get things rolling for David's admission, would you, please?'

'As soon as he's settled, I'll take the bloods,' Darcie said. 'What are we testing for?'

Jack reeled off what he wanted. 'Oh, add hypothroidism as well.'

Darcie frowned. Under-activity of the thyroid gland. 'That's more common in women, isn't it?'

'Perhaps.' Jack lifted a shoulder. 'But we can't take a gender-based view and not test for it. As a case in point, a couple of years ago at Mercy in Melbourne, they had a young *man* of twenty with breast cancer.'

'I guess it would explain David's continued lethargy to some extent,' she conceded.

'There were other pointers,' Jack expanded as they began to walk along the corridor. 'His heart rate was quite slow, plus his skin was as dry as old bones.'

'That could be because of a less than adequate diet and his iffy living conditions.'

Jack's mouth pleated at the corners. 'Well, we'll see when the bloods come back. Ask the lab to email the results, will you? We'll do a CT scan as well. We're equipped to do that here, aren't we?'

'Yes, but the technician is also the chemist, so I'll have to give her a call to come in.'

'Do that, then, please. Interesting case,' he said, as he handed her the chart and continued on his way.

It was a week before David's test results were back. Jack went to find Darcie and together they went along into his office.

When they were seated, she looked at him expectantly. 'So, was it the thyroid, as you suspected?'

'Mmm. Plus his iron stores are abysmally low. But we can treat him.'

'If we can find him,' Darcie warned. 'As you know, he discharged himself after only a day and went bush again.'

'You don't think he'll be at his shack?'

'Unlikely. He told me he has to get several paintings ready for a gallery in Melbourne a.s.a.p. He's possibly taken his swag and easel and gone somewhere to paint.'

Jack tugged thoughtfully at his bottom lip. 'Then we'd better find him and get him started on some medication. See if Maggie can draw us some kind of mud map for the general location where he might be. Fancy a ramble?'

Darcie looked torn. 'Should we both be away from the hospital?'

'It's quiet and it's not as though we're disappearing for the rest of the day.' He curved her a brief smile. 'I'm the boss and I'll take the flak if there's any. Look on it as doing a house call. If we can find David promptly, I'm hoping we may be able to persuade him to come back to the hospital with us.'

'That would be so helpful,' Darcie agreed. 'The sooner his condition is treated, the better.'

Jack got to his feet. 'That's why we need him here where we can monitor him and get his dose of thyroxine right.'

* * *

'That could be David's place through there.' Darcie pointed ahead to where a timber shack was just visible through the belt of spindly she-oaks. They'd been driving for about thirty minutes and Maggie's map had been spot on.

'Well, let's just hope he's home.' Jack brought the Land Rover to a stop.

Picking their way carefully, they climbed the rickety steps, stepping through a fringe of trailing vine to the landing. Raising his hand, Jack knocked and called out but there was no response and no sound from within. He placed his hand on the doorknob. 'Shall we?'

Darcie looked uncertain. 'Perhaps we're being a bit intrusive, Jack.'

'He could be ill and not able to answer the door.'

Jack's logic held up and Darcie nodded her assent.

The door was stuck hard and it needed extra impetus from Jack's knee to get it open. They stepped into the cool interior, which had light coming in from a glass panel at the rear of the building.

They stood there in complete silence until Darcie breathed, 'Oh, my goodness...'

'Wow,' Jack added, clearly awestruck.

The place was filled with artwork, unframed pictures of varying sizes and subjects, ranging from the simplicity of a handful of wildflowers in a jar to the dramatic wildness of a gathering storm.

Darcie's hand went to her throat. 'He's so talented.'

'Amazingly so.' Jack took a step backwards. 'We're treading on very private space, Darcie. I think we should go.'

They left quietly. Descending the steps, they stood for a moment and looked around.

'It's so still, isn't it?' Darcie sounded awed by the silence.

Jack's mouth folded in. 'Might be if the cicadas shut up for two seconds. But I know what you mean.'

It was the middle of the day, the sun high in the heavens, the feathery foliage of bush wattle trees clumping as far as the eye could see. Jack turned his gaze upwards, following the height of the eucalyptus that towered over a hundred feet into the sky. Then out to where the boulders rose up in uneven humps, their reddish-yellow tints like polished brass in the sun. He exhaled a long breath that turned into a sigh. 'David could be anywhere.'

'What should we do, then?'

'I guess we could try a coo-ee and see if we get any answer.'

Darcie knew he was referring to the Australian bush call. 'Go on, then,' she urged.

Jack needed no encouragement. Cupping his hands around his mouth, he called, 'Coo-ee-ee-ee.' The sound, high-pitched, reverberated and echoed back. And back.

They waited.

Nothing.

'Like to try one with me?' Jack's clear blue gaze suggested a challenge. 'Two of us might make a bit more of an impact.'

'Me?' Darcie wavered for a second. 'I've never...'

'Come on,' Jack encouraged. 'It's easy. Follow me.' She did and made a sound between a squawk and an out-of-tune trumpet.

Jack shook his head in disbelief. 'That wouldn't wake a baby! Let's go again. Ready?'

This time she did much better. 'Now I'm getting the hang of it,' she said, clearly delighted with her progress. 'Shall we try again?'

'Third time lucky?' His mouth quirked. 'Let's go.'

But there was still no answering call. Darcie turned away, disappointed. 'I hope he's not lying injured somewhere, Jack.'

'That's not likely. I'd guess he knows this part of the bush like the back of his hand. If he's heard us, he might simply have chosen not to respond.'

Darcie's gaze followed the myriad little bush tracks that ran off into the distance. 'Should we start looking then?'

'No.' Jack vetoed that idea. 'That's not our brief.'

'But David is ill, Jack. He needs treatment.'

'Yes, he does. I'll leave a note for him and shove it under his door.'

'Stress the urgency for him to come into the hospital, won't you?' Darcie looked concerned.

'Why don't you do it, then?' Jack flipped a spiral notebook and pen from his shirt pocket. 'Since David knows you, he might take more notice. While you're doing that, I'll give Maggie a call and check on things there.' Jack began moving to a spot from where he could get a signal for his mobile.

'Did you get on to Maggie?' Darcie asked when he returned.

'Nothing urgent on.'

'So we'll head back to town, then?'

'I think we could hang around a bit longer. David might show and it'd be a shame if we missed him. Let's give ourselves a break and find a shady spot where we can have our lunch.'

'Lunch? You brought lunch?'

He shrugged. 'I threw a bit of stuff together. It's always a good idea to carry food and water when you set out anywhere in this kind of country. Your vehicle can let you down, you can get lost, have an accident. Any number of unforeseen circumstances can see you stranded and waiting hours for help to come. And you don't venture out *anywhere* without telling someone where you're going.'

Darcie made a tsk. 'I *know* all that, Jack.'

'Just reinforcing the message,' he replied evenly. 'Can't have you getting lax.'

'As if!' she huffed, and set about helping him organise their picnic.

'That looks like a good spot over there.' He pointed towards some dappled shade provided by one of the gum trees. 'Bring the blanket from the back seat, will you, please? I'll just check there are no ants.' After a quick inspection he stated that it was OK.

'I see you've raided the hospital linen,' Darcie said, helping him spread the blanket on the grass.

He sent her a rakish grin. 'Are you going to report me?'

'Report you to *you*? Don't think I'll bother. Think of all the paperwork.'

He chuckled. It was brilliant to see her relaxed, upbeat and...happy. And he vowed to keep it that way. If he could. 'I'll just get the cooler.'

'I feel a bit guilty sitting here having lunch while our patient is missing,' Darcie said.

They'd eaten crusty bread rolls stuffed with cheese and cherry tomatoes and were finishing with coffee, from the flask Carole had thoughtfully provided, and some chocolate biscuits.

'We're just making the best use of our time,' Jack rationalised.

Darcie began gathering up the remains of their picnic. 'How long are we going to wait, Jack?'

'Darcie, it's been barely twenty minutes. Do you want us screaming with indigestion? We're entitled to time off but how often do we get it?'

'Not often...' Darcie made a small face. 'Well, not on a regular basis, I suppose...'

'So all the more reason to take it when the opportunity presents itself. And after all we could be considered working,' he said with a grin. 'We're waiting for a patient. Meanwhile, let's get more comfortable.'

When they'd settled themselves against the broad base of the gum tree, Jack turned to her. Raising his hand, he brushed the backs of his fingers gently across her cheek. 'This is good, isn't it?' he murmured.

'It's good...' Darcie voice faded to nothing. Almost without her noticing, he'd moved closer and gathered her in.

And in a second Darcie felt caught in a bubble. The world faded away and there was just the two of them. Her lips suddenly felt parched and she moistened them, her tongue flicking out to wet them.

Jack followed the darting movement and exhaled a long, slow breath. Leaning into her, he claimed her mouth. He tasted coffee and chocolate and was instantly addicted. A shot of adrenaline buzzed through his system. She opened her mouth on his, inviting him in. But he wanted more. Much more. He wanted to lay her back gently on the blanket. Make love to her here with nothing but the deep, rich smell of the earth and the sighs and sounds of the bush around them. His hand shook as it slid beneath her shirt and smoothed the softness of her skin where her waist curved into her hip.

At last the kiss ended. But not their closeness. Jack lowered his mouth to her throat, his lips on the tiny pulse point that beat frantically beneath her chin.

Darcie felt her throat tighten, fluttering her eyes closed as his fingertips idled, taking their time, delicate, like the finest strands of silk.

'Darcie...open your eyes for me...'

She did, every part of her aware of the heat of his body against hers, of that fathomless blue gaze and of a need as basic as her own. Lifting her hands to the back of his neck, she gusted a tiny sigh. 'I wish we could stay here for ever.'

They looked at each other for a long moment, unmoving until Jack reached out a finger and began to twine a silky lock of her hair around it. His gaze softened over her. 'Our time will come, Darcie.'

But obviously not today, she thought resignedly a second later as his mobile rang.

Jack swore under his breath. 'Whoever invented cellphones should be sectioned.'

'Then what would we rely on?' Half-amused, Darcie drew herself to a sitting position. 'Coo-ee calls?'

'Well, not yours.' He grinned, mock-swiping her with the offending phone and scrambling upright.

Activating the call, Jack said, 'Hi, Maggie, what's up?'

'Max Alderton's been injured. Severe neck wound.'

'What happened?'

'Apparently he was out on his motorbike, mustering.

He ran into a single-strand wire placed across the track.
Louise said it was put there deliberately.'

Jack whistled. 'What's the damage?'

'Profuse bleeding to the right side of his neck.'

'Can we expect arterial damage?'

'Lou isn't sure. Fortunately, Max had his mobile with
him. He was able to alert Louise. She's bringing him
straight in. I've told her to keep Max sitting up. But he
should go straight to Theatre, Jack.'

'Yes.' *In a perfect world.* Jack was thinking fast.
'What staff do we have, available, Maggie?'

'Well, I can scrub in. And providentially Brad Kitto,
one of the flying doctors, has just arrived, returning a
patient from chemo in Brisbane. He'll gas for you.'

'He's qualified?'

'Extremely.'

'Good.' Jack felt relief wash through him. 'Ask him
to scrub and get himself set up, please, Maggie. We'll
cane it back now.'

Jack filled Darcie in on the way back to Sunday Creek.

'Oh, how dreadful for Max! And Louise thinks it
was sabotage?'

'Seems so. Max has worked Willow Bend for over
twenty years. You'd think he'd know if there were any
single-strand fences about the place.'

Darcie shook her head. 'He could have been—'

'Decapitated.' Jack didn't mince words. 'If someone
was out to injure him, it's an appalling situation.'

'You'll take him straight to Theatre?'

'Yes. Maggie's on it. And fortunately we have an anaesthetist. A contingent from the flying doctors arrived,
returning a chemo patient.'

'Oh, that will be Heather Young. We like to keep her overnight and make sure everything's OK before she travels home.'

'And where's *home*?' Jack was concentrating on his driving, keeping the Land Rover at a swift but steady pace.

'Loganlea. About two hundred Ks out. Her family will be in to collect her tomorrow, I imagine.'

'What's Heather's prognosis?' Jack asked.

'Quite hopeful. But with cancer you never know.'

'Obviously you've been managing her care extremely well,' Jack said. 'I'll read the notes when I get a chance.' He glanced down at his watch. 'Another ten minutes should get us there.'

Darcie suppressed a sigh overlaying her concern for Max. In reality they were never off duty.

Already the enchantment of their magical time away from the hospital seemed light years away.

CHAPTER EIGHT

THEY ARRIVED AT the hospital almost simultaneously with the Aldertons. Max was groggy but conscious. In no time at all they were all inside.

'Didn't need this…Doc,' he slurred.

'Save your strength, Max,' Jack said gently. 'We'll do the best we can for you.' He whipped out a stethoscope, listening intently, checking his patient's breathing. 'Seems OK.'

Tossing the stethoscope aside, he very carefully removed the thick towel from around Max's throat, examining the wound with a clinical eye. 'Main aorta is intact. You've been very lucky, mate. Clamps, please, Darcie.'

Darcie handed him the instrument resembling a cross between a pair of scissors and a pair of pliers. Systematically, he began a temporary closure of the wound. 'Would you dress it now, please?'

Darcie was ready with several thick pads to staunch any residual bleeding. 'He's ready for oxygen.' She looked sharply at Jack. 'What capacity do you want it?'

He made a moue. 'Make it eight litres a minute. We'll see what that tells us.'

Darcie worked automatically, dovetailing with Jack as they carried out the emergency procedures. The probe was in place on Max's finger, allowing them to monitor the degree of oxygen saturation in his blood.

'We'll need a cross-match,' Jack said.

Natalie, who had been called in, said quietly, 'I'll sort that.'

'Thanks, Nat,' Jack acknowledged. He began preparing an IV line. 'How's the wound, Darcie?'

'Some seepage, but it's holding. Oxygen sats ninety per cent.' She gave a rundown of the BP and pulse readings. 'I'll get him some pain relief.'

When Darcie returned with the drugs, she could see Jack wasn't taking any chances. Max had been placed on a heart monitor.

Darcie shot the pethidine and anti-emetic home. 'He should begin stabilising fairly quickly. You should get to Theatre, Jack. Go,' she insisted, when he hesitated. 'I can monitor things here.'

'OK.' Jack ripped off his gloves and tossed them aside. 'And find Louise, Darcie. Give her as much support as you can.'

'Of course.' Darcie tamped down a prickle of annoyance. She'd have done that anyway.

Darcie found Louise standing beside the window in the patients' lounge, looking out as if fixed on a spot in the distance.

'Lou?'

Louise spun round. 'How is he?' she asked without preamble.

'He's stabilised. Natalie's just taken him along to Theatre. Come and sit down,' Darcie urged. 'I've asked Carole to bring us a pot of tea.'

'Ironic, isn't it?' Louise sent a distracted glance

around the room. 'I never thought when I organised for this lounge to be refurbished that I'd be one of the first making use of it. Max will be all right, won't he, Darcie?'

Darcie hesitated. In emergency situations no result was ever guaranteed. 'Jack is a fine surgeon.'

'Thank God we have him here.' Louise's statement was heartfelt. 'Otherwise Max would have had to wait hours for the flying doctor to come and then be transported miles away for surgery. How long will the operation take?'

'We can't know that until Jack assesses the extent of Max's injury. Oh, here's Carole with the tea.'

'I've made a few little sandwiches as well,' Carole said. 'Wasn't sure if you'd managed a bite to eat before Mr Alderton had his accident.'

'That's very kind of you, Carole.' Louise gave a trapped smile. 'Thank you.'

'You're welcome, dear.' Carole went on her way.

Darcie poured the tea. 'How did all this happen? Jack mentioned something about sabotage.'

'Something like this makes my blood run cold.' Louise shook her head as if in disbelief. 'Max is a generous and fair employer. I can't think why anyone would want to hurt him.'

Darcie frowned. 'So, you think it was someone who worked for you?'

'A couple of young farm labourers. Max caught them stealing petrol. We keep large quantities of fuel for the farm vehicles and machinery. Max gave them a warning and they told him they were sorry and they'd only wanted to top up their ute to go to a dance over at Barclay.'

'And Max believed them?'

'He put it down to them being young and wanting a

night out. And they offered to pay for it but Max said he'd let it go this time.' Louise took a nibble of her sandwich. 'Then two days ago he caught them at it again. But this time they were filling drums—obviously to sell. As far as Max was concerned, that was the end of their employment. He sacked them then and there and gave them an hour to be off the property.'

'Oh, lord.' Darcie gave her a wide-eyed look. 'So, they've got back at him in this awful way...'

'Looks like it. They knew his daily routine, knew where he'd be and when. They'd seen it often enough. They obviously set up the wire during the night.'

'That's so calculated. And so frightfully scary. Have you spoken to the police?'

'I've given them what information I had and what I surmised had happened. They'll take it from there. My concern has to be for Max and his recovery.' Louise rubbed a hand across her temple as if staving off a headache. 'You'll have to keep him in, won't you?'

'For a few days at least,' Darcie said. 'And Max will have to put up with his food being puréed for a little while. But as soon as he's able to swallow comfortably and if everything else checks out, he should be as right as rain again.'

Louise blinked rapidly. 'You can't imagine the relief to know you and Jack are in charge of our hospital, Darcie. And to have the theatre up and running. That hasn't happened in years.'

'Well, that was mainly Jack's initiative,' Darcie said fairly.

'But you supported it, surely?'

'Of course.' *Eventually.* 'Jack has far more experience than I do,' Darcie said carefully.

Nodding almost absently, Louise glanced at her watch.

'It'll be a while yet, Lou,' Darcie said gently. 'Would you feel more comfortable over at the residence? I'd come and get you when Max is back from Theatre.'

'No, I'm fine here. But thanks.' Louise managed a small smile, looking around her at the array of up-to-date magazines, the colourful mugs and facilities for making a hot drink. She flicked hand. 'Your little touches, I'd guess. Am I right?'

'Nothing worse than sitting in a dreary hospital lounge, waiting for news of a loved one.' Darcie offloaded the praise with a shrug.

'You feel in tune here in Sunday Creek, don't you.'

It was more a statement than a question. Darcie took a moment to answer. 'Yes, I do,' she said simply. And *safer* than she'd felt in her whole life. 'The outback has touched something deep down inside me.' Her downcast lashes fanned darkly across her cheekbones. 'That must sound a bit…odd.'

'Not odd at all.' Louise's green eyes grew soft. 'It's why most of us continue to live out here, through good times and bad. But don't let me keep you, Darcie.' Louise picked up one of the glossy magazines. 'I'll be fine. And you must have a hundred things to do.'

It was late afternoon. At the nurses' station Darcie began writing up her notes on Emma Tynan. The thirteen-year-old had been admitted the previous night with an asthma attack. Thank heaven she was stabilising, Darcie noted, but not as quickly as she would have hoped. 'You know, Nat,' she said thoughtfully, 'I have a feeling Kristy Tynan is still smoking around her daughter. But as usual Emma is totally loyal and noncommittal.'

Natalie shook her head. 'I sometimes wonder who exactly *is* the mother in that family.'

'Kristy works those awful shifts in the truckers' café,' Darcie said. 'It can't be easy for either of them. Do you know if there's a dad anywhere about?'

'Sorry, can't help you there. Kristy and her daughter landed here a couple of years ago. They live in that block of flats near the bowls club.'

Darcie replaced the file. 'Do you think Emma has to fend for herself, then?'

'Well, she'd certainly be on her own a bit with her mother's shiftwork.'

'Poor little thing.'

Natalie gave a frustrated click. 'I can't understand why Kristy can't just ditch the smokes and be done with them.'

'Some folk find it very difficult,' Darcie came in diplomatically. 'It's simply the drug they cling to when they're constantly under stress.'

'I guess so.' Natalie's sympathy showed. 'I could up the percussion on Emma's back if you think it would help. Just to keep an eye on how she's recovering.'

'Yes, it would, thanks, Nat.'

'Oh, look…thank goodness…' The nurse exhaled a relieved breath. 'Here come the guys at last.'

Darcie swung round. Although neither she nor Natalie had voiced their thoughts, she knew they'd been waiting for news of Max's surgery for the past hour. 'Oh, Brad's here!' Darcie was smiling.

'I thought you knew.'

Darcie shook her head. 'Jack just said one of the flying doctors was going to gas for him.'

Natalie leaned forward confidentially. 'Brad fancies you.'

'Brad's in love with life,' Darcie dismissed, feeling her nerves tense slightly, her cheeks grow warm, as the doctors crossed to the station.

'Hey, *Dee-Dee!*' Brad almost quickstepped to Darcie's side, flinging his arms around her in a bear hug. 'Good to see you, babe.'

Dee-Dee? Arms folded, Jack's gaze narrowed in speculation. What the hell was that about?

Feeling pink and flustered, Darcie disengaged herself from Brad's arms. 'I didn't realise you were the escort bringing Heather back to us.'

'You bet. I had to bribe someone to get the gig.' Brad's white smile flashed briefly. 'Couldn't miss the chance of seeing you. Harry's here too.'

Darcie nodded. 'I saw Harry earlier.' Harry Liston was one of the regular pilots for the flying doctors. 'Are you on turn-around or can you stay with us tonight?'

'Counting on it.' Brad did an impressive little drum-roll with his fingers on the countertop. 'Let's have a party, huh? We've brought seafood. Maybe we could gas up the barbecue?'

'Maybe...' Darcie gave a breathless little laugh.

'Natalie, you in?' Brad turned teasing blue eyes on the RN.

'Sorry, I'll have to pass.' Natalie propped her chin on her upturned hand and looked on amusedly. 'I'll be sharing dinner with my two-year-old.'

'That's too bad—'

'Where's Louise?' Jack cut in, his voice tripwire-tight.

Darcie blinked uncertainly. 'She's here, in the lounge.'

'Wouldn't she have been more comfortable over at the residence?'

Darcie's chin came up. He'd said it brusquely enough to sound like a reprimand. 'I offered,' she replied coolly. 'Louise preferred to wait here. I gather Max's surgery went well?'

'Brad will fill you in. I need to speak with Louise,' he muttered, before striding off.

Watching his retreating back, Darcie fancied she was dodging the invisible bullets he'd fired. But dropping innuendos was not Jack's style. If he had an issue with anyone or anything, he was upfront about it. So what was suddenly bugging him? She turned to Brad for enlightenment. 'There wasn't a problem in surgery, was there?'

Brad pursed his lips as if reluctant to get into it. 'Bit of a glitch when we were halfway through. But we were on it. Max will be just fine,' he confirmed.

Darcie couldn't help the relief she felt, both for Max and Louise but for Jack as well.

A beat of silence, until Brad continued quietly, 'It seems today's surgery was something of a litmus test for the viability of the OR.' He saw her tight little nod and added, 'Jack knows what he's doing, Dee. Trust me. I know a good surgeon when I see one.'

Jack swore silently and darkly as he headed towards the hospital lounge. Did Darcie have something going with Kitto?

Was she sleeping with him?'

He tried the shattering thought on for size. Did it fit?

He hissed a rebuttal through tight lips. That seemed inconceivable. Only a few hours ago *they'd* been as close as any two people could be without actually making love.

Something in Jack's heart scrunched tight.

Surely she wasn't playing him…

Pausing outside the door of the lounge, he took a deep breath, knocked and went in. It took a herculean effort to force his lips into a smile. But his eyes were unable to hide the mixed emotions that stalked him.

Deep in thought, Jack almost collided with Darcie as they made their way from opposite ends of the corridor some time later. He pulled up short. 'What are you still doing here?'

Darcie all but rolled her eyes. What did he think she was doing there? 'Maggie has to get off. We were just ensuring cover is in place for the night shift.'

'Shouldn't you be over at the residence, looking after our visitors?'

Darcie took a calming breath. There was that innuendo again. She had to be professional here. It was obvious *he* wasn't capable of it. 'They're well able to look after themselves. Lauren's there anyway and I imagine a few more folk will turn up if a party's in the offing. You look like you could do with an evening off yourself.'

Two frown lines jumped into sharp relief between his eyes. 'I need to be here to keep an eye on Max post-op.'

'If you're needed, you're two minutes away at the house.'

'It's fine.' His mouth drew in. 'I'd like to stick around for Louise as well.'

Darcie took a step back as if to regain her space. This was getting too petty for words. 'Why are you being like this?'

Jack folded his arms, leaning back against the wall,

challenge like a gathering storm sending his eyes to darkest blue. 'Like what?'

She raised a shoulder uncertainly. 'So…cross.'

'Cross?' The storm broke into harmless little showers and he looked amused.

Darcie sucked in her breath. 'You know what I mean. You're offside with me and with Brad as well. Surely, you should be thanking him for stepping up today.'

'We've debriefed,' Jack said shortly. 'I have no problem with Brad's medical skills.'

Darcie's thoughts were churning but this conversation was going nowhere. 'Lou will want to stay in town tonight. We're a bit full up at the residence…'

'She's made arrangements to stay at the motel. She knows the managers. They'll make her comfortable. In any event, she'll want to stay here with Max for a while longer.'

'Then what?' Darcie pressed determinedly. 'You'll come home and share a meal with the rest of us?'

In other words, pretend to be sociable? Pretend he was oblivious? 'No offence, Darcie, but as the senior doctor I should be here. Today's circumstances were…unusual to put it mildly. But we coped.'

But at what cost? Darcie wondered. Already there was an air of tension emanating from him. Her mouth thinned. If he'd allow her, she could massage his stress away in a second. But the way he was acting around her, he'd probably prefer a one-way conversation with Capone than let *her* anywhere near him. Instead, she held her head high and said clearly, so there would be no mistake, 'Since you've elected to remain on duty, I'll be here first thing in the morning to check on Max. Feel free to catch up on some sleep.'

* * *

Jack completed a final ward round and found nothing untoward with any of the patients. Max's status was stable and he'd been placed in the hospital's only private room. Ursula Cabot was a competent night sister so why wasn't he over at the residence, partying with the rest of the team?

Because he was being plain stubborn, wallowing in a pool of self-induced jealousy.

Jack passed sentence on himself, ploughing a hand through his hair in frustration as he made his way along to the hospital kitchen. Ten minutes later he was half-heartedly forking his way through yesterday's casserole, trying to ignore the tantalising aroma of garlic prawns wafting through the window. The seafood barbecue was obviously in full swing.

'Fool,' he muttered, giving up on the casserole and consigning it to the waste bin. He'd acted like a jerk towards Darcie earlier. But the fact was he'd hated to see her wrapped in another man's arms *Hated it.*

He wandered back to the nurses' station, realising the soft hush of night had crept over the hospital without him even noticing.

Ursula Cabot sat under the subdued lighting at the station, her blonde-grey head bent over a crossword puzzle. She looked up as Jack leaned across the counter.

'Would you like a cup of tea, Ursula?'

'No, thanks.' The senior nurse shook her head. 'I've already had several since I came on duty. And you're wearing out the floorboards, Jack. Go home. Isn't there a party going on at the residence?'

Jack lifted a shoulder indifferently. 'I'm just here to

keep an eye on things. Max Alderton had major surgery today.'

'And that's why *I'm* here,' Ursula said dryly. 'I checked Max only five minutes ago and I'll keep monitoring him regularly.' She sent Jack a reproving look over the rims of her smart black-framed glasses. 'There's no need for you to keep hovering, Dr Cassidy. I'll call you if I need you.'

Jack's mouth flattened in a thin smile. 'You're chucking me out.'

'Seems like it. Now, scoot. There's dancing happening, by the sound of it. Go and join the fun. Have a twirl around the floor with Darcie. I'll bet that girl's light on her feet.'

Oh, she was. As light as air. At least, that's how she'd felt in his arms.

Jack's thoughts were spinning as he made his way slowly across to the residence. Would he look in on the party? Perhaps. Perhaps not. As he opened the front gate, Capone stirred from his special place under the steps and came to meet him. 'Hello, boy.' Putting out a hand, Jack rubbed the dog's neck as he pushed in against his legs. Then, seemingly satisfied with the small show of attention, Capone gave a feeble wag of his tail, breaking the contact and wandering back to his hidey-hole.

Jack mounted the steps, hearing the music in the form of Norah Jones's husky voice urging someone to 'come away with me'. He dragged in a shallow breath, his normal good sense shattering by the second. Was Brad Kitto even now urging Darcie to do just that? And would she be tempted?

He didn't want to know.

Instead, he bypassed the rec room, where the party was happening, and made his way along the hall to his bedroom.

Minutes later, he was lying in bed, arms wishboned behind his head, staring at the ceiling. But all he saw was the hurt puzzlement in Darcie's eyes staring back at him. She hadn't understood his stubbornness earlier. Hell, he hardly understood it himself.

How could he have acted like that? As though he was some kind of martyred soul? Had what happened with Zoe destroyed his trust in women so thoroughly? God, he hoped not. Rolling over, he buried his face in the pillow. He had to try to keep his trust in what he and Darcie shared.

Somehow.

CHAPTER NINE

DARCIE CAME THROUGH the silent house, looking for Jack. She finally located him outside, where the morning's soft rays were illuminating the courtyard. He was sitting at the wooden table, nursing a mug of tea, Capone at his side.

'Morning.' She went briskly down the steps.

Jack looked up and felt something shift in his chest. She was dressed in cotton trousers and a pinstriped shirt that moulded every one of her curves. She was femininity in motion.

'I thought you were going to sleep in.' She pulled out a chair and sat down. It was barely seven.

'I did sleep in. How are things at the hospital?'

'Max was in some pain. Brad upped his meds. Otherwise he'd had a reasonable night.'

Jack sent her a mocking kind of look. 'Has our fly-boy gone?'

'He left a while ago.' Darcie kept her cool. 'He and Harry wanted to be on their way. We were up before five.'

We? Jack's mouth tightened. Hearing the inclusive pronoun, his worst fear seemed validated.

'So…' Darcie blinked a bit. He seemed suddenly distant, locked down. 'What are you going to do with your day off?'

'I wasn't aware I was having one,' he growled.

Darcie took a deep breath and threw caution to the winds. 'You're acting like a grumpy teen, Jack. I know you're the boss but you need a change of scene. And I'm quite capable of running things at the hospital. There's fishing tackle in the garage. Go and make use of it. Bunbilla Crossing is a good place to start.'

Jack moved his lips in a mocking little twist. 'So says the girl from England.'

Darcie refused to be drawn. 'Take Capone. You seem to prefer his company to that of the rest of us.' She stood and pushed her chair in. 'And I'll expect some decent-sized river perch for dinner tonight.'

Darcie inspected Max's wound. 'You're looking good, Max.' She smiled. 'We'll review your swallow in a day or so. But so far everything's textbook.'

Max managed a husky 'Thanks'.

She placed a hand on his forearm and squeezed. 'Lauren will replace your dressing now and Jack will see you first thing tomorrow.' At least, she hoped he would.

Darcie was thoughtful as she made her way back to the station.

'Jack for you.' Maggie held up the landline phone.

Darcie's heart skipped. She put the receiver to her ear. 'Jack?'

'Dinner in fifteen,' he said. 'Can you be here?'

'Just about to clock off.'

'Good. See you in a bit.'

'Wait…' Darcie sensed he was about to hang up. 'Did you catch my fish?'

He snorted. 'Of course I caught your fish. Hurry up.'

A trapped smile edged Jack's mouth as he put the phone down. She'd been right. He had needed to get away from the hospital, if only for a few hours. The break had re-energised him. He'd swum in the river, baked in the sun for a bit.

And caught her fish.

All things considered, he'd fulfilled all the requirements for a satisfactory day off.

Darcie had guessed what he'd needed and that had to mean something.

He couldn't wait to see her.

Darcie's feet had wings as she made her way across to the residence. A sense of relief washed through her. She'd been afraid she might have overstepped the mark, but it sounded as though Jack had accepted her suggestion without rancour and had taken himself off for the day. There'd been a lightness back in his voice. Suddenly life felt good again.

Making her way across the back deck, she popped her head in the kitchen. 'Hi.'

Jack looked up from preparing the fish. 'Hi, yourself.'

She smiled. 'Can you hold dinner for a few more minutes? I need to jump in the shower.'

He waved her away. 'I won't start cooking until you get here.'

Darcie was in and out of the shower in record time, the sweet sting of anticipation slithering up her spine. Bypassing her usual casual cargos and T-shirt, she pulled on a sundress in a pretty floral print, admitting she wanted to look special for Jack. They needed to reconnect. She knew that instinctively.

Taking a moment to look in the long mirror, she decided she'd do. The top of the dress was held up by shoe-string straps, showing off the light tan she'd acquired. And just wearing the dress made her feel cool and feminine—and something else.

Desirable?

She stopped for a moment and took a deep breath. There was so much going on between her and Jack. So many undercurrents. He hadn't spelled anything out. Neither had she.

She scooped her hair away from her neck and let it fall loosely to her shoulders. This evening was to be about relaxing. Not supposition. Closing her bedroom door quietly, she went along the hallway, passing the dining room on the way. Stopping, she peered in. Her hand went to her throat. 'Wow...'

'Darcie, you ready?' Jack's voice came from the kitchen.

'I'm here.' She stepped through the doorway into the kitchen.

Jack's eyes swept her from head to toe.

'We're eating in the dining room, I gather?'

'Well, a portion of it,' he countered with a dry smile. He'd set one end of the long refectory table after finding rather elegant placemats and cutlery in a drawer of the big old-fashioned sideboard and had thought, Why not?

'Can I give you a hand?' Darcie's eyes flicked over him, her gaze almost hungry. By now she knew all his features by heart—the clear blue eyes that spelled honesty, the dark hair, always a bit unruly, springing back from his temples, the strength of his facial features, honed to an almost hawk-like leanness. And his mouth— the gateway to the fulfilment of all her private dreams...

'You could pour us a glass of wine,' Jack said. 'There's a Riesling in the fridge. I thought it would go well with our fish. And Lauren's left some kind of salad.'

'Oh, that was sweet of her.' Darcie brought out the wine and the salad from the fridge. 'How are you cooking the fish?'

'I'll pan-fry it.' Jack raised a dark brow. And then let it rest in the oven for a minute or two. 'Is that all right with you?'

'Perfectly. I'm sure it'll be wonderful.'

It was.

Jack had prepared the fish into chunky fillets, leaving the skin on. Pan-fried quickly, the flesh was crisp, full of flavour and delicious.

'That's the best meal I've eaten in weeks,' Darcie said, replete.

Jack swirled the last of his wine in his glass. 'What about your seafood last night?'

'It was nice,' Darcie allowed, with a little shrug. 'But this was much more special.'

'In what way?' His dark head at an angle, Jack looked broodingly at her.

She swallowed dryly. Even in the subdued light from the candles they'd lit, she could feel the intensity of his gaze. 'Because you cooked it especially for me.' A beat of silence. 'Didn't you?' She felt her eyes drawn helplessly to his.

'I *needed* to do something for you.' He threw back his head and finished his wine in a gulp. 'After my boorish behaviour recently, I thought you might walk,' he admitted candidly.

'Leave?' Darcie almost squawked. 'Why would I do

that? Anyway, I have a contract. So unless you're boot-ing me out, Dr Cassidy, I'm not going anywhere.'

Jack couldn't believe the relief he felt. 'So…when will you be seeing Brad again?'

'I have no idea. But he's extended his time here for a couple of months so I imagine he'll be back and forth a bit.'

'You seemed pretty *cosy* with him.'

'And you couldn't wait to make a snap judgement.' Two spots of colour glazed Darcie's cheeks. She knew where he was going with this and felt like thumping him. 'I don't creep around keeping men on a string. That's not my style at all. And if you know anything about me, Jack, you should *know* that.'

'OK…' Jack held up his hand in acceptance. 'I admit to a streak of jealousy a mile wide. I'm sorry for thinking what I did. Deep down I knew it wasn't like you. I—just couldn't seem to get past the possibility…'

Darcie gave a sharp glance at the sudden tight set of his shoulders. So, someone, somewhere had stuffed up his ability to trust. It didn't take much imagination to know where the blame lay. She pressed forward gently. 'What kind of relationship did you have with your for-mer girlfriend? You gave the impression it was just a mutual parting of the ways. But I have to wonder if it was as simple as that…'

'I don't want to talk about it.'

Darcie *tsked* and gave a little toss of her head. 'So, it's OK to have me spilling the facts of my messed-up love-life but not you. How is that fair, Jack?'

It wasn't fair at all, Jack had to admit. But he'd been left feeling such a fool and worse. He dragged air in and expelled it. 'You want me to talk about this here? Now?'

'The place doesn't matter.' Her voice was soft, intense. 'The telling does. Begin with her name, Jack. And go from there.'

'Zoe,' he said after the longest pause. 'You already know some of the rest of it.'

'Some but not all,' Darcie said calmly. 'Go on.'

He rubbed a hand across his eyes. 'We met in Sydney through mutual friends. We hit it off. Pretty soon we were a couple. Our lives were busy, different, and that's probably what kept everything fresh.'

'But you had such diverse callings,' Darcie stressed.

'Yes.' Jack eased back in his chair, unaware his eyes had taken on a bleak look. 'Back then, Zoe had stage roles so she was working mostly at night. I worked mostly in the day. At first it didn't seem to matter. We grabbed what time we had. Made the most of it.'

Mostly in bed, Darcie interpreted, and felt a spasm of dislike for this woman who had obviously led Jack a merry dance and then for whatever reason had dumped their relationship and him along with it.

'Zoe wanted to try her chances for work in England.' Jack picked up the thread of the conversation reluctantly. 'It seemed feasible and obviously I didn't want us to be separated so I applied for an exchange. It took a while to organise and Zoe was over there for three months before I could join her.'

'But surely you kept in touch?'

'Of course, but, looking back now, I see it was mostly at my instigation. Zoe just said she was doing the rounds of the casting agents and I understood how much time and effort that took. Then, almost simultaneously, she landed a film part and my exchange came through. I texted her to let her know I was on my way. Told her what flight I was on.'

And he would have been full of expectation and excitement at the prospect of reuniting with his lover. Darcie's heart ached for him. She felt a moment of doubt. Perhaps she shouldn't have started any of this... She held out her hand to him across the table and he took it, clasped it and looked her squarely in the eyes.

She blinked. 'Stop now, if you want to, Jack. I think I know what happened.'

'I arrived in London a day earlier than scheduled.' Jack went on as though she hadn't spoken. 'I went straight to her flat. Zoe opened the door. It was obvious my arrival was unexpected, to say the least.'

Darcie took a dry swallow and tried gently to fill in the picture he was painting. 'She was there with someone else?'

He gave a hard laugh. 'Well, they weren't in bed but near as dammit. She was in a dressing gown and he was parked against the bedroom door, smoking one of those filthy cheroots. I wanted to smash the place up and him along with it.'

Oh, lord. Darcie took a breath so deep it hurt. 'So, it ended then and there? Did you not...talk?' Yet *she* hadn't, Darcie had to admit. She'd just cut and run...

'At that moment there didn't seem much point.' Jack gave a hollow laugh. 'But we did meet up some time later. Zoe simply said she'd moved on. That *Simon* was an actor, that he gave her what she needed. What I obviously hadn't been able to.'

Darcie heard the pain in his voice. 'You must have been gutted.'

His jaw worked a bit before he answered. 'I just got on with things. I had to. And I am *over* her.'

But there was still a residue of hurt there, Darcie decided. She ran her tongue over her bottom lip. 'That's probably why you didn't enjoy your time in England as much as you should have.'

'Possibly.'

'If you'd been with me, I could have shown you the most wonderful time, the magical places that make England so special.'

A beat of silence.

'I'm sorry you had to leave your country,' he said softly, his gaze, blue, clear and caressing, locking with hers.

'Don't be. Life happens, as they say.' Her smile was a little forced as she got to her feet. 'Now, what about a cup of tea?'

Jack felt his throat thicken. The need to hold her and kiss her was so urgent he almost jumped up from the table to make it happen. Instead, he let the avalanche of emotion wash over him. 'Tea sounds good.' His jaw tightened for a moment. 'And, Darcie?'

'Jack?' She turned back.

'Thanks for the talk. And the day off.'

They took their tea and some chocolate mints Darcie found and went outside to the courtyard. 'We seem to make a habit of this,' she said, as they made themselves comfortable.

'It's a good place to relax, listen to the night sounds. Are you used to them yet?'

'Mostly.' Darcie made a small downturn of her mouth.

'But the dingoes' howling at night still scares the life out of me. Thankfully, they don't come too close.'

'They're carnivores, for the most part,' Jack said. 'They hunt smaller animals. They only venture closer to civilisation when they can't find food.'

'So I wouldn't find one waiting for me on the back deck, then?

He chuckled. 'Unlikely. And even if you did, the dingo would be more scared of you than you of it.'

'Well, I hope so.' Darcie didn't sound convinced.

'Darcie, they're native dogs, not wolves,' Jack's eyes crinkled in soft amusement. 'The rangers keep tabs on their whereabouts so stop worrying.'

They lapsed into easy silence until Jack said, 'Would you mind if we talked shop a for a bit?'

Darcie gave a throaty laugh. 'I'd be amazed if we didn't. I've held off so you'd feel you'd had a *real* day off.'

'It was good.' Jack lifted his arms to half-mast and stretched. 'Very good.'

'So, where do you want to start?' Darcie said.

'How's Max's recovery?'

'So far, he's checking out well. Pain-free for most of today. I told him we'll review his swallow quite soon.'

Jack made a moue of conjecture. 'I'd like to leave it for a bit longer.' He paused and stroked his thumb across the handle of his tea mug. 'Brad filled you in about Max's surgery?'

'Yes, he did,' Darcie said slowly. 'He said it was your skill as a surgeon that got him through.'

'Generous of him.' Jack's mouth tightened. 'It was a joint effort. Brad's an instinctive clinician.'

'That's what makes him such a good fit for the flying doctors.'

'Mmm.' Jack's mouth curled into a noncommittal moue. He didn't want the obvious warmth she felt towards Kitto burning a hole in his skull. So, move on. 'The whole episode relating to Max's surgery got me thinking, though.'

'In what way?'

'We need to re-evaluate what kinds of surgery can be safely carried out here. And I want you to know I'd never have attempted Max's surgery without knowing there was a qualified anaesthetist on board. I'd have had Max flown out. You were right to be cautious about opening the theatre.' He held her gaze steadily. 'On the other hand, I was pretty arrogant about what could be accomplished here.'

Darcie's quick glance was very perceptive. As a proud man, she guessed it had cost him something to have admitted his lapse. 'But there was no harm done, Jack.'

'This time.' He gave a jaded laugh. 'I want you to know I would never put you in any position where you felt medically compromised, Darcie. In other words, only the very basic surgical procedures will be done here in future. And whether or not we decide to do them at all will in turn be a joint decision.'

'That's more than fair. Thank you.' After a moment, she continued. 'But I think we need to get this across to the board. And where Louise is concerned, gently, of course. But she took it as read that Max's surgery would happen here. She was grateful and relieved that he wouldn't have to be flown miles away.'

Jack gave a philosophical shrug. 'Well, I'll talk to her privately about that. As for the rest of the board, they'll have to be made aware that we call the shots about medical protocols.'

Which was what she'd tried to convey in the first place, Darcie thought. But she didn't bear grudges. She was just infinitely glad that the matter had been settled and that Jack had been the one to call it.

'Sunday Creek hospital is very lucky to have you, Darcie Drummond.'

'Pft!' Darcie dismissed the earnest look in his eyes and said lightly, 'It's a team effort between the doctors and the nurses. The practice only functions because of the efforts of both.'

His lips tweaked to a one-cornered grin. 'Well, that seems that matter dealt with. Any news of David Campion?'

Darcie shook her head. 'I'm still hoping he'll make his own way in to us.'

'If he feels grotty enough, he may,' Jack conceded. 'Let's hope your intuition is right.'

'Oh, it will be.' Darcie's lips turned up prettily. She got to her feet. 'Now, I'm going to do the dishes.'

'I'll help you.' Jack was on his feet as well.

'Uh-uh.' Darcie waved away his offer. 'You got dinner.'

'Oh, let's just leave it. I'll bung it all in the dishwasher later,' Jack declared, moving around the table toward her.

In a second she was in his arms.

'About before...' Darcie's look was contrite, her eyes glistening in the muted light. 'I didn't mean to pry.'

'It's fine,' he answered, meaning it. 'And you know what, Dr Drummond?'

She shook her head.

'You're a very good listener.'

'Oh. But I only—'

He kissed her into silence.

'You have the sexiest lips,' he said gruffly, looking down at her.

'Do I?' Her gaze widened and she saw the heat flare in his.

'You do,' he murmured, just before he claimed her mouth again.

Darcie made a tiny sound like a purr and felt a strange lightness, as if love and desire had rolled into one high-voltage surge, sweeping through her body and out to the tips of her fingers and toes. And with a half-formed decision of whatever would be would be, she curled her body into his, each curve and hollow finding a home, a placement, as though they'd been carved out and had been waiting to be filled.

When he pulled back, she felt empty, bereft. She looked up at him, warm honey flecks of uncertainty chasing through her eyes.

Looking at her, Jack felt all his senses go into free-fall. Was this the moment he asked her to go to bed with him? If not now, then when? He agonised for a few seconds, waiting for the words to form. In the almost dark the night air around them began snapping with cicada clicks and simmering with the sharp scent of lemon tea-trees.

'We could take this inside…' he murmured tautly.

Jack's meaning was clear and Darcie felt the nerves grab in her stomach, her mind zeroing in on the fact that they had the house to themselves and there was no one to disturb them. Whatever they chose to do…

'I want to be with you, Darcie. Let me…' His hands stroked up her arms before he gathered her in again, holding her to him so that she felt the solid imprint of him from thigh to breast.

'Jack…' She drew in breath, feeling his hands on her lower back, tilting her closer still, and the wild sting of anticipation pin-pricked up her spine.

'Just say the word.' His plea was muffled against her hair.

Darcie's arms went round his neck, images she'd dreamt about chasing sensible thoughts away. She longed to tell him what he so wanted to hear. But a little voice in her head told her that once they had taken that step, there was no going back. Nothing between them would be simple again.

And there'd be nowhere to hide if it all went wrong. Nowhere.

Wordlessly, she stepped away from him, wrapping her arms around her midriff. 'Jack—there's a thousand reasons why we shouldn't go rushing into things.'

'Who's rushing?' He made a sound of dissension. 'This has been waiting to happen for weeks. You *know* we'd be good together.' His voice was husky with gentle persuasion.

Darcie kept her gaze lowered, unwilling to let him see her fears, her vulnerability.

'You're scared, aren't you?'

She licked suddenly dry lips. 'Can you blame me?'

'No.' Jack thrust back against the lattice wall. 'But I blame that piece of work in England who took away your ability to trust your own judgement. But you have to trust again, Darcie. You have to trust *me*!'

Her heart scrunched tight and she shut her eyes against the surge of desire. This was what she wanted, wasn't it? To be a *real* part of Jack's life. Yet something pulled her back from the edge. 'Just give me a little space, Jack. A little more time.'

'Time for what, Darcie?' Jack's voice was without rancour but he was clearly frustrated. 'To start overthinking things. Imagining worst-case scenarios? Come on...'

'Come on, what?' She spun away when he would have contained her. 'You want instant solutions.' Her heart began beating with an uncomfortable swiftness. 'Well, sorry, Jack. I can't give you any.'

Suddenly the atmosphere between them was thick and uncomfortable.

'We have to work together,' she said without much conviction. 'Day in, day out.'

'So what?' He huffed a jaded laugh. 'Are you saying we can't have a personal life outside the hospital?' He pushed a hand roughly through his hair in irritation.

'I'm not being difficult for the sake of it, Jack.'

He shrugged.

Her eyes searched his face. 'We can't leave things like this.'

'I know.'

'How can we go forward, then?'

'I'll back off,' he said, as if coming to a decision.

'I— Thank you.' She forced the words past the dryness in her throat.

His mouth tightened for a second. An intensity of emotion he'd never felt before gnawed at his insides. God, she was so brave and beautiful. He curled his hands into fists to stop them reaching for her. 'The last thing I want is to be offside with you, Darcie. What can we do to make things right again?'

Her uncertainty wavered and waned. She couldn't doubt his sincerity. And she should remember that this was Jack Cassidy, proud and purposeful. And if it came down to it, she'd trust him with her life.

'I suppose we could kiss and make up,' she said softly.

Jack needed no second invitation. Keeping his hands off her by sheer strength of will, he bent towards her, letting his tongue just touch her lower lip as lightly as he could manage when every cell in his body wanted to devour the sweet mouth that opened for him so enticingly. Slowly, slowly, he drew back. 'Sweet dreams, then...' he murmured, and touched his forehead to hers. 'Just make them all about me, hmm?'

Darcie felt the smile on her skin as he touched his mouth to her throat. 'As long as you reciprocate, hmm?'

'Done.' He leaned forward and placed a quick, precise kiss on her lips. Hell, when the time was right, and they'd be able to make dreams into reality, he'd make her feel so *loved*, she wouldn't be able to see straight for a week.

CHAPTER TEN

WITHIN TWO WEEKS Max had been discharged and was doing well. David Campion had come to the hospital and been treated and was now following a health regime Jack had set out for him.

Life was good, Darcie thought reflectively as she updated Emma Tynan's chart at the nurses' station. And although they hadn't actually spelled it out, she felt as though she and Jack had reached a plateau in their personal relationship.

Everything was possible. And the thought lit her up from inside. She made a reflective moue, bringing her thoughts back to Emma. Was there something more she could be doing for the child's wellbeing? She was such a plucky little thing...

'Excuse me, Darcie...'

'Oh, Carole.' Darcie's head came up and she smiled. 'Sorry, I didn't see you there. I was away with the fairies.'

'That's all right.' Carole looked apologetic. 'I wondered, while it's a bit quiet, whether I could have a word?'

'Of course you can. Let's pop along to my office, shall we?' Darcie led the way, hoping Carole wasn't ill and needing medical advice.

'I won't beat about the bush,' Carole said in her practical way when they were seated. 'I'd like to give in my notice.'

'Oh…' Darcie looked pained. 'There's nothing wrong, is there? I mean, you're not ill or anything?'

'No, no.' The older woman waved away Darcie's concern. 'My daughter and son-in-law have asked me to go and live with them in Brisbane. Ben's just got one of these fly-in, fly-out jobs and he's away a lot. Nicole's feeling lonely and finding it hard to cope with the two little ones on her own.'

'So you're going to help out?' Darcie surmised.

'Well, I'd like to and I do miss the grandchildren. They're lovely little things.'

'Of course they are.' Darcie's tender heart was touched. 'When would you like to go?'

'Well…as soon as you can replace me. But I won't leave you in the lurch,' Carole hastened to add.

'We'll be sorry to lose you, Carole. But I realise things change and family should always come first if possible.'

'That's what I think too,' Carole said, getting to her feet. 'But I'll miss Sunday Creek and all you folk here at the hospital.'

'We must have a little send-off for you.' Darcie smiled, as they walked back to the station. 'And *we'll* do the cooking.'

'Oh—I never expected…' Carole looked suddenly embarrassed. 'But that'd be lovely, Darcie. Thank you.'

Darcie went straight along to Jack's office. As well as Carole's news, she had something else to tell him. She knocked and popped her head in.

'Hey.' He looked up, sending her a quick smile and beckoning her in.

'You were late home last night,' Darcie said. 'I just wanted to check in and ask how things went.' Yesterday had been the opening of their outreach clinic.

'Word had got out apparently.' He leaned back in his chair and stretched his legs out under the desk. 'We were swamped. Lots of follow-up to do. Thank heavens for Maggie's all-round skills. I couldn't have managed without her.'

'So we'll take her each time, then?'

'For the moment.' He rubbed a hand across his forehead. 'I imagine the other nurses would like a turn as well.'

'And me,' Darcie reminded him.

His gaze slid softly over her. 'Of course you, Dr Drummond. Maggie has a list of what else needs to be done to make the space more patient-friendly at the clinic.'

'Excellent. She's on shortly. I'll have a chat to her when she gets in. By the way, Carole's just told me she's leaving. We'll have to find someone to replace her.'

'Oh, no.' Jack made a face. 'I love Carole's spaghetti and meatballs.'

Darcie sent an eye-roll towards the ceiling. 'And on a lighter note, we had news yesterday the MD's house is finished.'

'Mmm,' Jack said absently. 'I know. Louise left me a set of keys.'

'Well, then.' Darcie's look was expectant. 'You should make a time to move in.'

He lifted a shoulder in a tight shrug. 'I'll think about it.' In fact, he had no real desire to move at all. He was quite happy to be living in the communal residence. The MD's house was meant for a family man, wife, kids, dog, the whole box and dice. He'd rattle around like a lost soul. He couldn't think why a needy family in the town couldn't be offered the place instead of him. But he was sure the board would have none of that.

'Meg McLeish will look after the domestic side of things for you,' Darcie said, 'so you only need to gather up your personal stuff and move in.'

One dark brow lifted. 'Keen to get rid of me, Dr Drummond?'

She flushed. 'Your moving doesn't mean we can't see something of one another outside work.'

He hadn't thought of that. 'Are you saying it could offer us a few *possibilities*?'

Darcie felt the slow build-up of heat inside her. 'Might.'

'We've unfinished business between us, Darcie,' he reminded her softly. 'Don't we?'

She gave a little restive shake of her head, her mind conjuring up a vivid image his evocative words had produced.

She got to her feet. 'If you need a hand with the move, I'm around.'

Darcie was thoughtful as she made her way back to the nurses' station. She found Maggie settling in for her shift. After the two had exchanged greetings, Maggie said, 'Jack tell you we need to organise a few more amenities for the outreach clinic?'

'Leave that for the moment, please, Maggie. I wanted to talk to you about something else.' Darcie swung onto one of the high stools next to the senior nurse, realising without her even knowing it that a possible solution for Emma and her mother had begun crystallising inside her head. 'Do you know anything about Kristy Tynan's personal situation?'

'I know she's a hard worker,' Maggie said. 'Been here a couple of years. Divorced. No man about the place. Keeps to herself.'

Darcie bit down on her bottom lip. 'I don't mean to be nosy here, Maggie but something's cropped up staff-wise.'

Maggie raised a well-defined dark brow. 'Someone leaving?'

'Carole. Relocating for family reasons.'

'And you're wondering whether Kristy would fit the bill?'

'My, you're quick!' Darcie grinned.

Maggie smirked. 'Just ask my boys. But, seriously, I think Kristy would jump at the chance to get out of that truckers' café. The hours she has to work are horrendous.'

Darcie looked at her watch. 'I think I'll go and have a chat to her now. The sooner we can get someone for the job, the sooner Carole can go to her family.'

'Working here would certainly be a nicer environment for Kristy,' Maggie reflected. 'And as we're supposed to be a caring profession, I don't imagine the board would object to Emma tagging along when necessary. And we could quietly work on a quit-smoking campaign for Kristy,' Maggie finished with a sly grin.

'You should be running the country,' Darcie quipped. 'But you've read my mind exactly. I'll see you in a bit.'

At the roadhouse, Darcie looked around and then made her way across to what looked like the dining area.

'Can I help you?' a young man, who was wiping down tables, asked.

'I was hoping to have a word with Kristy Tynan,' Darcie said.

'No worries. I'll give her a shout.'

Moments later, Kristy batted her way through the swing doors that led from the kitchen. Recognising Darcie, her hand went to her throat. 'It's not Emma, is it?'

'No, nothing like that, Kristy. Sorry if I startled you,' Darcie apologised. 'But I've come about a job at the hospital. I thought you might be interested in making a change.'

Kristy wiped her hands down the sides of her striped apron, agitation in her jerky movements. 'I don't understand…'

'Could you spare a few minutes?' Darcie looked around hopefully. 'Somewhere we could have a private chat?'

'I'm due a break.' Kristy pulled off her apron and placed it over the back of a chair. 'Let's go outside. There's a bit of a deck where we can sit.'

Quickly and concisely Darcie explained the nature of the job at the hospital. 'You'd be required to plan a menu but it would be nothing complicated, except now and again a patient might have special dietary needs.'

'Well, I could handle that,' Kristy said, looking almost eager. 'I actually did two years of a chef's apprenticeship in Sydney but then I got married and we moved away and I had Emma…' She paused and chewed her lip. 'You probably know I'm divorced now, Dr Drummond. There's just Emma and me.'

Darcie nodded. 'We could offer you more reasonable

hours at the hospital, Kristy. And if Emma needed to come with you, that would be fine.' Darcie smiled. 'You could have your meals together and I believe the school bus stops outside the hospital as well.'

Kristy blinked rapidly. 'It seems too good to be true…'

'It's true,' Darcie said. 'Carole, our present cook, is leaving. We need someone just as capable to replace her. And as soon as possible.'

Kristy's mouth trembled. 'So, would I have to come in for an interview or something…?'

'You've just had it,' Darcie said warmly. 'I'll run everything past the board and you'll need a couple of referees.'

'I can manage that.'

'Good. And if everything checks out, then the job is yours.'

'Oh…' Suddenly Kristy's eyes overflowed and she swiped at them with the backs of her hands. 'You can't know what this will mean to Emma and me, Dr Drummond. And thank you for thinking of me.'

'Folk in Sunday Creek have been very kind to me,' Darcie said earnestly. 'I'm just passing it along.'

Later that afternoon, Jack tracked Darcie down in the treatment room. She was suturing the hand of a local carrier who had received a deep wound when unloading roofing iron at a building site. 'Could I have a word when you're finished here, please, Dr Drummond?'

Darcie turned her head. 'Almost done. I'll come along to your office, all right?'

Jack merely nodded. 'Thanks.'

* * *

'So, what's up?' Darcie asked, having sent her patient on his way with a tetanus jab and a script for an antibiotic.

Jack stood up from his desk, his expression a bit sheepish. 'I—uh—thought, if you're not busy, we could go across to the house and take a look.'

Darcie's gaze widened in disbelief. 'You haven't been near the place since you arrived here, have you?'

'Didn't see the need.' He came round from behind his desk and began to usher her out. 'Want to come with me, then?'

She shrugged in compliance. 'I'll just tell Maggie where we'll be. By the way, I think I've found us a new cook. I've approached Kristy Tynan. She's keen and I think she'll do a wonderful job.'

Jack whistled. 'Well done, you. Nice footwork there, Dr Drummond.'

'So you approve?'

'Of course. It'll be an excellent move for the Tynan ladies.'

'It will,' Darcie agreed. 'I'll pass the whole thing along to Louise, and she can sort out Kristy's terms of employment and so on. And Carole can get on her way.'

'Oh, we're here already!' Darcie sent him an encouraging look as they pulled up outside the house. 'They've painted the outside as well.'

'Aw, gee,' Jack deadpanned.

'Stop that. It'll be fine,' Darcie said bracingly. 'Let's go inside and see what they've done.'

Inside, the house smelled of new paint and it was obvious the renovation was complete. They wandered from room to room, peered into the master bedroom with its

king-sized bed and en suite bathroom, down the hall to
two smaller bedrooms, both with their own en suites,
and then on to the living room and kitchen.

'It's obvious Lou has had a hand in the furnishings.'
Darcie was enthusiastic. 'It's wonderful, Jack, so clean
and bright.'

Jack merely looked unimpressed. 'What am I supposed to do with all this space?'

'Live here, one assumes.'

'I suppose I could offer it to the old woman who lived
in a shoe,' he grumbled, and sent Darcie a pained look.
'I won't be expected to *entertain*, will I? Give a drinks
party before the mayor's ball or something?'

Darcie gave an inelegant snort. 'Don't be pathetic.
And as far as I know, Sunday Creek doesn't have a may-
oral ball. And look…' she went forward and opened the
pantry cupboard '…Meg's already stocked up for you.'

'I just don't need this,' Jack insisted.

'Well, it comes with the MD's position,' Darcie
pointed out. 'The board is just fulfilling its part of your
employment contract. You have a certain position in the
town, Jack,' she reminded him. 'You don't want to be
remembered as the rogue medico who wouldn't live in
the doctor's residence.'

Jack dredged up a jaded smile. 'Do you think I could
coax Capone across to live with me?'

Darcie sent him a look of resignation. She imagined
Jack Cassidy could coax a herd of kangaroos to come
and live with him if he chose. Her heart dipped. Even
her. One day. 'I imagine Capone will probably opt to
settle here if you offer him a few treats. Oops, that's me.'

Reaching back, she pulled her phone out of the back
pocket of her cargos. 'Oh, hi, Lou,' she said brightly.

'Jack and I are just over at the house. It's lovely— Sorry, what did you say?' As she listened, Darcie began making her way slowly along the hallway and out onto the front veranda.

Hearing her abrupt change of tone, and fearing something untoward, Jack followed and waited until she ended the call. 'Darcie?'

She turned from the railings, her expression strained. She licked her lips. 'That was Louise…'

'I gathered that.' Jack went to her. 'Is someone hurt?'

'It's Jewel.' Darcie's throat pinched as she swallowed. 'She's stumbled into some kind of rabbit hole. They've only just found her. Her front leg's shattered. Sam Gibson's on his way…' She stopped and blinked.

'Oh, baby…I'm so sorry.' Jack hooked an arm around her shoulders and felt her shaking. 'Do you want to go out to Willow Bend?'

She nodded. 'Lou thought I might want to…' She bit her lips together to stop them trembling. 'My poor little Jewel.'

'Come on,' Jack said gently. 'I'll take you. Just give me a minute to lock up here and let Maggie know what's happening.'

'Do we have some idea where we have to go when we get there?' Jack asked quietly as they drove.

'Not far from the homestead. Louise said she'll keep a lookout for us,' Darcie answered throatily.

Jack put out a hand, found hers and squeezed.

A shadecloth had been erected over the little mare. Jack pulled to a stop a short distance away. 'Go ahead,' he urged gently. 'I won't be far behind.'

Darcie almost ran to where Max and Sam were standing just outside the shelter. Their body language told her everything she'd feared.

Max looked grim. 'Sad day for us, Darcie.'

Darcie turned to Sam, a tiny ray of hope lingering in her questioning eyes.

The vet shook his head.

'C-could I spend a few minutes with her?' Darcie's mouth trembled out of shape.

'Take as long as you need.' Sam's look was kind. 'And Jewel's not in pain, Darcie,' he stressed. 'I've sedated her.'

The little mare was resting on her side. Darcie knelt next to her. 'I'm here, sweetheart,' she murmured, touching her hand to the horse's neck, feeling the soft coat, the already fading warmth. Jewel's big dark eyes opened and Darcie knew she'd been waiting for her.

She touched the velvet ears, rubbed gently along the white blaze on the mare's forehead, her every action rooted in preserving life, until Sam returned to do what he had to do.

Darcie's goodbye was silent. Instead, she held Jewel's head for a moment before burying her face in her soft, shiny coat.

'Time to go, Darcie...' Max looked drawn.

Unable to speak, Darcie raised a hand in farewell and turned blindly into Jack's waiting arms.

He hurried her towards the Land Rover. Making sure they were belted in, he took off swiftly down the track. If there was a shot, he didn't hear it, and silently thanked Sam for his sensitivity. Darcie didn't need that last wrenching finality.

When they hit the main road back to town, he spoke. 'It hurts like hell, doesn't it?'

'Yes, it does.' Her voice broke. Tears made slow rivulets down her cheeks and she wiped them away with the tips of her fingers. Her thoughts spun and became muddled. It wasn't like her to be so emotional. Perhaps it was just past history and other losses, she thought bleakly.

When they neared Sunday Creek township, she asked, 'Could I come home with you, Jack?'

Jack felt his pulse tick over. 'To the new house?'

'If you wouldn't mind…' She didn't look at him, just stared straight ahead.

Jack placed his hand on her thigh. 'Of course I don't mind. I'll just swing by the residence and grab some whisky. I think we could both use a drink.' He flicked a glance at her and saw a solitary tear fall down her cheek. He tightened his fingers in a gesture of empathy. 'I know how bad it feels when you lose a favourite animal.'

'I…don't usually fall apart like this…' Her voice was low, throaty, the admission sounding as if it was wrenched from deep within her. 'I became so attached to Jewel.' She managed a jagged, self-deprecating laugh. 'Perhaps it was just wanting desperately something to love.'

Sweet God. Jack could feel the fine tremor running through her skin beneath his hand. '*I'm* here! he wanted to yell to the treetops. 'Love *me*!' But of course he couldn't.

Jack took down two whisky tumblers from the wall cupboard. 'I can have this neat,' he said. 'But what about you?'

'Is there any ice?' Darcie sat at the breakfast bar on a high stool.

He opened the freezer door. 'There is. Our Meg'
a legend.' He shook out ice cubes from the tray and
dropped several into her drink. Picking up the glasses
he joined Darcie at the counter.

'Here's to Jewel,' he said softly.

Darcie managed a small smile. She took a mouthful
of her drink and blinked a bit. 'It's probably crazy to get
so emotional over an animal, isn't?'

'It's not crazy.' Jack stroked her hand, which was
curled into a fist on the countertop. 'Animals are wonderful, with hearts as big as the sky. And they're ever
lastingly faithful. Something humans could learn from

A little while later Darcie felt the liquor begin to warm
her insides. The trembling had stopped. 'You really get
me, don't you, Jack?'

Jack paused giving weight to his answer. 'I think we
get each other.' He looked into her face and saw the honesty there. But he also saw the passion. So, what was she
telling him? What was she asking him here?

She lifted her glass and took the last mouthful of her
drink. 'I don't want to be anywhere else other than here
with you.'

Jack's mouth tightened fractionally. 'Are you sure?'

For answer, she leaned across and pressed her lips
against his, asking a silent question. She felt his resistance for a second and then he exhaled a breath and his
mouth softened. Then it opened and his tongue stroked
against her lips and she sighed as he lifted her off the
stool and gathered her in. Her whole body quivered and
she pressed herself in against him, snaking her arms
around his neck and opening her mouth, surrendering
it to his.

Passion like she'd never known flared inside her. She

pushed her hands into his hair, wanting more than anything to touch him. All of him. Her hands fell to the buttons on his shirt, pulling at them impatiently, almost desperate to feel his naked skin, absorb his heat and craving to get closer.

Jack was momentarily taken aback. This was a Darcie he didn't know. Yet hadn't he always known this was the woman inside the contained little shell she exhibited to the outside world? He could sense her loss of control but, on the other hand, he didn't want her to regret what they were about to do. Pulling away from her mouth, he kissed her throat, trying to slow their ardour. If they were going to make love, he didn't want it to be a hurried affair, over in seconds. He wanted them to *know* each other in the finest way possible.

'Come with me,' he murmured, taking her hands and bringing them to his mouth, pressing a kiss into each palm. He twitched a Jack-like smile. 'Let's try out my new bed, shall we?'

Jack closed the bedroom door softly and for a long moment they looked at each other.

Darcie couldn't believe this was really happening. Yet she knew she'd wanted him for the longest time. Wanted him as much as her next breath. 'Undress me,' she breathed, a tide of need overcoming her, shocking her in its intensity.

'I want this to be about us, Darcie,' he said with a rich huskiness that rippled along her skin. 'You and me. In the truest sense…'

Darcie gasped, feeling his urgency match her own as he flicked open her shirt, bending to put his mouth to the hollow between her breasts, peeling back the lace of her bra, tracing each tiny exposure of skin with his tongue.

With the last item of their clothing peeled away, Darcie couldn't wait a moment longer to burrow in against him. To hold him and be held in return.

'I can hardly believe you've come to me at last…' Jack's voice was rough-edged with passion held in check.

The softest smile edged her mouth. 'But you always knew I would, didn't you?' She reached out to carry his hand to her breast, standing full and proud as she straightened back.

'Feel. My heart's going wild.'

Jack's mouth dried. She was…magnificent. And soon they would be as one.

Lovers at last.

Darcie had never been so aware of her own sensuality. Leaning down, she patted the clean sweep of the bed. The invitation was in her eyes, her husky feminine laugh almost daring him.

Jack took her challenge, encircling her wrist and twirling her round so she landed on the bed on her back. In a second he was there beside her. Reaching for her, he gathered her close so that they were looking into each other's eyes, their mouths a breath apart.

'God—' Jack brought his head up sharply. 'I don't have anything with me.'

'I'm covered,' she whispered, dazed with emotion. 'Don't hold back, Jack.'

He didn't.

Darcie let all her emotions come to the surface. Soul-destroying scars from the past fell away and she felt as though she'd crossed to another time zone. Jack's touch was instinctive, seeking responses from her she hadn't known existed, touching her deepest senses, sculpting her body from head to toe.

'Let me now,' she whispered, deep in thrall, aching to discover him. His groan of pleasure pushed them closer to the edge and finally, irrevocably, they were lost in the taste and texture of each other, moving in perfect rhythm, climbing even higher where they met in the wild storm of their shared release, drenched in a million stars.

For a long time after, they stayed entwined. Quiet. Even a little amazed that they were there.

In his bed.

Lovers.

'You're smiling,' Darcie said.

'How do you know?'

She brought her head up from where it was buried against his chest. 'Because I am too.' Lifting a hand, she ran a finger along the shadow already darkening his jaw. And stared into his eyes and let her fingers drift into his hair.

Jack touched a finger to her lips, his gaze devouring her. 'No words?'

'No words,' she echoed, feeling her lips tingle where he'd touched them. She burrowed in against him once more.

'Hungry?' Jack asked after a while.

'Lazy, I think. But perhaps a bit hungry too. You?'

'I wouldn't mind a feed,' he admitted. 'But let's have a shower first.'

Darcie raised her head slightly and blinked. 'Together?'

'Of course together.' Laughing softly, he spanned her waist with his hand. 'I'm not letting you out of my sight.

* * *

'I'd rather not go out to eat,' Darcie said when they were dressed again and on their way to the kitchen.

'Me neither.' Jack placed a hand protectively at the back of her neck. Going out would somehow break the spell they were under. And that would come sooner rather than later, he decided realistically. 'Let's see what Meg's left us.'

'Left *you*, you mean.' She sent him an indulgent, half-amused look. 'Meg wouldn't know I'd be here.'

They found bread in the freezer, eggs and cheese in the fridge and a can of peaches in the pantry. 'Enough for a feast,' Jack declared. 'Cheese on toast, peaches for dessert.'

'And lashings of tea,' Darcie requested.

'Of course.' Tilting her face towards him, Jack kissed her gently on the mouth. 'English tea for my English rose.'

Cocooned in happiness, Darcie marvelled, 'I can't believe the phone hasn't rung.'

'I can.' Jack flexed a shoulder and grinned. 'I told Maggie we were not to be disturbed for anything less than a multi-trauma.'

'Oh, Jack…' A flood of colour washed over her cheeks. 'Does she know—about us?'

'She'd talked to Sam.' Jack seemed unfazed. 'Maggie got the picture. She said, and I quote, "I'm so glad Darcie has you, Jack."'

'Oh, heavens.' Darcie pressed a hand to her heart. 'Next thing she'll have us engaged.'

'No, she won't.' His mouth worked for a moment. But he thought the idea had real possibilities for all that.

'Will you take me home now?' Darcie asked, when they'd tidied up after their impromptu dinner.

'I'm coming with you,' Jack said. 'I'll move in here by degrees. When it feels right.'

'Oh…' Darcie felt a funny lump in her throat. She wasn't quite ready to share a bed with him on a permanent basis. And she guessed Jack understood that. *Even though I love him.* The realisation nearly tipped her sideways. She wrestled the startling thought back. Instead, reaching up, she placed her palm against his cheek.

Jack nodded. Message received and understood. Turning his head a fraction, he kissed the soft hollow of her palm. 'Let's go home,' he said, his blue eyes steady. 'It's late and I haven't said goodnight to Capone.'

CHAPTER ELEVEN

A WEEK LATER, Darcie and Maggie were sitting at the nurses' station, batting light conversation around, when the phone rang. Maggie turned aside to answer it. 'Bleep Jack,' she mouthed urgently, and began taking details quickly.

Jack came at speed to the station. 'What's up?'

'Another accident out at that movie site at Pelican Springs,' Maggie relayed. 'A stuntman hanging upside down from a tree. Apparently he's caught and they can't release him. They're in a panic.'

Jack swore pithily. 'Still no nurse on the set?'

'Apparently not.' Maggie spun off her chair. 'Let's grab some trauma packs, guys. You need to be gone.'

There was no use surmising anything, Jack decided grimly as they drove. But a few probable scenarios leapt into dangerous possibilities.

'If our patient has been upside down for any length of time, he's quite likely lapsed into unconsciousness,' Darcie said. 'It's going to be tricky, isn't it?'

Jack snorted. 'That's the understatement of the year. We could have a death on our hands, Darcie. Those bas

ards are obviously still ignoring normal safety protocols. But this time I'll nail them.'

Darcie felt the tense nature of the situation engulf
her. Every crisis they faced out here meant delivering
medicine in its rawest form. 'Should we run over what
we might find? We're going to have to think on our feet
from the moment we land there.'

'I've spoken to Mal Duffy.' Jack's response was
clipped. 'The SES are on their way, likewise the ambulance and police. Mal's wearing both hats. He's gone
ahead and contacted the folk at Pelican Springs. By sheer
good luck, the telephone company is doing some work at
the property. The phone techs have been using a cherry
picker to connect new wiring to the poles. They're on
their way to the accident site as we speak.'

'A cherry picker works like a crane, doesn't it?' Darcie's unease was mirrored in her questioning look.

'Mmm. It'll be mounted on the back of a truck,' Jack
explained. 'Usually, the operator stands at the control
panel at the side of the truck and directs the crane to
wherever it's needed. There's a cage-like platform at the
top of the crane, of course,' he added. 'The rescue team
will ride up in that.'

And that meant Jack himself would go up, Darcie
thought tightly. 'I hate this!' she said with feeling. 'We're
doctors—not monkeys!'

That brought a glimmer of a grim smile to his mouth.
It offends me too, Darcie, that these morons think they
can get away with treating their workers with such dis-
respect. Let alone the people who have to come and res-
ue them from their folly.'

Darcie bit down on her bottom lip. She could tell,
even without looking at him, that Jack was strung tight,

focused…almost driven. She only hoped he'd keep a cool head. But, of course, he would. They both would.

Because there was no other choice.

The accident site was in chaos when they got there. Automatically, the doctors donned their high-visibility vests and hard hats. 'Here's Mal,' Darcie said with something like relief. 'Perhaps he can tell us what's going on.'

Jack grunted. 'More than that clown Meadows, by the look of it.' Even as he spoke, the unit manager was screaming at the grips—the unskilled workers on the set—to do *something*.

Mal didn't bother with greetings. Instead, he cut to the chase. 'The flying doctors are within a two-hundred mile radius. We managed to catch them at Harborough station before they turned round to head back to base. If they cane it, they should be here within the hour.'

'Thanks, Mal.'

'Cherry picker's just arrived,' the policeman said. 'Two of the SES guys will go up with you. While you see what can be done medically, they'll start cutting him away.'

'Do we have a name?' Jack's gut clenched. This was a nightmare.

'Wayne Carmody. Sixtyish.'

'Oh, hell…' Jack shook his head. 'What's he thinking of, doing stunt work at his age?' Well, he already knew the answer. This whole set-up was nothing short of illegal. Understaffed and unsafe. Only people desperate for work would consider risking their lives here. 'Right, I'm ready.' Jack creased his eyes against the sudden glare as he looked up at the skeletal outline of the crane. 'Let's get that contraption moving.'

'I'm coming with you.' Darcie's voice showed quiet determination.

'You're not!' Jack's response was immediate and unequivocal.

'We're a team, Jack,' she reminded him, pushing down her own fears. 'We combine our skills.'

For a fleeting moment they challenged each other and Jack's mouth pulled tight. She was as pale as parchment. But as plucky as all get-out. There was no way she'd be left out of this. 'Just do what I tell you, then,' he stipulated, the edges of his teeth grating.

Darcie felt the nerves in her stomach pitch and fall as they were hoisted upwards. Nausea began gathering at the back of her throat and she almost made a grab for Jack. But she fought back the impulse. Instead, she anchored her panic by breathing deeply and holding onto the metal bars of the cage for dear life.

As they reached their target, Jack took in what they had to deal with. Trauma with a capital T. Poor guy. Wayne Carmody was hopelessly entangled, hanging onto consciousness by a thread, his face and arms almost purple with the pressure from his upside-down position.

The crane's operator directed the platform in as close as it would go. 'Best I can do, Doc,' he called from below.

'Thanks—just keep it steady,' Jack yelled back. Wayne,' he addressed the rapidly failing stuntman, 'can you hear me?'

The man's response was a bubble of sound.

'Don't lose it, mate,' Jack said. 'We'll have you down soon.' He turned to Darcie. 'Let's get a non-rebreathing mask on him. It's the only way we can manage the oxygen flow. His BP has to be off the wall. And getting an IV in nigh impossible.'

'I'll get an aspirin under his tongue.' Darcie steadied her position, delving into the trauma kit. It wasn't the ideal solution but the aspirin would begin lowering the injured man's blood pressure and at least alleviate some of the shock his body was undergoing. 'I think there's a possible femur fracture, Jack.' Her worried eyes took in Wayne's right leg, which was hanging at a very odd angle.

'Maybe not. But his circulation has to be critically impaired. We can't tell what we're dealing with until we get him down.' Jack looked up to where the SES team was vainly trying to separate and cut through the thick ropes. 'Come on, guys!' he exhorted. 'Lean on it! What's keeping you?'

'Doin' our best, Doc.' The hard-breathed reply came back. 'Five more minutes.'

The doctors exchanged a swift, tight look, both acknowledging that the time for a successful rescue was running out.

Darcie kept her gaze focused on their patient until her eyes burned. If they didn't reverse Wayne's upside-down position in the next couple of minutes...

Fear and anguish pooled in her stomach and froze the sunny afternoon, stretching the moments into a chasm of waiting.

'OK—we're about to cut the last of the ropes!' Chris, from the SES, yelled. 'He's all yours, Doc!'

Jack reached up, the muscles in his throat and around his mouth locked in a grimace as he took the brunt of the injured man's weight.

Darcie pitched in, her slender frame almost doubled

as Wayne's body descended heavily and fast into their waiting arms and they were able to guide him down onto the floor of the platform.

There were plenty of hands to help them once they were safely on the ground. 'I want the patient treated as a spinal injury,' Jack said tersely. And God knew what else. 'How's the BP, Darcie?'

'Coming down, one sixty over ninety.'

Jack hissed out a breath. He bent closer to their patient. Wayne was dazed and confused, babbling he couldn't feel his legs. Jack brought his head up. 'Will you do a set of spinal obs, please, Darcie?' he asked. As soon as she'd finished, he asked, 'Anything?'

She shook her head. There had been no feeling or sensation in either leg.

'Right, let's give Hartmann's IV, one litre. Stat, please.'

Darcie complied. Did Jack suspect internal bleeding? If he did, then they were hedging their bets here. It was better and safer to give a fluid expander if there was any doubt.

'Flying doctor's landed,' someone said, waving a phone.

'Almost ready for us, Jack?' Zach Bayliss hovered anxiously. This guy looked very bad. The sooner they got him loaded and away the better.

'Just give us a minute to get some morphine into him, Zach.' Jack brought up the dose. 'I'll come with you for the handover.'

'Right, good.' The paramedic looked relieved. 'Where are the flying docs taking him?'

'The Princess Alexandra in Brisbane.'

'It's the best place for him,' Zach agreed.

Jack nodded, proud of his old teaching hospital. The PA was outstanding. The leaders in immediate post-trauma care. And for Wayne it could mean the difference between life and death, or full or partial paraplegia.

'Darcie.' Jack touched her shoulder briefly. 'Check there are no minor injuries to be dealt with, please. I'll be back as soon as I can.'

Good luck, Wayne. The silent wish came from Darcie's heart as she watched the ambulance move away. She felt a shiver of unease up her backbone. This place was beginning to give her the creeps, the tree where the stuntman had been caught rising like some kind of grotesque giant. No, not a nice place at all, she decided. And the sooner they were shot of it, the better...

'I take it you've put in a call to Workplace Health and Safety?' Darcie said much later, as they drove back to town.

'And the local MP.' The tension in Jack's face had eased remarkably. 'If Meadows and his cronies haven't had their dodgy operations closed down by tonight, I'll raise hell.'

'Mal and his constables took statements from the film crew,' Darcie said. 'Blake Meadows had the hide to say that time meant money and that he wasn't going to hang about.'

Jack snorted. 'I'll bet that went down well with Mal.'

'He told Meadows that if he ignored a police directive, he'd be arrested,' Darcie said with satisfaction. 'Mal was brilliant.'

'So were you, Dr Drummond.' Jack reached across and found her hand, sliding his fingers through hers. 'I—uh—finished moving into the house this morning.'

'Oh—I hadn't realised…' Silence seemed to hang between them, a great curve of it, until Darcie gave an off-key laugh edged with uncertainty. 'Are you going to have a house-warming, then?'

The sides of his mouth pleated in a dry smile. 'I thought we'd already done that.'

Darcie lowered her gaze, at the same time feeling her skin heat up.

'What about coming for dinner?' Jack increased the pressure on her fingers.

Darcie tried to ignore the sudden leap in her pulse as his thigh brushed against hers. 'I think I can manage that,' she said slowly. 'Shall I bring something towards the meal?'

'Not necessary. Just come prepared to stay, Darcie.' Jack's voice had dropped to a deep huskiness. 'I want to hold you all night.'

The following morning Darcie asked if they could debrief.

Jack's dark brows flicked up. 'About Wayne?' They were sitting side by side at the breakfast bar, their mugs of tea in front of them.

'Have you heard anything?'

'I got on to the surgical registrar a while ago,' Jack said. 'Wayne's still with us.'

'Oh, thank heavens. Was it a fractured NOF?'

'Herniated L one, two and three.'

Lumbar vertebrae prolapse, Darcie interpreted. 'It must have happened in the initial fall when the rigging collapsed and left him hanging. Poor man. He must have been in such agony.'

'He's been put on a Fentanyl protocol IV. It's a strong narcotic so I guess his pain is manageable.'

'What about spinal damage? Do we know?'

'He's had MRI and CT scans. Seems OK. I'll check with the surgeon in charge later today.'

Darcie's eyes went straight to his face and slid away. 'Do you ever wish you were back there in the thick of it again?'

A small silence bled inwards, until Jack lifted his mug and drank the last of his tea. 'No, I don't,' he said. 'Why would I, when I can be here with you?'

'Same here…' She looked past Jack to the open window and beyond it, her eyes soft and dreamy.

Watching her expression, Jack took stock. I don't *ever* want to be away from her, he thought, unbelieving of the avalanche of emotion that arrowed into him. And recognising with stark reality that what he'd had with Zoe now seemed a pale imitation of what Darcie had brought to his life.

Jack Cassidy had fallen headlong in love. The thought scared him, delighted him, amazed him. 'Why don't we get married?'

Darcie's mouth opened and closed. She blinked rapidly. 'Married?' Her voice was hardly there.

'I love you,' he said for the first time.

She took a shuddery little breath. 'I know…'

'And you love me.' His jaw worked. 'You couldn't be with me the way you are, unless you did.'

'Marriage, though…' she countered inadequately. 'We're from such different backgrounds, different countries…'

'Happens all the time,' he drawled, his tone careful

and hard to read. 'Just please don't say we hardly know each other, Darcie.'

'No.' She gave a forced laugh. 'That would be silly. Marriage is an enormous commitment, though, Jack. Doesn't it scare you?'

'Not at all. We're perfect together and I love everything about you.'

'Oh, Jack…' She shook her head. 'I have so much baggage.'

'No, Darcie. You don't.' He lifted her hand and rubbed the knuckles against his cheek. 'You left it all behind at the creek, when we kissed for the first time.'

But it's still there, she thought silently, and carefully reclaimed her hand. 'I need some time to process all this.'

'In other words, you're going to tie yourself in knots.'

Self-preservation hardened her response. 'Well, I'm sorry I can't see everything in black and white like *you*.'

'You're taking this to extremes, Darcie. Hell! I've asked you marry me, not jump off London Bridge!'

Maybe that would have been easier.

'Why do we even have to talk about marriage?' Sheer panic sharpened her words. 'We're all right the way we are.'

He gave a snort of derision. '*Sometimes* lovers. Would you be happy with that?'

Meaning that he wouldn't. 'I'm just grateful for what we have.'

'But it could be so much more!' Sliding off the stool, he strode to the window and turned back. 'So, what do you need from me, Darcie? Just tell me.'

Her eyes clouded. 'I just need you to give me some more space. And no pressure.' She swallowed thickly.

'I don't want to hurt you, Jack, but I won't be pressured into making a life-changing decision.'

'On the other hand, if you could bring yourself to trust me, we could have something amazing together.'

Or broken hearts for ever if it didn't work. She got to her feet. 'I need your word about this, Jack.'

Jack stared at her for a long moment, his jaw clenched, a tiny muscle jumping. He flicked an open-handed shrug. 'If that's what you want…'

What *did* she want? In a moment of self-doubt she wanted to ditch her scruples and accept Jack's proposal. Make a life with him far from everything that had driven her here. But deep down she knew she couldn't make the leap. Not yet. *Perhaps not ever.* She swallowed the razor-sharp emotion clogging her throat. 'That's what I want.'

Three days later at the nurses' station Maggie asked Darcie if she was OK.

'Fine.' Darcie looked up from the computer. 'Why?'

'You seem a bit…distracted.'

The nerves in Darcie's stomach did a tumble turn. 'You're imagining things, Maggie.'

'I'm not,' Maggie insisted.

Darcie huffed a laugh. 'That carry-on the other day out at the film site would make anyone distracted,' she offered by way of explanation. 'I hate administering medicine on the trot like that.'

'Well, Meadows and his lot have left the district,' Maggie said. 'Packed up and gone apparently. And there's an investigation pending. You and Jack will likely be called as witnesses.'

That's if she was still here in Sunday Creek. Darcie felt her throat tighten. 'I thought you were going with

Jack to the outreach clinic today,' she said, changing lanes swiftly.

'I cried off. Ethan's not feeling so well.'

'Oh, poor kid,' Darcie commiserated. 'Would you like me to check him over?'

'Thanks, Darce, but he'll be fine. It's just a tummy upset. I'll pop home at lunchtime and take him some new DVDs. Lauren was keen to get a turn at the clinic so it worked out all right. Hey, great news Jack's organised for an ophthalmologist to take a regular clinic out here, isn't it? Quite a few eye problems among our indigenous folk, from all accounts.'

Darcie felt taken aback. 'He didn't mention any of that to me.'

The two looked at each other awkwardly. And then Maggie took the initiative. 'He's got a lot on his plate. Probably slipped his mind.'

Or perhaps he was just taking her request for space to extremes. Darcie felt her stomach dive. It was all such a mess.

And it couldn't go on indefinitely.

It was early evening the same day and Jack was sitting on his front veranda. Since Darcie's standoff, he'd felt like throwing things. He'd even considered howling at the moon once or twice but that wouldn't have solved anything.

Why the hell had he mentioned the M word to Darcie? Just because it had seemed a good idea at the time. He hated the panic he'd seen on her face. And knowing he'd been the cause of it made it even worse. Idiot! His heart lurched. He should be renamed *Crass* Cassidy.

He had to talk with her. Keeping this ridiculous *space*

between them was crazy. 'What do you think, mate?' Reaching down, he ruffled Capone's rough coat. Capone laid his head on his front paws and gave a feeble wag of his tail, before settling. Jack thought about it for one second. 'I guess that's a yes, then.'

Decision made, he got to his feet swiftly and went inside to locate his car keys. He'd go across to the residence now before he could change his mind. Making sure the house was secure, he pocketed his keys and walked back along the hallway to the front veranda.

About to close the front door, he stopped. Headlights lit up the street and a car stopped outside his house. He muttered a curse. Who wanted him now? Was it one of the board members? If it was, why couldn't they come to the hospital in daylight hours like normal people?

He blew out a resigned breath and waited. It was no use pretending he wasn't home as his silhouette was backlit from the sensor light on the veranda. As he waited, the driver's door opened and a figure got out. He blinked a bit. There were no streetlights but unless his eyes deceived him, it was…Darcie?

'Hi,' she called throatily, as she opened the gate and came up the path.

'I didn't recognise the car.' Jack winced at the mundane greeting.

Darcie reached the steps. 'My car wouldn't start. The guys from the garage lent me this one.'

Jack beckoned her up the steps. 'Any clue what's wrong with your car?'

She shrugged. 'One of the mechanics will sort it.' And why on earth were they talking about dumb cars? The nerves in Darcie's stomach twisted. Already, the tension between them was as sticky as toffee. Her shoulders rose in a steadying breath. She had to do what she'd come to do. 'Could we talk?'

Jack felt relief with the force of a tsunami sweep through him. 'Of course we can talk.' He swallowed the sudden constriction in his throat. 'As a matter of fact, I was almost out the door myself. I was coming to talk to *you*.'

'Oh…'

They looked at each other helplessly, unable to bridge the gap.

'OK if we sit here?' Jack waved her to one of the cane chairs on the veranda. 'Or we can go inside.' *Or I can take you in my arms and hold you.*

She shook her head. 'Here's fine.' She took the chair he offered.

'So…' His mouth tightened for a second before he hooked out a chair and sat. 'What did you want to say to me?'

Darcie ground her lip. 'I have some leave due. I'd like to take it.'

Jack sat back as if he'd been stung. This was *not* what he'd been hoping to hear. In the ensuing silence he scraped a hand across his cheekbones, took a long breath and released it. 'When do you want to go? In other words, do you need to make plans?'

'I've made them.' In fact, she'd spent the last couple of hours online, doing just that.

'OK…' He digested that for a minute. 'So, when?'

'There's a flight out tomorrow. I'd like to be on it.'

'To Brisbane?'

She nodded.

Jack suspected he should leave it there but couldn't.

'Well, that's probably a good call. Being in Brisbane will give you easy access to the coast.'

She met his gaze, startled. 'I'm not going to the coast.' She swallowed past the lump in her throat. 'I'm flying home.'

'Home?' Jack emphasised, feeling as though his heart had been cut from its moorings and was flailing all over the place. 'To England?'

She gave a tight shrug, wishing she'd used another word. But it was out there now. Front and centre.

'I thought you said Australia was home for you now?' A latent prickle of anger sharpened his response.

'I don't want to start playing semantics, Jack.' Suddenly Darcie felt apart and alone. 'This is something I have to do.'

'Why, Darcie?'

'You know why…' She met his gaze unflinchingly, although inside she was quivering. 'I hate the term but I have to say it. I need *closure.*'

'You're going to see *him*, aren't you?' Jack's eyes burned like polished sapphires. 'What, precisely, is the point of doing that?'

'Because I let him get away with everything! I should have stood my ground! Called Aaron on his despicable behaviour. Instead…' She paused painfully. 'I folded like an empty crisp packet. And bolted.'

'Which is what you should have done. God, Darcie…' Jack shook his head in disbelief. 'The cretin isn't worth the plane fare to England. Do you even know if he's still at the same hospital?'

'He's still there. I checked.'

Suddenly the atmosphere between them was crackling with instability.

Darcie felt the quick rise of desire, watching the play of his muscles under his dark T-shirt as he leant back in his chair and planted his hands on his hips. 'Here's another scenario,' he said. 'If you could delay your departure for a couple of days, I could arrange to come with you.'

Her teeth worried at her bottom lip. She felt guilty for not wanting him to accompany her. But he had to understand this was something she had to do on her own. 'Jack—my travel arrangements are locked in. Besides, the board would hardly approve your leave, would they?'

'The board can mind their own business.'

She gave a fleeting smile. 'The running of the hospital *is* their business, Jack. And, honestly, you don't need to feel responsible for me. I know what I'm doing.'

'Have you considered *he* might talk you into giving him a second chance?' Jack didn't look at her because he couldn't. The question he'd posed was too important. Just spelling it out opened a door on a future—their future— that was suddenly treacherous with deep, dark chasms and the crippling effect of stepping into a minefield.

Agitatedly, Darcie began stroking the edge of the table. Jack watched her hands, fine, delicate with short neat nails; doctor's hands.

'He won't, Jack.'

Jack looked up.

She brought her hands together and locked her fingers.

'Loving you has made me strong.' For a long moment she returned his gaze, her intent never wavering. 'He won't talk me round.'

CHAPTER TWELVE

AND THAT HAD been supposed to reassure him? The question ran endlessly through Jack's head for the umpteenth time as he scrubbed his hands vigorously at the basin. Well, he wasn't reassured. Far from it.

'Which one do you want to do first?' Beside him, Natalie began opening a suture pack. She was referring to the twelve-year-old boys who'd been brought in after crashing into each other while skateboarding. Neither had been wearing protective headgear. Both were bloody with split eyebrows and pale with shock at finding themselves in Casualty.

'Doesn't matter. Either one. Idiot kids,' he growled. 'And why weren't they at school?'

Natalie sent him a long-suffering look. 'It's Saturday, Jack.'

'Oh—is it?' he replied edgily. 'I've lost track.' But he hadn't lost track of the number of days Darcie had been gone. She'd been gone ten days and each had seem to last longer than the one before it.

'Perhaps I'd better take the kid with the egg on his forehead,' Jack reconsidered.

'Matthew,' Natalie supplied. 'Are you concerned he might be concussed?'

Jack shrugged. 'As far as we know, he didn't pass out but I'd like his neuro obs monitored for a couple of hours just to be on the safe side.'

'Need an extra hand?'

Jack spun round from the basin as if his body had been zapped by a ricocheting bullet. His dark brows snapped together. 'You're back.'

Darcie coloured faintly. He didn't seem very pleased to see her and it wasn't the welcome she'd orchestrated in her mind at all. 'I'm back,' she echoed.

'Good trip?' Jack's gaze narrowed.

'Wonderful.'

She looked fantastic. *Shining.* It was the only word Jack could think of to describe her. And she had a new hairstyle. A spike of resentment startled him. But surely it was justified? He'd been here worrying his guts out about her wellbeing, when she'd been off, obviously having a fine old time in merry England.

'Darcie, hi!' Diplomatically, Natalie jumped in to fill the yawning gap. 'Welcome back. It's good to see you.'

'And you, Nat. And I have presents for everyone,' Darcie singsonged.

'Oh, my stars!' Natalie's hand went to her heart. 'From London?'

'Of course.' Darcie was smiling.

'That's so cool.'

'Could we get on?' Jack yanked his gloves on. He'd had enough of the small talk.

'What do we have?' Darcie directed her question to Natalie.

'Two youngsters, two split eyebrows, two suturing obs.'

'I'll do one.' Darcie looked directly at Jack. 'Is that OK?'

'If you have the time.' Jack elbowed his way out of the door.

Natalie looked helplessly after him. 'I don't think Jack's been sleeping very well.'

And that was supposedly her fault? Darcie went to the basin. Suddenly her legs felt like jelly. 'Nat, if you've arranged to assist Jack, go ahead. I'm sure I can manage a few sutures.'

'Oh, OK...' Natalie's voice faltered. 'It's so great to have you back, Darcie.'

'Thanks, Nat...' Darcie blew out a calming breath. She'd been buoyed up by excitement, coming back. Now jet lag was suddenly beginning to catch up with her, leaving her flat. She'd sought to surprise Jack but that had obviously backfired. She gave vent to a sigh. Why was nothing in life ever simple? Drying her hands, she shook out a pair of sterile gloves from their packet and went to find her patient.

Darcie did her usual careful job, nevertheless. Placing four stitches in her young patient's wound didn't take long. She completed his treatment chart and handed him over to his mother with instructions to come back in a week to have the stitches removed.

Oh, boy. She wiggled her fingers stiffly. She must be more tired than she'd thought. But she was determined to wait for Jack. She looked at her watch. It was already late afternoon. Perhaps a cup of tea would revive her. Decision made, she went along to the hospital kitchen.

It was there Jack found her.

'You look like hell,' he said bluntly.

She brought her chin up. 'Fancy that.'

Jack's mouth crimped around a reluctant smile. He put out a hand towards her. 'Let's get you home.'

Outside the air was clear and sharp. Darcie felt a slight dizziness overtake her, the ground coming up to meet her. 'Oh…'

'You're out on your feet,' he growled, wrapping a supporting arm around her shoulders. 'When did you fly in?'

'Very early this morning,' she said, wondering why her eyelids felt weighted down. 'But then I had to coordinate two flights to get home to Sunday Creek.'

'No wonder your body clock's out of whack. You need sleep.' He stopped at his Land Rover and opened the passenger door. Scooping her up, he lifted her in.

'Did you miss me?' She mumbled the words against his shoulder as he settled in beside her.

'You bet I did.' His gaze softened. 'I should never have let you go without me. Did you miss me?' He turned his head, waiting for her answer, but she was already asleep.

Darcie woke to silence and the gentlest breeze wafting through the partly open window. Blinking uncertainly, she half raised her head. Where was she? She looked around at the unfamiliar prints on the walls, the white linen blinds. And then reality struck. She was in one of the guest bedrooms in Jack's house.

She muffled a groan into the pillow. He must have got her to bed after they'd left the hospital. What else had he done? Cautiously, she put a hand under the duvet and touched the softness of the jersey pants she'd worn on the flight. Except for her shoes, he hadn't attempted to undress her. 'Oh, Jack…' A smile curved gently around her mouth. 'You are such an honourable man.'

The sharp click of the front door closing had her sitting boldly upright, pulling her knees up to her chin. 'Jack?' Her voice came out throatily. 'Is that you?'

'Ah…' Jack's dark head came round the door. 'Sleeping Beauty's awake, I see.'

Darcie blushed, watching him amble into the bedroom, his powerful masculinity making the space appear to shrink to doll's-house proportions. 'Good sleep?' he asked.

'It was. Sorry I passed out on you,' she said ruefully. 'What time is it?'

'Five-ish.'

Darcie frowned. 'Five-ish when?'

'Sunday afternoon.'

'You mean I've slept the clock round?'

He looked at her with steady eyes. 'Jet lag will do that to you every time. How about some dinner? Hungry?'

'Starving.' She smiled a bit uncertainly. 'But at the moment I need the bathroom more than I need food.'

A wry smile nipped his mouth. 'See you in a bit then. Oh, I swung by the residence and picked up your suitcase.'

'Oh—thanks for that.' She watched as he slipped out and retrieved it from the hallway.

'I've made minestrone.' He hefted her case onto the end of the bed. 'Hurry up.'

Darcie threw herself out of bed and into the en suite. Were they back together? Properly back together? She ground her lip in consternation, letting the rose-scented gel drift silkily over her body and puddle around her feet. They hadn't parted on the best of terms. Jack had clearly not been happy about her reasons for going to England. But surely he wouldn't have brought her here to his home if he was still offside with her?

Air whistled out of her lungs, ending in an explosive little sigh as she dressed quickly. Conjecture was get ing her nowhere. She left the bedroom, an odd flutter of shyness assailing her as she made her way along the short length of the hallway to the kitchen.

Jack had set places at the table. Standing for a moment, she watched him, her gaze lingering, drinking in his maleness. He was wearing a black T-shirt that delineated the tight group of muscles beneath and a pair of washed-out jeans. 'Something smells good.'

He turned from the stove, eyeing with obvious approval her sleek black leggings and pearl-grey top. 'Feeling better?'

'Much.' She joined him at the stove. 'Anything I can do to help?'

He turned off the heat and gave the minestrone a final stir. 'Couple of bowls might be a good idea. And there's some multigrain rolls in that bag there. Then we'll be in business.'

'Another?' Jack's look was softly indulgent a little later as Darcie neared the end of her second bowl of soup.

'Heavens, no!' She gave an embarrassed laugh. 'But that was truly delicious, Jack. Thank you.'

His mouth pulled at the corner. 'You're more than welcome, Darcie.' He looked at her guardedly. 'Coffee?'

She shook her head. 'Perhaps later.'

He shifted awkwardly in his chair. 'Sorry for acting like a prat when you arrived yesterday.'

Eyes cast down, she made a little circle with her finger on the tabletop. 'Do you want to hear about my trip?'

Jack's heart was beating like a tom-tom. Lord, how he'd missed her! And now she was back, barely centimetres away from him, her faint, delicate fragrance teasing his senses, making a mockery of his control. 'I suppose we should get it out of the way.' Standing to

his feet, he collected their used dishes and took ther
across to the sink.

Darcie had the feeling of being dismissed. But no
for long. She rose from the table, moving purposeful
across to join him at the window, peering out. 'The rea
son I went, Jack, was to come to you whole. If you war
us back together, the least you can do is listen.'

Something in Jack's heart scrunched tight. He blinke
and turned his head a fraction. Her eyes were cast dowr
her long gold-tipped lashes fanning across her cheek:
He felt a lump the size of a lemon in his throat as h
swallowed. 'You're right. But let's get more comfor
able, shall we?'

They went through to the lounge room. Darci
switched on the two table lamps and a gentle glow c
light flooded the room. Jack held out his hand and guide
her to the big, squishy sofa. Once they were seated, h
looped out an arm and gathered her closely. 'OK.' H
took a deep breath and let it go. 'Fire away.'

Darcie's heart quickened and she edged back so sh
could look him in the eye. 'I saw Aaron.'

His jaw tightened for a moment. 'How long did yo
spend with him?'

'Not long. Needless to say, he was stunned to see m
I didn't bother with small talk. I just hit him with every
thing. I let him have it all—everything I'd been feelin;
How his behaviour had been reprehensible, how he'
sapped my self-worth and a whole lot more.'

Jack's eyes burned with a strange intensity. 'How di
he react?'

'He folded. Apologised. Several times, in fact.' He
eyes clouded briefly. 'I suggested he should get som

specialist psychiatric help. It's obvious he's deeply unhappy.'

Jack sent her a guarded look. 'How did he respond
to that?'

'He said he's already in therapy.' A breath of silence.
'I...said I hoped it worked. Then I got up and left.'

'Were you upset?' Jack asked carefully.

'Maybe a bit. But I felt free. It was a fantastic feeling.'

'My gutsy, brave girl.' Jack pulled her close again.
'I'm so proud of you.'

'Wait until you hear what else I did.'

'Good grief.' Jack shook his head. 'Better hit me with
it then.'

'I went to see my parents. They were actually home
for once.'

'And?'

'I had a very frank talk with them.' She sent him
a dazzling smile. 'On the flight over to England the
thought came to me that they hadn't shaped up very
well as parents. There was you and your big loving fam-
ly and you obviously had a happy childhood. Maggie
doing so well as a single parent, and Nat with her husband working away so much, managing to keep her little
girl safe and happy. And my parents took none of the responsibility that comes with parenthood. They're bright
people. They *should* have known.'

Jack blinked and blinked again. Sweet heaven, she
was lovely. His gaze slid softly over her. 'So, what was
the outcome?'

'For the first time we sat together like a family. And
we talked. Really talked.' Darcie's mouth wobbled a bit.
They both apologised for their lack of involvement but

assured me over and over that they'd always loved me.
And Mum cried. And Dad called me his *darling girl*.'

Jack's throat constricted. 'You continue to amaze me,
Darcie.' He held her more closely, his lips making feath-
ery kisses over her temple. 'So you had your big talk.
Then what? Dare I ask?'

'They're coming to our wedding!'

Jack looked at her, startled.

Her breath caught. 'That's if you still want to marry
me…?'

'Oh, God, yes!' he said hoarsely. 'With bells on.' In
one liquid movement he hauled them both upright. In a
second their bodies were surging together like breakers
dashing to the shore.

They kissed once, fiercely, possessively. And again.
This time slowly, languidly, taking all the time in the
world to savour each other. To reconnect.

On a little whimper Darcie burrowed closer, drinking
him in, feeling the absorption of his scent in her nostrils
through her skin.

When they drew apart, they stared at one another, the
moment almost surreal. 'We're getting married,' Jack
said.

'Yes.' She reached up and drew her finger along
his throat and into the hollow at its base. 'And I want
everything, Jack. A real outback wedding. I want our
little bush church decorated with masses of flowers, big
bows on the seats and the church filled with family and
friends.'

Jack looked bemused. 'And after?'

'We'll hire a marquee and find somewhere special
to put it. And we'll have fairy-lights and maybe a dance
floor and glorious food.'

Jack's eyes went wide in alarm. 'I won't have to cook, will I?'

Darcie snickered. 'Of course not. We'll fly caterers out from Brisbane if we have to. And don't look like that,' she chided gently. 'My parents are paying for everything. I bought a wedding dress in London,' she added shyly. 'I hope you'll like me in it.'

'Of course I'll like you in it.' There was a gleam in his blue eyes. 'And out of it too.'

Darcie laughed, feeling the warm flood of desire ripple through her body. 'We just have to make a date, then.'

'Let's leave that for tomorrow. Right now, we need to be doing other things. Don't you agree…?'

'I agree, Jack.' The catch in his voice told her everything she needed to hear. A slow, radiant smile lit her face as she slipped her hands under his T-shirt, loving the smooth sweep of his skin against her palms. Loving *him*. 'Now,' she enticed coyly, 'come and unwrap your present.'

CHAPTER THIRTEEN

It was a perfect day for a wedding.

'Darcie, could you possibly stand still for a half a second?' Maggie did a slow inspection around the now dressed bride. They were at the residence with barely fifteen minutes left before they were to leave for the church.

'I'm so happy I could burst, Maggie.'

'Don't do that,' Maggie pleaded. 'I'd have to fasten these tiny buttons all over again.'

'What do you think of the dress?' Darcie posed in front of the full-length mirror. 'Does it look OK?'

'OK?' Maggie's voice went up an octave. The dress was a stylish combination of silk and hand-made lace, with a fitted bodice, tiny cap sleeves and slim-cut skirt. 'Honey, you look stunning.' Maggie's gaze had a misty look. 'Jack's eyes will be out on stalks.'

'That's if he can see at all,' Darcie said dryly. 'I can believe his brothers hauled him off to the pub for a buck's do the night before the wedding!'

'Well, boys will be boys,' Maggie countered practically. 'And, anyway, Jack stuck to the soft stuff mostly, according to Sam.'

'Mmm.' Darcie didn't seem convinced.

'Oh, Darce.' Maggie laughed. 'Relax, would you

Even if Jack ended up a bit tipsy, he's had all day to sleep it off.'

Darcie gave a reluctant chuckle. 'Then it's lucky we decided to have the wedding in the late afternoon, wasn't it? For everyone's sake.' She paused and sobered. 'Maggie, thank you so much for standing up with me and for your endless kindness and friendship.'

'Oh, tosh.' Maggie shook her dark head. 'Friendship is a two-way street. And yours has been invaluable to me as well. Now, hush up.' She gave an off-key laugh. 'Or we'll both be bawling and ruining our make-up. Shame you're not getting a honeymoon, though.'

'Price of being doctors in the outback.' Darcie looked philosophical. 'But we're getting a couple of nights away. Jack's arranged for someone to fly us across to the coast. Posh hotel and all the trimmings.'

'Oh, yes…' Maggie waggled her eyebrows. 'Breakfast in bed?'

Darcie's face went pink. 'All that. I'm so happy, Maggie.'

'Sweetie, you deserve it.' Maggie's look turned soft. 'Oh, I meant to ask, how are your parents enjoying Sunday Creek?'

'They're loving it.' Darcie picked up their bouquets of red roses and handed one to Maggie. 'It was so sweet of Louise to invite them to stay at Willow Bend.'

'Willow Bend is such a beautiful property,' Maggie agreed. 'And they'll get a real taste of station life as well.'

'Your transport's here.' Lauren stuck her head in the door. 'Oh, my stars! Darcie, you look incredible!'

'Oh…thanks, Lauren.' Darcie gave a shaky laugh. Suddenly she was all butterflies. What if Jack didn't turn up? What if his brother, Dom, forgot the rings?

What if they both messed up their vows? With trem
bling fingers she reached up to touch the delicate silve
heart at her throat. Jack's gift to his bride. She blinke
back the sudden possibility of tears. 'Do we have tim
for a glass of wine?'

'No, we don't,' Maggie said firmly. 'It might be fash
ionable to be late but personally I think it's plain ba
manners. Besides which, Jack will be wearing out th
carpet and the priest will be getting tetchy.'

'Oh, he won't,' Darcie remonstrated. 'He's been lovel
to us.'

'Come on, guys.' Lauren began to usher them out int
the hallway. 'Your chariot awaits.'

'Do you have all our stuff, Lauren?' Maggie raised
quick hand in question.

Lauren held up her big purple holdall. 'Spares c
everything and the bride's pashmina in case it gets chil
later.'

'Thanks. You're a star.'

'Happy to be your lady-in-waiting,' Lauren said chee
fully, and the little party began to move forward to th
front veranda.

'Wh-what's that?' Darcie's voice squeaked wit
shock. She pointed to the buggy and two handsome gre
horses that were drawn up outside.

'It's your transport,' Maggie said. 'Isn't it fabulous'

Darcie's mouth opened and closed. 'But Louise prom
ised to lend us their Mercedes!'

'She did.' Maggie grinned. 'And it's for Lauren and m
You, my dear, are travelling in style by horse and coach

'You wanted a real outback wedding,' Lauren re
minded the bride.

'But horses!' Darcie looked helplessly between the two women.

'Aren't they a picture?' Maggie looked so pleased. 'Sam found them for us. And they're accustomed to this kind of thing, so you'll be quite safe.'

'Besides, the locals will want to wave to you along the way,' Lauren put in. 'You'll be like a princess.'

Darcie began to laugh. 'I can't believe you've all done this to me!'

'Oh, we're not devoid of innovation out here,' Maggie said innocently. 'Now, here's your dad come to escort you.'

'Good afternoon, ladies.' Professor Drummond greeted the little group and then took his daughter's hands, holding her at arm's length, his gaze suspiciously moist. 'Darcie…you look radiant. And so grown-up…'

'Oh, Dad…' Darcie choked back a slight lump in her throat and thought this was how it should be on her wedding day. It would have been unthinkable if her father had not been here.

'You look very lovely, Maggie.' The professor took his eyes off his daughter for a moment.

'Thank you, Richard.' Maggie acknowledged his compliment with a dignified little nod.

'Richard!' Lauren hissed in a shocked stage whisper. 'Isn't that a bit disrespectful? Isn't he a *lord* or something?'

'No.' Maggie snickered behind her hand. 'He asked us to call him Richard when he and Darcie's mum hosted a pre-wedding do a few days ago.'

'Now, are we ready, ladies?' Professor Drummond tucked Darcie's arm through his and proceeded to walk her carefully down the flight of shallow steps.

Darcie aimed her bouquet towards the horses and buggy. 'Are you all right about this, Dad?'

'It's really quite comfortable.' He turned his head and smiled at her. 'And our driver, Jay, is a very interesting chap. We had a most pleasant journey in from Willow Bend.'

'You came all that way in a buggy?' Darcie was astounded at her usually conservative father's easy acceptance of the rather *out-there* mode of transport for her wedding.

'Here, Darcie, give me your flowers while you hop aboard,' Maggie instructed. 'And don't panic. The seat is well sprung and it's spotlessly clean. You'll arrive in perfect order.'

'I'm just grateful I'm not wearing a hooped skirt,' Darcie vented as she placed her foot gingerly on the buggy's running board.

'Then we might have had a problem,' Maggie conceded, watching as Darcie settled back in the red leather seat and reclaimed her bouquet. 'Safe journey.' Maggie gave a jaunty finger wave and stepped back. 'See you at the church.'

Darcie's heart was cartwheeling as she stood in the church porch beside her father.

'You look beautiful, darling,' he said. 'Jack is a very lucky man. And a fine one,' he added with obvious approval.

Darcie took a steadying breath. 'Is he here, Dad? Can you see him?'

Maggie, who had arrived seconds earlier, said briskly, 'Of course he's here!' Lifting a hand, she brushed a tiny tendril of hair from Darcie's cheek. 'Now, are we ready?' she whispered.

Darcie nodded and swallowed.

'Good.' Maggie gave a smile of encouragement. 'Then let's do it.'

Standing in front of the altar, Jack felt his chest rise in a long steadying breath. She was here at last, his English bride, his Darcie, his love. She had almost reached him when he turned, lifting a dark brow in admiration.

Seeing the familiar broad sweep of her bridegroom's shoulders, the proud set of his head, Darcie stifled a whirlpool of nerves and found the impetus to walk the last few paces to his side.

'OK?' he murmured, reaching for her hand. Darcie nodded, and clung for dear life.

'Welcome, guys.' Standing in front of them, Father Tom Corelli beamed across at the bride and groom. 'Now, before we get on to the real business, I believe you have something personal you wish to say to each other.'

'Thank you, Father.' Darcie struggled with her prickling eyes and turned to face Jack. He smiled encouragingly at her and they took hands. Darcie drew in a steadying breath and began.

'Jack, you are my rock. You have listened to me and supported me both personally and professionally. My love for you is as wide and deep as the outback sky. You are my true north. And I will love you always and for ever.'

Raw emotion carved Jack's face and he wished he'd thought of something so poetic. But he'd do the best he could.

'Darcie, you are my true love. You are as strong and

brave as the finest trees of our forests, yet as tender and beautiful as our most delicate wildflower. And I will love you always and for ever.'

Darcie made the rest of their formal vows in a haze of happiness, hardly registering when she and Jack exchanged rings. When Father Tom pronounced them husband and wife, they kissed. And kissed again to a ripple of applause and a few whistles from one or two daring members of the Cassidy clan.

Smiling broadly, the priest ushered them to an especially prepared table at the side of the altar. And as they sat to sign the register, Lauren delighted them by singing a huskily sweet rendition of 'The First Time Ever I Saw Your Face'.

'I had no idea!' Darcie's whisper was shot with amazement.

'Just our little surprise for you.' Jack's expression was tender. 'And I have another for you as well, Mrs Darcie Cassidy.'

'Oh?' Darcie blinked and tried to speak and wondered if it was possible to overdose on sheer happiness.

Jack's smile began slowly and then widened. 'We're having a proper honeymoon,' he said. 'A whole week to ourselves. We've got us a locum.'

Darcie looked fascinated. 'Who?'

There was a gleam in Jack's blue eyes. 'One of the flying doctors.'

Darcie's eyes flashed wide in disbelief. 'Are we talking about Brad Kitto here?' she whispered.

Jack nodded. 'As a wedding present, he's kindly offered to give up a week of his leave for us.'

Darcie was dumbfounded. 'But Brad?' she emphasised in a stage whisper. 'You always looked on him as something of a rival.'

'That was then.' Jack seemed unfazed.

'But didn't you feel uncomfortable about accepting his offer?'

'Why would I?' Jack looked at his bride, his entire heart in his gaze. 'After all, my love, you'd chosen *me*.'

* * * * *

LET'S TALK
Romance

For exclusive extracts, competitions
and special offers, find us online:

f facebook.com/millsandboon

◎ @millsandboonuk

✗ @millsandboon

Or get in touch on 0844 844 1351*

For all the latest titles coming soon, visit
millsandboon.co.uk/nextmonth

Want even more
ROMANCE?

Join our bookclub today!

'Mills & Boon books, the perfect way to escape for an hour or so.'

Miss W. Dyer

'Excellent service, promptly delivered and very good subscription choices.'

Miss A. Pearson

'You get fantastic special offers and the chance to get books before they hit the shops'

Mrs V. Hall

**Visit millsandbook.co.uk/Bookclub
and save on brand new books.**

MILLS & BOON